Don't Shed Your Tears for Anyone
Who Lives on These Streets

Don't Shed Your Tears for Anyone Who Lives on These Streets

〉〉〉

PATRICIO PRON

*Translated from the Spanish
by Mara Faye Lethem*

 ALFRED A. KNOPF | NEW YORK | 2020

THIS IS A BORZOI BOOK PUBLISHED BY ALFRED A. KNOPF

Translation copyright © 2020 by Mara Faye Lethem

www.aaknopf.com

Grateful acknowledgment is made to the following for permission to reprint previously published material: New Directions Publishing Corp.: Excerpt from "Salutation The Third" from *Personae* by Ezra Pound, copyright © 1926 by Ezra Pound. Reprinted by permission of New Directions Publishing Corp.

LIBRARY OF CONGRESS CATALOGING-IN-PUBLICATION DATA
Names: Pron, Patricio, [date] author. | Lethem, Mara, translator.
Title: Don't shed your tears for anyone who lives on these streets / Patricio Pron ; translated from the Spanish by Mara Faye Lethem.
Other titles: No derrames tus lágrimas por nadie que viva en estas calles. English | Do not shed your tears for anyone who lives on these streets
Description: First edition. | New York : Alfred A. Knopf, 2020. | Translated into English from Spanish.
Identifiers: LCCN 2019032414 | ISBN 9780451493170 (hardcover) | ISBN 9780451493187 (ebook)
Classification: LCC PQ7798.26.R58 N613 2020 | DDC 863/.64—dc23
LC record available at https://lccn.loc.gov/2019032414

Jacket design by Tyler Comrie

Manufactured in the United States of America
First American Edition

The old world is dying, and the new one struggles to be born: now is the time of monsters.

ANTONIO GRAMSCI

Contents

>>>>>>>>>>>>>>>>>>>>>>>>>>>>>>>>>>

Don't Shed Your Tears for Anyone

Who Lives on These Streets

Ravenna,
Florence,
Genoa,
Rome

MARCH 1978

Interviews: Part I

〉〉

We poets in our youth begin in sadness;
thereof in the end come despondency and madness.

ROBERT LOWELL, "To Delmore Schwartz (Cambridge
1946)"

Oreste Calosso, Rome, March 16, 1978
The morning of April 21, 1945, broke with a magnificent dawn, like every other day that terrible month. I remember it perfectly, and I also remember how, when we found Luca Borrello's corpse, his eyes were open and he was looking up at the sky, as if a moment earlier Borrello too had been appreciating that it indeed was a splendid day.

Atilio Tessore, Florence, March 11, 1978
On April 21, 1945, it rained all morning and then the sun came out; ironically, by that time we'd all found shelter and no one had the slightest intention of going out for a walk; in fact, some of us were already leaving.

Michele Garassino, Genoa, March 13, 1978
I don't remember. I haven't the faintest idea what you're talking about and I can't even imagine how one would be able to remember such a thing, what the weather was like on an uneventful day more than thirty years ago.

Espartaco Boyano, Ravenna, March 10, 1978

On the twenty-first of April 1945 it rained all day and that made the search difficult. Gradually almost everyone gave up, except for me and a few others, who continued on despite the bad weather. Who can say whether their motive was curiosity, or the conviction that the missing person could have been any of them, or the speculation—right on target, of course—that searching would exempt them from the list of suspects. That was if, in the end, it turned out that Borrello had had an accident or been murdered, and hadn't just left on the sly.

Atilio Tessore, Florence, March 11, 1978

Why would I worry about being among the suspects? Hadn't I defended Borrello the day before, when he said we should take part in the impending regime change to keep our mission from ending completely? Haven't they already told you, you who are so young, that Borrello was accused of being a defeatist, that they claimed he was a mole, that they insinuated he'd gone crazy? Which is to say, he'd gone crazy with loneliness and weary saturation. Borrello's last project revealed how he'd walked a narrow, unclassifiable path; there were only rumors of the project's existence—persistent, curiously unanimous rumors, as if all those repeating them had actually seen Borrello working on it, or, more plausibly, they'd all accepted the rumors because they thought Borrello's body of work had grown diffuse, transforming and taking on increasingly singular, strange forms (as if *L'anguria lirica* wasn't singular and strange enough) as opposed to signaling a direction that only Borrello followed, a direction we said we wanted to follow but didn't, perhaps due to our understanding that art and life should never actually be combined. Art should be the disquieting or conciliatory dream of a certain wakefulness. Art and life coming together as one should only be fantasy, an impossible fantasy, an abyss it was better not to peer into, an abyss we retreated from in fear—understanding, as I said, that Borrello's work could only end the way it had (or the way the rumors said it had). Borrello was headed down a path that led to either art or madness and annihilation; exhausted, he had fallen only to look ahead toward the end of the path and discover that it had no horizon, just a wall of solid rock like the one they found him at the foot of, according to what I was told. Or maybe he'd encountered a stranger on that path, who'd laughed brutally at his ignorance and innocence. Or perhaps there was only a mirror, a mirror none of us, not even Borrello, would ever want to look into.

Turin

>>

We grant to the young all the rights and authority
that we deny and want to seize brutally
from the old, the dying, and the dead.

F. T. MARINETTI, "The Necessity and Beauty of Violence"

A few yards ahead, the old professor's back curves in such a way that it's impossible to see the nape of his neck; the hollow in his jacket is due to that curvature and to his habit of leading with his head as he walks. Pietro or Peter Linden—also called "Pitz" and "Peeke," though only by his mother—knows this is called "swan neck," a deformity that can be corrected, because he had it as a child and his mother corrected it in the style of those times, by placing a stack of books on his head and making him walk around the house without the books falling. From behind, Pietro or Peter Linden can see only the tip of the old professor's ears and, crowning his skull, a bit of white hair currently somewhat mussed by the wind. Winter seems to have come early and the city is subject to cold gusts— normal over much of the year—from the mountains surrounding Turin, which are already snowcapped. Pietro or Peter Linden knows the old professor well and doesn't need more than one or two cues to identify him: the color of the jacket he's wearing today, a leaden blue; or his hesitation when he extends his right foot, which Pietro or Peter Linden knows, because the old professor once told him in class (off the subject really) that it had had to be reconstructed after he got trapped in the collapse of a house where he and his wife were squatting in Milan during the last days of the war, which gave out when the building next to it, a school with some twenty-odd children locked inside, was hit by a grenade. This was enough for Linden to pick him out among the people gathered on

the corner of Giuseppe Verdi and Gioacchino Rossino waiting for
the traffic to thin enough to cross over to Corso San Maurizio and
toward the river; a corner that Linden and the old professor had
arrived at together—unbeknownst, of course, to the old professor—
after leaving the university building and crossing the Via Fratelli
Vasco, also together but with a certain distance between them.
There Linden only had to pretend to be one of the students in order
to follow the old professor from just a few yards behind. Further on,
the arcades of the streets offered him refuge, as did the crowds at
that time of day, rushing somewhat because the shops were about
to close, but still too slow for Linden, who often had the impression
that people never walk fast enough, so much so that he, who was
willing to assume important risks in order to bring about a new
world (one neither he nor his comrades could envision, and that
possibly would expel them when it arrived, if that ever came to
pass), has only two requirements that are, for him, nonnegotiable,
and which he is sometimes surprised to find himself musing about
with a malicious smile on his lips: one, in that new world there will
be books, and, two, people won't be allowed to stroll around, forced
instead to move at a steady, rapid pace or stay home. In fact, adopt-
ing the slowness required to tail the old professor without calling
attention to himself was the only difficulty that had arisen over the
last eight days, in which Linden followed him from the university to
his house every time on an almost identical route. The old professor hadn't stopped or turned around even once, as if no shadow of a
doubt hovered over him, as if he couldn't conceive of the possibility
that his words—some of his words that regularly appeared in a
local paper or were formulated in the classes Linden had attended
the previous year, which he'd found generally satisfying despite the
professor's numerous derogatory allusions to the factions and
political cells (almost all violent, almost all made up of young people)
of which Linden was first a sympathizer and later a member (though
his position is still uncertain, and therefore following the old professor has, for him, the importance of a test)—could come back to
haunt him. Linden particularly remembers something he'd said the
year before, when he was interrupted by a handful of young men

asking him to suspend class so that his students—barely five or six, including Linden—could take part in a demonstration beginning in the interior courtyard of the university, some students already shouting slogans and others piling up benches and tables so they could set them on fire if the police arrived. The police were already deployed, forming a wall erected on Via Po and on Giuseppe Verdi, and seemed willing to breach the courtyard at the slightest provocation. The old professor just looked at the young men and said: "I will not allow this class to be interrupted for political reasons." One or two students joined the interlopers and started down the stairs toward the courtyard, but Linden didn't follow them—at that point he didn't know that he would soon be one of them, that he would soon be advancing with them to a confrontation with history, that one of them would be his supervisor in his future cell, that another would convince him of the right moment to challenge the State, and that another, who usually hosted the political meetings that Linden didn't yet attend but soon would, would be murdered by the police a few years later in a confrontation—so he was one of the few present to hear the old professor mutter to himself: "We thought we were fighting for something too, but we were fighting only for ourselves and to preserve our youth, and we lost it," and that utterance had stayed with Linden in the same way other entire phrases of the professor's newspaper articles had, in which he usually advocated for greater firmness in the clashes with the younger generation and a return to values that are essentially religious and constitute a way of life similar to that of the professor's parents and grandparents. The professor, like everyone in his generation, had had to turn his back on those values because he'd had to take part in two world wars that annihilated his parents' and grandparents' way of life, the framework in which those values seemed useful and convenient. Perhaps, thinks Linden as he passes the Via Gaudenzio Ferrari—the old professor's back just a few yards ahead, sunken with the weight of his head and his indifference to the shop windows he passes—those values were conceived to prevent wars and the world that would result from them, but most likely they contributed to both, and thus became not exactly obsolete but useless for anything beyond a certain continuity of the existing state of affairs that, in Linden and his comrades' opinion, must be changed. The Italian Republic's status quo requires heightened confrontation, thinks Linden, and more—and more compelling—means of containing the State's powers, though it's possible that an increase in violent resistance contributes, as a justification, to the State employing increased force to avoid or repress it. Linden doesn't consider himself capable of determining what must be done, he is only interested in "doing." Behind that is both political conviction—the Italian situation must change, and it doesn't much matter what replaces it—and a feeling of personal inadequacy that isn't visible but which manifests itself in his blond hair, which makes him stand out on the Via Rossini (though there are quite a few blonds in Turin), and in his surname, both of which embarrass him because they reveal his German heritage—in other words, at least a part of him is related to those who caused the ruin of Italy in the war years—though the facts are more complex. He is not one of the Italians his age who were born of consensual (or not) relations between Italian women and Wehrmacht Germans, but rather his parents met years after the war, in Milan, when his mother was in her church choir and went on one of those endless tours that the German Evangelical Church organized regularly in those years to "strengthen ties" between the recent enemies and, more specifically and covertly, so that the Germans might be forgiven for the tragic events of the past, of which they were first perpetrators and then victims, or always victims in a way. His surname is actually that of a Swiss cabinetmaker who arrived in Turin some sixty years back, to work in the industry. Linden wonders if those facts are as important to him as the ones surrounding the escalation of violence in Italy that began on March 15, 1972, when the rhetoric became more radicalized, as did the methods of fighting the State. In turn, the State radicalized its response to the discontent and this wider vision of the political, because aren't radicalization and rejection political? Isn't it clear that, on that occasion, the old professor (now walking barely a few yards in front of him) was wrong, and that, if his class continued, it would mostly be for political reasons?

That the existence of a separation between political protest and the way knowledge is transmitted is, actually, a political problem? Linden is now reaching the Corso San Maurizio along with the professor and a fistful of other people he is indifferent to and to whom he devotes only the minimum attention required to not compromise his shadowing. He feels it is essential to seek out all means necessary to unify politics and experience, reflection and action; pursuits—including the artistic—and, for lack of a better word, life. Linden slows down deliberately and hides behind two women headed home with their groceries—tomatoes, bread, onions, something that looks like basil or maybe mint, bloody meat that's soaked through its wrapping paper and is starting to imprint a liquid stain on one of the women's bags—because the Corso San Maurizio is a wide street with few people this time of day. If the old professor were to turn around—though he hadn't done so up to that point and gave no indication he would, possibly ever: that is how sure Linden is of his stealth and of the legitimacy of his actions, surrounding him like some sort of padded wall distancing him from danger—he could recognize him as they crossed, slowly, in a route punctuated by the buses and cars lining the avenue, parked in the middle of the street, their drivers honking and shouting at the pedestrians who invariably move too slowly, particularly the two women returning home with their groceries and Linden, behind them. Linden lifts his head to not lose sight of the old professor, who is walking a few yards ahead and has almost made it across the corso and is now stopping for a moment in front of the window of a chocolate shop and hesitating, meditating it seems, on what he sees and perhaps whether it's necessary or appropriate to buy a box of bonbons, maybe not the biggest and most expensive but a small, modest one he can carry in his pocket unnoticed, but he resists and continues walking slowly, passes the Via Santa Giulia, approaching the street-car stop at a steady pace—streetcar number 16, a route Linden isn't familiar with—and then turns onto Corso Regina Margherita, pre-senting Linden with the same difficulties as on Corso San Maurizio, which he attempts to resolve by hiding behind someone; but the women with their groceries have already turned on Santa Giulia and Linden's lost sight of them, so he makes a decision—a risky one—that he'd already made once before when trailing him another day, the second or the fourth time, and he passes the old professor decisively. The professor doesn't realize, he doesn't know he is being overtaken by a former student, someone who remembers a situation when he stated he wasn't going to let his class be interrupted for political reasons; which is to say, for different political reasons than those he often defends in the press and in his classes, proposing a return to order and tradition, or to what he understands as tradition, which is basically the idealized version of the times that followed the revolution brought on by someone being nailed to a cross somewhere in Palestine. Linden crosses the street and takes shelter at a newspaper stand; he buys a couple of papers and then, on impulse, merely because his hand slides over in that direction, he buys a postcard of the Mole Antonelliana that he has no one to send to. He could have sent it to his father, if his father hadn't died a few years earlier, on the outskirts of a hospital located, in turn, on the outskirts of Milan, a hospital that seemed to Linden, the only time he visited, nothing more than a place to deposit old or crazy people and everything they had lived through, everything they'd seen or done during the war years. Linden watches the old professor pass the newspaper stand on the opposite side of the street, and he follows him with his gaze until the glass of its display case is interrupted by a column and the professor disappears from view; he stands there, watching him pass, and only emerges from this trance when the newspaper vendor, who thinks Linden has forgotten something or simply doesn't dare to put his next request into words, suggests, with a strong accent from Trieste—the accent of someone displaced, thinks Linden—that perhaps he is looking for something else, and from the depths of the counter pulls out some pornographic photographs that look like they could have been taken decades earlier, possibly before the war, reminding Linden of something he can't put a finger on, some sort of childish shame at his first stammering manifestations of desire for and curiosity about women, so he hesitates before saying he isn't interested, that he's just killing time, and he heads out onto the street, but not before hearing the Triestine murmur "faggot" behind his back: when he turns, he sees the man looking at the photographs himself, with an incomprehensible expression. The professor is already about halfway across the Ponte Rossini and, to avoid a man with a briefcase rushing in the opposite direction, suddenly swerves directly toward Linden, who dodges him and crosses the street only to keep walking behind the professor, who crosses Dora Firenze and then continues along Via Reggio to Via Pisa. There the old professor does something he hasn't done on any of the previous days, while Linden trailed him, wondering where the scheduled action would be carried out (at the bridge, which offers good escape routes, or at the old professor's home, or some point in between): he goes into the bookstore on the corner of Reggio and Pisa, which paralyzes Linden, who wonders whether to go in as well or wait outside, and in that case where, because the bookstore is one big window and it's hard to come up with a hiding place that isn't visible from inside; but then, as he slowly approaches the bookshop, he sees the old professor emerging and he understands; he gets what he'd gone in there to do and why he left immediately, and Linden makes a mental note and then continues to follow the professor, who doesn't again vary from his regular route. He walks along Via Reggio and takes a left on Via Parma, and heads even more slowly, because he seems exhausted by the walk, to number 49, where he stops and pulls a key out of his briefcase's back pocket and inserts it in the door of a building that—unbeknownst to Linden and the old professor, who, unlike Linden, won't live to see even the most immediate changes on the street, in the city, the country—will be demolished in a few years to make way for one of those modern, functional buildings that will spring up all over the neighborhood when the residents of the old palaces decide that times have changed and they have to find new homes and other ways of life. This is really the only thing Linden and his comrades want, even though they may end up regretting it: a new era, in which art and life have reunited after decades of a manifest mutual lack of understanding, a mutual disdain resulting from a time one could encapsulate in the figure of the old professor—and that, in fact, is what Linden and those who've assigned him this task of shadowing, which is finally nearing an end, do. The professor struggles with the lock, arduously opening one of the doors of the building's grand entrance, slips inside, and disappears from Linden's sight for the last time.

A few days later, the old professor is dead: he is gunned down in a warning action that—despite the rhetoric of the organization Linden belongs to, which takes credit for the execution and promises similar actions against other representatives of the old regime and the State—actually went wrong, horribly wrong. Linden—who didn't take part in the action, though, in a way, he did, by tailing the professor and sketching a detailed diagram of his routes, timetables, and any incidents that he handed over to his liaison, who later told him he'd done a very good job, and might be called upon again, and asked if he had experience with firearms—understands this as soon as he reads the news in the paper and learns that the old professor bled out, because all the bullet wounds were in the corpse's legs. They were only trying to scare the professor, but he bled to death in the doorway of his home waiting for an ambulance (called from the phone of a nearby bar by a regular who didn't want to give his name), which the Italian State he defended in his classes and in his newspaper articles didn't manage to send on time, which is ironic because it highlights that, while Linden and the members of his organization have chosen to be unprotected, the people who chose the protection of the State and chose to defend it publicly were also vulnerable. These people were forsaken by the State without any sign of bad conscience, possibly because the State also understood that times are changing and that the new can only be defeated by the new, disguised as the old and obsolete and legitimized by that disguise, by that aura of respectability Linden notices in many places; in Rome, for example, where he is sent by the organization shortly after the action against the old professor. In Rome, he reads the newspaper in a café near Termini Station, where he's sharing a safe house with another activist, who told him his name was Paolo and that he was a member of the Bologna jail front, although Linden doesn't believe that because, if he were in the jail front, he wouldn't be in a safe house and because his accent isn't Bolognese but vaguely southern, possibly Calabrian; also because he saw him counting large sums of money in his room and then hiding it in a safe concealed in the headboard of his bed, possibly waiting to close an arms deal, or perhaps as a test, so that Linden would feel tempted to rob the money and flee, for which the organization would make him pay with his life and which, obviously, Linden isn't considering doing; or maybe the "Bolognese" man is really an infiltrator, a plant waiting for someone important from the organization to come to the house so he can arrest him, because such things had already happened in the past and will continue to happen, eventually leading the organization to collapse, as all organizations do, dissolving its revolutionary potential in the thankless task of carrying out purges, chasing moles, listening to testimonies and arguments, executing or pardoning and using them. Which Linden knows because his father had talked to him about it dozens, possibly hundreds, of times throughout his life. His father was a partisan during the war and had to kill Germans and collaborationists and also, unfortunately, one or two infiltrators, though he was never sure they were infiltrators and that uncertainty and perhaps regret may have contributed to his downfall and desire to end his own life. His example served as a warning his son didn't want to heed except partially, because he also ended up becoming a partisan, or at least that's what he imagines himself to be. However, Linden also knows he is in danger in Rome, in danger of the divisions separating the sides beginning to seem more ambiguous than they actually are—if they even exist—so as soon as he can he goes back to Turin and there, before remobilizing, he remembers a mental note he took days earlier, and one afternoon he returns to the corner of Via Reggio and Pisa and enters a bookstore that's unusually dark in spite of its large window and approaches a glass counter, where an employee watches him, an employee who seems to be made entirely of glass from his spectacles to his hands. Linden asks if the books the old professor ordered have come in yet, and the employee observes him. Linden explains that he was the old professor's assistant and that the university sent him to pick up and cancel any orders the old professor might have made in his final hours of life, so the crystal clear employee, who may have also thought Linden and his intentions were crystal clear, asks him to wait a moment and heads into the back room, and then stammers out the old professor's name, as if he needs to invoke him while searching through the packages of books, and finally finds one of those packages and returns to the counter and hands it to Linden, who barely glances at it, pulls money from his pocket, and asks the employee to give him a receipt in the name of the director of the department library where the old professor worked because, insists Linden, that's what's done in these cases. Then he accepts condolences from the glass employee, a small curio about to burst into tears as he stammers that the old professor was a good customer, and Linden takes the package and the receipt, which he practically has to rip from those crystalline hands, then leaves the bookstore and heads down the Via Reggio and doesn't look back, not even once, as he wonders what to do next, and where.

Throughout his life, Linden has always thought of literature as something more than a distraction; in fact more like something inexcusably necessary. This conviction could be attributable to his mother's prescriptive exercises or his father's insistence, because his father, despite not having time for literature, never doubted its importance and transmitted that to his son. Occasionally his father told him he'd met a writer toward the end of the war who saved his life even though he didn't have to, which Linden found enigmatic and later considered simply another story of a war that, in some sense, is only made up of stories; and that is how, apart from what his father might have thought about literature and its usefulness—which for Linden can only exist relative to another question, that of "what to do" with literature—he once again puts aside everything else just to read, this time to read the three books the old professor ordered shortly before his death. In the coming months, he will on various occasions devote himself solely to reading, ignoring the possibilities of getting in touch with his organization, in no small part due to the fact that a few weeks earlier some activists were murdered or committed suicide in a West German jail, leading Linden's small world—the one he and his friends and acquaintances had created around themselves with the goal of eventually replacing the world outside, which they find increasingly strange—to shrink slightly while at the same time expanding with the hitherto unanticipated prospect of being murdered, as well as jailed and tortured. However, thinks Linden as he heads to a meeting where the cell plans to discuss the incident and possible reprisals, it may have been that those activists—whose names Linden, like many other young people throughout Europe, knows well: Andreas Baader, Jan-Carl Raspe, Gudrun Ensslin, and Irmgard Möller, who survived— weren't murdered but rather killed themselves because of the failure of the last action intended to liberate them, the hijacking of an airplane, with passengers and crew, that was diverted to an African city—a city, in fact, where in the future Linden will live for some time (although naturally he doesn't know that yet) and from whose airport he will depart on various occasions, wondering each time where the hijacking took place and whether any material evidence of it still exists—with the goal of starting negotiations with the West German government, which failed: the plane was attacked during the night, and the kidnappers were killed. That night, the members of Linden's cell gather in a safe house in the Mirafiori Nord area that Linden rented under a false name a few weeks prior and paid for with the cell's money but didn't bother to furnish, so it has only a radio and a table lamp left behind by some guy who spent time in the commune across from the San Salvario Church where, at least officially, Linden lives. He can't remember whether the guy left of his own volition or was kicked out. There are a few mattresses too, where the cell members recline to smoke and talk about the failed rescue of their German counterparts and their deaths in jail; but no conclusions will be drawn that night because they are all paralyzed by surprise and indignation and something similar to fear, as well as uncertainty about whether the deaths were murder or suicide, two options that have both supporters and detractors and that lead to different readings of the action as either a success or a failure. If it was murder, the confrontation with the State would only intensify, as the death of the German activists—whom the press, even the Italian press, were calling "terrorists"—clearly revealed the underlying violence of the State's institutions of justice, which would sway public opinion toward those who strive to replace these institutions with another kind of legality, one less tied to the empire of money and inequality; if it was suicide—though the possibility of suicide in a maximum security prison built to avoid that very thing, seems absurd—the action was also successful, or at least apparently successful, because that means the political activists remained masters of themselves even when in the hands of the State. That demonstration of independence, of tragic autonomy, can be interpreted as a mandate and a lesson for those, like Linden and the other members of his cell (whose noms de guerre are as absurd as the one Linden chose for himself and only reluctantly bothered to memorize) who look to them as role models, but also leads to the conclusion—which Linden doesn't dare posit openly that night, as his position in the organization is still precarious and continues to exclude him from armed actions, which is both a way to keep him safe until he has more experience and a tacit acknowledgment of the importance of his skills in another arena, in intelligence and investigation, in providing safe houses and commissioning false documents, for which it's preferable that Linden float in the vague region between legality and the illegality the other cell members are completely immersed in—that they left their followers behind, choosing to voluntarily abandon the struggle rather than continue to face its consequences, which Linden finds more dignified as well as more fatuous. There is personal defeat in that abandonment, which for years will remind Linden of the personal defeats of those who, at one point or another, had struggled and lost, like his father, who fought the German occupation of north Italy and fascism and later, somehow, ended up feeling nostalgic for them both, trapped as he was in a web of loans that suffocated him and the carpentry workshop he'd set up in the neighborhood on the outskirts of Milan where Linden was raised, thus—without realizing it—providing his son with reasons for his bitterness and frustration that served as a backdrop to the theatrical actions Linden had carried out since he was a boy (or at least that's what he thinks, tending to believe that everything, especially in childhood, is acting or posturing) and that led him to join the cell of political activists with whom he is sharing this particular evening. Linden doesn't dare confess his doubts about the relevance of the action against the old professor or, better yet, about the conviction, seemingly accepted by them all, that this sort of action will bring about a new world with values slightly closer to those his father and other partisans fought for and were unable to impose even in the confusion of the war's end. There is a possibility—which either no one realizes or they all prefer not to mention that night in the safe house—that the German activists achieved a, shall we say, posthumous victory by using their last dredges of freedom to make their suicides look like murders: putting the blame for their deaths on the State, obviously stained with blood since its very inception. While Linden understands and accepts this, it keeps him from imagining that the Germans might have faked their murders, because he believes—and this is, somehow, the line he doesn't and never will dare to cross—that constructive political actions always have the truth on their side. This will condemn him and his entire generation, who will end up having to admit that that line was crossed time and time again, mostly out of ignorance. Nor does Linden dare to confess that night that, days earlier, violating every safety regulation, he went to the bookstore and acquired, out of curiosity, the books the old professor had ordered; nor does he dare to confess that the action was legitimized or would be legitimized if they knew at least the titles and authors of those books, because the old professor had ordered three books by authors known in the history of Italian literature—if they're known at all, something Linden isn't sure of: he doesn't study literature but rather journalism, which he's always considered a type of literature detached from its transcendent vocation, and Linden agrees that its aim and uses are limited to a fleeting present it captures only to immediately release, hopefully explaining, clarifying, and eventually transforming it, to the extent that's possible—as fascist authors, writers who supported and celebrated fascism and collapsed with it. Yet Linden's impression that the action against the old professor was legitimized vanished when, as he read one of the books—whose author, Espartaco Boyano, he'd never heard of, like the other two, Ottavio Zuliani and Oreste Calosso—he found a familiar name. He, who knows absolutely nothing about nor has any interest in the literature of that period, had heard his father mention that name often when speaking about the final weeks of the war, when he accidentally separated from his partisan cell after an attack and dragged his broken leg through a ravine for a day (or two, he never was sure), directionless, until he reached a plain where he was found by a man who came out of the forest and saved his life and was not only his captor but also his friend. Then Linden thought he didn't have the full story, and should go see his father and ask him everything, but he immediately remembered that his father had died on the outskirts of a hospital on the outskirts of Milan, deciding himself when and how, which since then Linden considers a "good" death, though perhaps that was just a way to console himself—despite it being obvious to Linden that, had his father died some other way, that death wouldn't have truly belonged to his father, or to the man he'd known as his father, who volunteered for the Resistance and decided on each and every moment of his existence, except for his illness and debts. Linden could no longer talk to his father, and he'd have to find out everything he could about that man some other way: though he didn't know when or how, not as he was reading those books, nor on that night when he'd kept all this to himself.

During his only visit before his father's suicide, after an afternoon in the hospital gardens, his father, who could still walk, decided he should get back to his room. "Let's go along this path," he said, pointing into the hedges and prickly plants that stood between them and the hospital's main building. "What path?" asked Linden. His father, too proud to admit his error, too proud to admit any error, replied: "This one that hasn't been invented yet," and then he turned his back on his son to arduously make his way through the hedges and prickly plants, and Linden, understanding, comprehending everything for the first time in his life, began, in turn, finally, to walk by his side.

Some months after the death of the German activists in prison, Linden is assigned to create various profiles of local journalists. This time, he's told, he won't be trailing them but should go to a local library, give a false name, read newspaper collections, gather ideas. Linden does so, taking particular interest in one journalist whose articles stand out not for their rejection of Linden's organization— that's a feature of every, or almost every, article that mentions it— but rather for the (more humiliating and, were it to spread, more dangerous) idea that it is made up of common criminals and, therefore, no special laws should be created to judge its members. The idea, thinks Linden, is perverse: it feigns ignorance of the political nature of the crimes committed by the organization, their public manifestos, and the fact that the crimes are not the ends but rather the means, or one of the means, for the development of their political activity. Those articles intrigue Linden and leave him thinking, and for a second he believes he identifies with them, or rather identifies his contradictions with the contradictions of the author of those articles, who, of course, only pretends to have them, though that last part doesn't matter. Days later, in the local press, he reads that this journalist he researched—one of the most virulently opposed to the organization, precisely the one who seemed to hold up a mirror to him—was shot in response to the murder of the German activists in jail. Linden finds the action absurd, and believes it places him at personal risk, as he was the one who requested the articles from libraries, with a false name but still with his face uncovered; dozens of people had to have seen him reading those articles and he could very possibly be remembered by the librarians who provided him with the material. Linden sees, also in the local press, photographs of four of the six members of his cell, whose real names he reads there for the first time, and this breaks down the atmosphere of intimacy and complicity that Linden and the other members had laboriously created over recent months—the months since the action against the old professor and, particularly, the first few months of the new year, when they had met regularly in the apartment in Mirafiori Nord, prompted by their perplexity and fear around the murder or suicide of the German terrorists—as if the cell were some sort of refuge instead of a place of utmost exposure. When he sees those photographs of his former comrades, Linden suddenly understands that he is in danger and wonders what to do; he decides to take a trip in order to find out everything about the man who saved his father's life, and also to safeguard himself from finger pointing if the members of his cell are captured (all of them were, and in a relatively short period of time, Linden will recall years later, still perplexed), as well as to impose order on a confusing time that he believes to be definitively in the past, but also potentially in the future, if he finds, as he sets out to do, the remaining fascist writers and executes them the same way his organization did the old professor and the journalist, who is shot in mid-January and dies some twelve or thirteen days later, when Linden is already far from Turin. So Linden convinces himself that this is a private journey but also one taken in the name of his organization, which he doesn't want to abandon despite the errors that deep down he admits took place. He gathers his things and carefully cleans his room to avoid leaving fingerprints there or on the shared furniture in the house, whose occupants observe him with indifference, and later he rendezvouses with a member of the cell he met a few months earlier at the Milan train station, who gives him a safe-conduct for a haven in Genoa. In the station's bustling bar, which retains its former splendor and magnificence, though both are now seen as the manifestation of a dubious—at best—aesthetic taste, Pietro or Peter Linden is about to inform him of the possibility of initiating an action against fascist writers, but at the last moment he decides not to say anything. The other man tells him he's left something for him in the bathroom of the bar, then shakes his hand and leaves, and Linden won't see his face again until two years later, when the man is wounded and arrested by the police during a failed action. Linden will then recall what happened when he got up from the table and walked over to the bathroom and there, beneath one of the sinks, taped to the back, he found a brown paper bag that contained a fake identity, a bundle of lire notes, some handwritten instructions saying he should not be in Rome in March, and a loaded pistol, the first he had ever held in his hands.

Then the following things occur: Linden takes the train to Genoa, arrives at the local station, gets off the train, and decides he won't go to the safe house; he takes a hotel room in the neighborhood near the station where two Ethiopians and an elderly married couple from Voltaggio are staying. The couple is in Genoa because the old man has to undergo knee surgery: at some point he shows Linden his knee, one morning when they're both waiting in line for the bathroom, and it's an oozing stump on a joint devastated by cancer, wounds and operations hastily performed on the front during wartime. A few days later the couple will disappear from the hotel, and Linden will ask the owner about them when he returns from the job the Ethiopians got him, unloading cargo boxes in the back room of a bar at the station; the owner will tell him they went back to Voltaggio after the man's leg was amputated. Some time later, in Florence, Linden will meet Atilio Tessore, who will tell him that one day, during the war, he met a writer who lost a foot when accidentally crossing a minefield, and that the man wasn't as bothered by the loss of his limb as he was by the loss of all his money and a manuscript he carried hidden in his boot; by then Linden will have already read Tessore and the other Futurists from the Perugia region—and he'd know that they were Futurists and not something else; or that they were Futurists and fascists, in that order—but he won't have found even a single book by Luca Borrello. By that time, he'll have finally decided to interview Espartaco Boyano, with a false name and identity, slipping into the small, dark apartment the former Futurist poet has at number 23 Via di Roma, near the Santa Maria in Porta

Basilica, where he'll have arrived after consulting the telephone directory (and before interviewing the others—Atilio Tessore in Florence, Michele Garassino in Genoa, as well as Oreste Calosso in Rome—against the orders of his organization) and by following the directions several different people had given him. And Linden will have understood something, but by then this would no longer be his story but the story of a handful of writers and a conference meant to celebrate a republic in its death throes that had possibly never even existed, and the story of two good men, one of whom will become his father, and of two murders. But, as I said, that story will be other people's story, not Linden's, and it should be told—he will tell it, many years later, in Bologna, under woeful conditions he'll pretend to have forgotten—as something that didn't happen to him at all; or, at least, as something that didn't happen to him in his youth but rather shortly after it ended, after the deaths of the old professor and the journalist, deaths which he contributed to in no small measure. He didn't know what to think about his responsibility in those events and the ones that followed them, trapped between his convictions and the incidents that resulted from them, which he would never be able to frankly explain to his own son, even when that son asked him to as he was setting out along his own path. Linden will often think about that in the years to come, but he will also often think, without being able to explain why, about that man from Voltaggio who came to Genoa with his wife to have his leg amputated.

Ravenna, Florence, Genoa, Rome

MARCH 1978

Interviews: Part II

〉〉

The images should not show the crime in and of itself, but rather those who witnessed it.

CLAUDE LANZMANN, "What Is Memory?"

Michele Garassino, Genoa, March 13, 1978

Ah, yes, the Fascist Writers' Conference, sure: at one point we were calling it, among ourselves, the "Idealist Writers' Conference"; but now I think that "Autistic Writers' Conference," or "Imbecilic," or "Insane," would have been a more appropriate name.

Atilio Tessore, Florence, March 11, 1978

The idea, apparently, was Ezra Pound's. He convinced Fernando Mezzasoma that holding a conference of fascist writers would help mitigate the bad press that had plagued the Italian Social Republic since its founding, which is to say, since a fistful of German paratroopers rescued Mussolini so he could meet with Hitler, and Hitler, God only knows why, gave him a country. Actually, the problem with the Italian Social Republic wasn't propaganda, but more of a political and military problem: a small number of men were trying to sustain a national project that was threatened from the south by the Allied advance; from the north by the German occupation; and domestically, by despondency and incompetence, by disaffection, the ineptitude of its leaders and by those bands of criminals who called themselves "partisans" and wrote history in such a way as to make their crimes look like heroic acts. So, actually, what was threatening the Italian Social Republic on all sides, including above and below—in other words, truly on all sides—was reality, which is always the worst threat. Despite that, the idea of holding a fascist writers' conference wasn't the worst idea one could have in those days and it was fairly easy to bring about because Pound regularly corresponded with many people within Italy and beyond who aligned themselves, to varying extents, with the regime. What's more, we, the fascist writers, didn't have much to do in those days, as the paper shortage and the international siege condemned us to writing with the hope of publishing only after the war had ended. Of course it was clear to most of us that, once the war ended, and the various sides thought it over, we probably wouldn't be able to publish what we were writing, not to mention the quite plausible possibility that, once the war had ended, we would all be hanging from streetlamps on corners. So, I thought, why not attend a conference of fascist writers: a similar gathering held in Spain during the Civil War had produced some results, it seemed—of course those were "antifascist" writers, or so they said, although it's obvious that their conference did more for them than they did for their republic, another argument for taking part in our little fascist get-together. So the authorities of the Social Republic said yes to old Ezra, which was actually the simplest way to get rid of him: I know what I'm talking about, and there is no one who feels more sympathy for those poor nurses in that hospital in D.C. where they locked him up: we should have done it long before, but the truth is we didn't want to overwhelm our already meager medical staff. And Ezra accepted and put out a call for like-minded writers in a bimonthly newspaper called *Il Popolo di Alessandria,* which was where I first read about the conference in October 1944, although I obviously got more and more news of the event in the months following, from other writers and from Ezra himself, always so loquacious, and despite the fact that, I now realize, it would have been best, at least in retrospect, best and most convenient, if I'd never bought the newspaper that day.

Espartaco Boyano, Ravenna, March 10, 1978
Perhaps they'd made a list. But it's hard to imagine who could've come up with it, besides Ezra Pound himself. And in that case,

it's hard to imagine Pound was aware of our existence. We were a handful of Italian writers scattered across a shrinking country that was never properly a country at all. They called it "The Republic of Salò," but none of us ever used that name. For us it was simply the Social Republic, the remains of a shipwreck that, I now believe, we had a hand in provoking. Although, of course, the ship was a magnificent example of a very common kind of boat in the Italian naval fleet: beautiful and imposing when seen from the outside, but with engines that had broken down long ago, and holds filled with rats.

Atilio Tessore, Florence, March 11, 1978
"He often presents the appearance of a man trying to convey to a very deaf person the fact that the house is on fire," someone declared about Ezra Pound. Who? T. S. Eliot, who knew him well and who always knew which house was burning and when.

Oreste Calosso, Rome, March 16, 1978
I'm not sure there was a list of Italian authors, but I recall there being one of sympathetic foreign authors who could possibly participate in the conference, and I helped draw it up myself, at a meeting in Turin with hapless Ottavio Zuliani. Where? I can't even remember, although I haven't forgotten the jacket Zuliani was wearing, which was too big on him, making me think, I don't know why, that he'd taken it off a dead man. I may not have been better dressed, of course, but this isn't the time to go into Italian style in 1944, which was basically dead men's clothes worn by dead men, the former only separated from the latter by the thin film of a soap bubble that was always about to burst. One of the first names Zuliani and I mentioned was Richard Euringer, who had written an anti-Semitic play entitled *The New Midas* and had won the national prize for *German Passion*, whose subtitle was "A Hymn to Our Führer." None of us had read it, of course, but we imagined his convictions would be in line with ours; later, however, Philipp Bouhler, who was the head of something vaguely called the "Party's

Control Commission for the Protection of National Socialist Literature," rejected Euringer because he'd recently had problems with the censors. Bouhler announced that his office would pay the travel expenses for any German authors taking part in the conference, but in exchange he not only refused to invite Euringer and Hans Hagemeyer, possibly because of some sort of personal conflict, but also forced Hermann Burte on us. Burte had already taken part in a "European tour" of German writers in 1940 and was the author of a novel with the incredible title of *Wiltfeber, the Eternal German.* In any case, our list went through Bouhler's hands and was returned to us with some modifications; the definitive list of Germans (who were, in the end, the only friends we had left, although they were somewhat awkward friends, the kind who put their feet up on your table and criticize what's on your plate) was made up of Eberhard Möller, who had written plays and a novel about the Panama Canal, as well as reporting for the SS Propaganda Company; Hans Blunck; Erwin Kolbenheyer; Heinrich Zillich; and, of course, Hanns Johst, who had dedicated his *Schlageter* to Hitler. Some authors were simply never found, like the Austrian Josef Weinheber, who was an alcoholic in addition to being a great poet, and who committed suicide a month before the Red Army entered Berlin; Friedrich Bethge, who must have been somewhere writing chess problems for the soldiers' newspaper; and Felix Hartlaub, who was working in the office charged with writing the war diaries of the German Army's High Command and wasn't allowed to take leave.

Oreste Calosso, Rome, March 16, 1978
It's possible he wasn't allowed to leave his office even temporarily because they really needed him there, although it was already obvious that the war diaries of the German High Command were a version of history that wouldn't win out, just as the German Army wouldn't, so it wasn't necessary to be exhaustive: every entry in that diary was, actually, an argument in favor of condemning the army's survivors. Though maybe, in light of everything Hartlaub had learned at the main Wehrmacht headquarters, he wasn't

authorized to leave so he couldn't fall into enemy hands and possibly reveal relevant information; or perhaps it was the complete opposite, and Hartlaub's bosses were reluctant to let him go out of fear that he would run off. Shortly after the war we learned that, although seemingly a convinced National Socialist, Hartlaub was privately a dissident. That was revealed in his satirical drawings and the publication of his personal diary; unlike the texts he'd published during his relatively brief career, his private writing was dry, austere, harsh: the literature of the ruins, which constituted the primary line of German literature starting from the end of the war. Hartlaub had somehow learned to speak the new language, but he couldn't profit from it because he died or disappeared, which is the same thing, in Berlin, in April 1945.

Espartaco Boyano, Ravenna, March 10, 1978
Some of us—for example Oreste Calosso and I, in Turin and Ravenna respectively—survived by writing for the magazines published, for some reason, by the army. And for the newspapers that lost pages week after week until they were just tiny pamphlets, due to the paper shortage and transportation difficulties. No one expected anything of them anymore because the news unfolded at an unprecedented pace and, in any case, it had been years since anyone expected an Italian newspaper to say anything moderately close to the truth, whatever that was. So reading the press meant clinging to habit, in a time when all habits were crumbling. Mussolini had already said that bit about seeing the profile of the new Italian Republic in the air. He must have said it on a very windy day in Salò, since that profile was growing blurrier by the minute. While he was reading—supposedly—Plato's *Republic,* we were writing magnificent literary works, the best we'd ever written because they were truly literary. What I mean by that is they were written with a complete disregard for reality, so we would be immune to accusations of defeatism. They announced victories, surprise attacks, resurgences that were not only impossible but also unrealistic, but which we proclaimed with the conviction of those with no other

options. Who was it that said "A hungry dog believes in nothing but meat"? Nikolai Gogol? Ivan Turgenev? Take your pick; the point is it's true.

Oreste Calosso, Rome, March 16, 1978

Some other writers who were invited but didn't attend the conference: Hellmuth Langenbucher, known as the "Pope" of German literature, who had published two noteworthy books (or that was how it seemed to us) entitled *People's Poetry of Our Time* and *National Socialist Poetry*. He never responded to our invitation. Hans Jürgen Nierentz, who wrote for German television and was one of the few authors with any interest in technological changes, who knew how to sing the praises of the machine the way we did, and who was possibly already dead when we sent him the invitation, although there are those who say he lived in Düsseldorf after the war and worked as a publicist until 1955, when he died, for the first or second time. Georg Oedemann, who had written a novel entitled *City of Machines* and, before that, a celebration of highways, never sent any reply. Then there was Hans Zöberlein, who usually wrote about his experiences in World War I and became a member of the National Socialist Party very early on, in 1921; in the last weeks of the war he took part in the execution by firing squad of a group of people who wanted to surrender a town near Munich to the Allies. His response to our invitation was a handwritten note informing us that, aware he would be condemned by history, which would transform honorable people into execrable monsters and execrable monsters into liberators, he preferred to add to the list of accusations against him rather than chase the dream of literature.

Espartaco Boyano, Ravenna, March 10, 1978

I haven't forgotten a note handwritten by Hans Zöberlein, a German writer who—according to what I was later told—had declined the invitation to the conference by saying: "When this war ends, our invaders will bring with them their languages, which will be the languages of the victor, and they will impose them upon the German nation like Latin was once imposed, but they will also bring a new German language, and that new tongue will make our works illegible, like a dead language." Pretty true, don't you think? Our books do seem written in that language; I can assure you that, even if you wanted to, you wouldn't be able to read them. Anyway, how could you even comprehend the differences of usage, the heights some reached and the abysses others were mired in? Do you understand, for example, Chinese? I don't. Could I comprehend the stylistic differences in Chinese that exist between a poem and some camera instructions? No, I couldn't. The same thing happens, and will happen, to you. So why do you want to know about all this? Do yourself a favor: don't shed your tears for anyone who lives on these streets.

Oreste Calosso, Rome, March 16, 1978
Ah, yes: the Italians. It was no simple task drawing up the list, or it was incredibly simple compared to our other activities during that period, like surviving the bombings and scraping together a little meat, coffee, and sugar. (Some women gifted Pound with a few plums around that time, and he never forgot the kindness.)

Espartaco Boyano, Ravenna, March 10, 1978
We—the Germans too, by the way—usually rejected the use of motifs taken from ancient art and mythology, which we considered inappropriate unless they were subjected to major reelaboration. We ruled out any literature that wasn't, by definition, collective. In that sense, we weren't particularly interested in ambiguities or they simply seemed bourgeois to us, as did introspection. We considered literary experimentation a maneuver destined to conceal some disagreement with the times and with discourses that we believed should be imitated, because they emerged from the State as a collective voice. We rejected any hint of the fantastical, allegory, parables, and elegy, which reminded us of all we'd managed

to defeat with our works. What exactly had we defeated? The bourgeoisie's absurd, unfortunate recipe for a self-centered, mercenary, cautious peace and avaricious mercantilism. We opted for an aesthetics of violence and a spirit of revolt, and we thought that war was the only way to cleanse the world. We were interested in the beautiful ideas of technological progress and poetry, we were willing to die for them, because they seemed gloriously opposed to all the ugly ideas people lived and live for. Don't we all believe that at some point in our lives? Don't you believe it too, "Linden" or whatever your name is?

Atilio Tessore, Florence, March 11, 1978
It's not true: some of us thought the dehumanization provoked by technology was a way to overcome the limitations of the individual subject, and our books spoke to that, about the social order growing stronger through the destruction of certain people—for example, that's how I understand Franz Kafka's work, which I believe has been misinterpreted as a manifestation of humanist piety or some such idiocy. A second possibility, in other words, a second line, was documenting our own dehumanization, devoting ourselves to the destruction of subjectivity itself and realizing the losses you confront when destroying yourself: sometimes I think we all pretended to adopt the first alternative but were actually exploring the second; and at times I also believe that the only one who reached the end of that difficult path was the writer you've come asking about, who was the most extreme of us all.

Oreste Calosso, Rome, March 16, 1978
We also invited Carlo Olgiati, who in 1931 published a work in three volumes entitled *The Historic Metabolism,* which we were all careful not to read, although it was rumored to be some sort of attempt to explain an economic, biological, and social theory, which we all thought sounded quite Futurist. We did not rescind our invitation even when we found out that "La Redentina," which had published

his great work, was none other than Olgiati himself, who had fabricated a publishing house and named it after his candy factory in Novara. Olgiati's theory seemed to be that history is governed by biochemical laws that would fuse all of life's components into a single substance or nature called "olgiato"; when that happened, there would no longer be a State, laws, money, hunting, sex, police, salaries, or the transformation of energy into heat and mechanical labor, so I suppose there would no longer be history. I don't quite remember, but I think some of us were amused by the idea, and that's why we invited Olgiati, who somehow arrived from Novara. Shortly afterward, he received a telegram that converted the great prophet of the end of history into a quite desperate middle-aged man: his candy factory had been destroyed in the bombing. The fusion of everything that exists into a single magnificent sphere was of no comfort to him in those circumstances, and Olgiati returned to Novara the following day, I suppose to gather up the candies from the rubble, like a Mexican child dealing with a monstrous piñata. He hung himself shortly after that, at home, I think.

Atilio Tessore, Florence, March 11, 1978
A vision of the social classes that didn't condemn them to constant infighting but rather established agreements from alternative positions; the aspiration to full employment; the guarantee of property only if it didn't become an insult to the less fortunate; the protection of workers, the elderly, and the handicapped, of women and children; a certain idea of morality, always so necessary in Italy; the struggle against ignorance and servility through education; socialism, economic independence, the exaltation of pride in being Italian: that was what we believed in, first of all. Literature came after, not as a belief but rather as an instrument.

Oreste Calosso, Rome, March 16, 1978
Marinetti had died that year, and we thought about inviting his widow, the painter Benedetta Cappa, but we found her style too dec-

orative, in some sense serving a lifestyle we, at that point, still considered extremely bourgeois. Besides, she was a woman, which—as always—wasn't exactly an impediment, but it didn't make things any easier either.

Oreste Calosso, Rome, March 16, 1978
Our contact in Salò was Fernando Mezzasoma, the Minister of Popular Culture who was executed on April 28 in Dongo, on the walkway beside Lake Como: the ministry was in Villa Amadei, where Giorgio Almirante also worked, as did Nicola Bombacci, the person in charge of propaganda who'd been an important Communist leader before becoming a fascist. They were both approachable, but our contact was Mezzasoma.

Atilio Tessore, Florence, March 11, 1978
He combed back what little hair he had, making his forehead—with its crease typical of the lily-livered and the indecisive, contrasting strangely with his sharp jaw—look even bigger; he always wore dirty glasses, and he would take them off and clean them while he spoke, which perhaps was just a trick, a cunning ploy, to observe his interlocutors better, while they thought he couldn't see them clearly. However, he wasn't wearing his glasses when the partisans shot him in Dongo, on the twenty-eighth of April of that year.

Michele Garassino, Genoa, March 13, 1978
Ah, yes, Mezzasoma: he used to say that literature is better when it's the result of a group of conspirators communicating with and inciting each other, and, as such, he used to nurture quarrels and confrontations between writers, which he believed to be healthier for a lively literary scene than consensus and respect, which I suppose is true to a large extent. He would often turn his words over in his mouth before speaking, as if he were savoring them, and he moved his lips a lot when he talked, which gave the impression of

a film where the sound and the image were slightly out of sync. His entire existence was an invitation to a calamity, and one day, the invitation was simply accepted.

Espartaco Boyano, Ravenna, March 10, 1978
We wanted new ruins we could dedicate our poems to, ruins we could sing to like one sings to the Parthenon and other monuments to the glorious past. But soon we had too many, and we ourselves became ruins. And then it was over.

Oreste Calosso, Rome, March 16, 1978
And Princess Amélie Rives Troubetzkoy, an American-born novelist and playwright almost eighty years old who was married to a Russian. Troubetzkoy published twenty-four books, as well as hundreds of poems and a play in verse, but I can't remember a single line from her work. She died in June 1945, in Rome, where she lived because she was some sort of convinced fascist and because there was fresher fish there, even in times of war. We also invited James "Giacomo" Strachey Barnes, who called himself the "chronicler and prophet of the fascist Revolution" and wrote various books in English about fascism before disappearing after the war into a not-very-fascist but much more comfortable life. Strachey Barnes, of course, didn't respond to our invitation, and it's possible by that point he had already accepted what we later would: the end of everything we had, to varying degrees, believed in.

Atilio Tessore, Florence, March 11, 1978
It appears the preparations for the conference began in October 1944, around the time the publishing houses and newspapers were nationalized, and the proposed venues shifted as the country shrank. By then the Allies were already south of Bologna, and Milan, Turin, and Genoa were being regularly bombed: which is to say, what was left of Milan, Turin, and Genoa was being regularly

bombed, since the bombing had begun more than a year earlier, in August 1943; but almost every Italian city in the Social Republic had already been the target of raids, of aerial attacks—Taranto, Cosenza, Terni, Novara, Foggia, Salerno, Crotone, Viterbo, Avellino, Lecce, Bari, Orte, Cagliari, Carbonia, Civitavecchia, Benevento—and starting in February 1945, Trieste and Pola were also targeted. They bombed some city almost every day; almost every day there were statistics on the dead and wounded that were no longer reported because they were no longer news but rather an alternative form of normality; not just another form of normality, but the most Italian, at that time.

Oreste Calosso, Rome, March 16, 1978
Even though the natural choice would have been Milan or Turin, it was precisely that fact, that plus the bombing, that made us think of some other location for the event. In February 1945 we had already chosen the place, close enough to both cities so that travel wouldn't be an obstacle and far enough from Salò to make clear to the foreign press that the support for the Social Republic we were expecting from the authors taking part in the conference, which in some way they had already lent us by accepting our invitation, wasn't the result of any sort of coercion. We chose Pinerolo, a small city some fifty kilometers southwest of Turin, beside the Chisone River.

Oreste Calosso, Rome, March 16, 1978
"Pinareul" in Piedmontese, "Pineiròl" in Occitan, "Pignerol" in French; set against a curtain—white for a good portion of the year, and an unusual green the rest of the time—of the Cottian Alps and the Monviso Massif, in the Chisone Valley. Before naming Giorgio Almirante as his representative at the conference, Mezzasoma ordered we be given use of the main hall on the first floor of the Palazzo Comunale for the deliberations, and the Palazzo Vittone to house the German authors; the others would stay in San Germano Chisone, a nearby town.

Espartaco Boyano, Ravenna, March 10, 1978
The Palazzo Comunale? An enormous candle someone had brutally stuck into the cake of a mentally deficient child who could only see cubic shapes.

Oreste Calosso, Rome, March 16, 1978
Our list, Zuliani and I thought as soon as we started working on it, shouldn't be a list of our preferences; or, better put, it should be made up not only of authors sympathetic to the regime, who were, of course, our favorite authors, but also of writers who, having never declared their allegiances, could, potentially, lean toward our cause. Zuliani and I first thought of establishing a purely literary admissions criterion, related to the quality of their work, but later we understood that was no longer valid, since it was associated with a moral idea—as were all kinds of literary criticism and opinions on literary quality—that was collapsing under the weight of the military defeat and all the enemies assailing the Social Republic. I think that at certain historical moments there has to be some sort of interlude, long or short, doesn't much matter, in which one morality is replaced by another and, as a result, what was "good" is transformed into "bad" and vice versa: since this happens in the realm of politics, I don't see why it shouldn't also happen with literature, which is the artistic discipline most similar and most indebted to politics. So there should be a moment in every catastrophe in which there is no longer moral judgment, or it becomes inappropriate or incidental, or worthless for judging the new the way the old was judged, and in that brief or lasting moment—doesn't much matter, I repeat—the "good" literary texts must be equal to the "bad" ones, *The Iliad* must have the same value as the program for a mediocre play, and Dante's *Divine Comedy* must be equal to an instruction booklet for an electric toy train. In that moment, I think, one must no longer know what normality is and who the monsters are, and what drives, or hampers, a work's greatness. I think we found ourselves in that moment, which was why we invited Flavia Morlacchi, a Roman poetess who emitted some sort of crowing, like a laying

hen, when she read her poems, and Cosimo Zago, the rickety, lame poet from Venice who'd lost a leg in World War I, according to him, along with a manuscript in the boot he was never able to reconstruct. We considered both of them ridiculous, but it wasn't impossible that in the new times ahead they would make it big, which would be a catastrophe for everything we deemed worthy of reading and respect, but, nevertheless, was something we should take into account. I remember a fragment of one of her poems, Morlacchi's, God knows why, where she compared the ruins of the Palatino with "blind eyes / shaded eyes / of the fierce and glorious Roman specter / still open there in vain / on the hill / to the spectacle of / fascinating green life / of this April of distant times." Times that made those verses respectable deserved nothing more than contempt, but we were living in contemptible times and, who knows, maybe those were the verses that best reflected them.

Atilio Tessore, Florence, March 11, 1978
Zago had been poor his entire life except for a brief period when he served as a diplomat, possibly due to an error by the authorities, though it'd been some time since he'd been sent anywhere when Zuliani visited him in Venice. He hadn't left his home on the Lista Bari for days, and he confessed to Zuliani that he couldn't attend the conference because he didn't have any proper trousers. Zuliani went out and bought some, then took them over to his house to try on, so Zago got out of bed and struggled to get into them, hopping on the only leg he had. According to Zuliani, the trousers fit him perfectly but, when the time came, Zago still didn't come to the conference, and he didn't even send a telegram.

Michele Garassino, Genoa, March 13, 1978
It's not the strangest story I've heard about him, however: he believed he could speak every language, despite never having studied any of them. Once we put him to the test. "What does *Blume* mean, Zago?" we asked him. He puffed up his cheeks, as if the word

were a wine he was tasting, and finally replied: "Something aquatic." Some of us laughed out loud; we were finishing up dinner and had been drinking. *"Blume* means *flower,"* we corrected him, but Zago thought for a second and responded: "Yes: aquatic flower, like the lily."

Atilio Tessore, Florence, March 11, 1978
Naturally, Cosimo Zago worked for the secret police, as did many others.

Atilio Tessore, Florence, March 11, 1978
The line from Pisa to Rimini, which we knew as the Gothic Line or the Green Line, was the southern border of the Social Republic until April 1, 1945, like the Arno Line had been before it, and even before that, the Trasimene, which we used to call the "Albert Line" after Field Marshal Albert Kesselring, also known as "Albert the Smiling." Later we wouldn't have time to give the borders nick-names, except for the Genghis Khan Line and the Po, because the Allies were advancing so rapidly. It was all over by April 27, when the line reached Garfagnana, but by then we had taken refuge, to the best of our abilities, frightened but perhaps also forewarned by a death, a single death among so many others. Our conference was held on April 20 and 21, although it'd been scheduled to go on until the twenty-third.

Oreste Calosso, Rome, March 16, 1978
The idea was to break up the isolation that hung over the arts, par-ticularly literature, in the Social Republic; but while that would have been possible in, let's say, September or October 1944, it no longer was in April 1945, among other reasons because boats no longer headed toward the northern ports and traveling by land was dangerous and, largely, reckless. A handful of writers told us that they couldn't come, others we could never locate, since they'd

abandoned their last addresses and were in hiding or wandering through Europe; some never found a ticket: we could gather all their names into a list of the finest of world literature that you, perhaps, would call "fascist literature" although that term is imprecise or, at least, it shouldn't carry all the connotations someone of your age, and with what I imagine to be your political ideas, would give it. Those who couldn't attend the conference included the American Arthur Maddow; Justo Jiménez Martínez de Ostos, a Brazilian writer who loved jokes and had written "Ode to the Braying of Franklin D. Roosevelt," which consisted solely of donkey sounds and had to be performed in American English, according to Ostos, who was unable to convince any shipping lines to allow him passage from Rio de Janeiro to Europe: Ostos disappeared in Lisbon in 1956; he'd been born in 1897 in southern Brazil on an estate where he'd commissioned a gigantic statue of Mussolini that, according to what I'm told, was devoured by the jungle after his disappearance; Knut Hamsun, whose enthusiasm for the Germans seemed to pale beside his enthusiasm for us Italians, but who chose to decline the invitation and remain at his home in Nørholm, where he was arrested for high treason and died in 1952, seven years after writing an elegy to Adolf Hitler and nine years after sending his Nobel Prize medal to Joseph Goebbels; Juan Antonio Tiben, the Swiss man who had spent his youth in Florence and then in Rome, where he ran various literary journals in the 1930s after losing his money to an Italian film actress, and who never wrote a book but I can still remember part of one of his poems: "You will look through the porthole / at the two houses of God / and nothing will matter / beyond the lost gaze / with which from his two houses / God will be searching for you"; Louis-Ferdinand Céline, who had fled Paris, we couldn't locate him because he was in Sigmaringen Castle with his wife, a cat named Bébert, and Marshal Philippe Pétain; Robert Brasillach had already been killed on February 6 in Montrouge, but he had left us a letter filled with conviction and personal courage that we tried to read at the end of the conference but no one listened; Pierre Drieu La Rochelle had already committed suicide, though we didn't know it at the time, just as we didn't yet know his last words, which are terrible and accurate, and his rivals proved to be unworthy of: "Be as faithful to the spirit of the Resistance as I am to the spirit of Collaboration." Another one who'd died was Jacques Boulenger—in 1943 he'd written a book about French blood that could have been endorsed, word for word, by an Italian, particularly a northern Italian; Abel Bonnard had already fled, or was just about to, down to Spain, where he planned to hide out until his death sentence as a collaborationist was reconsidered or until he found the man of his dreams, which I think was what finally happened and, of course, was more feasible; Paul Morand, who by then was a representative of the Vichy government in Bern, although the Vichy government no longer existed, did try to come to the conference. He'd committed to attending, but in the end couldn't get across the Swiss border, which over those weeks seemed to be closed in both directions but particularly if you were trying to enter the country.

Atilio Tessore, Florence, March 11, 1978
Paul Claudel? An enormous Catholic cow, like Georges Bernanos, who was a mustachioed Catholic cow; and like Charles Maurras, a monarchical Catholic cow who'd already been arrested in September 1944. Strangely enough, Maurras was a cow with a goatee. Not Henri Massis, and that's why he was at the conference; as was Lucien Rebatet, who later wrote *Memoirs of a Fascist,* which we should have written ourselves and signed with our first and last names; which is to say, with our Italian first and last names.

Oreste Calosso, Rome, March 16, 1978
A sizable delegation of Spaniards also attended the conference. Not César González-Ruano, suspected by our German friends of having helped some wealthy Jews flee Paris, though more likely he just ripped them off . . . He also could have been a German spy, who knows. And not Ernesto Giménez Caballero, who at that point was the cultural attaché at the Spanish embassy in Paraguay but

also the closest to us: he'd invited Marinetti to Spain in 1928, he'd written about the connections he saw in Italy to Spanish national traditionalism (we took that last part as an insult, of course, but we mostly overlooked it), he'd made an important contribution to a general theory of fascism in Europe, and he was avant-garde, but he couldn't come. Nor could José María Pemán, whom we met on a visit he'd made to Rome in 1938 with a one-eyed general; nor Rafael García Serrano, even though we sent him money for his train ticket (he kept it and didn't come); nor Agustín de Foxá, who'd been banished from Rome in 1940 for espionage—although, of course, what else was a diplomat to do?—despite which he wrote some lovely *Poems to Italy*. But among those who did attend were Luys Santa Marina and Rafael Sánchez Mazas—who knew us well, who'd lived in Italy for seven years, and who was ugly, a horrible, frightful, possible moral ugliness—and Eugenio d'Ors and Juan Ramón Masoliver, who had been Pound's secretary in Rapallo and knew us well. Also Eugenio Montes, who a couple of years earlier had written *Italian Melody* and had visited the country on various occasions, with that one-eyed general or with some other one.

Michele Garassino, Genoa, March 13, 1978
The Spanish writers were contemplative: they were with the priests and the farmworkers, and aspired to be like them, in some obscure way. We were indifferent to the priests and the farmworkers, but the Spanish writers were our circumstantial comrades-in-arms, so their friendship was, as happens on so many occasions, inevitable. None of them knew what Futurism was, however: if they had known, they would have been very careful not to attend the conference.

Espartaco Boyano, Ravenna, March 10, 1978
They wrote *coplas*, from what I understand. Verses to a heroism that they, of course, lacked and to a rural life they probably had little knowledge of. Fortunately, God gave me the talent of not being

able to learn Spanish, which—from what I've been told by some—has saved me from having to read a ton of garbage.

Oreste Calosso, Rome, March 16, 1978
A Bulgarian novelist with the improbable name of Fani Popowa-Mutafowa came, and the Dane Svend Fleuron, and Rintsje Piter Sybesma and Henri Bruning from the Netherlands (Bruning was honored by the Dutch SS in September 1944 for his work as an author and a censor and, when he returned to his country after the conference, he was arrested and jailed for two years and three months), and the Romanians Ion Sân-Giorgiu and Niculae I. Herescu both committed to coming but only the first one actually did. The Norwegian Kåre Immanuel Bjørgen did not attend; he was in hiding, which meant we couldn't find him (though the Allies did, condemning him to three years of forced labor). Nor did Lars Hansen, the other Norwegian who had taken part in the Weimar conferences, and who died in July 1944. The Hungarian József Nyírö replied that he couldn't come because he was fulfilling governmental duties, but the following month he fled to Germany with the entire Hungarian cabinet.

Oreste Calosso, Rome, March 16, 1978
You see, the Allies were our enemies, but the Germans, whom the King had betrayed and who wanted to make us pay for that betrayal, were also our enemies. Everything in the middle was our enemy, but everything in the middle was everything, there wasn't anything that wasn't in the middle at that point in time. We organized that conference because we knew all was lost and that we would soon fall, but we wanted to fall honorably and remaining faithful to ideas that still seemed correct to us, or less erroneous than others, than the freedoms the United States offered based on money and usury, which was historically carried out by Jews, although, in that sense, I've always thought that our view of the Jews is a result

of usury, more than the usury is a result of the Jews and, as such, I don't believe it was necessary to murder them, particularly not the poor Jews, an idea I argued with Pound over, and which Pound ended up accepting at the end of his life. We also wanted to nationalize the factories, guarantee private property, and eliminate the bourgeoisie, as well as avoid the breakup of Italy, none of which was exactly furthered by bringing foreign writers to speak in favor of our idea, that's true; but our idea, I now think, was an aesthetic utopia, and those utopias should never transcend the realm of books, maybe they shouldn't have ever even left the heads of their authors: they had already left our heads, though. So we couldn't do anything else but organize the Conference of Fascist Writers.

Oreste Calosso, Rome, March 16, 1978
Shortly after being named by Mezzasoma as his representative at the conference, Giorgio Almirante took the liberty of inviting Julius Evola, but, as I expected, Evola replied that we weren't reactionary enough to benefit from his presence, something that, actually, was true: we were only carrying out the most revolutionary political experiment ever seen. As for the others, Pierre Gaxotte was crossed off our list by our German friends since he was against the Third Reich, and we rejected the Mexican Alfonso Junco, in that case for being against Italian fascism; in his place came the writer Pobre México. We waited for the historian Charles Petrie until the last minute, but he wasn't allowed to leave the United Kingdom and, from what I understand, he protested by grabbing the cap off of a policeman in the port of Bristol, which got him arrested for a few hours. Pablo Antonio Cuadra, the Nicaraguan, didn't want to come to the conference because he thought the political and aesthetic problems of the American continent should be resolved using their own cultural elements, which he informed us in a letter written in the European tongue Americans typically use to reject all things European.

Oreste Calosso, Rome, March 16, 1978

Almirante picked me up in an official car in Turin on the nine-teenth. Mezzasoma didn't come with him even though he promised he would, so Almirante was all the official representation we had. It wasn't much, and he knew it, so he was constantly apologizing. The car headed slowly toward Pinerolo along a highway devastated by bombing, with the remains of cars and dead animals on both sides of the road, and near Volvera we had a strange encounter with a group of Wehrmacht soldiers who stopped us to ask for identifica-tion. When we showed them our documents, one of them told us that the day before they'd seen a train passing by and that the train was made of cement and was immune to bombs, which sounded far-fetched, in part because it seemed hard to imagine what kind of a locomotive could have pulled such a train and because we couldn't conceive of someone wanting to travel through northern Italy in some sort of roving mausoleum. Almirante kept insistently preening his mustache, as if trying to shield his lips, and what might emerge from them, from my eyes, and told me later that he had heard talk of a similar project and also of some secret weapons Ger-many was about to use to change the direction of the war, which we were clearly losing—although there was no need for him to tell me that last part. He added that he knew because he had recently met with a Sicilian playwright—whose name didn't mean much to me, I've never been too interested in the theater, much less in the North African sort—who'd just returned from Germany. The playwright had been arrested by the Germans due to a problem with his papers in 1943, shortly before the Allied invasion, and he'd been sent to build some antiaircraft shelters in Salerno and later a barracks out-side Ancona and then to Germany to work in Wehrmacht arms fac-tories, without any of his attempts to clear up the situation being properly addressed. In Germany, in a factory outside Bochum, the playwright learned about the new weapons and found out about a plan the Germans had: they were going to make two passenger planes fall in the middle of New York City. The anticipated result wasn't so much human and material loss as it was plunging the United States into decades of paralysis and confusion that would lead the Americans to make successive terrible political errors that would stretch the country so thin it would start to fray, tensing over its empty shell, as had happened with the Roman Empire and all the other empires in history. One day, a few weeks later, the playwright managed to prove his identity to his supervisor, thanks to what we'll call fate: he'd heard his supervisor talking to someone else about a play he'd seen in the theater the night before and trying to remember the name of the playwright. "I'm the author, me," he had stammered out. The Germans checked their archives and confirmed the statement, and then sent the playwright on a troop transport train to Italy, to Salò, along with a recommendation letter they'd written as some sort of redress.

Oreste Calosso, Rome, March 16, 1978
"What are those weapons?" I asked him. Almirante looked at me, and then looked away, as if he were ashamed to tell me: "They're inside of us. They already put them in there, now they just have to activate them," he answered.

Michele Garassino, Genoa, March 13, 1978
His name was Emilio Carduccio, and he'd built up some prestige around the Strait of Messina and in Reggio Calabria, not so much in Palermo, where he was considered a regional author. I met him briefly when he was in Genoa accompanied by some local Party authorities. One of his plays was staged for a social excursion among authorities in the Spianata dell'Acquasola, to the east of the city. Maybe the actors were already drunk, or simply exhausted after the long trip they'd made, or perhaps I was the one exhausted, although I hadn't traveled at all, but I remember the play was a catastrophe. The actors shouted out slogans against the regime, one of them imitated Il Duce's mannerisms and cut his face and forehead with a knife, afterward they ordered us to sing the "Internationale," someone ate excrement onstage. Carduccio was the only one laughing, feverishly, as the sun dropped amid the park's trees and the wives of

the local Party authorities tried to herd their children and stunned husbands back home. After the war I learned that Carduccio was secretly a member of the Sicilian Communist Party and that he'd conceived of that performance as an act of revenge and perhaps suicide. Before that Giorgio Almirante told me Carduccio had been captured by the Germans and spent the last months of the war in an underground arms factory in the Ruhr basin, from which he'd also managed to escape. Of course, by then all of us who'd met him thought he was dead. In the area around the Strait of Messina, where his works had been performed with greater regularity though without any success, some sort of local cult had sprung up around him, and the Party had carefully, although secretly, promoted him as a martyr. One of the groups of insurgents who resisted the Allied occupation inland on the island, between Caltavuturo and Polizzi Generosa, had named a battalion after him, and the local section of the Party had already announced, from its—temporary, they claimed—refuge in Salò, that the main theater in Reggio Calabria would bear his name after the south of the peninsula was recovered. Of course, we never recovered the south of the peninsula, but all those gestures, the celebration of Carduccio as a martyr of the fascist cause, and his return to Italy courtesy of the Germans, were enough for the Allies: when they managed to get their hands on him, they condemned him to two years and three months for being a beneficiary of fascism. He died in prison, in 1946 or 1947.

Oreste Calosso, Rome, March 16, 1978
Pinerolo had managed to remain on the sidelines of the war by clinging to what seemed to be an unflappable indifference to everything that wasn't the nature surrounding it. At the entrance to town we were received by the authorities and a ton of little kids waving Social Republic flags and photographs of Il Duce, as if it were 1926 or 1934. Almirante found the reception as disconcerting as I did, and was about to ask the driver to speed up and pass it by. The formal greetings, of course, lasted for hours, which made clear, as if the flags and portraits of Mussolini weren't enough, that we were deal-

ing with Italians who were proud to be Italians and had no intention of being anything but Italians, not Swiss, not German, and not American. Finally, when we managed to be led to the room in the Town Hall where the conference would be held in a couple of days, and which was already prepared for the occasion, night had begun to fall. Outside, the town seemed to dissolve into the darkness that came from the mountains.

Oreste Calosso, Rome, March 16, 1978
The following day the conference guests began to arrive along the highways and railroad tracks; in fact, the participants had started to trickle into the city the night before, when Carlo Olgiati (in his private car), Henri Massis, and Lucien Rebatet arrived. The first of the two Frenchmen had a wide forehead and a thin mustache that sketched a black triangle beneath his nose; the other was clean-shaven and wore a wrinkled bow tie. I had the impression, when we were introduced, that Massis looked down slightly on Rebatet; but that was common among writers so I didn't think much of it. Naturally, I never asked them why they'd decided to travel together from France, if they had, nor how they got to Pinerolo and why they'd come two days before the start of the conference. I saw them strolling together through the Piazza San Donato, and it was the town's fascist mayor who pointed them out to me and made the introductions. Rebatet was carrying a small Italian phrase guide and was trying out the vocabulary with those around him. "Piacere," he said over and over again; there was something kindly about him, however it was obscured by his rabid anti-Semitism. The next morning, it seemed they had never left the piazza. When I approached them, Massis politely complimented the cathedral's bell tower, while Rebatet silently flipped through his phrase book, until he finally found what he was looking for and proudly exclaimed: "Torre." None of us bothered to clarify that the correct word for it is *campanile.* Just as the mayor was about to object, raising his right hand as if shooing away a fly, loud shouting from one of the plaza's side streets made us turn around, and a caravan of black cars drove in

and stopped in front of us. Two SS officers got out of the first vehicle and opened the back doors. As always, our German friends had planned a triumphant entrance (their retreats are usually quite different, from what I've seen). This one wasn't particularly magnificent, actually, because the black cars had turned the typical gray color of the dust on the roads, because the SS were sweaty, and because Hanns Johst, the most important literary man in the country that aspired to dominate the world, was also sweaty and covered in dust, like an obese pigeon.

Oreste Calosso, Rome, March 16, 1978
Some of the Germans were in uniform, but the impression they gave wasn't exactly bellicose. Eberhard Möller was wearing enormous glasses that he was constantly wiping on his sleeve, and Heinrich Zillich, in his Wehrmacht uniform, wasn't particularly imposing by his side. As they spoke, Hans Blunck's prominent jaw always pointed toward Johst, the man who had at least partially if not totally ousted him from his position of prominence in German literature, but Johst seemed to be paying attention only to himself, as if he were in a room lined with mirrors. In some sense, his presence was a relief to me, because he'd completely taken charge of the situation since his arrival: he assigned tasks to the others in his party, arranged the lunch and dinner schedules, sent some of the German authors (whom he didn't appear to like) to their lodgings, took a quick look at the Duomo, taking it in with what surely seemed—to him—a greatness comparable to that of the cathedral itself, entered the first of a line of cars, and disappeared.

Oreste Calosso, Rome, March 16, 1978
Ion Sân-Giorgiu arrived in the afternoon, at a moment when Almirante and I were arguing with the mayor about the decoration of the room where the deliberations were to be held. The mayor insisted it had to have an Alpine stamp, so he had some crossed skis hung to preside over the room. We recognized Sân-Giorgiu because

he was wearing a generic black uniform to which he'd applied some swastikas, and because he walked the way Romanians usually do, leaning slightly to the left. When I greeted him, I told him we were expecting his fellow countryman Niculae I. Herescu, and he replied he didn't think that ne'er-do-well would show up. He was right, but we didn't find that out until the next day, when a French policeman from the town of Ferrals-les-Corbières—who wasn't entirely without compassion, which is to say, a completely heretical French policeman unfit for duty—sent a telegram to Minister Mezzasoma saying he had a Romanian by the last name of Herescu who said he'd been invited to a writers' conference and was demanding we pick him up in France because he didn't have the means to cross the border. There was no need for the policeman to add that Herescu had drunk up those means on the train.

Oreste Calosso, Rome, March 16, 1978
It seemed the Spaniards had also been drinking on the train, or rather on the airplane. They arrived at night, as we sat at a large table presided over by Hanns Johst in one of the local restaurants; forgive me for resorting to cliché, but the truth is the Spaniards brought a bit of joy to a meal that had taken a gloomy turn right at the start, partly because Germans don't exactly light up social events—not even in wartime, it seemed—and partly due to Johst's words. We had to drink from his lips a panoply of reflections on "sacrifice," the "blood spilled," the "necessary effort we all must make," and the "purpose of the highest art" before he'd let us lay into the food. The Spaniards, on this occasion, uncharacteristically arrived, shall we say, right on time, but their enthusiasm waned as soon as they saw their German colleagues; only the food and drink—particularly the alcohol—managed to somewhat lift our spirits. Taking advantage of one of the inevitable pauses between the second and third courses, or between the third and fourth—in Pinerolo they didn't seem to be at war, and the dishes kept coming, as if they were rolling down the sides of the mountains around us, which, in a way, was actually true— Eugenio d'Ors stood up to inflict

on those in attendance a speech about classical antiquity, which he saw reflected in the faces of his Italian friends, he said, although, for the moment, his Italian friends were only Giorgio Almirante, the mayor of Pinerolo, and me. As you can see, I don't exactly have the face of a Polykleitos and, in that sense, can only serve to demonstrate how horrible classic antiquity was. D'Ors went on about the need to maintain those classical aesthetic canons, about the importance of those preservation efforts giving rise to an idea of authority, about that authority in turn guaranteeing access to a sexuality that is a matter for gentlemen, Catholic gentlemen in particular—I don't know why he said this; perhaps he was inviting us to a brothel and we didn't catch on—and about the superior nature of a classical, reasonable, and authoritarian lifestyle. When he sat down again, there was some timid applause, which wasn't seconded by Luys Santa Marina, who was absentmindedly stroking some embroidery on the front of his shirt: three skulls and crossbones with an inscription. I later asked him what the inscription meant and he told me: "It means 'it doesn't matter,'" referring to the three death sentences he'd been handed down in Republican jails during the Spanish Civil War. Rafael Sánchez Mazas didn't clap either, barricaded behind his glasses observing everything like an injured owl that would have flown off if it could. Naturally, I don't have many memories of how that night ended, but I do remember the embroidery on Santa Marina's blue shirt, Sánchez Mazas's gaze, the way all the German writers stood up at the same time and said goodbye to us with a choreographed nod of their heads and a succession of raised arms, how then Eugenio Montes and I were talking in low voices, with Montes asking me about the border situation in the Italian Social Republic. I also remember that, while we walked back to our lodgings through the already starkly empty streets of Pinerolo, Montes told me the story of Saint Genesius of Rome. According to the Spanish writer, Genesius was a Roman actor who was mocking baptism during a play when he had a revelation and asked to be baptized, and was then jailed and deported, and I think killed too, and that he's the only Catholic saint who's typically represented with a mask on. I don't remember why Montes started telling me about Genesius, but I do remember that I asked him how the audience had known that the request for baptism wasn't also just part of the show; by which I mean, how did they know that the play Genesius was performing wasn't about a Roman actor making fun of baptism during a performance when he has a revelation and asks to be baptized; I also asked him if perhaps the deportation and killing weren't also part of the show, its natural consequence or perhaps an accident, since it was unlikely that Genesius really wanted to die; but Montes, I recall, just looked at me strangely.

Espartaco Boyano, Ravenna, March 10, 1978
Why is it that everything we can say about those years seems untrue or, if it is true, seems like it didn't really happen? I don't get it, I don't really understand it even today.

Oreste Calosso, Rome, March 16, 1978
The next day Ottavio Zuliani arrived, as did some low-level bureaucrats from the ministry who were accompanying the Italian writers, who, once again confirmed the cliché—you can see this story is filled with them—by arriving late, in cars that the ministry had offered them in Genoa, Bologna, Salò, Venice, and Milan. Our German friends had taken their seats in the room at Town Hall designated for the early morning deliberations, long before the Italians and the Spaniards. When the Spaniards got there, they insisted on putting together work committees whose function eluded the French, the Germans, and me; they won out, however, and, at least nominally, the conference had five committees respectively designated as "Basic Procedures and Guidelines," "Translation," "Aesthetic Problems," "Classical Studies," and "Propaganda." We left open the question of who would be on each committee until everyone had arrived, but when they had—I'm specifically referring to the Italians, headed up by Zuliani with the octogenarian Amélie Rives Troubetzkoy on his arm, although she was dragging him

down to her pace, which was so slow they both seemed to be walking backward—we all pretended to have forgotten about the work committees.

Atilio Tessore, Florence, March 11, 1978
There wasn't time for introductions despite the fact that many of us had never met our foreign colleagues in person. Hanns Johst stood up and started to sing "Horst-Wessel-Lied" and then we sang our song "Giovinezza," after which there was some controversy, a bit of an argument, when the Spaniards demanded the chance to sing theirs and Johst and the Germans refused, claiming we didn't have time. Some Italians supported the Spaniards, as did Lucien Rebatet, but the proposal was set aside amid protests and murmuring, to move on to the election of the conference president and secretaries. Naturally, Johst was chosen for the top position: we Italians filled some of the secretariat positions as the hosts, and the others were filled by Spaniards, who were still insistently railing against the snub of not being allowed to sing their "Cara al Sol," though they'd toned it down somewhat, pacified by the secretarial positions and the presence of Johst's SS, who had taken their places at the back of the room, ostensibly guaranteeing the safety of the German writers. When I turned to look at them, at the very start of the conference, I recognized a face from the past, one I had known well and hadn't seen for years, that I believed to be just another of the faces of the war dead, and that was the face of someone, I thought, who'd come to commit a crime.

Espartaco Boyano, Ravenna, March 10, 1978
They drove us to Pinerolo in some vehicles that must have been previously used by the butchers of Salò because they smelled of animals and death. I traveled with Filippo Gentilli; our conversation started haltingly and died even before we'd left Milan, where we'd arrived exhausted. As we reached Pinerolo, Gentilli pulled one

of his books out of his luggage and scribbled something in it. When he handed it to me, I discovered he'd inscribed it to me. The dedication read: "To the poet of Ravenna, Espartaco Boyano, from his humble, devoted teacher Filippo Gentilli."

Espartaco Boyano, Ravenna, March 10, 1978
He was wearing—I remember it well—a ring on the middle finger of his right hand, so that whoever extended their hand to shake his would be reminded by its awkwardness that he preferred to be greeted in a different manner. That ring was a reminder that one should always raise one's hand, even in private, in the fascist salute.

Atilio Tessore, Florence, March 11, 1978
There was a story about Filippo Gentilli that he himself, for some reason, had spread, possibly as a warning. Gentilli lived in L'Aquila, where he had some family properties and made an effort to project an image as a royalist and traditional writer—which is to say, as a harmless writer, that is if being royalist and traditional isn't offensive, for example, to other people's intelligence. A few years earlier, he'd been confronted by a handful of writers who wanted to reinvigorate the local literary scene, which I imagine as small and possibly nonexistent. Gentilli chose the most talented among them, the most promising, and signed that writer's name to a handful of poems that he then sent to a Roman newspaper where he had contacts: the poems were clearly and unequivocally plagiarized from works by Gabriele D'Annunzio, who was the first to reveal them as such a few days after in the pages of the same newspaper that had published them, so the ringleader, the most talented of the young writers hoping to reinvigorate the local scene—a small and possibly nonexistent scene, I reiterate—was ridiculed in the press and literary circles for months. He could only publish once the scandal had blown over, seven or eight years later, and then only in a tiny house in Pescara; but by then it was already too late, for both him and his

readers. Meanwhile, Gentilli and his books dominated the literary scene in L'Aquila and would continue to do so for some time, although, as I mentioned, that scene is quite possibly negligible and perhaps doesn't even actually exist.

Michele Garassino, Genoa, March 13, 1978
That young man was named Giovanni Rossi; I met him briefly and he told me his version of that story. In it, in his version, he and others had read Gentilli's work and discovered dozens of poorly concealed plagiarisms—"Like the dead on a battlefield, buried hastily in shallow graves before the enemy troops returned," he said—and they denounced them in L'Aquila with the scant means they had and against majority opinion in the town, which considers Gentilli a local product in a way, like a cheese. Often, I suppose you already know this, we writers are merely local brands, due to the completely erroneous idea that we and our books can, and perhaps should, represent a country, a region, an identity of some sort. So Gentilli—to continue with the military metaphors—counterattacks and destroys Rossi, not only in L'Aquila but in the entire country, and not just for a short while but for the rest of his days. Those who read about Gentilli's plagiarism soon forgot about it, among other reasons because it is always easier to believe that a young man has plagiarized than that an older, recognized writer has, no matter how modest his recognition. When I met him, Rossi had published a second book of poems, a very slim one, which he gave me: the press, almost unanimously, described it as influenced by the poet from L'Aquila Filippo Gentilli; by then things had changed, however, and that attribution of influence was a form of disdain.

Espartaco Boyano, Ravenna, March 10, 1978
I didn't think the conference was going to happen, and I didn't know the republic's literary establishment considered my presence a contribution to the cause of European fascism. My books didn't seem

to be contributing. The invitation came in the form of two members of the Black Brigades bursting into my home here in Ravenna and demanding I quickly pack a suitcase because they had orders to take me with them. Neither offered any reasons and I didn't ask for any, as actually I'd been expecting their visit for some time. A few days earlier I had sent my wife and children to Lido di Dante, a town on the outskirts of the city where we had some acquaintances, to avoid any unpleasantness when they came for me. As I packed my suitcase in the bedroom, I heard the soldiers rummaging around in the house in search of something they could later sell. There must not have been anything of interest because they shouted for me to hurry up. I thought the suitcase was simply a ruse to avoid frightening the neighbors and that, really, where they were taking me, I wouldn't be needing it. So I just packed two shirts and a book I was reading at the time. Which one? Nothing particularly significant: a little romantic novel by Flavia Morlacchi that belonged to my wife. We walked down the stairs in silence, knowing that the neighbors were watching us from behind their doors. A cat owned by the caretaker wound around my legs as we crossed through the lobby. When it tried to do the same thing to one of the soldiers, he kicked at it, but the cat dodged his foot and walked haughtily over to its owner. When I went outside I found another soldier waiting in the driver's seat of a black car with no license plate. A moment before getting into it, I looked up at the sky and saw three low-flying planes pass over our heads. I didn't know if they were Italian planes, or German, or American, and I don't remember if I cared, but I do remember in that moment I thought of an aerial painting of Ravenna that Fedele Azari made in 1927. I couldn't bring up the image, however, just the title, which its author had whispered into my ear during an opening, and it was *The Will to Die Kissing His Children*. I thought the pilots of those planes were, in that moment, seeing what Azari had seen and painted and were in fact living inside his painting, except they didn't know it, and they were unaware that what was once art was now murder. I got into the car. Azari had committed suicide fourteen years earlier, by the way. In January 1930.

Atilio Tessore, Florence, March 11, 1978

There was another story they told about Gentilli, according to which one day, years earlier, Gentilli had written in the press about the "execrable" absence of works by the Jesuit priest Pietro Cecchini in bookstores, and how dozens of anxious—even desperate—collectors were willing to pay any price for them; a price, Gentilli figured, that could only rise. Naturally, no one had ever heard of a Jesuit priest named Cecchini, but the article and the subsequent confidence that his body of work was desirable and hard to obtain resulted in greater demand for his book. I don't have to tell you that economics is actually a certain mood, and the economics of literature even more so: the dozens of people who got a copy of Father Cecchini's book through relatives or contacts, which is to say, along rather unorthodox paths, paid a lot of money for it. Obviously, all those paths led to L'Aquila, where Gentilli sold Father Cecchini's books through third parties: just a few weeks before writing his article, he had acquired them all from a recently bankrupted press in Rome.

Oreste Calosso, Rome, March 16, 1978

Haven't I told you that already? Hrand Nazariantz, the Armenian poet who lived in Bari; Paolo Buzzi, who lived in Milan and who, despite his inscrutable political position, had published a "Radio Waves Poem" that we were big fans of; Enrico Cavacchioli, who was useful, like a huge portrait of an ancestor you can hang to cover up a stain on the wall; Alceo Folicaldi, the young Futurist poet who had gone to war with Marinetti in Africa; Bruno Corra, who in 1916 directed *Futurist Life,* which was a film of pain and death and luckily has been lost; Rosa Rosà, the Austrian-born Italian writer who had written the novel *A Woman with Three Souls;* Luciano Folgore, Francesco Cangiullo, Arnaldo Ginna, Bruno Munari, Emilio Settimelli, Mino Somenzi, and Filippo Gentilli. We wrote to Corrado Govoni inviting him, but Govoni declined the invitation because his son, a Communist, had been killed in the Fosse Ardeatine massacre in March 1944: Govoni, who had once composed a tribute to

Il Duce, couldn't get past his pain and astonishment, as if it were Mussolini himself who had slapped him across the face.

Oreste Calosso, Rome, March 16, 1978
We didn't invite Enzo Benedetto: we believed him to be among the fallen in Italy and many of us wrote obituaries and texts on his painting and poetry that, inevitably, deemed him a martyr to fascism or, more precisely, one of the few writers among us who had taken his ideals to their extreme. But Benedetto was alive: he had been taken prisoner by English troops and returned to Italy after the end of the war. I saw him shortly after, reading what we'd written about him, perplexed. He never really recovered from the shock, I now believe.

Oreste Calosso, Rome, March 16, 1978
Naturally we also invited the survivors of the Futurist writers' circle in Perugia that I had been a part of: Espartaco Boyano, Atilio Tessore, and Michele Garassino, about whom I could say so much—and I mean, so, so much—that perhaps it's better I say nothing at all.

Oreste Calosso, Rome, March 16, 1978
Ezra Pound, meanwhile—typical of him—had disappeared. We never found out where he was and he didn't attend the conference.

Atilio Tessore, Florence, March 11, 1978
That face had stuck in me like a black hatchet blade, many years earlier; seeing it again was like some sort of relief, a consolation; but it was also like scratching deep into an old wound. In other words, that black hatchet had split me in two: I had to pull it out, but I didn't know how to and, as you see, I wasn't able to. Although, actually, at that moment all I was thinking was that Luca Borrello had come to kill Michele Garassino; that finally, after so long, he was going to kill him.

Espartaco Boyano, Ravenna, March 10, 1978

Why would they arrest me? Either (a) because of my friendship with Aldo Palazzeschi, who had become an antifascist, and made no effort to conceal it; (b) because, unlike my Futurist colleagues, I had criticized the pact with Nazi Germany and the racial laws, although only in private; (c) because I had supported Marinetti in his effort to get an exemption for Ferruccio Parri's sentence for antifascist activities, something I did do publicly; (d) because I had opposed the campaign against "degenerate art"; (e) because, in the end, I was alive and it was a time when being alive wasn't enjoying much popularity. Remember, I'm talking about 1945: by then they had taken everything from us, except our fear.

Oreste Calosso, Rome, March 16, 1978

The first one to address us was Hanns Johst, who seemed to have taken over completely. Here, somehow, the action stops, as if what we'd experienced was part of a novel that one could put aside; but of course, if this were a novel, Johst's speech would also be part of it, though possibly a minor and at the same time central part, the kind of thing that one tends to skip—descriptions, for example, whose function in novels I've never understood—or just skim over but that are nevertheless key to understanding the book. In this case, it was key to understanding our actions before and after the speech, and to understanding what we believed in, or at least what some of us believed in, or wanted to believe in, or were forced by circumstances to believe in. Despite that, Johst's speech is impossible to reproduce, as it is lost in the circumvolutions of a memory that is like a room filled with competing echoes. There is nothing more unrealistic, I think, than those novels in which someone is able to remember, word for word, what was said five years ago, or one year ago, or fifty. To be honest, implausibility in literature doesn't bother me; it only worries me coming from a Nazi fanatic who's also a bad writer.

Michele Garassino, Genoa, March 13, 1978

Johst, I remember, talked about war and literature, and said that war wasn't provoking the collapse of Europe, but it was that collapse that had provoked the war, which had come to rescue our world; according to Johst, that collapse was not as a result of our negligence as writers, but rather more likely due to the fact that, even while we battled arduously for our voices to be heard, we'd been ignored for years. It had been the Jewish press and economic interests that kept our voices from being heard, he said; however, we had to be heard then, in Europe's most terrible hour, there, in the Italian Social Republic, where the battle between usury and economic independence was being fought, the battle between education and the stultification they tried to impose on us by destroying our cities, between the people and an enemy vision that saw everything as class struggle, between the protection of workers, the elderly and the disabled, women and children, and an economic system that plunged into misery those who couldn't support themselves. We were, declared Johst, men engaged in a mortal struggle against a better-armed enemy sustained by the unjust powers of usury and exploitation, men abandoned by those who should have been our allies and betrayed by those who claimed to be our defenders, and that was the reason our voices had to ring out louder than ever. This was the moment, he said, to set aside purity, which deep down couldn't satisfy us because it was antihuman, and the weak signs of creative individualism that were nothing more than usurpation, because our words belonged to a community to whom we had to return them revitalized, and adhere to a propaganda whose social need and simplicity of content should be enough for us. Johst said this was our opportunity to defeat Bolshevism and the empire of money; if we won the war but not that particular battle, the war and our lives would have had no meaning, as in the global conflict, what was at stake was not only our right to exist—the Germans and the Italians, brothers in the defense of the European values we ourselves had created—but also the struggle of poetry against the numbers brandished by our enemies and those who profit from usury.

Writers, he declared, had to take part in the conflict, and they would do so with metaphors, which only defeatists could consider inconsequential. It's true, he said, metaphors don't win battles; however they do last longer.

Oreste Calosso, Rome, March 16, 1978

There was a tall man standing beside me with a skeptical expression on his face. He gave me a look and then seemed to smile to himself while everyone applauded Johst's speech. The clack of military heels hitting the floor was heard as the Germans stood at attention and shouted in unison, several times, their Sieg Heils and their Heil Hitlers. The man—I later found out he was a Dutch author, Rintsje Piter Sybesma—murmured something as if to himself, that I, despite the clamor, could clearly hear. It was a quote from Pierre Gaxotte that I was already familiar with: "The history of Germany is the history of an unfortunate people."

Atilio Tessore, Florence, March 11, 1978

I didn't listen to any of what Johst said, and I don't think I missed much: we were like Achaeans trapped inside a Trojan horse, but the Trojan horse didn't move and Troy was still out of sight, and almost all of us knew it but pretended not to. At my back, near the entrance to the room, partially hidden by a column, was a man I had known and not forgotten, despite thinking he'd died months earlier. I suppose he wasn't looking at me—later I found out he hadn't even recognized me—but at the time I imagined that he was. Johst was speaking, and then Paolo Buzzi—up on tiptoes, looking like a supporting actor, as he always did, even after reaching an age at which one either takes on leading roles or gives up acting completely, but which Buzzi nevertheless seemed to enjoy, seemed to celebrate as if he knew that only supporting actors got the chorus girls and the buxom opera singers. As they spoke I thought of Luca Borrello and the things we'd done together and how it had all ended; I was also thinking, as I mentioned already, that he was going to kill Garassino and I wondered when he would do it, and how, and if someone, me for example, could or would want to stop him.

Oreste Calosso, Rome, March 16, 1978

"We want to glorify the war—the sole cleanser of the world—militarism, patriotism, the destructive gesture of the anarchists, beautiful lethal ideas, and contempt for women. We want to demolish museums and libraries, fight morality, feminism, and all opportunist and utilitarian cowardice," quoted Buzzi. It was unclear to us why, when he could have, for example, cited the 1939 text "Insecticidal Patriotism" or the 1942 "Song for the Heroes and Machines of the Mussolinian War," in which Marinetti said approximately the same thing in a similar way: variety wasn't exactly his forte and he always rejected stooping to what he considered the lowly position of changing his mind. While Buzzi was speaking, some of us couldn't stop thinking about him—not Buzzi but Marinetti. He had died on December 2 the year before as a result, possibly, of the suffering he experienced while with Italian troops in Russia between 1942 and 1943, and I had attended his burial in Milan along with thousands of others, unable to imagine even for an instant that the hysterical old marionette I'd met had once again, and for the last time, been stored at the bottom of the puppet master's trunk. There was almost a recognition of defeat in that memory, as I'd thought of the conference as an opportunity to see Marinetti and Pound in action again and neither of them was able to attend: Marinetti because he was dead; Pound because no one could locate him; he was lost somewhere possibly not even he, with all his nervous energy, recognized, with his vertical mass of red hair blowing in the wind, his eccentric attire, and those little bloodshot eyes that made him look like a lively, lewd monkey. We, the Futurists, considered war the "sole cleanser of the world," as Buzzi recalled, but those in attendance applauded only tepidly, already exhausted by a war that had given us more destruction and annihilation than we could reflect in our works. That war was, as Marinetti said in 1914, an immense Futurist painting. True, but apparently it was painted by an idiot.

Espartaco Boyano, Ravenna, March 10, 1978
Really, I now think, the best "cleanser of the world" is soap. But that was in short supply in 1945. So we settled for the war. What else could we do.

Oreste Calosso, Rome, March 16, 1978
The Spaniards also seemed weary of the war; they'd already had quite a long one themselves. Rafael Sánchez Mazas nodded in silence in one corner of the room, but his attitude was more that of someone distractedly listening to a lesson clumsily memorized by a child. Eugenio d'Ors, beside him, had asked for the floor a moment earlier, and was shouting himself hoarse in an imitation of, possibly, Francisco Franco—who, perhaps, was imitating Adolf Hitler, whose rhetorical skills were like those of a silent film actor who found himself in a talkie—in order to tell us that he was in agreement, completely in agreement, with his "friend" Paolo Buzzi and that it was "desolation, the exact, the utmost and the inexorable, the militia and the imperial, impassiveness, clarity, and heroism," facing off against "the barbaric, the murky, the shrill, and the sterile." War, he declared, was a "redeeming illumination" that proved (does an illumination "prove"? I'm not sure) that we writers must continue to put literature at the service of a higher cause, which was a nation at war. The prize, he said, was a paradise lost, an authentic, free, strong, meaningful life that can only be realized in death—as all paradises are only paradises once lost—in which "their dead are left alone. Not ours. Our dead are vigilant. They continue in the hot brotherhood of each heart." D'Ors added that it was precisely this we must laud in our works.

Espartaco Boyano, Ravenna, March 10, 1978

"That tide of foolishness, of insults, of lies, of heartless mockery, of dirty explosions of resentments is nothing more than the symptom of a fatal desire for dissolution," erupted Fani Popowa-Mutafowa. The excuse, she said, for making a literature of broad strokes, a literature of propaganda, when really, she declared, what was needed was a literature that forced people to shut their eyes to everything that wasn't literature. Some nodded, but the voice of Rintsje Piter Sybesma rose among the nay-saying in the Spanish and German sectors, to declare that for a writer there was no greater task—those were his words, I believe—than that of creating propaganda for a nation fighting for its survival, and that . . . But then Bruno Corra stood up and said that he could be a magician, a dance instructor, a diver, a paratrooper, a rugby player, a singer, a croupier, a jockey, a tightrope walker, a star of the silver screen, a radio commentator, a maître d', a chauffeur, a poacher, or a stock trader, but he would never be a propagandist, because he was against everything serious. His comments were met with some laughter, but then d'Ors stated that there was a misunderstanding of terms, or of opposites, as the difference between us and our enemies was that they said "representative, brother, and repose" and we said "captain, comrade, maneuver." "They say stupid fanaticism"—he said—"and we say faith. They, I: we, we. We say flag and they say torch, we vigilance and they discomfort, we shirt and they frock coat. They seriousness and we responsibility." Luys Santa Marina stood up and applauded frantically, but Johst shot him a cutting look and the Spaniard sat back down, while Henri Bruning interjected that, even if it were possible to write literature outside of our nations' struggle against freedom of enterprise (which wasn't freedom of expression) and against the government of everyone (which wasn't the government of everyone fit to govern), if, he said, one could write "pure" literature, literature written outside of the period and its battles, who would publish it, he wondered. Who was going to be interested in reading it. Bruning was accused by Popowa-Mutafowa of acting like a Bolshevik, but Eugenio Montes and Hermann Burte defended him. Despite which, and after a moment of hesitation, none of us was sure why he was being defended and at what point in the discussion we found ourselves. It was Johst who solved the problem by standing up, which meant the conference would be put on hold indefinitely. As I headed toward the exit, Almirante came over and asked me to release the conclusions of the conference's first session to the press. I have them somewhere around here. They said: "In view of the war, in view of the struggle of our peoples to maintain their national independence as their fundamental right, all that is not against them—all that is not lowly treason in support of capitalism devoid of a fatherland—is today felt in Italy as one and the same confronted with the essential, unquestionable situation in Europe, in the face of which we maintain our unshakable faith in victory." None of us had declared that, I objected. But Almirante shut me up, taking me by the arm and bringing me over to one corner of the room. "The declaration was written by the Germans; if we don't disseminate it, they'll shut down the conference and kill us all," he told me. In fact, while I was preparing the statement, I discovered that it had already been broadcast, by Johst or by one of his lackeys.

Espartaco Boyano, Ravenna, March 10, 1978
Do you really want to know these things? Isn't the little mentioned on the subject in the history books and documents of the period enough? All right, I'll tell you: we had nothing to say to each other, and we spent two interminable hours saying it.

Atilio Tessore, Florence, March 11, 1978
I hadn't seen Luca Borrello in four years but I had no trouble recognizing him; I say that with pride because he was almost unrecognizable. Borrello had gotten much skinnier and he seemed to have shaved his own head, leaving wide patches of gray, frizzy hair where he couldn't reach or couldn't be bothered. His hair seemed to follow a pattern set out by a barber who'd lost his mind, and his expression made me think he himself was the insane barber: his eyes had an otherworldly gleam, but his face, which had always

been gaunt, was now like the mark left by an ax blow in a tree trunk, and that was what most frightened me. "It's me, Luca," I told him, taking him by the arm, but Borrello looked at me for a moment, then started coughing uncontrollably and slipped off toward the door. I wanted to believe that his silence and the fact that he hadn't attacked me on sight were proof that our differences were in the past and that, somehow, Borrello understood—also, that he wasn't going to kill Garassino after all. But I instantly grasped that Borrello was beyond all comprehension and forgiveness, in a territory that only he inhabited. So I knew there was no possibility of an understanding between us. And whether you can believe it or not, that made me happy and, at the same time, filled me with a paralyzing fear.

Oreste Calosso, Rome, March 16, 1978
Lunch was uneventful, except for the fact that the Spaniards monopolized the entire conversation with a monologue about the Castilian landscape, its arid beauty, which to me was a contradiction in terms. Someone quoted Oswald Spengler, I don't remember who, and someone else, I imagine a Spaniard, made a reference to José Ortega y Gasset. This is all to say that the lunch was quite impoverished from an intellectual standpoint. Someone referred to his vision of a future Europe characterized by a "humanism endowed with religiosity"—as absurd as it seems, I think those were his exact words, or close to them—and another maintained that such a project would not come to fruition until it was accepted that the beauty aspired to by literary works was a combination of meaning, transcendence, and a certain moral order. Flavia Morlacchi hastened to agree, spitting out some tiny bread crumbs slathered in saliva as she did so. To her right, elderly Amélie Rives Troubetzkoy had fallen asleep shortly after the first course, with her head tilted back onto the chair, snoring gently. To my left, Alceo Folicaldi, who had gone to war in Africa with Marinetti, was talking about a visit to a brothel filled with young African girls where an extraordinarily comic incident had occurred, but he couldn't get

through the story because he was laughing too hard. Mino Somenzi, to my right, took advantage of the uproar Folicaldi had provoked to talk about the bombings in the oil refineries of Ploești and the train junctions in Brașov and Pitești, in Romania, making sure that neither Ion Sân-Giorgiu nor the Germans, who were eating in silence, heard him. Someone broke a water pitcher, I think it was Enrico Cavacchioli. Beside me, Morlacchi furtively pinched her cheeks to give them some color, since cosmetics were no longer obtainable; she had a camera and tried to get a portrait of us, but no one wanted to pose for fear that the resulting photograph would be used as evidence against them in a not-so-distant future. I knew, because Morlacchi had confessed it to me on some other occasion, asking me for help I was unable to give her, that she hadn't been able to get film for months. When she grew weary of attracting attention that way, Morlacchi took Mrs. Troubetzkoy and Cavacchioli back to their hotel in spite of their protests; alcohol had imbued them with a childish stubbornness. The author of the unforgettable ode to Palatine Hill, which began with the languid verse "Di questo Aprile d'un tempo lontano . . ." and which I'd almost completely forgotten, luckily, was dragging the two hoary relics toward the exit. They were both protesting and turning with broad hand gestures as if they wanted to grab on to some object to anchor themselves in the restaurant; seeing her, I thought she was looking fat and I told myself you can't trust anyone who gains weight during a war, particularly the Second World War. Then they served that drink that had replaced coffee a couple of years earlier in Italy and we all pretended it was coffee and drank it; later "Cara al Sol" and "Giovinezza" were sung. "Cara al Sol" was sung two or three times, due to the Spaniards' enthusiasm and as a redress, which the Germans approved with an indifference that is the best one can hope for from them, particularly when living in a country that borders theirs.

Espartaco Boyano, Ravenna, March 10, 1978
At first there were three: Atilio Tessore, Oreste Calosso, and Romano Cataldi. They constituted, at least according to them, the

vanguard of Futurist, and therefore fascist, literature in Umbria. None of them were from there, but they had all ended up in Perugia for various reasons, none of which were important. What I mean is, those reasons are considerably less important than the reason why they all left, only to end up meeting again in Pinerolo at that disrupted fascist writers' conference.

Atilio Tessore, Florence, March 11, 1978
I don't remember if I've told you about Romano Cataldi yet, and, actually, everything revolves around him, in a way. Before I tell you how we met him, I should mention some of the things we learned years later, which he revealed in bits and pieces and often only incompletely, without the slightest pride or enthusiasm—although they clearly thrilled us and made us proud to be his friends. He had lost his mother at the age of twelve and shortly afterward left home to live on the streets, in cellars, and on bales of hay between Cantiano and Foligno, to the east of Perugia. One day he stole some tomatoes, then a few potatoes, and then some apples that were still green; when he thought he'd perfected his methods, he tried to steal some eggs and got caught by a peasant farmer who beat him so bad he lost an eye; he kept stealing and spent fifteen days in jail after he got caught again. When he was released he went to Sassoferrato and got a job as an actor in a play but quit a few hours later over an argument with the theater owner, who reported him for theft when Cataldi fled in his Alpine hunter costume. The show was abruptly interrupted by one of Giuseppe Garibaldi's volunteers abandoning the battle of Bezzecca to flee toward the outskirts of town along the Via Roma. Cataldi told us that he had no better clothes at the time and felt the Garibaldian uniform was appropriate pay for the minutes he'd been onstage, because, in his opinion, he was enormously talented as an actor. However, the theater owner, the local police, and the audience disagreed. That made Cataldi a repeat offender and he spent a month in jail, and after his release he was served with another six months for begging in Fondiglie, in an attempt to get back to Umbria. Upon his release he spent five months work-

ing on a farm on the outskirts of Gubbio learning to raise pigs—and being treated like one, from what he told us. Then the clapper at one of the local churches disappeared and Cataldi was sentenced to three years in jail despite not having any religious inclinations and no clapper being found in his possession. From what he told us, during those three years in jail he learned to read and started writing, first his memories, which he was afraid he would forget if he didn't put them down on paper, particularly the years he'd spent with his mother, and later some short stories, tinged with a certain violence, which the prison authorities destroyed for indecency before his sentence was served. Which wasn't serious, really, as he was able to reconstruct them from memory soon after, and they were the first things he read us when we met him, many years after all that and at a time when Cataldi—who had enlisted in the army after leaving prison, gone to Africa, done hard labor, worked the grape harvest, spent ninety days naked in a wooden cage beneath the Tunisian sun, and managed to return to Italy after deserting again and walking forty-nine kilometers with an iron rod through one infected leg before having it removed at the hospital in Sidi Bel Abbès; he then escaped from the nurses by holding a knife to his throat and threatening to take his own life, allowing him to board a ship setting sail from the Port of Oran—was one of the leaders of the young fascists in Perugia.

Espartaco Boyano, Ravenna, March 10, 1978
Cataldi had an obsession with counting the number of times the letter *a* appeared in the books he was reading. His literary opinions usually consisted of a statement such as *"The Factory Owner* by Romano Bilenchi has 78,342 *a*'s" without making clear in any way whether he'd liked the book or not. In fact, it is quite likely that his vowel counting had completely distracted him from its content, to the point that he was incapable of declaring a positive or negative opinion. On the other hand, I recall that Cataldi wanted to write like Bilenchi. He was very skilled at spelling entire sentences backward, after only a quick glance and without a single mistake. In his

head, literature was ruled by symmetry, and it's possible his decisions were as well, as he tended to make them in pairs, sometimes with a long time between the first and the second. One day, for example, a farmer's house on the outskirts of Foligno burned down. On another occasion a pig farm was destroyed during the night on the outskirts of Gubbio. Those two incidents did not form a pair, even if their author—never found, by the way—was the same person, but rather each formed a pair with other incidents in the past.

Atilio Tessore, Florence, March 11, 1978
Michele Garassino and I were studying Italian literature at university, in Perugia, at the time. My literary background, if at all relevant, is of no interest here; it's much less interesting than Garassino's, as his is, unfortunately, criminal. His father had an imports store in Arezzo and made a trip to Algiers that allowed Garassino to get his hands on a copy of the only published book of poetry by Arthur Maddow, an American who renounced his family's money and lived in Sicily and Tunisia. Maddow published that book in 1931 and not, as is often said, in 1938. Garassino read Maddow's poems with the help of a dictionary and thought—or this is what I believe he thought—that the fascination and enthusiasm provoked in us by certain works involve a transference, and the property of the works shifts from the creator's hands to the reader's; in other words, Garassino made Italian versions of the poems, learned them by heart, published them in the magazines within his reach, those small magazines that proliferated in places like Arezzo and Perugia, and read them publicly. He read them to Borrello and me and Oreste Calosso and Romano Cataldi so many times that we too ended up believing that, being his, they also belonged to us in some way. They were lovely, terrible poems that spoke of cities in Sicily and Tunisia and in the United States that Garassino had never seen; in the absence of firsthand information about all those places, we found added merit in those poems, which made us think that literature creates even when it pretends to imitate. Garassino was

our best man, we thought at that time, and it's possible Garassino thought so as well, in the same way it's possible he still thinks so, years after a presumptuous young man studying in Rome discovered the books of Maddow and of Garassino and unmasked him, perhaps in the hope of creating the sort of scandal that nothing any of us—writers who were relevant in the 1930s—say or do could possibly provoke now. Garassino responded, I remember, by writing a long article in the *Corriere della Sera* that wasn't exactly a defense against the accusation of plagiarism—which he, therefore, admitted to—but rather he maintained that everything, absolutely everything, is plagiarism, appropriation, starting with the very words we use. While not bad, his article wasn't very original either: Garassino had more or less copied his statement from Bruno Giordano Sanzin's 1931 defense against accusations that his poem dedicated to Umberto Boccioni, *Modernolatria,* was, actually, a slightly bulked-up plagiarism of some lines Boccioni had written in the margins of his painting *The City Rises.*

Oreste Calosso, Rome, March 16, 1978
Actually, the story is more complex than that. Some time later, also in *Corriere della Sera,* Sanzin admitted, to everyone's surprise, that he had enjoyed Garassino's article very much, and he wondered if that was because it was so similar to a text by Filippo Tommaso Marinetti, which he had plagiarized, undiscovered, some years earlier as an experiment, with the consent of Marinetti himself. No one likes to lose, and it seems that plagiarism is invariably a losing game, except that its rules are different than they seem, and known only to a very few. Perhaps the sole innocent party in this story was Marinetti, with whom the chain of borrowing and theft began, but perhaps he too had plagiarized someone and his deception is yet to be discovered. In my opinion, no theft has occurred until you miss what's been taken from you, and that almost never happens with texts. When Garassino plagiarized Maddow, he made us believe we had a genius among us, which led us to strive to match his level. Was

that not a magnificent gift? And we were all children then, and that is exactly what children do: they appropriate what they like, or they break it.

Michele Garassino, Genoa, March 13, 1978
OK, when I stop laughing I'm going to tell you something about Atilio Tessore that he apparently didn't mention: all of his work, all of him, is the result of the publication of the complete works of his father, Filippo Castrofiori. At fifty years old, in 1934, Castrofiori, who had up until then lived off of earnings from an unclear source—Castrofiori is a Jewish last name, I guess you know what I'm getting at—self-published the six thick volumes of his *Complete Works,* which none of those close to him knew he'd written, except his family. The first volume was devoted to his collected poetry; the second his prose, composed of two novels and an essay about a perpetual motion machine he'd invented; the third his plays; the fourth his correspondence with the primary European intellectuals of the century—Miguel de Unamuno, Hermann Graf Keyserling, Max Scheler, Oswald Spengler, Rabindranath Tagore, Charles Maurras, José Ortega y Gasset, those are the names that come to mind right now; the fifth was an opera libretto he'd written about the "anthropogeography" of Friedrich Ratzel; and the sixth gathered a selection of his private diaries. Castrofiori was surprisingly popular in the years following the publication of his works, and Tessore—who adopted a pseudonym in order to make it look as if he had no desire to profit from his father's success, which he actually did as much as possible—took advantage of the circumstances to print a somewhat premature book of poems. It's not that he didn't have talent—actually, I think he does—but rather that his talent was encumbered by great anxiety about profiting from what his father had achieved and, at the same time, being judged on his own merits, which were significantly inferior to those of his prolific, somewhat disconcerting progenitor. Of course, that is something his own father had foreseen and hoped for: after the publication of his *Complete Works,* Castrofiori never published anything again,

and devoted what remained of his life to promoting his son's work among his friends and acquaintances. He didn't ask for anything in exchange, as far as I know, but he crushed Tessore with his generosity and enthusiasm, which were those of someone who, in order to guarantee his family patrimony, gives his children a property completely disproportionate to their abilities, which they have to manage and multiply whether they want to or not: I think I've already mentioned that Castrofiori is a Jewish last name. He financed the performance of his son's erotic play in a Roman theater in 1937, which got awful reviews, as well as the publication of his next two books, which his father insisted on writing the prologues for—without reading them, I imagine. He paid to have a lot of postcards printed up and mailed out, with his son's face and an advertisement for his work on the back. Perhaps by then he understood that his son lacked a talent in keeping with his father's ambitions and he set out to destroy him with massive exposure before he could bring down the family legacy, or perhaps he still believed in him and was supporting him gladly. It doesn't matter which is true; what's relevant here is that, if Atilio Tessore and his work are anything, they are merely offshoots of his father's opus, even if they engulfed him unwittingly; but I'll tell you all about that when I've finished laughing about his so-called moral integrity. Just give me a moment to catch my breath.

Espartaco Boyano, Ravenna, March 10, 1978
Tall and thin. Very tall and very thin, that's the first thing I'd say about him. After that, I would say that I met him in medical school, where we were both students, and that he was an inexhaustible source of words that one day, I don't know how, just dried up, though that happened later. The likely date of our first meeting is March, or maybe April, 1931. The famous Futurist dinner at the restaurant Penna d'Oca had taken place in November of the previous year and Marinetti had already published his "Manifesto of Futurist Cooking," which I'd been quite interested in, for some reason I can't recall. Although, if you force the issue, I'd admit that I can remem-

ber why, that what interested me about Marinetti and the other Futurists was their vitality and sense of humor. In that moment I believed those both to be youthful characteristics, but now it seems obvious that youth tends to take itself terribly seriously and isn't exactly what I'd call vital. In that era there was a magazine in Perugia called *Lo Scarabeo d'Oro,* whose entry into literary history is disconcerting to me because the magazine was bad, bordering on dreadful. It was run by a Perugian writer named Abelardo Castellani, who had enjoyed some limited but still significant success a few decades earlier: since then he'd been a professor of literature. He didn't have much to teach, but he was adamant, and his influence, which I consider negative, is visible in all of us who studied under him. That negative influence is, of course, the only phenomenon that ever takes place in the teaching of literature. Castellani was a huge fan of Edgar Allan Poe, which, according to some, is a symptom of intellectual immaturity. The range of his literary interests was considerably smaller than the range of opinions he held about alcoholic beverages: mostly positive opinions, though all preferences were put aside when any alcoholic beverage entered into his line of sight. Castellani wore a messy mustache that gave observers the impression they had caught him eating a rat, and when he drank, the rat drowned beneath his nose. Explaining how I met Borrello involves having to tell you these things. One day, despite having no interest in him, Castellani sent me to interview Marinetti, who was staying at a local hotel, and ask him to contribute to our magazine. I had read everything about the Futurists, and most of their books, including all of Marinetti's. So, if I had to describe my emotions as I went to meet him—all, incidentally, quite puerile, and therefore perfect material for a novel, which is what I believe you've come here in search of: nervousness, expectation, a sense of opportunity, joy, worry—the description would go on too long. I will merely say that Marinetti received me in his room, which was dark. The room became darker and darker as the minutes passed. We had set the interview for 7:00 p.m., shortly before a dinner at which the city's dignitaries were set to honor him, which obviously pleased Marinetti. As we spoke about his work, or he spoke, my pulse calmed, but it also grew harder for me to write in my notebook as I could scarcely see it. Marinetti seemed to have no problem with the scant light. He was pacing from one side of the room to the other, often stopping in the cone of light on the carpet beside the window in such a way that it illuminated his shoes and his trousers up to the knees. He had magnificent shoes. I mean magnificent Italian shoes, or just Italian shoes, if you prefer. I don't remember much of what he told me, though it all must be somewhere in his manifestos. For some people, quoting themselves constantly is a sort of flirtatiousness. In Marinetti it was more of a necessity: on the one hand, all of his ideas were contained in his dozens of manifestos; on the other, it was hard for him to imagine anyone could have better ideas. He was like a theater impresario who'd been abandoned by his cast some time ago, so he'd decided to play all the roles himself in a drama that, of course, he himself had written. When he finished speaking he stared at me, as if I should applaud or attack him—often his audiences did the latter, frequently with eggs—so I set aside my notebook and asked him to contribute to *Lo Scarabeo d'Oro*. If I had to guess what Marinetti was feeling in that moment, I would say that, judging from his gestures, he felt relief. He sat down on the bed and wrote some words on a piece of paper he rested on the night table. He wrote as quickly as he spoke, and then stood up and said that his wife was waiting for him. We shook hands in the doorway, with what I believed to be a strange emanation brought on by a transfer of some sort, possibly of talent, but it was just my nervousness, my perception of my own, entirely imaginary, importance. When I got to the lobby I pulled out of my pocket the page Marinetti had given me. The lines were written on top of each other and the words made a jumble of ink. He'd folded it before the ink was dry and it was no longer possible to make out anything of what the great man had written. I turned around, about to ask him for another contribution, or for him to read the page to me, but just then I saw the writer and his wife being pulled from the hotel by the local dignitaries. A moment later, it was impossible to see where they'd gone.

Espartaco Boyano, Ravenna, March 10, 1978

Some young men stopped me as I left the hotel. It seemed they'd been there for some time, smoking cigarettes. The butts lay at their feet, making a sort of stain with vague borders. I didn't know any of them, but they addressed me familiarly. "Did you see that clown Marinetti coming out of the hotel?" one of them asked. I nodded. "That insufferable fool makes a mockery of Italian literature," added another. "Because of him, the younger generation doesn't read our great writers, like Enrico Cavacchioli," pointed out another. "Don't forget Flavia Morlacchi," chimed in another. "How could I? How could anyone forget the author of those immortal verses comparing the ruins of the Palatine with 'blind eyes / shaded eyes / of the fierce and glorious Roman specter'?" "You aren't a Marinetti supporter, are you?" interrupted the first young man, with a glare. Just then I noticed that he wore a patch over one eye. I can't recall exactly what I thought at that moment, not even when I really try to, but I answered with the first thing that came into my head: "I deeply admire Mr. Marinetti and consider Futurism one of the most important artistic movements of our time." For a moment, the four of us remained in silence, possibly surprised by my audacity, and I remember thinking I should cling to that moment because whatever happened next would be terrible. But just then one of them laughed and the man with the eye patch held out his hand. "My name is Romano Cataldi," he said, "and we're all Futurists here."

Espartaco Boyano, Ravenna, March 10, 1978

For some time, the four of us—Tessore, Calosso, and Cataldi, who, because of his age and his experiences in Africa and other places, was our leader, and I—worked on sowing discontent in Italian literature. A point in our favor: unlike our opponents and rivals, we had the general press on our side, not just the literary reviews, and that gave us more power of persuasion. Of course, by then, the general press, particularly what had come to be called "the cultural press," wasn't what it is now: writing about literature so all those who don't want to read but *do* want to have "opinions" can formulate one. Shortly after meeting and joining the group, I stopped working with Castellani, but first I handed in my interview with Marinetti along with his contribution. Not the one Marinetti wrote for me in the darkness of his hotel room, which was still illegible days later despite my best efforts, but rather the one Atilio Tessore, Oreste Calosso, Romano Cataldi, and I wrote one afternoon in a café, using sentences from Futurist manifestos and placing them randomly on the page, which gave us a good laugh. Of course, *Lo Scarabeo d'Oro* published our contribution by Marinetti in the next issue, which made us laugh even harder. The forgery only brought us closer together, although now I'm a bit ashamed to own up to it. The following year, in 1932, Marinetti published it in one of his books, I don't know if that was because he didn't remember what he had written up in his hotel room or if, despite remembering it, he had identified his tone and his word choice in our text and they'd seemed sufficient to make it a recognizable text "by" Marinetti. If I had to choose between those possibilities, I wouldn't because, actually, there is another, third possibility: that Marinetti understood that, in the end, a writer's work is everything published under his name, even if he hasn't written it. I mean the work is the writer himself, and all the rest—by which I mean the literary texts—is barely an appendix and utterly unimportant. This last perspective seems very modern, I don't know if Marinetti would sanction it. But I think it's the vision of a great many writers and every editor who exists and has existed in recent years. It's also the manifestation of a somewhat secret triumph for us, the Futurists: we wanted to give art back to life, and we did so to the point that they ended up conflating, so that the lives of writers are now all that seems to have any relevance in literature.

Oreste Calosso, Rome, March 16, 1978
Atilio Tessore and I met Cataldi at a fascist meeting held near the university, in Perugia. Espartaco Boyano joined us later, as did Luca Borrello, eventually. We considered ourselves the fascist and

Futurist literary vanguard of Umbria and maybe we were despite the obliviousness of the Umbrians. We made a real effort to believe that we were writers and part of a passably secret society that each day should come up with a plan and not carry it out. One of our many contradictions was that we repudiated art, or at least conventional art. In other words, anything written by someone who wasn't us or the authors we admired, mostly Futurists. But we also repudiated life and often even repudiation itself. Someone would propose something like "Let's break Abelardo Castellani's teeth." He was a Perugian writer whose work, luckily, has been lost to posterity. We would all vote and if the motion was approved—as was always the case—we would jot down the action in our minutes and not follow through with it. Among the actions we deliberately did not carry out: the aforementioned breaking of Abelardo Castellani's teeth (he wasn't even a fascist); visiting Venice, bursting into the house of Cosimo Zago, the lame poet, stealing his orthopedic leg, and then throwing it into the Grand Canal; sodomizing Flavia Morlacchi while a bunch of blind men bellow out her poems, particularly that one that compares the ruins of the Palatine with "blind eyes" and with "shaded eyes"; visiting all the bookstores in Perugia and, furtively, tearing out the last ten pages of every copy of every book by Enrico Cavacchioli; getting some famous musicologist to publicly discuss the work of "Giacomo Porcini," mispronouncing the supposed last name so that he understands it as "Puccini" and then creating a scandal; stationing ourselves outside of a bookstore, stopping each shopper on their way out, inquiring about the book they've acquired, and telling them the ending, completely inventing it just so they won't read it; using planes to skywrite Tessore's mother's risotto recipe, while explaining to viewers that there is much more literature in it than in many of the works marketed as such; etc.

Atilio Tessore, Florence, March 11, 1978
There was one action we did carry out, among all the others we didn't: we stationed ourselves near bookstores and places where

some sort of literary event was taking place and pretended to be arguing; when someone who seemed like a good target passed by, we would ask their opinion on the subject, generally Futurism, skywriting, or the new trends, which we would pretend to be opposed to. That was how we met Oreste Calosso, once when our action didn't go over well, although generally they did; I mean, generally they went well. When we had the person embroiled in our conversation—usually an older man we'd chosen for his conservative appearance—and it seemed we were all in agreement, we would start shouting out "Long live Futurism" and "Long live Marinetti" and, on an order—usually from Cataldi—we would beat our victim unconscious and then run off. Although Perugia is a small city, and on one or two occasions we met up with our victims again on its streets, none of them ever reported us, perhaps out of fear of having to admit to the police that they'd lost one or two teeth in a literary dispute with some young men. And this, I believe, I understood later: at the time we thought we had performed a transubstantiation on them, a transformation of some sort, and that now they were Futurists like us although reluctant to make public their conversion. At least once, and to encourage him, as Futurism was primarily an attitude and not merely an aesthetic ideal—although it was that too—we addressed one of those men with shouted slogans in favor of Futurism and Il Duce. The man was so terrified that he was speechless for a moment, and then he timidly raised his arm in a poor imitation of the fascist salute and shouted the slogans with us, weakly. Then we made him lend us some money to have coffee at a nearby bar we preferred he didn't accompany us to. We never paid him back, actually, so—I now think—perhaps that loan should be called by a different name; but, as you know, we Futurists generally supported each other and weren't particularly scrupulous about money. Those who crossed our path at least learned that about Marinetti's great movement.

Oreste Calosso, Rome, March 16, 1978
By the way, one of those plans was to create a "bad" art museum; in other words, a museum where the pieces were chosen not for their artistic quality but rather for their absolute lack of it, for the clumsiness of their execution, for their adherence to ideas we considered "bad"—we particularly disliked Mary's "immaculate conception," but there were other bad ideas, like perspective, solemnity, the appearance of angels, landscapes, and still lifes—and for other completely mysterious reasons that the visitor would have to discover for himself; the list of works and artists for the museum was extensive, although I can only recall Rosso Fiorentino, the unsettling painter of religious eroticism whose work is filled with erections, masturbation, and fainting.

Oreste Calosso, Rome, March 16, 1978
Then, after lunch, we went back to the Town Hall and discussed whether art should create or imitate. I don't remember our conclusion, but I do remember that we were all firmly opposed to Soviet art and that at one point we grew silent when we heard a bomber squadron passing over our heads: it came from the other side of the mountains, possibly from France, and was headed to bomb some city in the north of Italy, perhaps Milan. In the silence that followed I could hear, for the first time, Luca Borrello's coughing as he stood at the back of the room. Some feigned indignation and others, disquiet at the bombers' passing overhead, but I'm convinced that the only thing we all truly felt was relief at not being the target of the air raid. Someone talked about American jazz, which we firmly rejected, and then someone alluded to the tarantella, which we also, mistakenly, in our nervous state, repudiated as well.

Espartaco Boyano, Ravenna, March 10, 1978
Luca Borrello was scarcely a teenager when he read about the latest Futurist scandal in a newspaper and felt drawn to it. For a time he even tried to impress other inhabitants in his town by saying that

he too was a Futurist. But he didn't actually know anything about the Futurists, except that they provoked scandals and were in favor of a new art. To one living in Sansepolcro (which owes its fame to Perugino and Santi di Tito, but above all to Piero della Francesca, who was born in Sansepolcro and also died there, if I recall correctly), that must have seemed strange, yet also essential. Perhaps Borrello didn't need to know what a Futurist was in order to be one, as the things that interest us are always those we know the least about and there is some triumph, but also some forfeiture, or at least a forfeiture of interest, when the actual knowledge is acquired. What I mean is that if Borrello's interest didn't fade, it's because there in Sansepolcro he had no way of knowing what a Futurist was, although he would soon find out.

Atilio Tessore, Florence, March 11, 1978
I remember the story well, although I should say that I only have Borrello's version of it, which he told us a few years after we met him, as if he hadn't dared to tell us before or as if he'd invented it, to explain something to us. Borrello told us that one evening a Futurist gathering was held at the restaurant La Taverna Toscana in Sansepolcro, headed up by the Florentine poet Aldo Palazzeschi. Borrello attended, and what he saw, in some sense, cannot be told, or at least cannot be told without taking into account the emotions it inspired in Borrello, and those were lost along with him. What did he see? Alternating provocation and indulgence, seriousness and humor—don't forget that Futurism was the only artistic movement with a clown among its ranks—and proselytism and the senseless defiance common to Futurist gatherings, but all degraded, somehow, as if it were a facsimile of a Futurist evening rather than a true one. Years later, when he told us, Borrello admitted that at the time he was unable to say what it was he was seeing and in what sense Palazzeschi's performance was a degradation or an unfortunately incomplete or mutilated echo of something, but the intuition of that other thing, and what there was of it in Palazzeschi's gathering, interested him deeply. At least its ending was exactly the same

as those of other Futurist evenings: since it culminated with the poet being pelted with eggs and tomatoes, which, being Sansepolcro, were all of the finest quality, as I'm sure you know. Borrello—obviously—wasn't among the attackers: as soon as they'd calmed down, he slipped into the restaurant's kitchen and found the poet smoking in silence, seated beside an enormous pot of boiling spinach. Palazzeschi asked him: "Have you also come to slap the new art in the face?" Borrello shook his head, but didn't know what to say. Finally he asked what hotel he was staying at. "None," replied Palazzeschi. "The owner of the hotel I was at was in the audience and told me he no longer wants me in his establishment; he sent someone to fetch my things." Borrello and Palazzeschi remained in silence for a moment, looking at the pot of spinach. "Are you a Futurist?" the Florentine poet finally asked. Borrello nodded and said to follow him, he knew a place where he could stay.

Atilio Tessore, Florence, March 11, 1978
Palazzeschi lived in Borrello's parents' house for several weeks, in the attic. Borrello's father, a doctor, had begrudgingly consented to the arrangement. Borrello told us his father never really liked Palazzeschi, although it's possible his dislike lessened, at least slightly, when Palazzeschi demonstrated an unnervingly deep knowledge of brick arches and, with his own hands, repaired the partially collapsed one at the house's entrance. He and Borrello would take long walks through the outskirts of Sansepolcro avoiding all contact with the paintings of Piero della Francesca and the visitors who flocked to town to admire them, whom they considered strident imbeciles. Borrello never told us what they talked about, except for the following story, which he mentioned in another context when referencing another matter altogether. According to him, Palazzeschi met Marinetti once when Palazzeschi asked him to sign a manifesto against Filippo Gentilli's publication of some apocryphal letters by Alessandro Manzoni. Marinetti analyzed the style of the letters and proved that they weren't written by Manzoni and, what's more, that they weren't written by Gentilli either, who must have

assigned the writing to a third party. Marinetti showed Palazzeschi the originals the signatures had been traced from, then handed over this vitally important evidence to a Venetian businessman in exchange for a sum of money that wasn't entirely negligible. Later, however, Palazzeschi discovered who had sold naïve Gentilli the letters in the first place: it was Marinetti himself, who'd convinced him to publish them only to denounce them immediately, thus earning some money and the moral satisfaction of having publicly opposed a forgery that would have damaged Italian literature and one of its greatest figures, the immortal author of *The Betrothed*. Gentilli never spoke to him again, Palazzeschi told Borrello, which was a third source of satisfaction for Marinetti, no less important than the previous ones.

Michele Garassino, Genoa, March 13, 1978
Oh, yes. Borrello used to say that everything he knew about Futurism he'd learned from Palazzeschi, but it's possible he was joking and only really thought that when he began to distance himself from the movement, when the wellspring started to dry up, because Palazzeschi, in his opinion, didn't know much about the movement either. Palazzeschi would contradict himself, he didn't know the publication dates of certain texts or he would confuse them along with their authorship and a large part of their content; he often didn't even seem to remember who was a Futurist and who wasn't. Borrello felt somewhat confused when these things happened, and experienced a sort of restiveness he had no way of expressing; but the restiveness and confusion always dissipated when Palazzeschi showed him a poem of his that had just been published in the press, a reference to his work in an article by another writer or, more often, the letters written to him by Marinetti, or Ardengo Soffici or Giovanni Papini, which Palazzeschi would pick up at the main post office in Sansepolcro, on long walks he preferred to take alone, in order to, as he would say, give free rein to the profound emotions that would take hold of him when he read them for the first time.

Atilio Tessore, Florence, March 11, 1978

That arch, the arch at the main entrance to Borrello's parents' house that Palazzeschi had repaired, collapsed a few weeks after he left, killing the family dog, who usually lay beneath it to watch the scant traffic that passed through Sansepolcro. Even before that: one day Borrello read in the newspaper about a banquet in Rome to celebrate the Florentine poet Aldo Palazzeschi's return after a few months in Paris; in the paper was a photo of Palazzeschi, a person Borrello had never seen in his life. Perhaps "his" Palazzeschi had never seen him either; he refused to give any explanation and fled the city as soon as possible, but not before insulting his hosts and their son and cursing the dog, who, alarmed by the shouting, awoke from his usual drowsiness to bite Palazzeschi's calf, ruining his trousers in the process.

Oreste Calosso, Rome, March 16, 1978

Perhaps "Palazzeschi" had tried to explain this to Borrello when he told him about the forged Alessandro Manzoni letters; maybe he understood there isn't much difference between falsifying some texts and falsifying their author and he wanted, somehow, to tell him that. Perhaps he had also succumbed to the fascination with Futurism—like Borrello, like all of us—and had decided to live out that fascination in his own way, in the only way available to him; maybe he was crazy, although, in general, madmen prefer to live their own craziness rather than other people's, which is the only thing that distinguishes them from the so-called sane. Perhaps he was simply teaching Borrello a lesson, a lesson with no definitive conclusions, from which one could learn a lot and, at the same time, practically nothing at all. In some sense, the "fake" Palazzeschi continues to be a mystery; for a time there was a suspiciously high number of Futurist evenings put together by Florentine poet Aldo Palazzeschi in the small city of Veneto and later in the area around Pescara, before ending abruptly not long after.

Espartaco Boyano, Ravenna, March 10, 1978

That was how we met him. One day, the Florentine poet Aldo Palazzeschi visited Perugia. In the crowd at the gathering, scattered among those who insulted and threw rotting vegetables at the poet, there were some who defended him. Arguments broke out constantly in one part of the room or another, and were stifled with difficulty by those in favor of things not getting out of hand, who were impeded by scandalmongers and those anxious to see a good fight. We were there, of course; we were fans of Palazzeschi but also of scandals and brouhahas. At a certain point, one of the spectators challenged Atilio Tessore, who was short and wore glasses, and was, let's just say, an easy target. From the other side of the room, Romano Cataldi stood up and headed over with two of his friends. But he stopped short: a fist had flown through the air and the man who'd tried to punch Tessore was on the floor. Beside him stood a very tall, very thin young man. We later found out his name was Luca Borrello and he came from Sansepolcro. That was how he became one of us. His passion for Futurism made him our ally, and his facility for winning fights and confrontations, the savage energy he gave off in those situations, turned him into Cataldi's best friend.

Atilio Tessore, Florence, March 11, 1978

That night, as on many previous as well as future occasions, we were defended by the workers in the room, who didn't understand Futurism but understood and sympathized with its revolutionary potential; toward the end of the night—I repeat, like many other times—the police burst in and carried off Palazzeschi amid booing and applause. The next day, the press gave us completely free publicity, us and Futurism and the vanguard of fascist literature in Umbria. It was a special occasion for us, because we met Borrello, who would years later become so important to us—in some sense, obviously, he saved our lives. Likely it was also special for Luca Borrello himself, not only because he met us (if he hadn't before then, at least via word of mouth) but also because for the first time he had the opportunity to see Aldo Palazzeschi, whom, actually, in a certain sense, he'd lived with for several weeks in Sansepolcro a few years earlier.

Oreste Calosso, Rome, March 16, 1978
One of our German friends, I believe it was Hans Blunck, took the floor to discuss a certain "theory of discontinuity" created by Professor Hans Jürgen Hollenbach—I think that was his name—which, in his opinion, made clear that art neither creates nor imitates, but rather exists as a force in the bosom of the history that gives rise to it and endows it with meaning. In order to understand this, one merely had to observe the interstices between series of events, more than the series of events themselves, maintained Blunck. Hrand Nazariantz stood up and tried to call our attention to how, in his opinion, Hollenbach's theory, which he had never heard of before, was linked to the representations of history that can be found in Armenian churches; he tried to explain them to us, but his explanation came up against the limitations of his vocabulary and the strong Bari accent he'd acquired. What saved us, in some sense, from having to continue enduring that was a telegram of support that Ezra Pound had sent from Sant'Ambrogio. It was read, eliciting some discussion, by Juan Ramón Masoliver, who'd been his secretary. I remember the text of the telegram because when Masoliver finished reading it I asked him to give it to me; it said: "Here are their tomb-stones. / They supported the gag and the ring: / A little BLACK BOX contains them. / So shall you be also, / You slut-bellied obstructionist, / You sworn foe to free speech and good letters, / You fungus, you continuous gangrene. / Come, let us on with the new deal, / Let us be done with pandars and jobbery, / Let us spit upon those who pat the big-bellies for profit, / Let us go out in the air a bit. / Or perhaps I will die at thirty?"

Atilio Tessore, Florence, March 11, 1978

Perhaps not even Ezra Pound himself knew what that meant, but he repeated it, literally, word for word, during his trial in Washington some years later; which is to say, after having been arrested, locked up like a caged animal in an internment camp in Coltano, or in Padula, or in Laterina, I can't remember which; after having thrown himself onto the electric fence, according to what he told me; after having been deprived of the possibility of writing, transferred to the United States against his will, locked up in a psychiatric hospital where, this time, he did almost go mad, and where twentieth-century poetry almost went mad with him.

Espartaco Boyano, Ravenna, March 10, 1978

Marinetti sent us a telegram shortly after our intervention at the Futurist evening organized by Palazzeschi. "Art, before you, was memory, anguished evocation of the lost Object (happiness, love, landscape) and therefore, nostalgia, ecstasy, pain, distance. Now, with Futurism, art becomes art-action, in other words, will, optimism, aggression, possession, penetration, joy, brutal reality in art," it read.

Atilio Tessore, Florence, March 11, 1978

Perhaps Ezra Pound's telegram was some sort of reprimand, since it went on to say: "It has been your habit for long / to do away with good writers, / You either drive them mad, or else you blink at their suicides, / Or else you condone their drugs, / and talk of insanity and genius, / But I will not go mad to please you, / I will not flatter you with an early death, / Oh, no, I will stick it out, / Feel your hates wriggling about my feet / As a pleasant tickle, / to be observed with derision, / Though many move with suspicion, / Afraid to say they hate you; / The taste of my boot? / Here is the taste of my boot, / Caress it, / lick off the blacking." Years later I still think there is much truth in that, and not much madness; although, really, who could possibly know.

Michele Garassino, Genoa, March 13, 1978

Pound was arrested by two partisans on May 3, 1945, shortly after our conference—or, better put, after the hasty end of our conference days before its scheduled closing ceremony—in his house in Sant'Ambrogio, in Rapallo, not far from Genoa: he was translating Mencius, the Chinese philosopher, disciple of a disciple of a grandson of Confucius. "Ashes of Europe Calling" was the title of the radio program he offered to do for his captors; he had already done some one hundred and twenty, each ten or fifteen minutes long, from December 1941 to July 1943, but Pound, for whom bragging was an essential activity, used to say that he'd done three hundred plus the articles in the press. If that were true, the author of the *Cantos* would hold the dubious honor of being the person who most wrote about fascism; even more than Mussolini himself, who perhaps wasn't as well acquainted with it despite having created it. For Pound, the war was against the banks, usury, arms sales, and international capital, an activity carried out, he maintained, by Jews. "This war is part of the secular war between usurers and peasants, between the usurocracy and whomever does an honest day's work with his own brain or hands [. . .] The peasant feeds us and the gombeen-man strangles us—if he cannot suck our blood by degrees," he said. Perhaps he was a spy, or a double agent, or perhaps he subscribed to some other mode of literature; I can affirm that, at least since 1943, Pound was trying to escape Italy. During the war, foreigners were obliged to periodically come in to the police station and would be stripped of their ration cards at the slightest sign of disaffection for the regime; their bank accounts would also be blocked, which made it difficult, if not impossible, to leave the country. According to Pound's calculations, one would need something like eighteen hundred dollars to escape Italy in 1943, and he didn't have the money, which may have been the Jews' fault, although most likely wasn't. He admired Walt Disney and watched *Snow White and the Seven Dwarfs* several times in 1938, in a movie theater in Rome with his daughter, and I prefer to remember him that way, smiling in a dark cinema.

Atilio Tessore, Florence, March 11, 1978

Perhaps it was the influence of Pound's words, a result of exhaustion after a day of deliberations; or, more likely, we were all going crazy, like the author of the *Cantos* had; but the fact is in that moment, for the first time, I was aware of the ridiculousness of how we were all dressed, which didn't spurn elegance, at least superficially, but if you scratched the surface of that elegance it revealed that we were all survivors: wrinkled yet perfectly knotted ties over dirty but still starched shirts, with rings of filth and desperation at the necks. Someone, I believe it was Lucien Rebatet, wore a child's eyeglasses, mended at the bridge and then smeared with shoe polish to cover up the repair: they pressed tightly on his temples, drawing a sort of scar on either side of his face. Luciano Folgore, who spoke next, was wearing a wrinkled jacket with wide greasy lapels on which a lone fascist insignia floated, less useful at that point in the war than the handkerchief that peeked out of the jacket's chest pocket, but all suspended, in time and in space, just like him, with his cuffs rolled up and a severe expression or, better put, beyond any adherence to a moral attitude, in his own tiny—or enormous, I don't know which—world. It's not that any of this was surprising: actually it was all we had seen in the last year, when on the sides of the roads in northern Italy cars abandoned for lack of gasoline were crowded alongside gutted, rapidly decomposing horses, and families trying to escape God knows where dragging carts filled with children and mattresses, or sometimes just small suitcases. What was surprising was for it to show up there and in those circumstances, at the conference, which had been conceived to deny all that, as a demonstration of the possibility of a victory that, if you examined the faces and attire of those of us in attendance, seemed, for the first time, impossible no matter how blind you were.

Oreste Calosso, Rome, March 16, 1978

I saw him again years later, during the Fascist Writers' Conference in Pinerolo, in April 1945. Even though he hadn't changed substantially, I had trouble recognizing him. Only did after Michele Garassino pointed him out to me during the afternoon session. And only because of his feverish gaze behind metal-framed glasses whose temples seemed to have been twisted again and again, as if they were a child's toy: I knew that gaze, which I had last seen when Borrello shot Garassino and thought he'd killed him. He had scars on his forehead and at the corners of his mouth, and his face, whose features seemed to have been distilled by the sun and the cold and perhaps hunger, looked like a plowed field.

Espartaco Boyano, Ravenna, March 10, 1978
About five years, from 1931 to 1936. That was how long our friendship lasted. It was also how long we were on the cutting edge of Italian fascist literature in Umbria, if such a claim can be made. There were six of us: Atilio Tessore, Michele Garassino, Oreste Calosso, Romano Cataldi, Luca Borrello, and me. Just like all the other Futurist sections in Italy, we were organized as a political party but shied away from the better known aspects of such institutions. There was no out-and-out obedience, no seriousness, no struggle for internal power. What's more, our structure was complex and I never really understood it fully. Cataldi was the leader, of course; he was older than us, had been in Africa and returned, and he spurned publication. Below him were Tessore and Garassino, who had already published their first books and were, for all intents and purposes, "our" writers. After them, I think, came Calosso and me. Borrello was always with us—calling what he did studying would be even more of a lie in his case than in ours—but his situation was more complex. He was the one closest to Cataldi, who had brought him into his fascist group, but he was also the most Futurist of us all, which, tacitly, created a conflict between him and Tessore and Calosso, who were somewhat conservative in both aesthetic and political terms, although that last part we only found out later. Garassino was closest to Borrello in aesthetic terms, but we now know that wasn't entirely true, because the poems he published under his name in those years weren't his own, nor were the ones

he published later. Garassino was the most fascist of us, along with Cataldi, and, therefore, also the closest to Borrello in that sense. But the truth is that Borrello seemed to float on the margins of our structure, and that—which should have been obvious to us from the beginning, and a cause for alarm—we only grasped some time later.

Michele Garassino, Genoa, March 13, 1978
What did Borrello write? Nothing, everything, horror after the horror, I suppose, fear.

Atilio Tessore, Florence, March 11, 1978
The invasion of Ethiopia, also known as the "Second Italo-Ethiopian War," wasn't, in my opinion, an invasion exactly and perhaps wasn't a war either, but rather a campaign to recover a territory traditionally claimed by Italy and, as such, already part of the Italian territory, at least in symbolic terms. Although, now that I say it, I realize I can't think of any way a territory can belong to a state except symbolically, despite it being obvious that there are different degrees of symbolic possession, and that those territories where it operates most visibly, burying itself into the territory, to put it one way, are those in which there exists a symbolic possession without any political sovereignty, which gives them, again in symbolic terms, greater significance than those territories where political sovereignty is guaranteed and, as a result, need no recovering, as happened in Ethiopia when the recovery some people called a war began, on October 3, 1935. I'll spare you the details, because if you've ever been anyplace where a war of recuperation broke out, a patriotic war in some sense, whose objective wasn't expansion and acquisition of territory but rather its reclaiming—in other words, the reparation of what can only be seen as an injustice—you already know firsthand about the ubiquitous grand declarations and statements of support, the reconciliation of people who'd been mortal enemies just days earlier, the enthusiasm of the press for what is finally news, the popular displays of joy (all more or less sponta-

neous, more less than more), the flags, the chanting, the euphoria of those who enlisted voluntarily to contribute to the war effort. Luca Borrello was one of those volunteers, but he was rejected due to his poor vision. Paradoxically, Cataldi, who was missing one eye and had a file crammed with disciplinary actions that culminated in desertion, was accepted. That war was ours, it belonged to us somehow because it was a war we had prepared for with so many skirmishes, in many confrontations, not only literary ones. It's possible that, if there'd been time for such a thing, Borrello and Cataldi would have ended up enemies over the fact that the latter was able to carry out what had been denied to the former, but that never happened. Instead there was some sort of transferral, in which Cataldi was to take part in the conflict in a way that Borrello had been denied while Borrello was to remain in Italy and ensure that Cataldi's work reached readers. This transferral wasn't metaphorical in any sense. When Cataldi left for Africa, he dragged along with him a large part of the young fascists in Perugia—although perhaps "dragged" is too strong a word: his influence over those young men was great, but they would have enlisted anyhow—and he gave Borrello a box containing everything he'd written to date and Borrello promised to take care of it but didn't fulfill that promise, which perhaps was beyond him. The next thing I knew he burst into the dinner where we were celebrating Michele Garassino's new book, with a pistol in his hand, and shot Garassino in the face.

Oreste Calosso, Rome, March 16, 1978
Between October and December 1935 I only received one letter from Cataldi, from Aksum, the former Abyssinian capital. In it he spoke of the Church of Our Lady Mary of Zion, where, according to him, the Ark of the Covenant is located, and about the Ethiopian women he had seen in the city, whom he found very beautiful, unlike the men, whom he said were a cross between monkeys and rats: he didn't understand how a race could have such different exponents, being the product of the union between the two. At the end of his letter, Cataldi suggested putting to a vote an idea he'd

had for our archive of unrealized artistic actions. This was the idea: in order to clarify why Arthur Rimbaud had wanted to disappear in Africa, and what kind of experiences he'd had there, we should travel to Paris and be as bored as possible; then, of course, we had to travel to Africa, where we would also be bored, but at least we'd be together. Perhaps it was his way of saying he wished we were there, although, under normal circumstances, Cataldi would never have said, or even insinuated, something of that sort. Obviously, war isn't a normal situation, though I think it will end up seeming that way before too long, and Cataldi was an orphan, which perhaps has some importance in relation to our group, the leading edge of fascist literature in Umbria, in central Italy. The idea wasn't a good one, incidentally, but we never gave it a try either; it would have been included in our minutes and you should be able to read it there, if they exist, or still exist: another advantage of our methods.

Espartaco Boyano, Ravenna, March 10, 1978
I never received any letters from Cataldi after he went to Ethiopia, to war. But I think Calosso got one, and Luca Borrello probably got one, or maybe two; he was the person closest to him in our group, as well as the guardian of his literary work while he was away. In exchange, Cataldi was going to experience the war that Borrello wanted to and was going to tell him the story of it upon his return and, possibly, before that, in his correspondence. Of course he never did return, as perhaps you already know.

Michele Garassino, Genoa, March 13, 1978
Very possibly, and without any of us knowing it until then, what united us was our admiration for Cataldi and his work. Between October and December 1935 we only met formally on one occasion, and it was a brief gathering. Calosso read us a letter Cataldi had written him, of which I can't remember a thing, I don't think. Someone said Marinetti had joined the African troops, which seemed to us a confirmation of Borrello's determination and then Cataldi's,

but also a reproach to those who, like me, despite being a Futurist and having sung the praises of war and its cleansing properties and the machines that made it possible, hadn't made a single attempt to experience it firsthand, not a single one.

Oreste Calosso, Rome, March 16, 1978
Borrello and Garassino started to meet up shortly after, I believe; almost always in the room Borrello rented in the house of a Perugian family who lived off the sale of tourist postcards of the cathedral; they were very religious, but mostly they were poor.

Espartaco Boyano, Ravenna, March 10, 1978
Perhaps his relatives in Sansepolcro received some sort of official notice. We only learned that Cataldi had died when the list of Italian casualties was made public, at the end of that war. Because we'd won, meaning that Abyssinia was recovered for the Italians, not many wept for the dead, and there were even those who envied them. The next war would destroy all those illusions, but in 1936 wars were still pretty popular. Very possibly, Borrello envied them too. The news of Cataldi's death took us all by surprise despite our not having received word from him since October or November 1935. However, it's likely that Borrello, who, if I'm not mistaken, thought that Cataldi went to Africa in his place (if I can say that I ever understood what Borrello thought), had known ahead of time how things would end. But I'm convinced he didn't know what would happen next.

Atilio Tessore, Florence, March 11, 1978
Michele Garassino had to publish a new book because the previous one had gone to press in 1934, almost three years prior. The poems he'd published in the Futurist magazines during that period, which he'd read to us in their earliest versions and polished and worked on for months, hadn't been well received: many of them repeated

the images from his first book, and almost all of them had the same structure and showed the same influences. Some people maintain there are two types of writers: those who make different books, or books that aspire to be different, each time; and those who try to always write the same book, or rather a book that is the same yet better, that gets closer to the personal vision they want to make public. The first group are working out of the erroneous belief that a single individual existence—and particularly, the kind we writers usually lead, which tends to be brief and generally disappointing—can produce more than one vision of that existence, and that it's possible for a writer to totally or partially change his ideas, his interests, and those filigrees we call "style." The second group work out of the erroneous belief that the life of a writer is a repository that holds a single, Platonic ideal of a book that can be extracted from him, and that this book wouldn't change with the vicissitudes of individual existence, which tend to produce, at least in those who aren't writers, visible changes of interests and ideas. Those of us who were his friends simply assumed Garassino belonged to that second group of writers and never, not for even a single moment, did we ever have the slightest intention of thinking the opposite.

Michele Garassino, Genoa, March 13, 1978
That same year, 1936, Borrello tried to join the Italian detachment headed into combat on the nationalist side in the Spanish Civil War, however, he was rejected again because of poor eyesight.

Oreste Calosso, Rome, March 16, 1978
Perhaps he felt some relief at being once more allowed to demon-strate his desire to know war firsthand while at the same time being exempted from actually doing so, or perhaps he already had that desire to lose himself, to disappear, that we would see later on, and he truly did want to go to war. While he unquestionably wanted to disappear, his desire to go to war seems doubtful, particularly

considering that, ever since the official announcement of Cataldi's death, and perhaps even earlier, Borrello had only one objective, which was organizing Cataldi's work and delivering it for publication with the help of Garassino, who became his confidant and a familiar presence in the house where Borrello lived, the house of the postcard sellers. Going to war would have been perfectly reasonable given that we all aspired to conflate our lives and our work; it would have been, to put it one way, an obligation, but in that moment it seemed that Borrello chose the work, although his friend's work rather than his own. Of course, we later understood that he'd actually chosen life, although not his own life either, but others' lives. However, we didn't know that yet, and wouldn't know it for a few years.

Atilio Tessore, Florence, March 11, 1978
Do you know what a monster is? Have you ever seen one? Do you know what happens to those who cross a monster's path? Seeing a monster is as dangerous as being a monster yourself because seeing one and turning into one are the same thing, of that I can assure you.

Oreste Calosso, Rome, March 16, 1978
Maybe it was something we owed Cataldi; I mean, something Borrello owed him, and perhaps Garassino as well, though, from what I understand, he hadn't yet incurred his debt. Perhaps Borrello and Garassino grasped that they needed a martyr but didn't yet know they would be the martyrs, or one of them would, or maybe all these interpretations are false, or maybe all of them are true each in their own way.

Oreste Calosso, Rome, March 16, 1978
They may have been preparing Cataldi's book between May and August 1936, or perhaps earlier, since March or April. If I'm not

mistaken, Garassino read us some texts during a dinner in June. I remember well how magnificent the texts were, absolutely extraordinary: they began timidly, but then unfolded to reach heights that none of us, or at least not me, had ever thought Cataldi capable of. They were texts that transcended Futurism, that took its themes and led them in another, unexpected direction; they weren't raucous, but they were surprising, and I remember that the one most surprised by them, or more precisely by the reaction they provoked in us, was Garassino. I remember that he read them to us and then collapsed in his chair, as if disappointed or exhausted, although it actually must have been exactly the opposite. Then he tried to light a cigarette, but his hands—I was beside him and saw it clearly—were trembling. Borrello, on the other side of the table, took the texts and put them away in a cardboard box. Perhaps he too assumed these were emotions provoked by the work of art and by the disappearance of a friend, because, when he could, after having carefully put away the texts, he placed a hand on Garassino's shoulder and left it there for a while.

Atilio Tessore, Florence, March 11, 1978
In July and August I wasn't in Perugia, I was at my parents' home in Florence. I don't have much to say about that except my father was also a writer, not sure if you're aware. At the end of August I returned to Perugia and in September Borrello tried to kill Garassino; in July the box where Borrello stored the poems, maybe under his bed in the house of the Catholic stamp sellers who stationed themselves at the doors to the Cattedrale di San Lorenzo in Perugia, simply disappeared, and Borrello never found it again. Actually, he did find it, in a way, but only in September, and only, if you'll allow me to phrase it this way, when it was already too late for almost everything, except for trying to commit a crime, if the crime hadn't been committed earlier, with more lasting, permanent effects, and by someone who wasn't Borrello.

Atilio Tessore, Florence, March 11, 1978

Then we headed to the dining hall where the first dinner of the conference was to be held; it was in the center of the city, in a somber basement that the owner (who, if I remember correctly, was from Venice) had equipped with a long table that looked like a gangplank, and gas lamps. The precariousness of the setting clashed with the table's solidity, which made me believe, once again, that there wasn't a war going on out there and that the months of rationing and scarcity had been nothing more than my misapprehension. Before the food arrived, even before we'd had anything to drink, Henri Massis stood up and proposed a toast for closer ties between France and the Third Reich. The proposal seemed to catch the Germans by surprise (they stood up despite having empty glasses and feigned taking part in the imaginary toast), except for Johst, who merely nodded. Of course, ties between Germany and France couldn't get any closer, as the former had been raping the latter for some time, so the attempted toast wasn't met with much enthusiasm from anyone, not even Lucien Rebatet, who must have been thinking that if relations were any closer, France would be left gasping for air. Then Svend Fleuron tried to explain something about the tailoring of the gloves he was wearing, which were fairly inappropriate for the climate. If I remember correctly—and believe me, the story is hard to forget—the gloves had been made with Russian astrakhan lambskin that had been manipulated inside the sheep even before her offspring was born, so that, marinating in the placental juices, the leather took on a softness that—it can only be described this way—was not of this world. Because cadavers decomposed rapidly even in the harsh Russian winter, both had to be handled as quickly as possible, and the gloves had to be fitted onto their owner's hands as soon as they were pulled out of the sheep: otherwise, they were discarded. When crafted this way they were so good that no modification was necessary, and the glove makers merely had to measure the hands of the future wearer, a task they devoted enormous attention to, in order to later produce—blindly, and guided only by their sense of touch, with just a few tiny instruments introduced into the sheep's uterus through her vaginal canal often even before she was sacrificed, when the calf was already completely formed—the ordered gloves, extracting the leather using those tools when the lamb was still alive, which, according to experts in the field, gave it a particularly vibrant color. "Well," concluded Fleuron, "we do something similar with our ideas and thoughts: we are their manufacturers and their murderers at the same time," he said. Though for me the conclusion of his story pointed more toward the purity of an art that can only be achieved through crime. How did I react? I congratulated him on his gloves, of course.

Espartaco Boyano, Ravenna, March 10, 1978
If you run with the pack, you don't have to bark. But do wag your tail.

Oreste Calosso, Rome, March 16, 1978
I wasn't in Perugia when I got the news, which was conveyed over the phone by the doorman of the house I lived in there, that Borrello had showed up and tried to force his way in. The doorman had kicked him out rudely, according to what he told me. In some sense, the news wasn't a surprise: those kinds of things were common between us, especially when we were drinking, and Borrello was the one with the lowest alcohol tolerance. I wouldn't have been surprised if the doorman had told me that he'd tried to come in through the window, but later I learned, from the others, that he'd also attempted to get into their homes. It seems he'd spent an entire night wandering through Perugia, making incomprehensible accusations, fueled by what we imagined was alcohol but was actually—and we only found this out later, when most of us had returned to Perugia, at the end of August—desperation and urgency, because Borrello had lost the box that held the texts Cataldi had given him, he had lost it or it had been stolen, he imagined (mistakenly), by me or someone else who was out of town. At the end of August, when we saw each other again at a sort of partial, secret gathering, without Garassino, who was still away, and without Borrello, who we

couldn't find despite various efforts, we decided that we would do something for him, that one by one we would open up our rooms so he could see we didn't have what he was looking for, and that we would do so consecutively and in the course of one afternoon, to show him we weren't hiding anything, we trusted him, and that we were hoping he would trust us as well, so he would know that the loss of Cataldi's texts was also a loss for us.

Espartaco Boyano, Ravenna, March 10, 1978
Atilio Tessore and I were in agreement. We had to bribe the post-card sellers so they would let us into his room. It wasn't hard, as they seemed used to providing certain services in exchange for modest sums of money, something we verified a few days later with more serious consequences for everyone. When we went into his room, we found Borrello lying in bed in a disastrous state, wearing clothes it didn't seem he'd changed in several days. Tessore must have been unaccustomed to that sort of thing, and possibly surprised himself when he kicked Borrello in the back to check if he was alive. We watched him in horror, but then Borrello turned and asked us what we were doing there. Calosso explained everything, and it looked as if Borrello was smiling, actually, not because he was surprised by our behavior, our generosity if you prefer, but rather because of his absolute lack of surprise. Because (and I thought this later, some time later) Borrello in fact knew we were going to do that: allow him into our rooms to search them with a fine-tooth comb. And he knew (this I also understood later) he was going to refuse to do so. At some point we found ourselves all standing there, in his room, in front of the small window. Two pigeons had built a nest in the cornice of the building across the street and were gently, but regularly, cooing, in a way that I found irritating. Tessore, Borrello, Calosso, and I looked at each other. Actually, Borrello looked at the three of us, and told us that he appreciated it, but that it wasn't necessary. That he already knew who had stolen Cataldi's texts, and it was all his fault, that he had thought about it and now knew that it was

all his fault. Then he turned around and asked us to go and leave him there alone.

Oreste Calosso, Rome, March 16, 1978
Garassino returned to the city, if I remember correctly, on September 2. The day before he sent us a note saying that the publishing house of the magazine *Artecrazia* was going to publish his new volume of poems; he added that some of them would be featured in that week's issue and that he'd brought us some of the first copies. He asked us to meet him in a restaurant called Il Letto Caldo, very close to the entrance of the city's walls, at eight the following evening.

Espartaco Boyano, Ravenna, March 10, 1978
Il Letto Caldo was a small restaurant, but quite popular among the students at the University of Perugia. It had a cheerful atmosphere generally, but I don't remember anything cheerful about that night. When Calosso and I arrived at the restaurant, Garassino was already settled at a table in the back and waved us over. As he did, I noticed that he was trembling slightly and the magazines he held shook as if rocked by the wind. There was an urgency in his gaze and his gestures, which I mistakenly interpreted as enthusiasm. "Where are the others?" he asked, looking over our heads. When we explained that Tessore was expected to arrive a bit late and that we hadn't heard anything more from Borrello since the day of our visit, he seemed relieved. Then he held the magazines out to us. In them were his poems. One could say.

Atilio Tessore, Florence, March 11, 1978
I was taking a class that usually ran late and that night, once again, luckily, went overtime. It was taught by a bald, terribly shy teacher whose light eyes were always looking away, lost at the back of the

classroom, on the exit door—which he insisted be closed at the start of each class—or on the floor of the room, or on its ceiling. He had a measly bit of fluff beneath his nose that danced each time he addressed us, which was all he did the whole class, because he didn't allow questions or answer them. But where some saw arrogance there was really just shyness, and the consequences of a quite serious case of tuberculosis he'd suffered as a child. It had affected his spinal development, so he, whose name, by the way, was Luigi Bagiolini, had a defect that meant he stood at a seventy-five-degree angle. It was that stance, which many judged artificial, simply an affectation, that was most natural for Bagiolini and, as such, he gave his classes leaning forward, looking at the ceiling or the back of the room or the exit, and always seemed to be bowing before his own lectures, as if he were venerating himself or, better put, what he was saying, which was always or almost always disconcertingly and brutally brilliant beyond any doubt. Although, as I mentioned, had there been any doubts, they couldn't have been raised as Bagiolini didn't allow for them. On the other hand, that prohibition opened the door for abundant doubts, if not about the subjects he was teaching, then about Bagiolini himself. It was said, first of all, that he'd discovered that a large part of the posthumous poetry of Lucio Piccolo, from Capo d'Orlando, was written not by the poet but rather by a professor from Messina who, upon realizing Piccolo's work wasn't important enough to justify the publication of his complete works he'd been planning, had written poems in Piccolo's style to round out the volume. Bagiolini had uncovered the ruse but chosen not to denounce him, and only mentioned it as a warning to his students when he taught Piccolo's complete works. He would linger particularly on the poems written by the professor from Messina, which he considered the finest of the Sicilian poet's oeuvre; in his opinion, Piccolo's work could be derided as mediocre, or superficially mediocre, only when considered in its entirety or through each poem individually, as neither way was how Piccolo would have wanted his work to be read. Bagiolini insisted that Piccolo's work was the result of the poet's understanding that innovation in literature was, in the best-case scenario, incomprehensible to contemporary readers and acknowledged only when read in later times, by the readers of the period the writer had anticipated and in the context of other works that had emerged from it. To avoid alienating either his contemporary or his future audience, Bagiolini said, Piccolo had decided that his literary project should consist of a series of an indeterminate number of mediocre poems among which would appear fifteen or sixteen extraordinary poems, spaced out to avoid any hasty interpretation. They would be the best poems written by any author of his generation: poems, of course, that he had already written. His intent was that someone would find them among all the others and use them to reconstruct the book he'd originally conceived, without the mediocre poems placed around them as cushions so that lazy readers or those threatened by visionary literature could rest comfortably on the work. That book was published yet invisible, and of course only Bagiolini had been able to locate it. Incidentally, the poems written by the professor from Messina that completed Piccolo's body of work were absolutely necessary because they abetted his project of obliterating, of hiding, the fifteen or sixteen good poems that had been written for readers of the future; the others were for the present, which is always brief, too brief in almost every case, and not particularly generous with writers.

It was also said that Bagiolini had spent years working on the reconstruction, minute by minute, of the day in which Giacomo Leopardi had composed his poem "Brutus the Younger" in 1821. Bagiolini had already lost hope of finding—amid all the irrelevant details he'd located in Leopardi's correspondence and personal diaries, and the statements of those who knew him, particularly those who visited him that day—an event of some importance that explained and justified the writing of the poem, which he considered a masterpiece (an opinion that, actually, was his alone among the experts on Leopardi's work). He had found only minor, banal, entirely trifling events, which possibly even Leopardi had forgotten about by the next day, showing that the triviality of everyday life has no effect on literature and perhaps even stimulates it or turns out to be its necessary flip side. People also said that Professor Bagiolini endured his authoritarian and extremely violent wife, whom he'd married only for her money and who forced him to sing in a choir despite his hating music and, even worse, having no talent for it in the slightest.

Oreste Calosso, Rome, March 16, 1978

The poems were extraordinary, they had such power and, in a sense, the rigor that Garassino's first book, about Africa, had lacked. They also managed something only good poems do, which is to establish a completely particular time and space, a self-absorption, apart from where and when they are read, which in our case, I will remind you, was at a restaurant frequented by students, in Perugia near the city's ancient walls. It was possibly the least appropriate place to read poetry and, therefore, the ideal spot to test what the poems could actually have achieved anywhere, including a brothel, a public library, or a church. Their immense quality, their power—which situated them, to put it one way, outside of this world—was extraordinary. In that sense, for us, reading those poems was flattering, as Garassino was one of us, and his personal triumph was, or should have been, ours as well, or at least something that belonged to him but we could use, or at least recognize as the product of something we had been part of, even if only as witnesses. I later understood that our reaction was typical of all those who know and spend a lot of time with a writer whose achievements become, through proximity, something that also belongs to them. It is precisely that which a writer most resists, because he considers his achievements his alone. Often they are nothing more than the results of his efforts—tedious, as anyone who's attempted writing knows—to impose himself on his circumstances, which the writer generally finds irritating and stupid. Yet those circumstances are what the others feel so proud of because they constitute them. I would later understand that the last thing a writer wants is for his achievements to be shared and seen by others as a source of pride and with a certain sense of ownership, and that's the reason why so many of a writer's friendships end after (and in fact due to) a book's publication. If they had truly understood what I wrote, the writer thinks, if they'd done the work of carefully reading what I wrote, then they would feel ashamed, they would realize that I did it to offend and ridicule them, that I wrote it behind their backs, against them and what they represent, so that they could never feel proud of themselves, so that they would never dare to believe a personal achievement in spite of them and to humiliate them was an achievement of their own. What I'm trying to say is that they were good poems and that, as we read them, all of us there with Garassino—who watched us with nervous expectation, and sometimes hid his face behind a glass of wine he was pretending to drink—searched for the words to best express our admiration and our astonishment. Until a certain surprise seeped into that admiration, followed by a paralyzing perplexity and later an insistent, even burning, desire for what we were reading to not be true. It was like in the nocturnal schisms of nightmares where you are aware you're dreaming but yet, at the same time, immersed in fear, you believe everything that is happening. Boyano was the first to lift his gaze from the page and ask Garassino what he had done. Garassino—who perhaps at that moment felt relief at someone finally asking him that question—responded that he'd used what another man no longer had any use for, and that it was all literature; that through literature and in his poems—as they were now his—the dead man's memory would be perpetuated, his work would be read, finally, and perhaps read the way he would have wished, as things belonging to the world of the living, untarnished by the burden of premature death.

Atilio Tessore, Florence, March 11, 1978
Because of Bagiolini's class, and as I'd foreseen, I was late to the gathering at Il Letto Caldo. When I finally arrived, no one was there and the scandal had already died down, although it was still being discussed at the tables. A student I knew, who was aware of my friendship with the Perugian Futurists, told me everything and then showed me where the incident had occurred, and the bullet holes in the back wall, next to a photograph of a man with a pen-

etrating gaze who was perhaps the owner's father, a local politician, an actor, or some other figure of no consequence.

Espartaco Boyano, Ravenna, March 10, 1978
Garassino had taken Romano Cataldi's texts and had broken them up into verses. He'd made literal poems out of some of them, merely transcribing the original texts into a poetic language that, admittedly, reflected a great talent for rhythm. But in other cases he had "broken" the texts into units that he'd shifted around, as if they were pieces of a puzzle that could be put together many different ways—by which I mean, generating new images each time or simply the same ones. In either case, there was talent in it and I had to admit, and I believe anyone would have to admit—meaning, anyone who could read the book outside of its context—that the poems, which were brilliant, were now Garassino's poems. Perhaps that was what upset and hurt us more than the theft, which is simply one in a wide range of literary practices. The fact that Garassino had improved Cataldi's texts, which, as he told us, he'd gotten by bribing the postcard vendors Borrello was living with so he could steal the box from his room. What is there to say when that happens? Probably a few things. But we couldn't say them, not then nor, unfortunately, much later, which is when we should have, because just then Borrello came into the restaurant. I stood up and headed toward him on reflex, habit if you will, but he seemed not to see me. When he reached our table, he pulled a pistol from the back of his waistband and shot four or five times at Garassino, who was still sitting down, leaning against the restaurant's rear wall. Let's just say that what saved his life was what kept Borrello from dying somewhere in Africa or in the skirmishes of the Spanish Civil War: his terrible eyesight. After emptying the pistol, with no time and perhaps no desire to confirm whether or not he'd killed the man who had been his best friend and collaborator in the months prior, Borrello threw the latest issue of *Artecrazia* onto the table and left through the front door of the restaurant before anyone managed to catch him. By the time I stood up—we were all on the floor, which,

obviously, wasn't very heroic but was quite sensible—Borrello had disappeared and I didn't yet know that I wouldn't see him again for almost ten years. Nor that, when I did see him, he and I, in some sense, would be other people.

Michele Garassino, Genoa, March 13, 1978
I'm not going to answer that, not because I'm offended by the question, which I understand perfectly, but because I think it is poorly formulated. What is truly important in literature? The authors or the texts? If you believe it's the former, you have no reason to read and therefore no opinion to offer about literature: you live with your back to literature, in a world of shadows. On the other hand, if you believe that what's important is the texts—which is exactly what the word *literature* comes to mean, or came to mean; God only knows what the authors of your generation think it means, if they've even bothered to pose the question, which I doubt, particularly as I made the mistake of trying to read them—then in that case you have nothing to reproach me for, because what I did was give those texts new life, a life unburdened by their author's untimely death that instead would benefit from the existence of an author who could sign them, promote them, and, eventually, if necessary, defend them. That this author had my name is the least important part of it, although I will say, the fact that those texts did indeed bear my name was as beneficial to them as it was to me, or at least didn't do me any serious harm. Besides, isn't that how things are done? Don't we spend our lives manufacturing books like pharmacists manufacture prescriptions, simply pouring things from one vessel into another? Don't we all spend our lives braiding and unbraiding the same twine?

Oreste Calosso, Rome, March 16, 1978
We were later able to reconstruct the hours prior to his abrupt appearance at Il Letto Caldo with the help of a map of the city and by asking some people who had seen him. Borrello left his house

in the early afternoon—soon after waking up, it seems—and headed to the train station: like the rest of us, he had received Garassino's announcement of his publication in *Artecrazia* and the celebration that night; unlike us, he couldn't or didn't want to wait for Garassino to give him a copy of the issue, and he bought it himself when the train from Rome arrived with the first copies of the day's press. Perhaps he read the poems "by" Garassino in one of the bars at the station, but most likely he couldn't resist reading them right there on the platform, because by the time he reached the bar, according to the waiter, Borrello was already beside himself. He ordered a coffee and a grappa and read or reread the poems; when the waiter brought his order, he asked for a second grappa. What was going through his head in that moment is hard to know and, in general, given that we're talking about Borrello, impossible. He paid, went back to his house, and confronted the couple who sold postcards in front of the cathedral. The owner of the house, who was in the kitchen preparing beans for supper (which was the main food in that home, she insisted when we interviewed her, as if that were somehow proof of her decency), denied everything, to Borrello and again when we questioned her, but her oldest son—he had a scar covered with ointment that ran across his left shoulder blade, possibly the result of a fight with other vendors in front of the cathedral, nothing unusual in those days—admitted it. In other words, he admitted that his mother had sold the box of Cataldi's texts to Garassino, and for a relatively small sum of money. We never found out why he'd confessed, whether it was to get rid of Borrello, to aggravate him, or to aggravate his mother, or perhaps for some other reason. I can think of one now that we didn't consider at the time: that he'd had something against Garassino, whom he'd met on his periodic visits to the house and perhaps didn't like for some reason or another. However, it's obvious that Garassino could only have gotten the texts from Borrello, who never would have handed them over willingly and who, by the way, was seeming quite desperate in those days. As far as I know, Garassino never admitted to paying that woman for the box of Cataldi's manuscripts, but, at least in private, he never denied the fact that those poems had "originally"—I think that was the expression he used—been what Cataldi had entrusted to Borrello before setting off for Africa. Nor did he offer any explanation as to how he could have acquired them in some other way apart from theft: Borrello never would have lent him the texts or allowed him to copy them. Those texts had an importance to Borrello that transcended their literary quality. They were memories of his dead friend, but also some sort of amulet guaranteeing him something, possibly luck or fortune; more likely, a purpose for his life, the conviction that he had something to do and he was doing it. I don't know. In any case, what happened next, according to the son, was that he admitted they'd sold Cataldi's texts to Garassino, at which point Borrello became furious and punted the pot where dinner was cooking (navy beans, insisted the woman). Then the son hit him and a neighbor soon joined in, and between the two of them they kicked Borrello out of the house, then went up into his attic room and threw his belongings out the window. He said that by the time they threw out the first few things Borrello was gone, he'd left without waiting to gather them up.

Espartaco Boyano, Ravenna, March 10, 1978
I don't know about you, but it seems ignominious that it was postcard sellers who sold Cataldi's texts to Garassino. What is a postcard, in any case? An object that, apart from what's depicted on it, means nothing until it's been received by its addressee. What I mean is that it's a souvenir with no memory—or just a provisional memory—behind it. In that sense, we saw Cataldi's texts as diametrically opposed to the postcards those miserable wretches earned their living selling, when they weren't committing crimes: the texts were the basis of a memory we'd already acquired. A rarity, a souvenir with a real memory behind it, as opposed to some potential, still incomplete one.

Atilio Tessore, Florence, March 11, 1978

It seems he was drinking later somewhere; by the time he visited one of his *fascio* comrades and asked him for a revolver, Borrello was completely drunk, according to the man's testimony. He also said that, of course, he gave him the pistol: that was how things were done in those days, then Borrello headed to our meeting point and shot Garassino. I don't know what he did in the ten years following, so you'll have to imagine it yourself, but perhaps, in order to do that, you need to know this: I didn't see him again until the interrupted Fascist Writers' Conference, and by that time, I thought, it was already too late to tell him, in case he didn't know, that I hadn't taken part in the theft of Cataldi's texts. It was also too late to tell him that I wished—as I think the others, except for Garassino, did too—they'd never been stolen, for the sake of our friendship, for the sake of Cataldi, for the sake of our role as the vanguard of fascist literature in Umbria, but also out of a certain vision of what could be called—for lack of a more appropriate, less puerile term—"poetic justice." Of course, at the conference, Borrello showed us that it wasn't too late, at least not to redo what had been done badly, what was twisted and seemed beyond repair. Even today I still regret not having told him that I wasn't what he'd thought, that at least among all the people attending that conference I wasn't, although the truth is that I was. I only ceased to be—if you can name the date when you change your mind, or at least perceive you have—after that conference; more precisely, on its second day, when it ended, tacitly and precipitated by circumstances, without anyone lowering the stage curtains, or saying any words. Borrello was to blame for that ending and for my change of heart, obviously.

Oreste Calosso, Rome, March 16, 1978

Alceo Folicaldi pushed an upright piano in from the restaurant's kitchen, where the owner probably hid it so it wouldn't be played. Folicaldi must have known where it was since the start of the dinner, or perhaps he'd discovered it on one of his trips to the bathrooms, which were next to the kitchen. Several people swooped down on him as soon as he entered with the piano and again an argument arose about who had the right to play their songs in the first place. Once again, Johst solved the problem by standing up and demanding that, that night, we would only hear songs that would allow us to forget we were at war, at least for a few hours, and that was why in the end it was Mencaroni who played.

Atilio Tessore, Florence, March 11, 1978
You probably don't know this, but Mencaroni was not only a writer, but a filmmaker as well: an unusual filmmaker who composed the melodies for his films and, before sound—by which I mean, in the silent film era—he would play the tunes himself on the movie theater's piano, often introducing comments and observations about what the viewers were seeing or explaining the plots, as if they were incomprehensible to the spectators. The arrival of the talkies put paid to that practice, which was, at least in Mencaroni's case, an activity so extraordinary, its unfinished nature so complete, that the talkies often seemed impoverished without his music and commentary, less satisfying, as if they were some sort of a regression. Then the war put an end to all Italian cinema that didn't serve as propaganda, and Mencaroni, who was unable or unwilling to meet that requirement, hadn't made a film since 1939; so when he began playing that night, it wasn't the familiar melodies he'd composed for the films that we'd seen, but rather ones he'd created for the films he hoped to one day make.

Michele Garassino, Genoa, March 13, 1978
Borrello had taken a seat at the far end of the table and remained in silence the entire night, slowly eating with one hand while the other covered his neck, as if it was hurting him or he didn't want the others to see it. Arnaldo Ginna addressed him a couple of times, and Rosa Rosà spoke to him as well, but Borrello exchanged only a few words with them, interrupted by coughing. None of us dared to approach him, and then Mencaroni started to play and I forgot

about him. Only later, when I thought about it again, did I understand why Borrello had spent the entire night covering his neck: his shirt had no collar, it was the typical shirt of an Italian worker of the time, and that, it seems, embarrassed him.

Espartaco Boyano, Ravenna, March 10, 1978
All I can say about Mencaroni's film—I mean, the music for the film Mencaroni told us about that night—is that it was like a blind man's drawing. Have you ever seen one? The blind's perception is tactile and, as such, sequential, in the sense that they are unable to comprehend an object in its entirety, at a glance. Imagine a cube. You and I can see most of its faces simultaneously, and because of that we know it's a cube; the blind, on the other hand, can only hold and touch its faces one after the other. Their understanding that it's a cube comes from a succession of tactile stimuli, as they confirm the cube's faces are regular and there are six of them, and that's how they represent it if they have to draw it; as a series of six squares laid out one after the other. Something similar happened with Mencaroni's film. The narration was linear, but the object it referenced, the hypothetical film, seemed set in a hard-to-imagine place in which time did not exist and description was not sequential. A place where words did not follow one another but rather could be spoken out loud all at once. In some sense, Mencaroni's description of his film was saying that there's a way to escape the linearity that affects music, literature, ballet, cinema—not the visual arts—and that is to conceive of the description as a lost entirety, or as an object we're unable to comprehend. One that we have to touch and approach from different angles, describing one after the other, knowing they make up a whole, even if it's an incomprehensible whole. Mencaroni's art took place in time while rejecting time. His art made us walk feeling our way, as if we were blind. And as a result, it was exceptional art, only accessible through a multiplicity of simultaneous perspectives that's said to only be visible through God's eyes, if God exists. I am not God—I think that's pretty

obvious—so I can only imagine such art, but I think it's the art of the future, if, once again, a future exists, something I'm also dubious about. So, here, these are my blind drawings.

Atilio Tessore, Florence, March 11, 1978
The music was all noises, as I recall, music that could only have been tolerated in an era without noise, a time without bombs or airplanes flying over cities, without antiaircraft alarms or explosions.

Oreste Calosso, Rome, March 16, 1978
Naturally we were all very drunk by then, including me, and I don't remember much. If anyone was sober, however, it was Borrello, who approached first Espartaco Boyano and then Atilio Tessore, leading them out of the restaurant to speak on the street. I couldn't hear them from where I was, but I did see that Borrello spoke first and they shook their heads and then spoke and he made emphatic gestures of refusal, there in the middle of the street, as if he were talking to himself like a madman, and then he spoke again and the others shook their heads and then he left; Borrello headed toward the end of the street and the other two stood there for a little while before coming back inside. He didn't approach me, and he didn't approach Garassino either; while his reasons for not wanting to speak to Garassino seem obvious, I don't understand why he didn't want to speak to me. That was the penultimate time I saw him; the next time was a day later, but then, of course, it was too late for me to ask him.

Pinerolo

APRIL 1945

>>

We are inhabited satellites.
A falling man
is creation
collapsing.
But we keep spinning
with the weight
of those who perish.

ARMAND GATTI, "Death/Worker"

Oreste Calosso, Rome, March 16, 1978
The morning of April 21, 1945, broke with a magnificent dawn, like every other day that terrible month. I remember it perfectly, and I also remember how, when we found Luca Borrello's corpse, his eyes were open and he was looking up at the sky, as if a moment earlier Borrello too had been appreciating that indeed it was a splendid day.

Atilio Tessore, Florence, March 11, 1978
On April 21, 1945, it rained all morning and then the sun came out; ironically, by that time we'd all found shelter and no one had the slightest intention of going out for a walk; in fact, some of us were already leaving.

Michele Garassino, Genoa, March 13, 1978
I don't remember. I haven't the faintest idea what you're talking about and I can't even imagine how one would be able to remember such a thing, what the weather was like on an uneventful day more than thirty years ago.

Espartaco Boyano, Ravenna, March 10, 1978

On the twenty-first of April 1945 it rained all day and that made the search difficult. Gradually almost everyone gave up, except for me and a few others, who continued on despite the bad weather. Who can say whether their motive was curiosity, or the conviction that the missing person could have been any of them, or the speculation—right on target, of course—that searching would exempt them from the list of suspects. That was if, in the end, it turned out that Borrello had had an accident or been murdered, and not just left on the sly.

Oreste Calosso, Rome, March 16, 1978

Giorgio Almirante turned to me during breakfast and whispered that Borrello had disappeared. "What are you talking about?" I asked him. Almirante told me the woman who ran the hotel had informed him that Borrello hadn't returned from dinner. "It seems he checked in before heading over to Town Hall," he said, "but never came back." Almirante and I were silent for a moment; then both opened our mouths to speak at the same time, as so often happens. "What's most important is that this doesn't get out," I said, "that we deal with it amongst ourselves." Almirante replied, "That isn't possible, or at least not anymore, because the woman reported it to the police. She said she had to." "Which police?" I asked him. Almirante shrugged; by that point there were dozens of more or less secret police forces, with contradictory objectives that were never very clear, even to their members, whose primary motives I imagined to be personal convenience, along with some sort of loyalty to their most immediate superiors. Wasn't that also how the legions behaved, and later the condottieri? Perhaps it's the only form of social organization that we Italians are willing to accept, the one that best matches our nature, as all the others have failed. "I don't think we need to worry," I said. "Borrello might've just gotten distracted somewhere along the way. He'll be back." Almirante didn't answer; he got up and asked to be put in touch with Salò.

Oreste Calosso, Rome, March 16, 1978

Later I went up to my room and stretched out on the bed to think about what to do; the second day of the conference would start in an hour and I was still thinking that Borrello was fine, wherever he was. Maybe he'd simply left the conference, angry over something or with someone, and gone back to where he'd been living, possibly near Perugia, in Sansepolcro or wherever he'd been spending those months we all—even those who, in some sense, wished it weren't the case—knew were the final months of the war. It was strange to register his absence as an exception, a problem, because up until that point it had been, for lack of a better word, normality—at least for someone like me, who at one point had seen him frequently and then hadn't seen him for years; it was as if, for the first time, an ominous portent lingered over his absence. Now I know that it was the situation itself that was ominous, and I wonder if Borrello had planned it that way—his disappearance and reappearance and new disappearance—so that our lives (completely desensitized to the pain of others, and even our own pain, after so many years of war) would be disrupted by an ominous situation that forced us to flee, to break with the stasis we found ourselves in (of which the conference was merely a manifestation), in order to seek refuge (those of us who could) from what we ourselves had created.

Espartaco Boyano, Ravenna, March 10, 1978

People say that when someone close to you dies, you don't dream of them as soon as you'd like. I think I dreamt of Borrello just a few days later, although it's possible, probable even, that it was weeks or even months later. Dating it precisely is no longer as important for me as the fact that in the dream I was irrationally convinced it was taking place the day before Borrello's death. I mean I knew that what I was seeing and doing was all part of a dream, and I believed that the dream was taking place the day before his disappearance and not months or years later, as was perhaps the case. It doesn't matter. This was the dream: I was walking through a park. It was autumn, a clear day. Then I saw Borrello. He was seated on a bench and waved me over. As I approached, he got up and quickly moved to a different bench further away, where he sat down and again waved me over. I continued my approach and he stood up and moved to another spot, further on, where he yet again waved me over. This went on a few more times, and I experienced a growing feeling of powerlessness. Finally, when there were no more nearby benches, and Borrello could no longer continue to flee, he remained sitting in his spot but raised both hands to his face. I asked him why he was doing that. They stole my face, he said through his fingers. And then he vanished.

Oreste Calosso, Rome, March 16, 1978
When I came down from my room I found the source of the noise that had awoken me: some members of the Black Brigades had come to the hotel to interview the conference participants, who were firmly refusing to answer or had stated, with varying degrees of truthfulness, that they didn't understand Italian. Apparently Troubetzkoy had fainted or had a dizzy spell a few minutes earlier while being questioned by the police, and Morlacchi and Hrand Nazariantz were working hard to bring her back to life. A life that, frankly, if it were up to me, there was no need to bring her back to. I remained standing on the staircase, observing the scene, not daring to descend completely, and it was in that moment that I saw Almirante, who was trying to mediate between the soldiers and the conference attendees, particularly the French, who were shouting and refusing to answer questions, and Almirante saw me too, in the same moment, and shook his head. Years later, as you perhaps know, Almirante became a politician of some importance, with a career that, despite what people say, was based on intelligence and his eye for opportunity as well as a certain loyalty that some people consider useless and that serves not so much fascism as the ideas and ideals that made fascism possible. Those were the ideas and ideals of our youth, which, in some sense, fascism later betrayed, because all it could do was betray them. Almirante's political career

is maintained more by that foolish loyalty (which must be intrinsic to his character) than by votes, at least beyond southern Italy, which seems to be his fiefdom. In that situation, with that gesture, Almirante was being loyal to something perhaps not even he understood: he turned his back on me, and drew a one and a four with his hands, and I understood what he meant and went back up the stairs.

Oreste Calosso, Rome, March 16, 1978
Naturally, the bed hadn't been touched, and there were no clothes or personal effects in the room, except for some sort of large chest that must have been dragged there by someone much stronger than Borrello, or at least that's what I thought at the time. Both the door and the window were open. I stuck my head out the window; it overlooked the hotel's interior courtyard, which adjoined some homes with clothes in the windows that must have been hanging there all night. I wondered if Borrello had taken in the same view, at least out of curiosity, and I told myself that he must have in order to open the window, although his reason for opening it was and continues to be unclear, at least to me. A woman emerged on one of the balconies over the courtyard and I ducked back instinctively. I realized I didn't have much time: I took the chest and, with great effort, as it was even heavier than I'd imagined—which again made me think Borrello couldn't have dragged it there to the middle of the room, although he may have—pulled it out of the room and into the hallway. I heard familiar voices in the stairwell, including Almirante's, which was yelling and crackling in an attempt to impose itself on the other voices, taking part in the argument but addressing me exclusively, in warning. I struggled with the handles of various doors until I found one that was open: it revealed a storage room piled with brooms, rags, some tools, and a half-drunk bottle of grappa, which shocked me—though, of course, I had no reason to be surprised. There was a key: I pushed the chest inside and locked the door. Almirante was leading the group of soldiers up the stairs just then. His gaze was filled with terror; I had never seen him like that before.

Michele Garassino, Genoa, March 13, 1978

I was late coming down from my room: by the time I did, all anyone was talking about was Borrello's disappearance, which I learned of from Bruno Corra or Arnaldo Ginna, I can't remember; more likely it was Bruno Munari or Alceo Folicaldi; or, perhaps, Paolo Buzzi or Luciano Folgore.

Michele Garassino, Genoa, March 13, 1978

Two groups formed very quickly, the first mostly made up of Italians and Spaniards: we argued about the possible reasons behind the disappearance, knocking down other people's theories and defending our own in a chaos where both sets of arguments were similar or exactly the same, though we didn't notice that so it didn't trouble us in the slightest. It was this first group that came up with the idea that Borrello could have been kidnapped by partisans, in other words, by criminals operating outside of Salò's laws, an idea we all accepted despite its relative improbability, in the sense that the scofflaws who would later create the myth of the Resistance could have chosen a more noteworthy representative of European fascist literature to kidnap, if that was what they had done: Henri Bruning, Ion Sân-Giorgiu, Paolo Buzzi, or Hans Blunck. Besides, kidnappings weren't common in those days; the prevailing dilemma was between indifference and murder, with no intermediate terms. For some reason, however, that argument won out over the others, even over the idea that Borrello could have simply left, which is what I had originally thought. In the second group, on the other hand, Rintsje Piter Sybesma had gotten a detailed map of the Pinerolo area from the hotel owners and was studying it, surrounded by the Germans, who were tracing possible search routes. No one spoke except for a few whispers, there were no arguments about the reasons for his disappearance, just the enviable practicality of those who see in tragic events—for some reason, everyone agreed that, whatever had happened to Borrello, we should expect the worst, that he wouldn't be found alive—an opportunity to exercise a talent or ability, in this case map reading and missing person searches. We southern Europeans also saw Borrello's disappearance as an opportunity to exercise our talents—the only ones we had—which were, and are, a gift for controversy, unprovoked rejection of others' arguments, and stirring up scandal. I probably don't need to tell you that we employed another of our talents—perhaps the most important one: as soon as the Germans had divided up the territory and established search routes, we all set aside our arguing and obeyed them, as if obeying were the only thing we knew how to do.

Espartaco Boyano, Ravenna, March 10, 1978
Maps always provide a different perspective. Have you noticed that certain people seem bigger the further away from us they are? The exact opposite happens with maps, in relation to what they represent. Things are always bigger than they appear on a map, and more complicated.

Atilio Tessore, Florence, March 11, 1978
Why didn't I join the search? It didn't seem necessary. I went back to Florence that day, in a car Hanns Johst made available for me, along with Ion Sân-Giorgiu, Henri Massis, and Erwin Kolbenheyer, who, by the way, I never saw again after that: it seemed obvious that the conference was over.

Espartaco Boyano, Ravenna, March 10, 1978
I don't know if you've ever seen a topographic map of the region Pinerolo is in. To the west is a simple plain, but to the east there are all sorts of challenges: high mountains spread out all over the territory creating complicated passes and hollows that intersect two streams, the Chisone and the Pellice. If Borrello had been kidnapped, we thought, we wouldn't ever find him in that complex terrain, which only the rebels, or "partisans" as they called themselves, knew how to move through without being seen. If, on the

other hand, he'd been murdered already, most likely the "partisans" would have disposed of his body somewhere on the outskirts of one of the region's cities: Pinasca, Bricherasio, Luserna San Giovanni, Torre Pellice, or Pinerolo itself. If, in the end, he was wounded, he could be anywhere, probably to the east. So four groups were created: one headed north, toward San Pietro Val Lemina; another followed the Via Nazionale to San Germano Chisone; a third went southward following the Chisone, and a fourth southeast through Miradolo and San Sebastiano. The groups were made up of members of the Black Brigades who'd been sent from the surrounding towns by order of the ministry in Salò and joined by some of the conference participants, whose reasons for aiding in the search must have all been different. I was part of the third group, the one following the course of the Chisone. I don't know why I did it. Perhaps out of fear that I would be accused of passivity or even complicity. Maybe out of fear of staying by myself in Pinerolo, where Borrello's absence was, for lack of a better word, omnipresent. And possibly also due to a bad conscience, because the previous night I had rejected his arguments and accused him of being a defeatist. I'd said that to his face and then gone back to the table and repeated it. Borrello is a defeatist, he believes the republic is done for, I'd said. The next day he disappeared and the rain was making the search for him difficult.

Atilio Tessore, Florence, March 11, 1978
Why would I worry about being among the suspects? Hadn't I defended Borrello the day before, when he said we should take part in the impending regime change to keep our mission from ending completely? Haven't they already told you, you who are so young, that Borrello was accused of being a defeatist, that they claimed he was a mole, that they insinuated he'd gone crazy? Which is to say, he'd gone crazy with loneliness and weary saturation. Borrello's last project revealed how he'd walked a narrow, unclassifiable path; there were only rumors of the project's existence—persistent, curiously unanimous rumors, as if all those repeating them had actually

seen Borrello working on it, or, more plausibly, they'd all accepted the rumors because they thought Borrello's body of work had grown diffuse, transforming and taking on increasingly singular, strange forms (as if *L'anguria lirica* wasn't singular and strange enough) as opposed to signaling a direction that only Borrello followed, a direction we said we wanted to follow but didn't. That last project sounded like one of those nightmares in which you're both victim and assailant, weapon and wound, at the same time.

Oreste Calosso, Rome, March 16, 1978
It seemed obvious that the soldiers didn't know what they were searching for, nor how to go about it. They questioned me at length, first in the hallway and later in Borrello's room, which Almirante had the hotel manager open, though it was clear to me we both knew the room was unlocked. The manager was crying the whole time, covering her mouth with a dirty handkerchief, as if the missing man was one of her relatives and not a complete stranger who had been staying in her establishment for less than twenty-four hours. The soldiers seemed anxious to slap her across the face, and only restrained themselves because of Almirante's presence and the orders they'd received from Salò to treat the case with the utmost speed, discretion, and efficiency. It was evident both to us and to them that the authorities didn't want anyone to disappear at a conference whose function, if it had one, was to create solidarity with the cause of the Italian Social Republic instead of sabotaging it. The head of the soldiers was a hirsute man appropriately called Macellaio, meaning "butcher," who seemed to derive some pleasure from the fear he elicited in his subordinates. He ordered them to organize a search that, as we immediately confirmed, had already been organized by the Germans, so Macellaio placed his men under German orders. He didn't allow me to join them, however: when they had all left, he sighed deeply, as if he had been holding his breath, convinced that the air exhaled by writers is tainted—which of course it is—and demanded that we sit with him. Almirante and I took our seats and he asked the hotel manager to bring us three

glasses and a bottle of wine; I told him I preferred not to drink, but the man pretended not to have heard me. When the woman arrived with the glasses and the bottle, he demanded she stop crying and the woman began to cry harder. Macellaio smiled and poured the wine. His gesture forced us to drink with him, and Almirante and I reluctantly took sips. Then the man fell silent: he seemed to enjoy our not knowing what to say, and between the three of us some sort of tense calm was established, which made us aware, I think for the first time that day, of our present moment, of the wine we were drinking, of the rain that was falling on the other side of the window, in a city that feigned indifference to Borrello's disappearance despite being cognizant of the commotion it had provoked at the hotel. Along with the calm established by Macellaio's silence there was also a certain resignation, as if the search for Borrello was already a thing of the past and we were merely reminiscing; I wondered if that wasn't Macellaio's way of lessening the drama of his investigations, giving the impression to those most interested in the case that it was actually already solved. When the time seemed right to him, and without any warning, Macellaio said: "Nice wine." He poured some more and insisted, with a gesture, that we drink. "What do I need to know about the missing man?" he finally asked us. Almirante improvised a response, but the other man wasn't listening; he interrupted with a wave of the hand and stood up clumsily before Almirante had a chance to finish. "Let's go," he said, and we followed him.

Oreste Calosso, Rome, March 16, 1978
Now it all seems like a dream, a dream of more or less identical rooms that the hotelkeeper opened for us before retreating and languishing in the hallway until we were finished. But there was nothing to finish. Macellaio gestured, the woman opened the door to a room, and he and Almirante and I would enter; then we watched Macellaio as he studied the room, sometimes leaning over to catch some detail, the outline left by a body in the bed, the papers accu-

mulated on a desk, the clothes laid out on some piece of furniture, the placement of personal objects or lack thereof; his investigation lacked any methodology, any scientific nature, or intensity, and gave the impression that he wasn't ever lingering over anything. Macellaio didn't seem interested in the objects themselves as much as in the relationships between them, as if those relationships were some sort of clue that we were obviously unaware of but he wasn't: when he believed he'd grasped that clue, or its absence, he would leave the room and we would follow, the hotelkeeper would close the door behind us and open up another when he signaled to her. Macellaio wasn't known for his adherence to established police protocols but neither was he known for creating new, more effective ones; in fact, he seemed to have opted for an absence of protocol, and that absence created in others a compulsion to speak, to tell all. If I had been guilty of Borrello's disappearance I would have confessed it at the first opportunity, to break the silence and escape his clutches and, for lack of a better expression, fall into the hands of the State, whose laws at least I would be familiar with. But at the time I didn't know he was an improviser and, in that sense, better suited to understanding an improvised life than those who struggle to make life, to make the always contradictory and mostly absurd facts of life fit in with a predetermined process and baseless hypotheses. Macellaio knew, of course, that anything left empty when it should be full will be filled by others for appearances' sake, as giving meaning to something is always less effort—and more reassuring, no matter what they say—than accepting a lack of meaning in something that should have it. In that situation, as Macellaio ran his gaze over the sequence of rooms, forcing Almirante and me to witness something we didn't understand, I deemed him to be of exceptional intelligence, with brilliant investigative methods that involved feigning indifference at all times. Even when the hotelkeeper tried a key in a door—number 14—and stepped back and said, with some surprise, "It's open," and then allowed us into a room that I was seeing for the second time in the span of a few hours and that Almirante had perhaps already seen though he didn't mention it, but which Macellaio was seeing for the first time and which should have been particularly interesting to him, being as it was the room of a missing, possibly dead person, yet he didn't seem interested in the slightest. Macellaio was known among his colleagues for his fondness for wine, for leading one of the most brutal of the Black Brigades, and, as I told you, for his lack of method; in other words, for dispensing with the formalities they sought to restrain in that era, but which they actually only covered up: extortion, torture, and murder. It seems that when the partisans entered Turin, he headed to the woods behind La Venaria Reale, to the north of the city, and fired a shot into his mouth. Perhaps he avoided an act of revenge that way, probably an inevitable one in his case, maybe also in Almirante's case, though Almirante was more intelligent, or less brave and skillful, and he went into hiding for a few months until things had calmed down, which he knew would happen sooner or later. Macellaio may have known that too, irrespective of which he committed suicide in the woods, perhaps with the same callousness with which he seemed to scorn all method. Although what I'm saying isn't really true, as Macellaio did have a method, which could be called "waiting," and which he employed for Borrello's disappearance, but this only occurred to me after the phone rang at the hotel reception desk. The older son of the hotelkeeper—who kept breaking into brief, unfounded crying jags as if suddenly remembering that something had occurred in her establishment that she, for lack of a better word, would deem an ordeal—answered the call and then went up the stairs two by two and stood before us and told us what Macellaio might have already known, or considered quite likely, so that not much more than just waiting was necessary. This waiting was the only method he possessed and, it seems clear to me, yielded the best results for him. It unfolded before my eyes in all its—one could say—shrewdness, which I can only compare with the shrewdness of a peasant, which Macellaio may very well have been before joining the Black Brigades. The facts of life, as I've already said, are always contradictory and absurd, which is also what Atilio Tessore would've said and I say it to you here with his exact syntax and mannerisms to see if you recognize my old friend in me, something that, actually, I hope doesn't happen. The woman's elder son, as soon as he caught his breath, told Macellaio that they'd found a body to the southwest of Pinerolo, on the edge of a village called Rorà.

Espartaco Boyano, Ravenna, March 10, 1978
The Chisone begins in the Cottian Alps, more precisely in a mountain called Barifreddo, and it ends in the river Po, of which it is a tributary. Although it is quite deep in certain stretches and seasons, particularly in May and June, its most notable characteristic is the deafening sound of its rushing water. Because of that, but also because of the nature of our search, we didn't speak much. At some point, however, we took shelter from the rain beneath the overhang of an abandoned building beside the torrent. It seemed to have once housed a mill, whose wheels had been dismantled and dragged along the riverbed, and all that was left to bear witness was the pillar where its axis had rested. Between the pillar and the building there was a fissure, a void like a gap in the teeth of someone laughing at us, mocking our objective. We were joined in our search for Borrello along the riverbed by Eberhard Möller, Hrand Nazariantz, Alceo Folicaldi, and Luys Santa Marina. Some sort of military complicity had been established between those last two and the soldiers, which was revealed in small gestures. When we took refuge in that house, Folicaldi and Santa Marina sat with the soldiers and gave them cigarettes. The soldiers leaned their rifles against a wall to smoke. Later they took off their raincoats, exposing mended, ill-fitting uniforms that looked like they'd previously belonged to other, now dead, men. They spoke in low voices, as if conspiring, and I only heard the words "Africa," "two months," and "blood." I didn't know whether the second phrase referred to how long the speaker had been a soldier or to the time he had left to serve. In the latter case, he, obviously, would be referring to the end of the war, but I couldn't tell if that was with disappointment or with joy. When they'd finished smoking, the soldiers stood up and Nazariantz went over to ask them to stop the search: it had started to rain harder and it was practically impossible to make out any-

thing beneath the dense curtain of water. The soldiers looked at each other, unsure, but only for a brief moment. Folicaldi nodded and the soldiers began to follow him back toward Pinerolo. There was nothing in the place we'd stopped that led us to believe we'd turned a page. Nothing that made us think of a break after which there should be a second phase, or a third, and, because of that, because it didn't actually seem that we had finished anything, I had a clear, devastating awareness of the futility of our search.

Michele Garassino, Genoa, March 13, 1978
I didn't know that Tessore had left until I returned to Pinerolo that evening, along with the others who'd taken the Via Nazionale to San Germano Chisone: the heat had been scorching that day, and we were exhausted and dirty. Near Porte we'd heard shots in the mountains, and in San Martino some boys had thrown rocks at us from a roof: Bruno Munari had had to go back to Pinerolo with a soldier because of a head wound that, I suppose, he did his best to play up. Does Tessore's hasty exit from Pinerolo seem suspect to me now? No, not really. Did it seem that way to me then? No. When we reached the hotel we got the news that Borrello's corpse had been found almost five hours from Pinerolo, which made it unfeasible for Tessore to have gone to the site of the crime and returned in such a short period of time. There's no reason to stoke that suspicion, in my opinion.

Oreste Calosso, Rome, March 16, 1978
The corpse was at the foot of a cliff, beside a spring that ran between some large rocks; the rocks must have come loose not long before, which explained why the winter snow hadn't yet crushed them into pebbles like those that covered the riverbed until it disappeared from view, in a place where the mountain seemed to spin like a ballerina. We didn't have time for much: a car had taken us to Luserna San Giovanni and from there we'd had to climb up some paths forged by goats and, seemingly, the transport of heavy objects

on skis, which had left two deep furrows, one on either side of the trail. Almirante and I were sweating profusely, and Macellaio and the soldiers were too, although unlike us they weren't sweating because of the climb but rather because of the knowledge that they were in partisan territory, behind regional enemy lines that had been drawn practically since the start of the war: Italian fascists and Germans governed the cities and towns, but the mountains belonged to the rebels. Knowing that, the beekeeper who had found the corpse that morning had refused to take part in the search, leaving us with only a sketch to orient ourselves in that territory, which none of us were familiar with, not even the soldiers, who clung to their rifles and machine guns as if they were sacred icons and rosaries. I couldn't tell you what I was expecting exactly: the idea that Borrello was dead seemed absurd to me for the first time in many years, since I had given him up for dead that night in Il Letto Caldo. Perhaps the only thing I wasn't expecting was what I found when we finally reached Borrello's corpse. He was lying against a big rock drenched in blood and small clots of gray matter, in a position that made him seem to be merely sleeping, despite his eyes being open.

Michele Garassino, Genoa, March 13, 1978
I never saw Borrello's corpse. They told me it was left in the mountains, a few yards beyond where it was found.

Atilio Tessore, Florence, March 11, 1978
Someone told me they found him with his eyes wide open, as if contemplating those who observed him, trying to unravel some mystery, although it seemed obvious to everyone that the mystery was him or was in him and could no longer be solved.

Oreste Calosso, Rome, March 16, 1978
Macellaio stopped beside me, inside the circle the other soldiers had formed around us. "Is it him?" he asked. I nodded; but, although

it was obvious that the corpse belonged to Borrello, I couldn't have said then, and I couldn't say now, if it was him; by that I mean, if it was the Borrello I had known years earlier, in Perugia. In some sense it wasn't, of course, just as I wasn't the same person he had known, but understanding how Borrello could have changed, and under the sway of what influences, seemed as difficult to me as understanding how I myself could have changed. Macellaio lifted his head. "He fell from there," said the soldier, pointing to the top of the rock wall. "Could he have slipped?" I asked. "No," he replied. "He didn't drag anything along with him, no rocks or vegetation." "Could he have been pushed or thrown?" asked Almirante. Macellaio didn't reply. One of the soldiers came over and whispered something in his ear: the forest around us was dense and dark and the soldiers seemed uneasy. The light had started to wane and barely penetrated the treetops. Although I didn't think it then, I now believe we were being watched by the partisans, and I wonder why they didn't attack, when we were in such a vulnerable position. Was there a nonaggression pact between the enemies when they were recovering their dead? I've never heard of anything like that; and, in any case, if such a pact existed, the fascists didn't respect it so why should the partisans? It's not an easy question to answer; in other words, it's not easy for me to answer with the convictions I held in 1945 and prior, but perhaps that's the whole point.

Oreste Calosso, Rome, March 16, 1978
Macellaio turned to Almirante to ask him what they should do with the body. "Let the men bury him to one side of the path," replied Almirante. "We should get back to Pinerolo."

Oreste Calosso, Rome, March 16, 1978
The most terrifying police were the so-called Special Service of Republican Police, also known as the "Banda Koch" for their leader, Pietro Koch. Their first headquarters were in Florence, in a building called Villa Triste but at that point they were located on Calle

Paolo Uccello, in Milan. Koch was captured shortly after, in Florence, on the first of June 1945; on the fourth he was condemned to death; he was executed by firing squad at Forte Bravetta the following day, at 2:21 p.m. The filmmaker Luchino Visconti—an aristocrat, by the way—recorded his execution, which I suppose some would consider an honor. The Banda Koch was linked with what was called the "Ettore Muti Mobile Autonomous Legion," which killed rebels, and with the Voluntary Militia for National Security, or the Banda Carità—for its leader, Mario Carità—which not only strove to eliminate fascism's enemies, but also sought to cleanse fascism itself of its moderate elements, including intellectuals; but, really, all those groups acted autonomously and pursued different, often contradictory, political and criminal interests. When he reached Luserna San Giovanni, Almirante sent a telegram to Salò saying that Borrello's body had been found, but the authorities in Salò had already sent a handful of Pietro Koch's men to Pinerolo; when we got back to the hotel, they had already warned the conference attendees not to talk about what had happened; for that reason, and others, no one did and we all forgot about it, or pretended to. The war ended about ten days later, on May 1, 1945, and then something else began, this new normalcy, which I don't suppose is really worth discussing. In fact, it's possible that you, who didn't live through the period before, consider it as disastrous and irredeemably failed as I do, that we agree on that, even though I—along with others—took part in a project that you most likely also condemn. Dare I say that this is the disadvantage, to put it one way, that you and your generation have compared to mine: we contributed to an alternative project that is absolutely incomprehensible to your generation. And it doesn't matter how hard you try to create another alternative, even one imposed by violent means. Do you think I haven't noticed the pistol you're carrying under your jacket, very poorly concealed, by the way? Do you think that one can survive a war without developing a certain ability to judge people at first glance, to determine how dangerous they are and, to the extent it's possible, neutralize that threat? Why do you think I've told you all this? Because of the debt I owe the dead, on all sides. And my debt to Borrello, who showed us something that almost cost us our lives, and cost him his, in one way or another.

Michele Garassino, Genoa, March 13, 1978
I'm of the opinion that Borrello tried to escape through the mountains, to France or perhaps Switzerland, and just had an accident. Many people attempted the same thing and died in similar ways, especially those who traveled at night to avoid patrols by partisans or regular troops, either Italians or our German friends, who were particularly visible and very violent in those final days of the war. The mountains in that region are complex and difficult to navigate during the day; during the night they are even more dangerous, especially for someone who didn't grow up there. In some sense, the irregular geography of the Alps is a good metaphor for those times, when everything was irregular and we had no orientation whatsoever except for what could be culled from the contrast between our personal convictions and the way events turned their backs on them. The Italian Social Republic lasted six hundred days, although its existence was called into question almost immediately. Perhaps Borrello didn't believe in it either; in fact, I don't even think he was a fascist until the last moment of his life. A Futurist, sure, maybe, but not a fascist. His flight was evidence of that, and it's possible he tried to carry it out with the help of the criminals hiding in the mountains: he could have gotten into contact with them, he could have paid them to get him across the border, he could have been abandoned by the partisans or pushed over the cliff, he could have fallen on his own while running away from them.

Espartaco Boyano, Ravenna, March 10, 1978
I don't think he fled. There was something pure in Borrello, a decency and a sort of tempered savagery. There was also a certain secrecy. A habit of turning inward that could be seen as a tendency to engage in the type of inner drama we Futurists didn't commit to paper: on the one hand, because it went against the grain of the

politically provocative literature in the first person plural that we believed in; on the other, because we soon had more than enough outer drama, which we inherited but also contributed to in large part. I don't know if Borrello wrote those inner dramas he seemed prone to by nature, and I suppose now we'll never know because, from what I've been told, he left behind no written work. But the retreat into himself that he seems to have carried out somewhere in central Italy during the years before the conference and his death, is sufficient proof that he had a talent for it. It also seems proof that there was something broken inside him. It's possible not even Borrello himself could put a name to what was broken, but it was clear to everyone, including myself, who had known him and seen him again in Pinerolo during the conference. It was not only a physical change, though the physical change was notable, but also one of a, shall we say, moral nature, as if his inability to protect Cataldi's work—whatever one thinks of it, and whatever is said about what happened to it—had hardened into a sort of rod that had served as his spine for years. Seeing him in Pinerolo, I had the impression that rod could only break beneath the weight of the moral standards Borrello had chosen for himself. Although all of us who called ourselves Futurists and fascists should have had those same standards, now it seems clear to me that only Borrello lived with them right up to the very end, beneath the added weight of disappointment and hatred. A hatred of himself and possibly also of others, although that hatred was never expressed in a violent way. Perhaps this was a manifestation of his purity, which was no longer the purity of violence.

Oreste Calosso, Rome, March 16, 1978
What are you going to do now? Kill me? Maybe it's not such a bad idea, particularly considering that I would have done it, at your age and in your situation; but first I have to ask: What do you know about Luca Borrello? What can you tell me about him, because I've discovered I know nothing about him, I practically never knew him, I only thought I knew who he was and what he believed in.

Michele Garassino, Genoa, March 13, 1978

Why wasn't it investigated? It's not hard to imagine for someone like myself, who lived through that time when the regime and the country were putrefying. Borrello disappeared on the night of April 20; the next day they found his body in the mountains beside a spring, if I'm not mistaken. April 21 was also the day the government of the Italian Social Republic tried to reorganize their forces in Como, and failed. Three days later, on the twenty-fourth, Bologna and Ferrara fell, and on the twenty-fifth, Genoa. Also on the twenty-fifth, the partisan rebels rose up in arms against the Germans and began to come out of the mountains and head to the cities in the north. For days, those cities had been covered in smoke but, for the first time in a long time, that smoke wasn't from bombing but from all the files, documentation, and Party membership cards being burned. Anything incriminating was destroyed, as if fascism had to die twice, first crushed by the military forces divvying up the country, then at the hands of its own followers. Of the two defeats, the second was the one that made us fascists feel ashamed, and as such was worse, although we would have preferred not to have had to live through the first either. Borrello's death was not investigated for various reasons, all of them linked to what was happening at the time and to the specifics of his death. If it was suicide, a hypothesis I don't subscribe to, there would be no reason to investigate, because the Italian Social Republic rejected the idea that people killed themselves there and they would deem such deaths accidents. If it was a murder perpetrated by the partisan rebels—either because he'd been taken for a spy, or because he'd mistakenly entered their territory on his way to France, or simply because of some error in calculation: maybe Borrello was betrayed by rebels who'd offered to get him across the border; because, after having agreed to do so, they'd somehow discovered he was a fascist writer—then the investigation of the crime was impeded by the impossibility of finding those responsible for his death, which took place at night and in the forest, not to mention the fact that it's difficult and, of course, inconvenient to judge those who, with some quick sleight of hand, were about to dole out justice instead of submitting themselves to justice doled out by others. And if he'd been killed on the orders of the government of Salò or by someone at the conference with the authority to kill one of their colleagues or have them killed—which seems relatively improbable in my opinion—it was in someone's best interest that the death remain unsolved. There are more reasons, however, and I would like to mention them. First of all, Salò had already been abandoned and there was a marked perception among the various security organs of the republic that its authority then stemmed only from the use of force and, as a result, was short-lived; its armed forces, those of the so-called Banda Koch, for example, were the last ones clinging to an idea before dissolving, disappearing, and seeking some sort of refuge from the victors' revenge, which, naturally, the history books always call "justice," for some reason that escapes me. Secondly, one more death was completely insignificant in a moment when death's proliferation—on the cities and battlefields, when they weren't one and the same—had led to its devaluation, for lack of a better term. Thirdly and finally, because Borrello's death, and this is something very telling, I suppose, gave the conference attenders a feeling of finality: the end of the conference itself, but also the end of the idea of fascist literature, or, at least, the end of the idea that it could somehow help governments that could no longer help themselves and had given up trying. The Fascist Writers' Conference—or "Idealist Writers' Conference," "autistic," or "idiotic," or "crazy," or however you want to describe the writers—had come too late, something none of us had been able to grasp, possibly due to the fact that, in general, literature always arrives late, even literature that strives to anticipate events. In some sense (I would say, if the comparison weren't a bit ridiculous), the conference was the last desert island for a handful of sailors shipwrecked from an idea about politics and an idea about how literature and power could mutually nourish each other. Borrello's death exposed that, and it became immediately clear to all of us. No one officially ended the conference: the participants gradually dispersed, first in government cars that took most of us to Milan, which was as far as they could get, and then along back roads, like the mountain passes Borrello took in a futile search for his salvation, finding his death instead.

Espartaco Boyano, Ravenna, March 10, 1978
A couple of years ago someone insisted on seeing me. Someone like you who said he wanted to know everything about the conference in Pinerolo. I didn't meet with him, but what he said reverberated inside of me for some time. He told me there was documentation about what had happened in Pinerolo and that documentation was available in a local archive in Salò. One day, months after his call, I visited the archive and discovered he was right, a large part of the conversations that took place during those days was secretly recorded. Not only the official conversations that had to be used by the press and the cultural authorities of the Italian Social Republic and, to a lesser extent, by the other European fascist governments, but also the private conversations that had taken place during the meal and in the hotel hallways over the brief hours the conference lasted. Even though the reports were signed with pseudonyms and code names that, I imagine, were used by the participants in their role as informants to the secret police, I had the feeling I could recognize some speaking styles, certain intonations and word choices. However, I didn't recognize myself in my own conversations, which seemed like they'd been formulated by someone else; I didn't blame the informants for that, just my own memory, which obviously modified, altered, or obliterated events. The hours I spent in that archive were unusually intense, though I doubt that was visible to anyone who happened to glance over at me, a man sitting in a chair in a corner of the reading room. When the light from the large windows grew slanted, I remained there in the darkness, sitting with my legs curled around the chair's legs because I've always sat that way, for as long as I can remember. Reading a more realistic, and therefore more real, version of my life than the version I could recall, learning something about the past and the way we

remember it. I'm not mentioning this so that you'll draw any particular conclusion about me, as I'm not at the center of this story, but so that you'll understand the official surveillance that went on at the conference. And you should be aware of something I only learned from those reports: Borrello had opposed the government a few years earlier, in other circumstances, in the framework of another attempt by the republic's authorities to discipline writers who shared their ideology.

Atilio Tessore, Florence, March 11, 1978
Another possibility is that Borrello was killed to undermine the fascist writers from within; which is to say, to plant distrust that would lead us to disagreements, to confrontation. It doesn't seem likely, but, at this point, hardly anything from that period does.

Espartaco Boyano, Ravenna, March 10, 1978
Which is to say that any of them, any of the secret police informants or their proxies, any of the many bands and organizations more or less tied to the republic's authorities, could have killed him: anyone could have believed he had betrayed someone or something. What's more, it could have been a revenge murder or a botched theft, though it seems clear Borrello didn't have anything that could be of interest to anyone at all.

Espartaco Boyano, Ravenna, March 10, 1978
Borrello refused to sign an accusation against a handful of Umbrian writers who had, a few weeks earlier, attempted—in fact, demanded—to be allowed to continue to be considered fascists despite not adhering to the aesthetic agenda. We will never know why he did that. Perhaps due to personal ties, though they were younger authors, authors we hadn't met—at least I hadn't—and who hadn't published yet: their text on subscribing to fascism but

not its aesthetics was their first publication. It was also their last, because rejection of the fascist aesthetic was a strike against them while fascism was in power yet supporting fascism condemned them after its fall, all of which must have been obvious to Borrello, and perhaps—I'm thinking now of the self-destructive tendencies so common among writers—also to the young Umbrians themselves, who disappeared shortly after the accusation. Of the writers denounced for deviance, I can only remember the name Corrado Govoni, probably for all the wrong reasons. There's something I can't stop thinking about, however, and that's what Borrello told us that time in front of the restaurant, in Pinerolo during the conference, when he asked Atilio Tessore and me to step outside with him for a moment. He told us—and this happened, as you may recall, a few short hours before his death—that we had turned literature into politics and politics into crime, and that it was our fault.

Oreste Calosso, Rome, March 16, 1978
Why did he head to the southwest instead of the southeast, by which I mean back to Umbria, where he may have still been living, or to the north, toward the Swiss border? Was it a mistake? In the north was freedom or something close to salvation, the same salvation sought by Benito Mussolini and many officials of the republic, who were arrested by irregular forces when they headed in that direction; toward the southwest were only Allied troops and, therefore, arrest and likely execution. So why did he walk those twenty or twenty-one kilometers from Pinerolo to the place where his body was found? How many hours did it take? Four? Five? Why did he walk at night along roads that are difficult even by day and that descend and rise along the silhouette of the mountains? Did he want to turn himself in? I doubt it. Borrello was the one out of all of us who had best understood that Futurism wasn't simply an aesthetic, a posture in the literary scene, or inclusion in a clique, but a combative attitude toward all of life. Renouncing that attitude and the idea that life can be, to put it one way, "used" as a transforma-

tive tool, like a weapon, had led him to question everything, including his own identity. I don't know. Perhaps it's something I'll never understand.

Espartaco Boyano, Ravenna, March 10, 1978
I don't need to make any effort to remember that conversation. In fact, I found it reproduced perfectly in those papers in that archive, in Salò. The report was signed with an initial, which matched—by the way—the one on most of the reports the secret police had had drawn up about the conference and which their secretaries hadn't burned, perhaps because they ran out of time. But finding out who had written it wasn't difficult and, as far as I was concerned, it could have been signed with its author's real name, because the only people involved in that conversation, the one in front of that restaurant in Pinerolo, at Borrello's request, were Borrello, Tessore, and me.

Atilio Tessore, Florence, March 11, 1978
Why are we fascinated by monsters? Is it because we understand, since they have nothing to lose, having already been excluded from humankind and the sorts of commitments and loyalties humankind demands, that monsters speak the truth? Is it the intuitive conviction that monsters reveal our own monstrosity and in that way protect us from something worse? And what would that something worse be? Becoming them? Wouldn't that in itself be the liberation promised by the monsters and the reason they fascinate us? Luca Borrello was a monster, but what is a monster anyway?

Espartaco Boyano, Ravenna, March 10, 1978
At this point I don't remember the conversation as much as its transcription, which was a summary, so I also feel obliged to summarize. He didn't want to discuss the past with us, said Borrello, but rather the immediate future and the types of problems it would pose to

Futurist writers. He had taken us over to a streetlamp, which gave off a dim light that fell on us like a fine rain. When the war ends, he said, with the Italian defeat—which is to say, with the defeat of both the partisan rebels and the Italian authorities, he said, which surprised me—Futurism will be over, along with the regime that was so inseparably identified with it. On the other hand, he maintained while still coughing—a cough that made his entire body shake, I recall—Futurism had always been too revolutionary and anarchic to represent the art of the fascism in power and we hadn't understood that. The end of fascism, he added, garnering some mild, purely formal objections from us, doesn't have to be the end of Futurism. But in order for that to happen Futurism has to distance itself from fascism, it has to see fascism as its inflation and perversion, the perversion of the absolute faith in art to which we Futurists are committed. We needed to save ourselves and save the ideas of compassion and solidarity that had buoyed us, and also save the ideas of individualism and freedom that, contradictorily, we had also fostered, and which had given meaning to Futurism, and we had to do it before the fall of fascism dragged us down with it. "Fascism is made up of all fascists, not just Mussolini," objected Tessore, "and we all do it in our own way. It will survive," he added. Borrello looked at him as if he didn't understand. "But will we survive?" he asked him. "And will what we believed in survive, or will individualistic art take over again?" If we didn't want to see a return to that art, he added, we had to plot a peaceful, public conspiracy to save what could be saved. We had to witness the collapse of history without collapsing along with it. "What do you want to save?" I asked him. "Us," he replied in a frenzied coughing fit. "There is no us," replied Tessore, turning his back on him. "What we believed in," Borrello insisted. "Are you afraid of dying?" Tessore asked him. Suddenly, it seemed that he was the one who was afraid, and I was too. Borrello closed his eyes, as if dazzled by the light, and then smiled. "It's not death that worries me, but the deaths we carry inside and the holes they've left within us," he replied. "We turned literature into politics and then we turned politics into crime," he said, "and we have to save what can be saved, save our ideas before they are transformed into terror," he added. Then he moved a little, outside of the streetlamp's cone of light, and when I looked again he was no longer there, he was already gone.

Atilio Tessore, Florence, March 11, 1978
A monster, it seems clear to me, is someone who was born before their time, someone who forces us to look our period, which is not theirs, straight in the face, even if that glare dazzles, even if it permanently blinds us.

Oreste Calosso, Rome, March 16, 1978
"Don't you see," Macellaio said to Almirante when we were finally inside the car. "If he had been pushed he would've tried to hold on to the rocks and he would have fallen feetfirst. If they had tied his feet and hands so he couldn't escape, or so he couldn't try to grab on to the rocks, we would have found the ropes, and marks on his wrists and ankles. If they'd shot him, we would have found bullets in his body." "What do you think happened then?" Almirante asked him, but Macellaio didn't answer: he didn't hear him or pretended not to.

Espartaco Boyano, Ravenna, March 10, 1978
After Borrello's death, when the conference dissolved—for lack of a better word, spontaneously—each of us kept searching. But the nature of the search changed after Borrello's death. From that moment on it was no longer a search for death and the end. The Fascist Writers' Conference, conceived as support but also as the manifestation and conclusion of a project that would bring together art and life, literature and politics, was prevailed over by death, I now think. Our later searches came out of changing plans, out of desperation, but also out of the desire to save something, not just ourselves. That something could be called by different names, but for me it was Borrello and Cataldi and what they both believed in

and what I believed in too and, to be completely frank, I still believe in: the idea that literature is life, but improved, and that literature should strive to embody what is most alive.

Atilio Tessore, Florence, March 11, 1978
I believe Luca Borrello was a monster. What happens to monsters when they've been cornered, when they can no longer distract us from our monstrosity with their own?

Rome

MARCH 1978

〉〉〉

*Laws are against the exception, and I'm only
interested in the exception.*

FRANCIS PICABIA

Pietro or Peter Linden jumps when the tape recorder stops: Oreste Calosso has been silent for a few moments and Linden looks over at him. "What are you going to do now?" the man asks. Linden doesn't respond; in fact, he doesn't know, as he is still lost in the past and in Borrello's story. He is aware that he was the one who insisted on getting involved despite having maintained and continuing to maintain that he and his generation should be concerned not with the past but with the future—and the reparation of the past in the future, as well as the task of preventing the past from repeating in the future, although the past never actually repeats itself. People often say past events will repeat themselves in the dearth of some sort of intervention, but it never happens in the way one expects. Political totalitarianisms come back in the form of economic imperatives, and social oppression comes back through an invitation that, by its very nature, cannot be refused: to consumption and perhaps to commerce. Linden can't think about it at that moment, while he is trying to decide how to respond to Calosso, but in the following moment he will theorize that his concern for the past imposed itself, somehow, when he went against all of his organization's security measures and directives (though the organization isn't aware of what he's doing and likely never will be) and returned to that bookstore on the corner of Reggio and Pisa to find out what books the professor had ordered, and took them home. In them he read a name that rang a bell and then he visited some of the writers whose names appeared in that book and then again in the Italian phone books. At first he thought the ones he didn't locate there were already dead or were unlisted or lived abroad, but those last two options now seemed unlikely. The writers he did visit (as a result of his personal investigation but also the tips and contacts offered by the writers themselves, which led him to Ravenna, Florence, Genoa, and Rome, as if they were his guide dogs, he thinks—despite him wanting to believe that it is obvious *he* is not the blind man in this story) all wanted to talk. That could be interpreted as a desire to clarify the story, a conviction that by telling everything they knew, or everything they claimed to know, they were doing justice to Borrello's resolve to be a writer and to his desire to save his friends and colleagues long after they'd ceased to be either, or it could have been a decision designed to keep them off the list of suspects in his death. Another possibility, thinks Linden, is that the writers he interviewed, whose testimony readily creates a narrative (certain facts converged with others, so all it took was composing an ordered story, even if that story couldn't be further from the essential truth, which was betrayed by forced logic), had simply wanted to talk about themselves, and had accepted his offer to do so despite not being the main focus of the conversation. Although, thinks Linden, it's possible that they were the main subject of the conversation, in some sense, and that all the interviews were the result of Linden's desire to talk about Borrello's death coming up against their determination not to, or to do so only if in exchange they were able to talk about themselves, leading to a mutual satisfaction that followed the initial disappointment of, after years of writing, being interviewed not about themselves but about someone else, regardless of what they thought about that someone else. This revealed the futility of the sort of effort Michele Garassino had spoken to him about a few days earlier, when he told him—Linden now thinks he was being too honest, possibly in an attempt to hide some greater, more important dishonesty—that day after day he would sit in the same chair and imagine that finally someone would visit to interview him about his work. In preparation, he would rehearse his answers, which meant also rehearsing questions that, in a fit of overzealous scrupulousness, he tried to make as bad as the ones journalists usually ask when interviewing writers. "Yours are bad too, but at least they're unexpected," he said, adding, "despite that, I would prefer not to answer, although I invite you to ask me more: I'm going to pretend you don't exist and that I'm the one inventing your questions. That way I won't interrupt my routine: every evening, year after year, in this same chair, in front of this window. You see that window there? I've seen two people die in that house, two old people; I saw their children get rid of the remains of what had been their parents' lives, paint the walls, and put the house on the market; and later I saw how the house was rented out and someone else died there too and the children of that someone got rid of their things and painted the house and it was for rent again and in all that time I haven't run out of questions." Pietro or Peter Linden doesn't know what to do with that but he has the impression that, in some sense, the story told by Garassino and the other writers (who embody the type of thinking he's always loathed, ever since he became acquainted with the meaning of the word "fascist," a word he'd heard hundreds of times from his father and his father's friends, mostly in a disdainful tone, though sometimes he'd also heard his father maintain that it was pernicious to judge all fascists equally, in a rare gesture of moderation, thinks Linden, who would listen with some surprise, just as his father's friends did; those were friendships he'd made after the war, when he tried to set up a carpenter's shop in a neighborhood on the outskirts of Milan, and before, in the years when he fought the fascists in the Piedmontese mountains), sometimes he thinks that story has provoked a series of schisms in his way of seeing things. He's unable to predict the consequences of this, although it's obvious that as a result the boundary between the fascists and a varied "us" (in which he and his organization are located probably to the farthest left of the spectrum) is blurred, and may never be clear. If he is correct, and the schism really exists, it manifests in various realms: in literature, where it now seems obvious to him that his way of thinking about books, organizing them around his political ideas or in some cases lack thereof, is mistaken; also in the idea that the fascists, including the fascist writers, made up a homogenous front, as well as in the idea that they make up one now. In Ravenna, in Florence, and in Genoa, Linden wondered if it was up to a revolutionary like him to finish off those fascists—he was armed, it wouldn't have been hard to do—however, something always prevented him, and Linden thinks at that moment it could be that he's not a murderer, that he lacks the skills if not the motivations of those who carry out such tasks within his organization. It's also possible—but Linden doesn't even consider this—that he's a coward. Another possibility, however, is that Linden was unable to kill the people he found—Oreste Calosso, for example, who at that moment is observing him from the opposite side of a low table, without the slightest regret for having been and, in fact, continuing to be a fascist writer—because one of the schisms the story has provoked in his life and ideas now divorces a certain idea of justice from the conviction that justice can actually be carried out by individuals or even the organization. What do we call "justice"? Revenge? wonders Linden, but that question, which he's been asking himself since the old professor's killing, is impossible to answer. Some time later, in jail or after his release, Linden will read about people's regrets about trying to achieve justice with violence, and he will recognize a face or two from his years in Turin, but he won't know if what they regret is having resorted to violence or having believed that using it for political agitation could bring about change of some sort; in other words, if what they regret is having killed or having believed in the transformative potential of death; at that point, Linden hadn't killed, but he would pay the price as if he had and, more importantly, he would remember the story of Borrello, whose death was, in some sense, transformative, and had the nature of political action, whether that was deliberate or involuntary. By that point, Linden would have gathered all the fragments of the story and imagined the parts that were missing and would conceive, finally, of the story as a crime, a view of the events that didn't actually offer him any comfort. He would think about all that during the years in jail that he won't mention, or barely, to his son, when he has one; by that time, Linden will have the impression that Borello's story had all taken place in some distant, very distant, past, and in some sense that would be true, since it was more than thirty years earlier than now, when he sits before Calosso, in what he believes is the end of his investigation. On the other side of the table, the writer clears his throat and Linden thinks he's about to say something, but he remains silent. Linden remembers what Calosso asked him a moment earlier, but prefers not to respond; he'd like to redirect the situation, in some sense, and make Calosso the main focus of the conversation, if he wasn't already, right in that moment when he believes there is nothing more to say, but he can't help asking him, even though the question seems superfluous: "So, do you believe that Borrello committed suicide?" Calosso has a big head supported by a strong neck and wide shoulders; when he speaks, his voice seems to emerge from his chest, or further down, from someplace near his solar plexus, from where a strength—which hadn't seemed aggressive to Linden until that moment—emanates. But just in that instant, when Calosso tilts his head, observing him, in a gesture that could seem submissive or acquiescent in someone else, it makes Linden think that Calosso is stronger than his outer shell and could destroy him. Despite that, what Calosso says next isn't violent, it doesn't include the slightest hint of violence. "You see," he says, "Borrello knew how to make people act in a certain way. In that sense, if you prefer to look at it this way, he knew how to manipulate people; but 'manipulate' isn't exactly the right word, not when you look at its connotations, which are almost all negative. Borrello had learned to write using events as an alphabet, and in doing so he reached a more authentic and important fusion between art and life than the vanguards had. His death could be interpreted as a text to be deciphered, it's true, but only because it was part of a life that aspired to be read as such. We knew this already but his death proved it, later, when we were all forced to 'read' that death somehow. Maybe he had an accident trying to reach France, there's no way of knowing for sure, but that's much less important than the perplexing state his death plunged us into, along with the feeling that an era was ending and that we had to do something to save ourselves from that end. If Borrello hadn't known how to get people to act in one way or another, his death wouldn't have had so many consequences; but obviously he did, and his death did, because that death seemed to form part of a body of work. Shortly after I met Borrello, he showed up one day with two versions of a lecture on literature as forgery that Marinetti had given a few days earlier in Rimini; both transcriptions had problems: the first and fourth paragraphs didn't match and their contents were problematic: in the first version forgery was considered a literary practice and in the second, an execrable activity, more politics than literature. Determining which of the versions was the correct one, which hadn't been corrupted by the transcription, meant analyzing the styles and holding their contents up to our own views—the views we held about what Marinetti could have said on the subject and, indirectly, what we ourselves thought about him—and arguing, most of all arguing. So that was all we did for weeks, until the subject got replaced by some other, possibly more relevant subject. After Borrello's death, when we returned to Pinerolo, we were told we should go back to Milan immediately; the order was really just the confirmation of the premature end to the Fascist Writers' Conference, which we all knew was coming. The Germans had provided some cars, and they were already waiting outside the hotel, blocking traffic on Pinerolo's main street, which hadn't been overwhelmed yet by the anguish of the end of the war, but which would succumb that very day with the news that the operations in Como had failed. The urgency and expectant anxiety at the Americans' arrival would break the calm that still reigned in the city, in contrast with what was going on inside the hotel, where we were all hastily gathering up our things, myself included. Someone on the lower floors had started burning papers, possibly documents, and smoke was spreading through the hallways, particularly on the upper floors, which was where my room was located. Almirante had sent a young soldier to help me move my things to a car. There was fear in the soldier's face, a stark fear that he may have hoped looked like military rigor but was clearly fear of what was happening in that hotel, of the screaming in the hallways, of the maneuvering of the woman in charge to hide all objects of value (presumably negligible value), of the writers who were rushing down the stairs with suitcases and without saying goodbye, anxious to leave that conference and return to Milan and then to their home countries, in the case of those who weren't Italian, before Milan and those countries collapsed on top of them. The soldier was very handsome and looked as if he were sculpted in stone, like one of the many sculptures in those days that wavered between reproducing the classical ideal and its geometric abstraction while striving to represent bold, vigorous, deeply Italian masculinity; but in his face there was fear, something that was never shown in those statues, and the impression the fear gave was that the sculpture could collapse at any moment. I didn't give him time to, however, and ordered him to follow me. 'You see that box?' I asked, opening up the broom closet at the end of the hallway. 'Bring it down,' I ordered, and the soldier's shiver of terror made me realize something I hadn't understood before, and it was the fact that the box looked like a coffin."

"What happened to the box with Borrello's manuscripts?" asks Linden. Calosso points, smiling for the first time since the interview started. "It's right there, at your feet." Linden leans over to stroke it; he thinks he can tell it's made of ash: the years have darkened the wood, and the pale rose that must have been its original color has shifted toward red; otherwise, the wood is in good shape. It seems significant to Linden that the box was always there, on the carpet, between the chairs where he and Calosso are sitting. He wants to say something more, or say it in a tone that doesn't reveal any sort of childish anxiety, but all he can do is ask if he can open it. Calosso gestures with his hand, as if waving away an insect flitting in his face. "Before you do, I want you to know something else," he answers. "In there you'll find everything Borrello produced from his break with the Perugian fascist writers until his death in Pinerolo. Everything, except for an annotated index of his works I made shortly after the war (in April or May 1947, I can't remember which), was written by and belongs to him. I'd like to think that the study of these works will solve the mystery of Borrello, but I'm afraid it only deepens and intensifies it. In the box you'll find, among other things, some ten or twelve pages handwritten in pencil on both sides; it's a short story, one of the few Borrello ever wrote. Its plot is the following: someone comes across two versions of a lecture on literature as forgery; it's impossible to reliably determine which of the versions is correct; the first is a defense of the practice and the second deems it unbefitting; there are other divergences between the two texts, which are the subjects of study by a handful of young writers; the writers are young, and passionate about literature, each one of them is, to put it one way, willing to give his life for the others. The portrait offered of them is moving, it makes you think that literature and friendship, or a certain idea of friendship, always go together and always unfold in the same way, despite people imagining themselves unique, thinking that everything happens for the first time with them. At one point in the story, the action jumps ahead several years to when a surviving member of that group of young men meets the lecture's author in a banal social situation; they chat about dozens of subjects, and find they have things in common (surprisingly, due to their age difference). Then, the young man, who is no longer that young, asks the other about his text on forgery and the other admits he has no idea what the young man is talking about. 'I've never written a text on forgery,' he says, so the young man, who, as I mentioned, isn't really that young anymore, tells him the story of the two texts and their divergences, and then their supposed author (who actually isn't, as we've seen) says that the differences between the two stances defended in the two texts, which the young man and his friends found extremely significant, are, actually, nonexistent, seen in perspective. He goes on to say that forgery is literature thrown at life, completely in and against life, as both versions maintain in different ways, and that, really, his friend had involved him in a story that had forgery not as a subject but rather as a process, showing that that friend understood how to write literature into life, how to make those two things into one. I believe there's no need for me to tell you that Borrello's story is a belated justification of his forgery of Marinetti's supposed lecture, and that, as he has his literary copy of Futurism's inventor say, the subject is not as important as the process, the trick that sustains it. I don't suppose I have to tell you that the discussions between the young men in the story are the ones we had when Borrello brought us the alleged texts by Marinetti. Maybe there's a story here inside another story or a story reflected in another story, but that doesn't matter, except in relation to the fact that, as one of his characters says, it was about writing literature into life, and Borrello learned how to do that. Why not think of his death as the final sentence of his book? Out of some misguided survival instinct? Borrello seems to have been interested only in the survival of ideas and their projection onto a hostile world. Hostile because those ideas revolved around 'literature,' which is supposedly removed from life; but Borrello's life and death revealed that there is no life beyond literature." When Calosso goes silent, Linden observes two things: night has fallen, there is no longer any light in the room, and the sounds of the elevator, which he hadn't noticed until then, can be heard unusually vividly, as if the elevator is going up and down right in the middle of the room; he thinks he sees that Calosso has shrunk, as if emptied of some air he'd been holding in that whole time, and that the threatening energy emanating from him has dissipated. Linden has an intuition, or a certainty he prefers to disguise as an intuition, that has paralyzed him since he saw the box for the first time. Calosso stands up and walks over to the wall, where he flips a light switch, and Linden leans forward and sees it: his father's signature, so recognizable to him, delicately engraved on one of the corners of the box. Calosso doesn't sit back down, and Linden understands that the interview is over: he knows he'll have to make up the rest, but he doesn't know he'll have plenty of time, an unthinkable amount of time when, in jail, he thinks about everything, and thinks long and hard about who could have turned him in to the authorities, telling himself, every time, that it must have been the man in front of him at that moment. "Can I open it?" he asks him. Calosso answers: "You know full well it's yours: it has been since the first moment you stepped into this room. Now take it with you."

Valsesia

OCTOBER 1944

>>>

He feels the pain before opening his eyes; he knows he must escape, but he's almost intoxicated by the pain running through his entire body: his right side is paralyzed; he knows he should open his eyes and locate the wound, try to treat it if possible, but thinking about the origin of the pain terrifies him, so he remains still, with his face against the ground, which he starts to perceive as damp; he's not sure if it's the ground's own dampness or something else, nor does he know the height from which he's fallen. He continues to wallow in the pain, hearing the last orders given in German and, from a distance, a few orders in Italian; when he finally opens his eyes, he sees only darkness around him and he tells himself he must have lost consciousness for just a few moments; but then he sees the sky through the leaves of the bushes and branches he pulled down on his fall, which are partially covering him, and he realizes the sun has already started to come up.

Someone descends along one of the walls of the ravine toward him; their impatient panting, their muttered curses with each misstep, dragging with them dust, rocks, bits of bush and branch, make him think the task is difficult and unrewarding; the footsteps stop several meters above his head, and then he hears a shout he doesn't understand from the mouth of the ravine and, from even closer, above his head, another voice responds "Tot" and adds in a whisper: "Bald." The first word, the man knows full well, means "dead"; the second, "soon." The footsteps head up the ravine with difficulty; when he opens his eyes again, minutes or perhaps hours later, the man discovers that it is already day and that he is alone. Intoxicated by the pain, which feels like the equivalent of some very strong liquor he'd never tried before because of his youth and obliviousness, or maybe just luck, he finally overcomes his resistance and runs his eyes over his body, which he still doesn't dare to move: the only thing he sees is his right leg twisted at a grotesque angle; the pant leg is tattered and stained with blood; at the height of his tibia something sticks out that looks like, and is, a bit of bone: when he sees it, he loses consciousness again.

Before opening his eyes he feels the pain, but that pain is already part of a story and, as such, has meaning; in the distance he hears shots, a brief succession that makes him realize that the Germans are executing the partisans they've captured. He's surprised they're doing it there, in the forest; usually they shoot them in the main squares of the cities and towns, to dissuade the population and terrorize them. He doesn't hear screaming, but does hear a braying. It could be La Petacci, one of the mules the group used to transport weapons and supplies, enjoying, finally, the freedom she must have always longed for, especially during the forced marches through the mountains and the forest: if he could call her without attracting the attention of the Germans who are still around, he could get the mule to carry him; but then he'd have to think of where to go, and he can't. When he opens his eyes, even before glancing again at his broken leg, he chooses one of the branches around him that he can use to make a splint and some sort of crutch to use if he can't find his rifle. In order to do so, he relies on knowledge that predates the war and his entrance into what, as you're fully aware, the fascists call "the rebel delinquency": before all that, and after, though he doesn't know it and can't even imagine it yet, he is, and will be, a carpenter.

As he stands up, the pain is unbearable, and he lies back down, as he once saw a newborn foal do.

He accepts the fact that he won't be able to scale the walls of the ravine; in the last few hours his right leg has swollen up despite the tourniquet he made and, although it's no longer bleeding, he can't put any weight on it: the pain is so intense that it's giving him visions, flashes of situations and conversations that took place before the war, and before he joined it, a year all in all, not much but also not something to be written off easily. The visions make him think for a moment that he's somewhere else, in some other moment. Maybe he's starting to run a fever, but the decision he makes isn't a product of that: he decides to follow the ravine. He can't know where it will take him except in general: it will lead him downward, toward the valley, where there'll be doctors and hospitals, but also the German authorities and their Italian allies, and he can only expect he'll fall into the hands of one or the other. In his moments of lucidity his preferences are obvious; in other moments, his desire to be somewhere else is all he needs to continue on, sometimes dragging himself and other times, less and less as the hours pass, on foot, with his weight on his left leg, using his rifle as a crutch.

Sometimes he wakes himself up, believing he's answering a question he's been posed, by mumbling out a reply to a nonexistent listener.

At midday he stretches out under an apple tree growing in a dry riverbed. Who could have betrayed them, he wonders, how did the Germans find them, in these convoluted mountains where they themselves—who know them as few do—still occasionally get lost? Who could have betrayed them just when they thought they'd eliminated the mole and moved to a place he couldn't know about, higher up in the mountains; how did it all start for him?

The first action consisted of robbing a carabinieri station to get weapons and ammunition before heading into the mountains; they used a small pistol they bought off a Jew trying to cross into Switzerland with his family in the autumn of 1943; everything happened so quickly that he couldn't remember anything about the incident, except the fear in the faces of the carabinieri and the fear he felt himself, which would have been greater, in fact boundless, and would have completely impeded his ability to carry out the action if he had known—as he would later discover during target practice at an abandoned windmill at the foot of a small stream, the Torrente Pellice—that the lever on the bolt that sends pressure from the trigger to the hammer was broken, so the gun didn't work, it was useless.

Maybe it had always been broken, and had circulated among the members of the family as a private joke until the joke aspect was lost and all that was left was the delivery of the object as an expression of good wishes and the desire to protect; or the bolt's lever broke over time with use, though it looked like the gun had hardly been used; or the Jew disabled it as a precautionary measure, to keep from being killed or robbed with the gun after selling it; or the lever came loose some other way: anything is possible.

In addition to the pain, his other most pressing problem is thirst, which has glued his tongue to his palate, and heat; and also birds, of which there are many in that part of the forest, and which give off sounds that seem to him warnings or censure.

.   .   .

The laughter of the partisans during that target practice was hysterical, as was his own; ever since then he carried the weapon with him as some sort of amulet, but he no longer has it: he must have lost it in the fall down the ravine or before that as he fled, when he heard the first shouts.

He remembers the laughter and the jokes and the weapon that the political leader of his brigade then put in his hands, a rifle from World War I that someone took with them when they deserted the army. Later he had a 9-caliber Beretta and after that a Mauser, but the morning of the attack he could only grab a rifle that someone had left as they ran off.

He chews on some gentian root as he's seen his comrades do to bring down a fever; later he brings a fistful of bilberries to his mouth, but they aren't ripe and are unbearably bitter; they do calm his thirst for a few hours, though.

He sees the town first; its lights bounce off the cloud cover that's formed over the valley at dusk; it could be Borgosesia, Quarona, or Varallo, he doesn't know; he sees the house somewhat later, to his right and closer than the town: a whitewashed brick construction, a wooden shed beside it, weeds invading everything, there's also a patch of land that was part of a vegetable garden; it all looks abandoned; he takes a step toward it, and then he feels a push, or he slips and falls again, onto rocks and pebbles and dust and branches that he can't count or distinguish from each other, down to the foot of the ravine; and there, finally, he once again loses consciousness.

Before opening his eyes he smells a deep mustiness that surprises him: he opens, or thinks he opens, his eyes quickly only to discover that he is in a dark, possibly underground room; but when his eyes get used to the darkness, he sees a thread of light slipping beneath the door and others between the wall's planks, which makes him realize he isn't underground. He is lying on a wool blanket, in one corner of the room; to his right he finds only a bare wall, to his left there is a narrow but unusually long wooden table: he cannot determine whether there is anything on it, and soon loses interest in trying. Someone has taken off his shoes and cut off his right pant leg at knee length. He sees a clean bandage and a splint and thinks that someone must have set his bone while he was unconscious; for a moment he holds his breath, wondering if the pain will return, but he doesn't feel much: the intoxication of the pain has already passed. The man tells himself that, given the angle of the light coming through the wooden planks of one wall, it must be approaching evening, but he can't know what day it is and how much time has passed since his fall in the ravine during the attack; he should figure that out, he thinks: figure out who dressed his wound and, eventually, determine if it's someone trustworthy who can direct him back to the mountains and his group of partisans. Perhaps the group no longer exists, he tells himself, and he feels fear and hatred run through him, depleting him. Fear and hatred are not the same thing, he tells himself, although he knows that they are. He looks around but doesn't see his rifle, he knows he needs it or will need it in the immediate future; he tries to stand up, but collapses back onto the blanket: he didn't put weight on his wounded leg, wasn't able to because of the chain that someone, perhaps the someone who dressed his injury, was using to hold him there.

He sees no sign of life around him at any point that night, except for the typical little rodents and nocturnal birds he's grown accustomed to over the last few weeks; he can't get free of the chain, which is around his right wrist and linked to a metal clamp meant for animals that is hammered deep into the wooden floor; if he had the right tools he could pull out the clamp, but the tools, which he discovers at one end of what appears to be a shed, are out of his reach.

. . .

He hears a train passing, not very far from him; it could be a train carrying armaments, he says to himself at some point in the night: it had been some time since he'd heard a train.

He must have fallen asleep, because he feels himself waking up when he hears noises at the shed's door; when it opens, the light that enters blinds him for a moment, despite which it's clear that the sun isn't high yet. A man approaches him and places a plate of soup at his feet; he is tall and wears metal-framed glasses whose temples look like they've been twisted many times; as he stands up, the man coughs and observes him from a seemingly great height. "Thanks for this and for fixing my leg," he mumbles. The other man doesn't respond; when the man on the blanket finishes the soup, he takes it from him and heads toward the door. "Do you speak Italian? Sprechen Sie Italienisch?" asks the injured man; but the other man has already left.

He tries not to think. He avoids it. He learns once more the meaning of the expression "killing time." He mostly sleeps, but he doesn't remember a single one of his dreams, if he has any.

The man returns at dusk with more soup and a piece of bread, which he places beside him; this time, as he does, he leans over to check on his leg injury and then another bandage on his head that the wounded man hadn't noticed before: he nods in both cases, and the prone man has the opportunity to get a closer look at him. "My name is Francesco Linden," he says. "Do you speak Italian?" The other man doesn't respond. "Wie heißen Sie?" asks Linden. The man shakes his head, without making eye contact. "My name is Luca Borrello," he finally responds. Linden begins to interrogate him: "Where am I? Why am I chained up? Where are my belongings?" he asks, but Borrello has already left the shed. By his belongings, of course, he is referring to the rifle he used as a crutch during his descent along the ravine that he was carrying when he lost consciousness, but he doesn't think that requires explanation.

The clamp is nailed decisively into the wooden floor and impossible to rip out: if Linden had some sort of metal implement he could try to chip away at the wood around it to loosen it, but there is nothing in reach. The night is particularly cold, and Linden hears Borrello coming and going from the shed, dragging objects and sometimes stopping to cough violently. He also hears the train, but that's less worrying to him.

He doesn't hear anything throughout the course of the following day, and thinks Borrello has abandoned him; he feels horribly hungry and thirsty, and afraid when an animal—a boar or a dog, he can't be sure—wanders around the shed and tries to get inside by destroying one of the door planks: just as the animal is about to burst through, it gives up, for some reason, and runs off.

Borrello returns at night. When he comes in he doesn't notice the damage to the lower part of the door and heads directly over to Linden; he comes in empty-handed except for an object Linden can't see, and circles him: a moment later, Linden hears the chains fall onto the wooden floor. "You could freeze to death if I leave you here. It's going to be very cold tonight," Borrello says to him, and then asks if he thinks he can stand. Linden nods and the other man helps him up. They walk out through the shed door with Borrello holding Linden up so he doesn't lose his balance, and they're greeted by a gust of freezing air: in it float some stars that Linden is familiar with, yet they surprise him as if he were seeing them for the first time. Neither of the two men stops to contemplate them, however: they quickly enter the building located a few yards from the shed, the one Linden saw from the top of the ravine a few days earlier. Inside it, Linden can only make out a bed, a larder, a small table with a few papers on it, and two chairs. Someone created a makeshift mattress out of blankets beside the bed, and next to that there is a woodstove. "You'll sleep here," orders Borrello, pointing to the blankets; when Linden lies down on them, Borrello takes a rope and ties his hands. Linden shoots him a questioning look, but the other man doesn't seem to notice. Linden notices that Borrello always looks at the ground when they are together; when he finishes tying him up, he hands him a spoon and a plate of cornmeal or polenta with bits of chestnuts and a few strands of meat. "I'm sorry I can't offer you anything better," he says.

Borrello throws some more wood onto the fire and turns off the kerosene lamp before removing his shoes and getting into bed with his clothes still on, including his jacket. Linden realized a moment earlier that the other man had given him all the blankets he had and sleeps only covered by a sheet. Even though he is used to sleeping next to other men, in the improvised shelters thrown together by the members of the Resistance or the buildings they happen upon, that night Linden can't do it. Neither can Borrello, bothered by his virulent cough and the other man's proximity. Not much time has passed before Linden understands that the chains in the shed and the ropes that night mean that Borrello is afraid of him, and he wonders why; up until that point, he'd thought it was the other way around. "The planks on the shed door are loose, I can fix them if you want: I'm a carpenter," he says finally, breaking the silence. But Borrello doesn't respond.

When he wakes up, he sees Borrello cutting a piece of bread with a knife he puts away in his pocket: the air in the room smells of coffee, although only weakly; the coffee he is served also seems weak, but it's been so long since Linden's had any that he finds it delicious. "What is your job?" he asks, but Borrello doesn't answer. "What do you need to fix the door?" Borrello asks instead. Linden thinks for a moment. "A hammer, nails, some wire, some planks," he says. Borrello nods: when Linden's finished his coffee, Borrello refills the cup and leaves, locking the door behind him.

Linden sits up with difficulty and opens the larder. He expects to find something he can use as a weapon or, at least, something that will allow him to get out of the ropes, but all he finds are a couple of pewter mugs and books, a lot of books. Some of them are by fascist writers whom Linden's never read but has heard about or read about in the press, authors that he and his comrades would kill if they had the chance, along with their readers.

Borrello opens the door and helps him stand up; when they're outside, Linden sees that the other man has taken the door off the shed and placed it on two sawhorses in front of the entrance, where the sun shines directly but is still just warm; on top of the door he's placed some nails and some wire; there are some new wooden planks leaning against the outer wall of the building. There was a frost overnight. Borrello tells him, "You'll work better in the sun," and moves a few steps away, but Linden calls him over and shows him his wrists. Borrello comes back and unties him; then Linden leans over and takes a long sniff of the wood, as if that aroma could transport him, for a brief instant, back home.

Earlier he saw something that surprised him and it comes back to him then, a handkerchief on Borrello's bed covered in mucus and blood.

Despite the sun not being very high in the sky yet, Linden starts to sweat a little once he's begun; some time later the effort of standing and working on the door makes him feel like he is going to lose consciousness: he drops the hammer and leans against the wall of the shed; a minute later he feels himself slipping toward the ground.

Borrello comes out of the house when he notices the hammering sounds have stopped. He sees Linden laid out, and approaches and picks him up. Linden leans against his shoulder and together they enter the shed, where Borrello has him lie down on the blanket: he studies the bandages on his head for a moment and then the one on his leg, which has gotten muddy. "Are you going to change it?" asks Linden. Borrello shakes his head no. "We don't have many bandages," he replies. When he stands, Linden looks up at him from the blanket the way he had the first time. Borrello turns and observes the hole where the door had been. "What could have broken it?" he asks. "I don't know. An animal, maybe," responds Linden. Borrello leaves the shed and the other man hears him working on the door, stopping occasionally to cough violently. At some point Linden falls asleep.

He wakes up when he hears Borrello trying to fit the shed door onto its hinges; he gets up with difficulty and helps him put it in place. Then they both stare at the door, one on either side. From outside Borrello says: "Take it easy. It's normal to feel faint." Linden nods, and only later realizes that Borrello couldn't have possibly seen the gesture.

In the shed there are some tools. Linden weighs them in his hands and decides he'll use them when he's stronger, if the other man doesn't turn him in first: he's heard stories of people who buy the protection of the authorities by handing over a member of the Resistance, usually a relative; in the valleys, half of Italy has been turning in the other half, and—Linden figures—things will only get worse as the Italians are forced to adopt one position or the other.

An awl seems ideal for his purposes: he just has to sharpen it in secret, without the other man realizing; and then come up with a way to reunite with his group in the mountains, if his group still exists and he can figure out where they are. It can't be that difficult, he tells himself: the Germans pulled it off handily, for example.

Borrello helps him out of the shed; he takes him behind the house, where he's set up two chairs facing each other: he sits him in one and lifts his broken leg onto the other; then he leaves and comes back with two plates of boiled cabbage and potato soup. He hands Linden a spoon and sits down to eat by his right side, kneeling against one of the walls. They eat in silence, Borrello coughing only gently and without choking. Then he stands up, gathers the plates and spoons, and goes back into the house for coffee; when he gives him the pewter mug, Linden observes his hands. "How long have you lived here?" he asks him. "You're not a peasant." Borrello, who is again kneeling by Linden's right side, is slow to answer. "I've been living here for a few years. I found the property abandoned and I've been trying to restore it." Linden notices or thinks he notices that the other man is lying to him, but he can't imagine what about. Borrello's next answer is even slower in coming. "I used to be a writer," he finally says. Linden is immediately intrigued. "What's in the shed doesn't look like the work of a writer," he says. Borrello looks at him with curiosity for the first time. "What does it look like then?" he asks. "I don't know," stammers Linden. "Like paper objects. Drafts. Blueprints for buildings. Nightmares. Like nothing I've ever seen before." Borrello nods. "Nightmares," he muses to himself, and Linden doesn't sense disdain for his comment but rather some satisfaction in Borrello's voice, something close to pride.

That afternoon they see the dog for the first time: it has some tufts of white fur that are particularly visible behind the bunches of weeds where it is trying to hide, but its coat is almost entirely gray;

it has long legs with haunches that must have once been strong, although now the animal is squalid. Borrello and Linden watch it for a long time; when the breeze changes direction and stops blowing at their backs, they can hear the animal's whimpering from the edge of the property. Sometimes it remains lying down and sometimes it wanders along a line dividing Borrello's property from the others, which only the animal is still able to recognize. The dog seems to vacillate between a desire to come closer and a fear of doing so, and Linden is about to make that observation out loud but then fears that perhaps the other man will think it's improper to attribute desires and fears to an animal, so he stays quiet. Borrello is the writer, he thinks; he knows how to put these things into words. But he also thinks the writer doesn't have all the words: for example, he doesn't know what words they used to communicate up there, in the mountains, nor the words employed in the trial that took place days earlier and cost a man his life and those up in the mountains a disappointment about the integrity of the "Resistance" and later, when the Germans found them, in the middle of the night, also cost them their lives. If the other man knew those words, thinks Linden, he would be, like him, a slave to them. At nightfall the dog trots off toward the mountains.

At night they watch the trail of sparks the train leaves behind in the valley, a trail that dies out immediately but remains recorded on the retina awhile longer: if Linden closes his eyes, he sees the train at one end of the darkness behind his eyelids; when he opens them, the train has moved a few millimeters. "They adapted the gasoline engines to run on wood," observes Borrello, bringing his handkerchief to his lips. "It may be carrying weapons," says Linden after a moment, but Borrello shakes his head. "It's moving too fast. It might be transporting refugees from the south, or perhaps from Rome. A lot of people will try to cross into Switzerland," he says. "Why don't they band together?" The question arises naturally on Linden's lips, without his being able to control it. "There's a new government in Salò. Isn't that what you and your German allies wanted?" Borrello doesn't answer right away. "What's it like up there, in the mountains?" he asks finally, but Linden doesn't say a word.

Borrello helps him into the house, but ties up his hands before turning off the lamp. In the darkness, Linden lets his thoughts wander again; inevitably, he wonders once more who could have betrayed them, and he reviews the moments of the trial—which was very short, actually—and who spoke and the testimonies of those who most decisively maintained the guilt of the accused man, a baker from Aosta who had joined up with them a few weeks before. Perhaps one of them did it to cover up their responsibility, or maybe knowing that blaming a newcomer would be easier and would involve fewer drawbacks than blaming one of the other fifteen men in the group who, more or less around the same period, had left Milan and Turin to meet in the mountains, all for very different reasons whose differences history will erase in a few years' time. But then Borrello's breathing, and the sudden violent coughing that interrupts it again and again, suspends those thoughts.

The next day Borrello locks him in the shed with some coffee and a bit of bread and says he'll be back that afternoon. Linden hears him leave and then struggles to stand up and head over to the place where he hid the awl the day before: he starts sharpening it against the edge of a shovel he holds between his knees; soon he feels exhausted and stops; he lets his gaze wander around the shed, pausing to observe the swirls drawn by the dust in the air where some light slips between the wall planks. Despite it being October, according to Linden's calculations, the cold is only unbearable at night. During the day the air is pleasant and the sunlight warming until the sun drops behind the mountains, which, from the house at the foot of the ravine, give the impression of a perfectly vertical wall. Shots are heard somewhere, still very far away. Linden goes over to the table and, almost distractedly, as if it were inevitable, starts to read.

. . .

I could destroy it all, he thinks; the pages written in a cramped, awkward handwriting that seems to convey urgency, the paper constructions gathered by the other man, which must be meaningful to him, must be a source of nostalgia or pride. Linden thinks destroying the man's work would hurt him in an irreparable way, but later he understands that, in some sense, the other man has beaten him to the punch.

An animal wanders around the shed for a good part of the day and Linden realizes it's the dog they saw the day before; seeing it start to scratch at the door he and Borrello fixed, he also realizes the dog is the one who broke it in the first place. This time the planks are new and the animal can't break them; after failing, it starts to scratch beneath the sill, sending dirt and splinters to one side in the attempt. Linden can hear the dog snorting each time it rests its snout on the ground, and something similar to Borrello's cough. The dog's urgency to get inside is incomprehensible to Linden: it can't be hunger—though the dog is obviously starving, and may have been abandoned and hungry for days—because there's nothing to eat inside the shed. The animal has chosen him, he thinks, but that doesn't give him any joy. During his first days in the mountains they had a dog who spontaneously joined them when they attacked the carabinieri station in Ivrea; they had to kill it because they were afraid its barking would give away their location: they took a vote and the task fell to Linden, who tried to ensure the animal suffered as little as possible; but it did suffer because he wasn't able to break its neck in one blow. He'd found the decision to kill the dog overzealous and, in general, a mistake; he remembers the animal's eyes and having killed it pains him more than having killed people. In the skirmishes that took place when they went down into the valley or in the forest, his opponents were armed, so their deaths took on, in some sense, a necessary quality, and besides they were done from a distance, without it being clear who killed or wounded whom, which allowed those who wanted to brag to do so and those who wanted to avoid responsibility—like him—to also do so. But the dog, of course, wasn't armed, it wasn't at a distance, it hadn't been taken down in any specific action, in no act of justice or vandalism that could later be justified as an act of liberation; the animal had died by his hand, looking into his eyes, and only after a long while in which it had tried to defend itself without hurting him, which seemed to Linden an awareness on the dog's part that its survival didn't depend on eliminating its aggressor. The dog's death is one of the many mistakes they made, but it's the only one Linden laments, even though—in a different way—he also laments not knowing who betrayed them, and having condemned an innocent man in a secret vote that now seems completely unfounded. Maybe they're all dead already and no one is responsible for these mistakes, except him and the mole, if the mole is still alive. Linden throws the pewter mug against the door and the dog whimpers off. Linden closes his eyes.

Borrello returns that afternoon; his cough gives him away as he climbs the path that leads to the house. After stopping there, he opens the shed door and helps Linden out, limping, and then sits by his side in the same spot as the day before. "I was in Borgosesia," he tells him. "The Allies bombed Milan again; two hundred children died in an attack on a school in Gorla." Linden doesn't say anything; he has the impression the other man would rather he didn't. "The Allies have taken Aachen, but they haven't broken the Gothic Line between Florence and Bologna, so they still haven't reached the Po Valley," he continues. "There are only refugees in Borgosesia, but the government seems to be holding firm, and there are rumors they'll pay a certain amount of money per head to anyone who turns in partisans," he says. "Are you going to turn me in?" asks Linden without looking at him. Borrello doesn't answer: the dog has returned and is again traveling the imaginary line that separates the property from those around it. Seeing the animal, Borrello stands and heads over to the house. Linden tells himself he doesn't want to see what will happen next, but he sees it before it even happens, when his mind flashes back to the slow death of the other dog, in his arms. When Borrello comes out again, however, he is carrying a knife and a bit of pork fat; he sits down, cuts a piece, and flings it far, in the dog's direction. The animal lowers its forehead, heads cautiously over to where the piece fell, and gobbles it up. Borrello titters; it's the first time Linden's seen him do that; he cuts another piece of pork fat and tosses it somewhat closer. The animal lets out a snort and swallows the second piece: forehead lifted, it's sniffing the air while moving its head from right to left, trying to guess where the next piece will land. Borrello drops the fat almost at his feet and the animal hesitates for a moment, then slinks through the grass and gobbles it up while keeping an eye on him. Borrello extends one hand and the dog approaches and takes the piece from his palm with the utmost delicacy. The animal begins eating while it looks in turn at each of the two men. Linden can see that it's young, little more than a puppy; it must have belonged to one of the families in the area who left seeing that the war was headed their way, or for some other reason. When Borrello runs his greasy hand over its back, the animal lets out a thin stream of urine.

When Borrello returns from this next trip, he pulls some dark corduroy pants from his backpack and spreads them out. "Here you go," he says, looking away. "This was all I could get." Linden considers the offer for a moment and then starts to take off the pants he's wearing, which the other man cut to one knee so he could put on the splint; as he does, he drops the awl. Borrello hears the sound it makes when it hits the ground and he turns: he looks at Linden as if for the first time. The object lies on the ground at an equal distance between the two men, completely inert and senseless, Linden realizes. Borrello takes a step toward him, picks it up, and chucks it in the direction of the mountains. That night he locks Linden in the shed again, while he sleeps in the house.

He attacked the carabinieri station with a young guy who worked at Fiat, while on their way into the mountains; they had been introduced to each other by an engineer who'd lived in the same house as he did, in the north of Turin. The single engineer had never hidden his antifascist feelings, but he swathed them in a jokiness that kept him safe from reprisals, as if he—a single guy who often wooed the young ladies who lived in the building, sometimes giving them perfumes as gifts—had the ability to pass off his criticisms as just venting among the obviously like-minded. Every manifestation of discontent on his part actually seemed like contentment and each rejection, support. Linden never heard of his having success with any of the young women in the building but, in some sense, he was successful with Linden, as Linden really believed he was a fascist; so his invitation to head into the mountains was a surprise. The best word to describe him was perhaps "meticulous"; he always had his hair and mustache perfectly trimmed, and he usually shaved twice a day, in the morning and at night, which was very annoying for the young women who shared a bathroom with him when they were trying to prepare for their dates, which were never with that single engineer, who tried to stay fit and young—though the last time Linden saw him, he seemed surprisingly aged.

The young Fiat worker died six days later during an attack on a truck heading up to the Luserna San Giovanni quarries transporting explosives. The truck was guarded, and the guard opened fire.

A day before he died, the young man had confessed that he was the one traveling around the outskirts of Turin at night, destroying fascist symbols, for example, ripping the fasces off of houses built by the government. The police had been looking for him for weeks, with no success; he'd also been mentioned in the press.

He said something had to be done. But he never said what, and Linden never asked. Never.

. . .

One morning, two days later, Borrello discovers that the dog has dug under the shed door and slipped inside during the night; curled up in Linden's blankets, it observes Borrello without surprise when he opens the door. Borrello had gone back down into town the day before; he'd also bought a newspaper, which he read in the house, in silence, with a worried expression printed on his face. Before passing it on to Linden, he carefully cut out an article, without comment; he'd bought some lamb bones for the dog, which he hung overnight from one of the house's overhangs, in a net, so the cold would keep them fresh and the dog couldn't reach them. Now the animal is pacing around them and looking up at them with a worried expression that reminds Linden of Borrello's and makes him think of a statement often repeated by some members of the Resistance: that the volunteer militias of the Salò regime, and its informants and collaborators, fought only for money. Maybe it's true, thinks Linden, but Borrello, who is obviously a fascist, or was, contradicts what his comrades-in-arms said, as he doesn't seem to receive any remuneration for his ideas; in fact, he seems to have renounced all remuneration and everything superfluous in order to hold on to something essential that Linden doesn't even understand. In that renunciation he seems to be inflicting a punishment on himself, but Linden doesn't know what Borrello renounced or how much what he renounced and the renunciation itself meant to him; and Linden doesn't know anything about the other man's life, except that he wrote books, which Linden has been studying over the last few days without understanding much of anything, and made objects, which don't look like books but maybe can also be read somehow. Linden also knows that the other man studied medicine at some point: Borrello told him that to distract him or perhaps to distract himself as he changed his bandages the previous day. "The head wound is already practically healed," he told him; the leg wound, on the other hand, is still open, though the bone is no longer visible and he is feeling less pain. Borrello had started to cough more than usual, and sometimes seemed to be choking.

While he dressed Linden's wounds, the dog remained at a distance, as if it feared that the wounds or the deep, violent coughing could be contagious.

Borrello leaves him in the shed again that night, but he goes without locking the door, and Linden believes it to be some sort of message: he can escape, if he wants, he can leave when he wants to and is able. Borrello was more absent than usual throughout the day: he dug up some potatoes and some spinach that was practically covered by weeds and he washed up behind the house with water from a pump. Linden watched him, absorbed in his thoughts: on a few occasions Borrello pulled a newspaper clipping out of his jacket pocket and read it, over and over, as if it were written in an incomprehensible language. That night he left Linden a few extra blankets, the ones he'd used to make a bed in the house, but Linden's main source of heat during the night comes from the dog, who sleeps curled up at his feet and sometimes snorts and growls, as if facing enemies in its dreams, enemies that are sometimes strangers and sometimes familiar.

What could they hope to know about the motivations of someone like Borrello, he'd wondered a couple of times. What could they know about events happening in Rome and places like that, they, who had never visited those places, who remained isolated in the mountains in a state of permanent tension, all of them in the mountains for different reasons and fighting against different enemies, sometimes strangers and sometimes familiar: a disrespectful work supervisor who happened to be a fascist, a neighbor who reported them to get a little bit of property, someone luckier than they were, who'd managed to rise slightly above the irrelevance all lives transpire within, and get a political post or something like that. The orders they received came from the political headquarters in Turin, through a mail system that muddled their justification, if they'd ever had one, and all they could do was act accordingly. None of them had much schooling, which filled them with a mix of shame and pride, the latter because they—those who've been excluded from history—now find themselves making history. He likes to remember the monikers of his brigade members and their professions; he'll forget the names over time, but not the jobs: there was a miller; a Communist typographer; a former carabinieri officer who'd deserted the Royal Army when the situation became untenable; a lathe operator; two bricklayers; an accountant from Turin; two local brothers, about whom they said one was a man of few words and the other even fewer; the brigade's political leader had worked in the Olivetti factory; there was a fourteen-year-old orphan who took care of the food and the mules, including La Petacci; five workers from the quarries who had joined them after an attack and were specialists in explosives; a British paratrooper they'd liberated from a police station; and a carpenter—him.

One of those men had betrayed them, however. Linden has no doubt about that.

He is woken by screams; they're coming from the mountains, but rebound off them and seem closer than they actually are. Linden doesn't yet understand the significance of the words, but he recognizes the familiar sound and violence of orders in German. The voices get close enough that he can also hear the stomping of half a dozen boots approaching along a path of rocks and pebbles, as well as some words in Italian. Someone kicks opens the door to the shed. It's Borrello. "Whatever happens, don't go out," he orders, frightened.

The six men are Waffen-SS, so Linden imagines most of them will be Italians, but actually only two are. When they approach, skirting the ravine, and enter the visual field offered by the slits in the shed's walls, he sees that the SS have a man with them: he is dressed like a peasant, but Linden immediately understands that he's another partisan. When the SS arrive, the dog escapes: it stops and watches them all from the property line, sniffing the air with its head lifted, pacing uneasily, expectantly. Borrello comes out of the house and goes over to them; he doesn't speak. The German sergeant does, and one of the Italians rushes to translate; however Linden doesn't need the translation. The sergeant asks to see Borrello's papers, and he hands them over; after the sergeant verifies that they're in order, he demands to know if he's seen anything unusual in recent days. Borrello says no. The men look around and their gazes land on the shed. Linden holds his breath and instinctively withdraws from his lookout point as if they could see him there, but then immediately returns. The Italian suggests to the German sergeant that they investigate, but his superior officer seems not to hear him. "Do you live alone?" he finally asks through his interpreter. Borrello doesn't respond. "He lives with the dog," says one of the German soldiers, pointing to the bag of bones hanging outside the house. They all laugh and the situation seems to ease for a moment. Linden whispers to himself that they'll end up just leaving, and the heat of his breath surprises him when it ricochets off the wall planks and hits him in the face: it's a heavy breath, sullied by sleep and lack of food, but also by fear. The soldiers have formed a semicircle around the hanging bag of bones and are pointing at it, smiling, when one of them leaves the group and moves in Borrello's direction: Linden gets a look at him, and almost cries out. "You don't remember me, but I remember you," the man says. Borrello looks at him for a moment. "Take off your helmet," Borrello orders: the other man does, while the remaining Italian translates for the Germans, whose interest has moved off the bag of bones and onto the two men. "You used to have thick black hair," says Borrello finally, "so we all called you 'Blondie.' You were with us when we expelled the rector from the university and put one of our own in his place. You once punched a young Communist and he came back with his comrades: word spread and we went to your aid. It was in the square, in front of the cathedral. They brought sticks, but we had pistols. And there were more of us. You were always with the guy they called 'The Roman,' who died in another scuffle, at the Porta Trasimena," he says. (You pretended to be a former carabinieri officer who had deserted, thinks Linden in silence. You said you were a Communist and that your name was "Monaci Luigi" but you asked us to call you by your nom de guerre, "Zosimus," which you'd chosen because you were the oldest in the brigade and the most experienced. You gave us military training, you were in charge of target practice and weapons.) The other man nods. "He's one of us, I know him," he says, returning to the circle where the other men are. "He's one of us?" asks the sergeant sarcastically; when he takes his pistol off his belt, the dog, expectantly silent on the property line, starts to bark, as if wanting to warn someone of the danger, but Borrello doesn't move. The sergeant puts the pistol in Borrello's hand and orders the interpreter to translate; then he says, pointing to the prisoner: "Kill him. If you are one of us it won't be difficult for you. He's a rebel bandit. We captured him last night. Or kill the dog, if you believe this man's life is worth more than his. You decide."

Borrello observes the pistol. Perhaps he's remembering the last time he had one in his hands (though Linden can't know that); he lifts his head and looks first at the dog, who whimpers and barks on the property line, and then at the prisoner, who is a young man, practically a teenager. Linden had asked himself many times what he would do in Borrello's place, if he were one day captured by the fascists or the Germans. Of course this was hypothetical: he wasn't expecting to be captured, he expected to die in some action or not die at all; but, if he were captured, he'd always thought he would die as he's tried to live, with some dignity. In that moment, however, Linden realizes he wouldn't be able to; if he ever is captured, he will die like that teenager, crying in silence, shaking, on the cusp of losing consciousness, at the hands of someone who knows nothing about him and won't even remember him a moment later— someone who will never know his name.

·   ·   ·

Borrello looks at the pistol in his hand again and then, quickly, unexpectedly, he brings it to his own temple. One of the Italians pounces on him and, after a brief struggle, wrests the gun away just as Borrello is about to cock it. The men, including the prisoner, look at him in horror: one of them lets out a hysterical laugh, but the laugh dissolves in the air immediately when the German sergeant grabs the pistol from the Italian and puts it back in its holster. "He's crazy, that guy is crazy," he murmurs, and he makes a sign to the men, who begin to head downhill behind him, dragging the prisoner. Borrello will see him the next day, hanging from one of the balconies overlooking Borgosesia's main square: they executed him shortly after arriving in town, without a trial of any sort.

As they resume their march, the man Borrello knew as "Blondie" and Linden as "Zosimus" stays back and turns to Borrello to say: "You've humiliated me. You're an embarrassment to fascism. If I ever see you again, I'll shoot you." Then he goes off with the others.

When Borrello opens the door to the shed, he finds Linden curled up among the blankets. The dog slips through his legs and starts to lick Linden's face, and Linden allows it. Borrello closes the door slowly and gently.

He has a coughing fit, the worst one Linden has witnessed.

That afternoon Borrello begins speaking: he tells Linden it wasn't random chance that brought him to the house, it once belonged to his father's family; he had only heard tell of it during his childhood, which took place in Sansepolcro, in the region of Umbria, where his father moved for some reason he's not privy to. Borrello found it a few years earlier thanks to a distant relative; the house had been looted by neighbors and was in ruins. He tore down what remained, leaving only one room standing—the house's firewood storage—and got rid of everything he found inside because it all seemed too laden with meaning, he says mysteriously: he kept only what seemed meaningless and waiting for him to imbue it with meaning. His father was a ceramicist; he made small statues of virgins to sell to women who visited the Madonna del Parto to ask for an easy birth. Borrello hadn't inherited any of those talents: he was a writer, he says. In Perugia. There he met the best writer of his generation, but that writer died and Borrello failed in his attempt to protect and promote his work: he lost it, he says, and now that work belongs to someone else, someone who used to be his friend but no longer is, obviously.

Something seems to have broken in Borrello and his words burble out, with no need for questions, as if every question, thinks Linden, would be inopportune. The dog sleeps at their feet, immersed in dreams that occasionally send a shiver through its body. While Borrello speaks, the sun abandons its zenith and ceases to give off heat. The days are shorter and colder, and there's a certain urgency in the air, related to the war but also to the physical changes Borrello is experiencing before Linden's eyes. He watches him grow thinner and waste away. Borrello told him the night before that he's going on a trip, but he didn't say where to, and Linden didn't ask.

He blew up a bridge, he attacked a convoy of Germans heading from Novara to Biella, Linden tells Borrello; he sabotaged the phone line that linked rural Piedmont with Turin; he also had skirmishes with Italians, but they were brief and chaotic and he never knew for certain if he was responsible for the deaths that occurred. Linden went into the mountains in October 1943 despite the opposition of his father, a Swiss cabinetmaker from Bern who had arrived in Turin some thirty years earlier following a brother and his promises of work in Italy. There's no need to meddle in Italian affairs, Linden's father said, in spite of the fact that his wife and son were Italian, and in spite of the racial laws, the lynchings of the opposition, the conscription and collaborationism not being necessarily Italian affairs but rather involving an idea of justice that his son didn't consider limited by a national jurisdiction. Naturally, Linden couldn't formulate his thoughts that way from the beginning, but any objections were surpassed by the pressing need to do something, anything. Borrello could understand that. Later Linden was able to explain it because his comrades-in-arms explained it to him, those who'd had some sort of political education. He fought in Issime; in the Gressoney Valley; in Torrazzo; in Ribordone; in Cuorgnè, in the battle where Italo Rossi, whom his group was supporting, died; and in Valperga. He's suffered hunger and cold, and believed he understood something. They never had much; Linden can still remember the last inventory they carried out, four days before the attack: eleven military capes, six submachine guns, eight rifles, five hand grenades, a typewriter, a calculator (both completely useless artifacts in that situation), ammunition, and fourteen pistols, including one that was inoperable and carried just for show.

The ammunition was considerably reduced the night before the attack, when "Zosimus" made the surprise announcement that they would do target practice; he also ordered that the grenades be tossed to test their effectiveness, claiming more would arrive the following day from the French border. Now Linden knows there were never any new grenades and the reason "Zosimus" ordered target practice was that he wanted to reduce the group's resources and limit their ability to respond to the attack the next day; the grenades also allowed the trackers to find them more easily in the mountains. At daybreak, when the Germans attacked, the partisans were exhausted and without ammunition, Linden tells Borrello. He prefers not to say anything about the execution of the supposed traitor the day before the attack not just because of what the other man might think, but also because he prefers not to remember it: the secret trial, held without the accused in attendance; the sentencing; the march through a clearing in the forest; and the shooting in the back, which the partisans, for some reason, called "the

Soviet method." The supposed traitor had been one of them from almost the beginning; he was a mechanic from Aosta, he had gone into the mountains to avoid the draft, so he must have been eighteen or nineteen. "Zosimus" was, Linden recalls, the main instigator of the execution, but they drew straws for the actual shooting and the Communist typographer was chosen. He vomited afterward. "Zosimus" walked up to the young mechanic's corpse and delivered the coup de grâce and, gradually, the other members of the brigade approached the body as well. One of them, the political leader of the group, ordered him buried beneath a twisted pine that grew in a hollow and commanded them to make note of the execution in the journal that the brigade kept at the request of the political leadership in Turin, but he also ordered that the grave be unmarked, so that only they knew where it was and there could be no possible posthumous tribute to the traitor.

Linden tries to push away a thought that comes over him every time he remembers Borrello with the pistol at his temple: in the last year he'd discovered that all corpses are equal, no matter what their owners believed in before dying; as such, every death is equal to every other one and could be—in fact is—his own.

A few years later he will see a photograph of the young mechanic from Aosta in a newspaper; the article remembers him as someone fallen in the fight against fascism, but it also says that he died during the German attack on his brigade, a few days after his real death in completely different circumstances. Linden will write a letter to the newspaper, slowly and with difficulty, hesitating and going back and forth, in order to explain how events really played out, but in the end he will never send it.

The next day he starts building a chest with some ash wood he found in the shed; most of the time he works seated so as not to tax his broken leg. The dog lies beside him, and sometimes plays with the wood shavings that fall to the floor, licking them up and then spitting them out with a sneer. Borrello has gone down to Borgosesia and Linden works at his own pace: he nails the boards and runs the plane over them to the slow, regular rhythm of his thoughts. He can see himself doing it and thinks, to his surprise, that taking up his old habits again makes him happy. He hasn't worked as a carpenter for a year and enjoys returning to it, restoring a meaning to his actions that he can only deem authentic: as if the year spent up in the mountains had been a parenthesis, not necessarily false but at least distanced from his true nature, a parenthesis in which Linden played a part, somewhat begrudgingly and with growing displeasure as the dead piled up on his conscience, weighing heavier and heavier collectively but blurring grotesquely in individual terms. In the end he will only remember one face, he thinks, made up of scraps of all the faces of the war dead, and he won't know if that face is an enemy's face, or the face of one of his own.

The only thing he cannot understand is why Borrello wanted to take his own life and what that has to do with the trip he's thinking of taking. Does someone attempt suicide when he has a task ahead of him like a trip, wonders Linden, contemplating the ash box. He still has to make a lid, he thinks, but the size is fine, or at least it seems so to him.

When Borrello returns it is almost nightfall; the dog is first to realize he's approaching and runs to meet him. When it reaches his side, it leaps up and Borrello runs a hand over its head. The animal follows him, sniffing the tracks left by the man and, sometimes, glancing behind him, toward the valley; it barks at the houses in the distance, as a sign of self-importance or of something that is perhaps happiness. Borrello seems exhausted: he coughs hard once or twice before he can speak; when it finally seems he can, however, he remains silent. Linden had pumped some water a moment earlier and offers it to him, but the other man shakes his head. They've entered the house and the dog stays at the threshold, whining, not daring to follow. Seeing the animal, Borrello pulls something wrapped in bloody paper out of his backpack. Pig's lungs. He puts them down on the ground outside the house. The dog pounces. Outside, in the valley, a train passes. The sound is familiar but still gives them each a shiver.

Borrello has brought a large round loaf of bread and some salted meat, and the two men eat in silence; afterward, before lying down on the bed, he instructs Linden to heat some water in two pots. When the water's ready, Borrello sits up and asks Linden to come over with the lamp and the pots. He puts everything on the table and then slowly removes the bandage on Linden's head and studies his wound, standing by his side. "The gash on your forehead is closed now," he says, "but it could open up again if you're not careful." Borrello pulls a strip of bandage and a quarter of a bar of purple soap out of his backpack. He wets the bandage in the hot water and then rubs it over the soap, making foam. He runs it all over Linden's forehead with quick, short movements and then takes another strip of bandage and soaks it in the second batch of hot water: he rinses and dries the wound and applies an iodine tincture. Then he has Linden extend his leg over his lap and removes that bandage: the wound is still open, but a small layer of fat and skin has begun to form over it, obscuring the bone. Borrello repeats the procedure and teaches Linden how to clean and dress his wounds himself. "There's no necrosis or infection," he says with pride, "and the bone is set in place. You'll feel some pain for a while, but it will heal; however, it's important that you keep your leg immobilized for another month, at least. I'm going to teach you how to do it," he says before cleaning the wound and replacing the splint. The scene seems to Linden to have some religious significance, but he doesn't know what exactly: when Borrello finishes, the two men remain in silence. Linden stands up to head toward the shed, but the other man indicates that he can sleep in the house, where he'll be less vulnerable to the night's cold. He stands up, opens the door, and tosses out the water he used to clean the wounds. Then he throws some wood on the fire and turns off the lamp, removes his jacket, shoes, and glasses, and gets into bed. Linden hears him cough a couple more times and then clear his throat. "I'm leaving the day after tomorrow," Borrello starts to say. "At dawn, if possible." Linden wants to ask where he's going, but he doesn't because he believes Borrello would rather not tell him. Instead, he asks how long he'll be gone. Borrello doesn't answer. "It doesn't make any sense." Borrello seems to be arguing with himself, as if hallucinating, between fits of coughing. "They want to defend the idea that things don't collapse, but things do collapse." Linden doesn't know what he's talking about. "A noble impulse, something pure." Borrello's turned his face and is speaking directly to Linden, who doesn't know how to respond. "Perhaps that could be saved, perhaps there's a way to reconstruct it later, for the others: what we did, but without those of us who weren't up to the task and ruined it." Linden waits for the other man to continue, but he doesn't; he asks him once more when he expects to return, but Borrello doesn't speak again that night.

The next day Borrello gathers his things. The dog seems to know that something in the situation is about to change, and is uneasy. Linden has finished the ash wood box and, after carving his initials into it and carefully placing all the papers he found in the shed inside of it, gives it to Borrello. "I don't know if you're still a writer or not, but this way you can save what you've written," he says. Borrello is pensive for a moment and then thanks him: he seems flattered that the other man thinks his work deserves saving, but he also seems overwhelmed, as if Linden had added more weight to the burden he's been trying to cast off, unsuccessfully, all this time.

Borrello has a wheelbarrow he sometimes uses to gather firewood and he now spends some time greasing its wheels. The next day, he says, he'll go down to the valley to board the train, if it comes. He'll go to Turin, he says, and, if that's not possible, to Milan. From there he'll figure out how to get to Pinerolo, which will take him two or maybe three days. Linden nods in silence: on a map of the region he indicates as best he can the areas Borrello should avoid if he doesn't want to run into partisans and then he gives him his safe-conduct. Borrello thanks him and leaves the house. A little while later, Linden finds him sitting in front of the path that leads to the valley, observing it and playing with the dog, who gently nips at his shoes. "Will you take care of him?" he asks. Linden nods. "What will you do when your leg's healed? Will you go back to the mountains?" he asks. "I don't know," replies Linden; the idea of killing again repels him, but he thinks that if he doesn't return to the partisan fight the sacrifices of the last year and the deaths of his comrades-in-arms will have been meaningless. Perhaps, he thinks, that's all war is, inertia provoked by a series of revenges that overlap until the first humiliation—the origin of it all—has been forgotten. Killing demands more killing, thinks Linden, but it also demands not knowing who is being eradicated, and maybe because of that ideologies are necessary, a ton of words designed to confuse in such a way that those who hear them forget the intimate knowledge they have of their enemies, who start to seem like dangerous strangers. Ideologies are designed to make you forget, he thinks, that the face of the enemy is your own, disfigured by a relatively minor detail or two. He crossed a line by getting to know Borrello, he tells himself; he understands he probably shouldn't have ever crossed that line, and now he will no longer be able to kill those who are fascists like Borrello; or those who aren't fascists like him but could have been. Soon, when the war is over, the Italians will find a way to continue living together, you don't have to be an expert in history to understand that, he thinks; fascists and antifascists will end up pretending that nothing happened, and it's possible that actually nothing did, nothing relevant in relation to the long periods over which history is written, which exceed men's individual existences as well as, probably, their comprehension. One day, the accountant from Turin confessed to him that he was afraid, and what he feared was not capture or death but the advent of a time when the partisan struggle would be betrayed by its leaders and its own violent, anarchic nature. At the time Linden told him he didn't think that was possible, that the difference between them—what they believed in—and the fascists was so vast that not even history, when written many years later, could ignore it. But the accountant replied that the only difference he could see was between those men who had done bad things voluntarily and those who'd done them unwittingly, and the partisans and the fascists fell into both categories. The difference, he said, was clear to him, but only on a personal level: he would never be able to explain that difference to anyone and he'd have to live out the rest of his days with that inexpressible conviction. Linden saw him fall during the attack on their brigade and since then he's thought on a couple of occasions that, unlike him, the accountant from Turin would never recant, he wouldn't ever hesitate and he wouldn't see the Resistance betrayed, but even still Linden prefers not to be in his shoes. Something in the partisan fight is unquestionably, irreducibly pure, he tells himself; and that purity is simply not of this world.

"Maybe I'll wait for you here," says Linden finally. "I'll keep the house in order, and I can fix up the garden for when you return. In the spring we'll plant potatoes and maybe onions and peas; maybe some pumpkins too," he adds. Borrello addresses him wearily, as if he resents having to put into words something he feels he's already made clear, though of course he hasn't. "I'm not coming back," he finally says before returning to his silent observation of the valley.

Linden watches him leave from the door the next day; he would have liked to accompany him at least to the main road, but he still has trouble walking and, besides, it's better if he's not seen. Borrello gave him his ration card and told him how to use it, pretending to be him. Of course, he won't be able to do that in Borgosesia, where Borrello is known, but, once he's recovered, he can use it in Coggiola, or Serravalle Sesia or Biella, if he thinks he can get there without being recognized. Borrello obtained a new document in Coggiola that Linden can use as if it were his own, and he bought a bag of rice, some potatoes, and conserved meat so he can survive until he can walk better and use the ration card. Before he leaves, Borrello lifts one of the floor planks and pulls Linden's rifle out from beneath it: he had hidden it there about eleven days earlier, on the night he found him wounded and unconscious on the edge of the ravine. He also pulls out a pistol and hands it to him: he tells him he once wanted to kill someone with it, but wasn't able to pull it off, and no longer needs it. Linden nods; later he has to tie up the dog in the shed so it doesn't follow Borrello. When he's finished, and goes outside, the other man has already left, dragging the wheelbarrow containing the ash wood box along the road with some difficulty, stopping at times to cough. He didn't say goodbye, and Linden thinks that's best if that's how he wants it. Borrello taught him something, and Linden won't be able to forget him or what he learned from him. The dog's panicked barking can be clearly heard outside the shed and maybe Borrello can hear it too, amplified by the echoes in the mountains; if that's the case, maybe Linden could shout something out to him too, thank him or convince him to stay, but he doesn't. Borrello doesn't look back even once.

At midday, when he's already untied the dog and fed it, Linden and the animal can hear the sound of the train crossing the valley. The dog remains in a dreamy haze, lying there at his feet, but Linden, intuitively, smiles.

Florence

APRIL OR MAY 1947

>>

Like lost children we live our unfinished adventures.

GUY DEBORD, *Howls for Sade*

The typewritten transcription of a talk; the speaker and date and the location are not noted in the text.

The manuscript of what, despite its fragmented and somewhat chaotic nature, seems to be a novel. There are two alternating plotlines. In the first, a handful of people about whom we know only their largely unrealistic nicknames, are confined in what is perhaps a hospital or, more likely, a prison. There, somehow, the circulation of a drug among the inmates allows the authorities to extract and by some means profit from their pain and perhaps their memory, though how they do this is never explained. In the second plotline, a man drives along the highways of a country he says nothing about; at some point he picks up a violinist or a cellist—the author alternates the two terms, as if he were unaware of the differences in timbre and especially in size between the two instruments; or, more likely, due to the fact that the novel was never revised—he meets along the road. Predictably, he strikes up a romance with the musician, about whom we never learn anything, not even her name. The protagonist, at least, is called "P." Over the course of what seem like days or weeks, the young musician tells P. a story that turns out to be a lie, though perhaps not. It's unclear what relationship there is between the first plotline and the second: maybe there isn't any, or maybe

P. is one of the characters that appear in the hospital or prison (it would be more appropriate to call it a "concentration camp," though, given what appears to be the date of the manuscript, the early 1930s, that would be an anachronism, or shocking and terrible prescience on the part of its author), and he shows up there shortly after the events of the second plotline, with his mind already completely destroyed by insanity or the drugs they're giving him or the nature of his forced internment. Maybe he was institutionalized by the young violinist or cellist for some reason, or perhaps P. killed her and was found out and sentenced; maybe the second plotline is a fever dream or delirium of one of the characters in the first one, possibly the guy known as "Rusty." None of this is explained at any point in the short novel: some one hundred and forty typed pages, double-spaced and with wide margins. The manuscript is headed with the phrase "Shakespeare Machine" and the very ambiguous: "'What have you done with William Shakespeare's dog?' she shouted." Either of the two phrases could be the title of the work, more likely the first, its succinctness making it more appropriate for a title.

A play some six pages long entitled "Woodpecker." The action takes place in the dining room of a middle-class home decorated with the exuberance and bad taste typical of wealthy homes in the early decades of the twentieth century. The scene is banal: the father reads the newspaper, the mother sews, the children—she is older than he is, almost a young adult already—are looking at a photo album. They exchange brief comments, casually formulated and in connection with each of their activities; but despite the actors talking and moving, no sound comes out of their mouths. After a few minutes, the first act ends. In the second act, the action again takes place in the family dining room, but it is of a completely different nature: the man hits the woman, spits in her face, throws her to the floor, and drags her around by her hair, stopping to kick her; the children also slither around on the floor, kissing each other, the young woman masturbating her brother to give him an erection. Although they all seem to shout and moan, none of that is heard: in its place, and thanks to a recording, the audience hears the polite and somewhat childish exchanges of the first act, which contrast significantly with the action onstage. When it ends, giving rise to the third act, the situation has recomposed, the characters are in their original places, and a fifth actor bursts onto the scene and is greeted with displays of recognition and affection by the father and, to a lesser extent, the children: his visit clearly seems to upset the woman, however. None of what they say can be heard by the audience: in its place— and via a recording—we hear the insults, shouts, and moans that correspond to the previous act. The final act takes place on a dark stage devoid of actors; the dialogue from the preceding act is heard, with the visit of a family friend who turns out to be, and this explains the woman's discomfiture at his arrival, the wife's lover. The audience should understand, from the stage directions at the end of the text, that the second act is really the third and vice versa, and that the dialogue of the second is really that of the first and that of the third, the second. The author suggests the possibility that the play be circular, reproducing the dialogue of the third act during the first, which is mute in his version; he also proposes adding a fourth act, in which the audience "hears" the characters' thoughts. In a handwritten note added later, the author realizes another possible way of interpreting his work, in which it was all the wife's dream, as she considers bringing her lover into the family home, with the predictable consequences for all concerned: in that sense, the play would be a denunciation of Italian women's situation in the first half of the twentieth century. In the same handwritten note, the author adds that the title of the piece comes from the anonymous poem "Woodpecker / Sad Industrialist / Undertaker," scrawled on a wall in the town of Sansepolcro in 1923.

"Kaidmorto," a comic piece for one actor; length, eleven pages.
  In the notes for its staging the author indicates that it was

specially created for Emilio Ghione and that he is the only actor who has a right to perform it; an addendum dated January 10, 1930, notes the actor's death a few days earlier, and goes on to state the author's wish that the piece never be performed. The note is particularly disconcerting: indeed, Ghione, who was an exceptionally popular actor and film director in the 1920s, as well as a novelist, died in January 1930; but the piece's original concept made it impossible to perform with Ghione alive or not, as it consisted of two simultaneous and contradictory speeches, one in English and the other in Italian, that were to be spoken "at the same time" by a single actor. Both texts cover several pages in two columns with hardly any stage directions. The material impossibility of an actor performing two monologues simultaneously, not to mention that of the audience understanding both at the same time, isn't brought to light at any point in the play, though it's implicit in the title, which references the being of the same name described by Diodorus of Sicily who "had a tongue split half from root to tip, so that it could speak to two people at once, in different conversations and different languages." The texts in the play differ, and describe two dreams in which the kaidmorto appears. The link to Emilio Ghione and the description of the work as a "comic piece" are presumably ironic references to the actor's dour and occasionally terrifying appearance, even in the rare comedies in which he performed: again, there is a reference in this to Diodorus of Sicily, who wrote that the kaidmorto "would bite laughing."

Luca Borrello's theater pieces seem to follow two of the relatively vague general guidelines of "The Futurist Synthetic Theater" manifesto (1915) by Filippo Tommaso Marinetti, Emilio Settimelli, and Bruno Corra, with its string of restrictions and jabs: "*it's stupid* not to rebel against the prejudice of theatricality when life itself [. . .] is largely antitheatrical"; "*it's stupid* to pander to the primitivism of the masses"; "*it's stupid* to want to explain with minute logic everything taking place onstage, when in life we can't grasp events in their entirety"; "*it's stupid* to submit to obligatory crescendi, prepared effects, and postponed climaxes"; "*it's stupid* to allow one's own genius to be burdened by a technique that everyone (even imbeciles) can learn by study, practice, and patience"; etc. (The hysterical italics are the author's.) An example of B.'s adherence—not without its contradictions—to the Futurist theatrical aesthetic is found in his work "Depressa" [*sic*].

In "Depressa," two characters who strongly resemble each other are
   arguing in a hotel room; one of them is the shadow of the other,
   which detached when its "owner" was run over by a streetcar,
   which seems to have happened just minutes before. The shadow
   is dying, but it's never clear why it's the shadow in its death throes
   and not the man who was run over. The interesting aspect of the
   piece, if there is one, lies not in its mimesis of a reality that B. may
   not even believe in, nor in its adherence to its own guidelines—as
   confusing as they inevitably are—but in the confrontation
   between the shadow and its former owner, in the course of which
   the shadow reproaches the man for various decisions he made
   in the past, including rejecting a woman, making a poor choice
   of profession, and something only described as "confusing and
   terrible" that took place in the cathedral plaza in Perugia. In the
   notes to the piece—some sixty-two pages typed on both sides,
   a length that is anomalous in Futurist theater, which tends to
   be brief and even extremely brief—the author states that the
   physical resemblance between the two characters can only be
   guaranteed by choosing twin actors for the parts, something
   naturally difficult or impossible to find on the Italian theatrical
   scene of the period and, in general, in every period and country,
   despite which—as the author specifies—that is a nonnegotiable
   aspect of the work. The piece must be performed by twins or not
   performed at all. As for the rest, its title comes, as the author
   notes in a perhaps superfluous stage direction, from the poem by
   M. S. Oliver of the same title, which reads: "Depressa fugen les
   hores / depressa y no tornan més. / Aprofita l'hora / dels encants

primers, / aprofita l'hora que no torna més." No information was found about the aforementioned M. S. Oliver, who is perhaps fictitious; beyond that, as far as is known, the author did not speak Catalan or know anything about Catalan literature.

Despite the aforementioned difficulty of finding a pair of identical twins on the Italian theater scene, the next two plays by Borrello again require them.

The first, entitled "Red Red Balloons" [*sic*], consists of a series of completely meaningless dialogues that are to be performed while the actors hang off an iron structure: from the description offered in the long note that begins the play, the structure is similar to a scaffolding typically used in the construction and repair of buildings, to which dozens or hundreds of balloons have been tied (the author exaggerates here, despite not giving exact figures). The actors have to untie the balloons and let them float up to the stage ceiling: because they're performing upside down, the balloons' ascent is perceived by the actors as a fall, which they find disconcerting, and which gives rise to situations that should be comical and, yet, aren't, or aren't very. Instead, the audience may be overcome by boredom, which was possibly the author's desired effect.

A similar piece, with completely different characteristics, offers greater narrative development and a deeper engagement with the aforementioned mood. The work, entitled "Abel, Cain, Seth," offers only half a dozen pages of dialogue that is diagrammatic. Most of the manuscript consists of performance notes that are, unlike the dialogue fragments, highly precise: according to them, the piece should be performed on a large stage with a double bed placed on an inclined plane, a sewing machine with its respective chair, an umbrella stand filled with umbrellas, a dissection table with its surgical materials, etc. All these objects should be laid out in such a way that they create different, clearly defined spaces around them through lighting that comes up when the action is taking place there and hides them while it's on another part of the stage. The action begins in the bed, where, at the start, a woman should be having sexual relations with a man. Yet the man, designated simply by the letter P, should be played by three actors, brothers, if possible, insists the author (in other words, triplets). The author's insistence stems from the fact that the entire play revolves around this plot: three brothers are born joined at the waist—and because of that rejected by their parents, who hand them over to circus performers who, due to a series of events that the author insinuates in the notes but refuses to clarify, are now their owners. As teens they fall in love with a woman, one of the circus midgets. In spite of, or perhaps due to the sexual possibilities offered by these conjoined triplets—three heads, four arms, six legs, three penises, three tongues, etc.—the midget accepts the lover or lovers into her bed. But each of them longs to possess the woman exclusively, which is—in this and similar cases, or not—anatomically impossible. The arrival at the circus of a surgeon who offers to separate the three brothers, despite the obvious risks, changes everything; the brothers argue: one of them refuses to take part in the experiment in the name of everything they've been through together; another, in the name of all they have left to go through together. (The spectator understands, or should understand, that each of them "embodies" a verb tense, states the author: past, present, and future.) Only one of the brothers, the third, clings to the idea of separating from the others: he gets them drunk with the help of the woman and the surgeon, so that the operation can be carried out. That third brother dies. The initial situation—the woman and her lover, now double, are in bed, etc.—is repeated; when they are done, and as in the first act, the woman sews. Shortly after, the brothers argue: the elimination of one of them doesn't allow either of the remaining ones to exclusively possess the woman; it doesn't even mean they enjoy a greater percentage of her despite sharing her between two instead of three. One of the brothers, the taller one, now claims to fear the operation's future consequences; for the other brother—of course—the future is inconceivable. Once again, the latter convinces, or is convinced by, the surgeon to perform another operation, and the second act ends with the two brothers lying on the dissection table, one of them drugged by the other. In the third act they have already been separated, and the woman frolics with one of the brothers in bed: she is apathetic, however; when they finish the sexual act and each heads to an opposite end of the stage—the woman goes back to her sewing—the other brother bursts onto the scene. He's survived the separation but doesn't seem to understand what's happened; in one of the more comic scenes, he tries to join up with his brother again by inserting himself under his clothing, hopping onto his back, etc. The other brother, who has no arms because he was the one in the middle, fights him off, they tussle, he kicks his brother on the floor over and over again. His concern for the future made no sense: the young man has no future. The murderous brother realizes, understands, regrets, but when he looks to the midget for comfort, she rejects him. Beside him he finds the surgeon, naked and, for the first time, completely bald, like the brothers. The midget has finished sewing what turns out to be a suit: it is made of blue latex, similar to the one worn by the brothers: the surgeon gets into it; the suit has two dolls, one on either side, that represent the other brothers. The midget kills the surviving one and goes off with the surgeon, who takes the triplets' place in the circus hierarchy. The curtain comes down.

Sketches for a building on whose faces are written, in giant letters, *ARDITA*, ANTISOCIALIST, ANTICLERICAL, ANTIMONARCHIC, and the corresponding rejection letter sent to the author by the Fascist Cultural Institute on September 4, 1938, a day before the enactment of the first racial laws. The proposal recalls that texts, specifically Futurist texts, invaded the regime's buildings during a certain period—it should be noted that our texts in turn became more architectural—for example in the Foro Italico. The work also seems to be inspired by, or ironizing, the Book Pavilion designed by Fortunato Depero for the publishers Bestetti, Tumminelli, and Treves in 1927, whose facade was made only of uppercase letters, which, in turn, were perhaps Depero's send-up of the textual excess afflicting Italian society of that period, as the coauthor of "The Futurist Reconstruction of the Universe" had quite the sense of humor.

A theater piece—this one finished—for two actors, entitled "The Competition / The Sea." The actors need not be brothers, according to the staging notes. Unlike those previously listed in this catalog, the piece does not show any rejection of family or bourgeois lifestyle; nor is it a drama born of the fleetingness and simultaneity of events that Marinetti described as the epitome of Futurist drama, despite which the author defines it, following M., as "dialogued hilarity." "The Competition / The Sea" places emphasis on the range of interpretations of an event and the way that range is, in itself, the drama. The work is bound in such a way that, between the title page and the cover, a bathtub unfolds in the middle of a deserted landscape. Sixty-two signed and numbered copies have been found.

An addendum to "Abel, Cain, Seth," possibly written at a later date, in which B. maintains that—contrary to what one might think— the piece is not a drama but a pantomime and what the author calls, once again following Marinetti, a "synthetic deformation." The note offers a minute description of how the actors should move and act, and of both suits, the one worn by the three actors playing the brothers and the one the woman is sewing throughout the play. The former, it says, should be made out of latex or a similar material in blue, and must allow the actors some freedom of movement: for example, they must be able to get onto each other's shoulders so that, during the coitus at the start of the piece, they can simulate the man in bed being unusually tall, etc. It is essential, maintains the author, that the suit be elastic enough for each of the actors to get far enough away from the others while still being inside the suit to realize an "aside" onstage. The interpretative possibilities are directly dependent on that aspect, states Borrello. The addendum includes various drawings: of the stage; of the blocking of the man in bed and other objects; of the suit and the actors' range of movement inside it—successively on each other's shoulders, extended on the floor with the middle one's head beneath the first one's feet and his feet brushing the head of the third, etc.

A long narrative poem entitled "The Sleepwalker," three typed copies. The first one has no alterations; the second, on the other hand, is filled with handwritten marginal notes, which, as the notes explain, correct or complete the poem's verses; the third copy reproduces just the notes—the main text has been erased so that, in some sense, the notes seem to float in the air of the page. About the poem itself, not much can be said, except that the writer of this text had the opportunity to hear it read by Borrello and to discuss it with him and others in a certain student bar in the Italian city of Perugia. I can't recall the exact date, despite remembering, or believing I remember, that the marginal notes are the result of that discussion. In the one that begins with the statement "It's not about occupying a territory, but about 'being' the territory," the author seems to recognize his choice of words and the ideas he defended circa 1933 and earlier.

A short piece—three pages—for two actors; on this occasion they should be not only brothers but also older. The work alternates the two actors' monologues, each placed on one side of the stage. Neither ever addresses the other directly, but they interrupt each other, to correct or expand on what the other has said, which is vaguely related to a fire on a boat they both witnessed when they were young. For some reason, the title of the piece is a short, anonymous poem: "The old men and women / are / poor Argentines / in the comedy of / the theater of life," despite none of the characters being explicitly Argentine or any other nationality.

A variant of the piece by F. T. Marinetti "Simultaneità" in which the flowers received by a woman from her beloved are actually from the middle-class man who sits to her right and visits her later: a single actor should play both characters, though that is materially impossible. Two pages.

An abandoned sheet of paper on which the author attempted to embroider a text onto the page: the text consists of the words "We men / make towers / and women / make / poor / children," perhaps part of a poem or a poem in itself, by the author or by someone else.

A ninety-page novel entitled "Continuation of the Fire," in which two lunatics try to clarify events in an unnamed place at some point prior to a fire that occurred at some vague date. The story digresses time and again toward a discussion of the existence of certain strange characters belonging, perhaps, to the oral traditions of the author's native Piedmont region, or the Arezzo province where he lived (in a town called Sansepolcro) before moving to Perugia. "Continuation of the Fire" could be described as dreamlike except—despite the diffuse logic running through its pages, its repetitions and inconsistencies typical of two such alienated characters—it's possible to infer from reading it who committed the events described, as if the novel were a simple, conventional thriller, perhaps the first sign of Borrello's interest in that genre. The novel follows the guidelines sketched out by Luigi Scrivo, Piero Bellanova, and the ubiquitous Marinetti in their "Manifesto of the Synthetic Novel" of 1939, according to which it must be brief and original, including in its typographical presentation and layout on the page; and it should present situations dynamically and simultaneously and show some love for urban life and mass society. However Borrello's novel doesn't fulfill that last aspect, and may have been written prior to the manifesto, suggesting the possibility that the manifesto was the product of reading B.'s novel—which could have been delivered to Scrivo, Bellanova, or Marinetti himself, though there's no proof that Borrello had met or known any of them; in fact, there's no proof that Scrivo or Bellanova ever existed—instead of the other way around.

"A Fat Woman," short story. The first two pages, typed; then three photographs that show the author destroying the story's final page; an attached note indicates that the work's subject matter (as well as the work itself) is testimony to the incomplete nature of all artistic work and that, if the story—meaning the piece that includes the story and the documentation of its partial destruction—is a work of art, this is because it's been mutilated, leaving just the residual limb, or "stump," Borrello's term. The "stump" should include all other texts, every text that makes up our country's culture and literature. (The identity of the photographer who took the pictures of the author destroying the work is not mentioned.) The piece is one of the first examples of the gradual "hollowing out" of B.'s work.

Some sort of untitled, possibly incomplete visual diary: it includes photographs of a chair, a table, views of a mountain town; images of the dismantling of a house, the elements that made it up—beams, bricks, some furniture, mosaics, a photograph—laid out in rows or lists on the floor, an image of the beams being turned into firewood by the author, etc. The photographs seem to have been taken during a brief period of renovation of some kind; they were gathered in a box obviously made by the author out of the remains of a milk carton.

The following two "pieces" are another part of the effort to leave some sort of visual record of the conditions in which Luca Borrello lived during his final years and, in general, throughout his entire life. The first, also stored in a box, brings together plans of different homes and rooms of various sizes, mostly small; then there are maps of the cities of Milan, Sansepolcro, and Perugia, and of northern Piedmont, and then some notes by the author indicating that the plans are of houses he's lived in over the course of his life: the author tells his reader where each house is found—hence the maps—and adds a few words about his life there. The second piece consists of the mechanical superimposition of the city maps so that, as possibly is the case in the author's memory, they make one single city. In an attached piece, the maps of the houses have been put together to make one sole, large property, which would be the "only" house in which its author lived throughout his life, divided over various cities. (Which could be a reflection about the relationships between space and memory, or space and presence, or something else.)

Some photographs gathered in a box with the title "Rustic Nature": a city skyline, a mountainous landscape, a house, the paths of a botanical garden, a car, etc. According to the corresponding note, they all depict the contents of a novel entitled "The Narrathon" [*sic*]; however, the images don't represent parts of the plot, rather they are metaphors: in a pretty confused way—in the opinion of this writer—Borrello maintains that the city represented in one of the photographs, the mountainous landscape of another, the house, the paths of the botanical garden, the car, are not "part of" the novel, but the novel itself. To prove it, the author suggests a quick summary of the book, which includes an inland expedition on horseback in an unnamed country at some point in the nineteenth century, the playing of sound documents with political messages, an English linguist who lies dying in a room, the monologue of a young man who narrates all the stories of that unnamed country, some confusion, an accident, etc. Despite that, it's impossible to determine how the novel's plot fits with the gathered images, either individually or as a group. Borrello doesn't expound on this in the author's note but he does go into detail about the idea, formulated as a justification and perhaps apology, that this and other pieces of his shouldn't be considered experimental but rather avant-garde, by which the author must have meant that his intention was not only to put forth new, rarely used narrative forms but also to "rewrite the text in life"; in other words, create a total fusion between art and life as part of the avant-garde and, more specifically, Futurism. Besides that, and as the author indicates, the work's title comes from the poem—it's immaterial whether it was written by Borrello himself or someone anonymous—"Rustic nature / whence words die / and music / is born." Once again, what relationship music has to the novel "The Narrathon" is not specified by the author.

"Vita," a piece that consists of the life story, birth through death, of a young man named "Giuseppe Bicchiere" [*sic*], who was born in 1901 and died in 1918 in one of the last actions of the Great War. The story is told through a succession of advertisements, obituaries, and news items and without the author's apparent intervention, though we shouldn't rule out the possibility that he was the one who published the texts in the newspaper in the first place in order to be able to present a coherent story that way.

A book composed of nine strips of paper folded in such a way that they make up the phrase "Escape from." When they are unfolded, we discover other phrases on the back of each one. In this order, the phrases are "Escape from the light," "Escape from death," "Escape from life," "Escape from yourself," "Escape from irony,"

"Escape from your friends," and "Escape from the possibility of escape."

A map of Perugia's city center circa 1934 in which the street names are replaced by crosses that represent the number of dead that should be attributed to the historic person or event the street is named for. In a note on the back of the map the author explains that only the red crosses represent a single death; the rest follow this progression: a blue cross represents ten deaths; a green one, a hundred; a yellow one, a thousand; a black one, ten thousand. Ulisse Rocchi Street, for example, has only two red crosses, for the suicide in 1905 of a couple of medical students, who threw themselves off the top of the polemic aqueduct built during R.'s mayorship of the city; Francesco Guardabassi Street has only one, which marks his death sentence given in absentia in June 1859 for his participation in the so-called provisional government of Perugia that year; but the Biordo Michelotti Square has three yellow crosses—the author doesn't reveal his sources for attributing three thousand deaths to the famous condottiero, though the figure likely isn't at all exaggerated—and a red cross denoting Michelotti himself, murdered in 1938 by order of his rival Francesco Guidalotti. The note specifies that if the map had included the total number of deaths "behind" the events and characters honored by the city of Perugia, there would have been such a proliferation of crosses as to be illegible. This map is the first of a series produced by B. between 1934 and 1945; the series is made up of subseries.

A succession of plates entitled "Self-Portrait" that show summaries of statistics and physical data. B.'s "self-portraits" include a chart with the physical description of a whale—the weight of its heart, lungs, liver, eyes, etc; the weather report for the Italian town of Bordighera for the week of February 8 to 15, 1941; and the technical details of a Junkers Ju 52 plane. The last piece in the series, which seems to have been added later, consists of a test for *Mycobacterium tuberculosis,* or TB, for the Italian writer Luca Borrello; while the information is real—blood and lung tests, etc.—and, in some sense, the realest data possible, it doesn't allow us to form an idea of who B. was, of course, though it does allow us to infer that the breakdown of the concepts of author, book, linearity, and reading in these pieces matches, due to his illness, the decomposition of B. himself.

A map of the city of Perugia in which the author, with the help of an eraser, a scraper, and some white paint, has obliterated all references, leaving only the houses where he lived, his friends' houses, and the places he frequented during the years he spent in the city. A series of notes on the back of the "piece" contain descriptions of this, including a general description of the project, designated as "emotional cartography," though it could also be called "a solipsism" as all that remains of Perugia is merely what's significant to a single one of its inhabitants, the author. On the other hand, the writer of this text feels obliged to correct him when he maintains that a deer head hung on one of the walls of the Osteria Santucci, with a Juventus F.C. scarf draped over its antlers by a fan during the celebration of that team's 1930 championship win: it wasn't a deer's head but a boar's, and it wasn't Juventus F.C. that won the Serie A Championship that year but the Società Sportiva Ambrosiana, also known as the Internazionale, and therefore it wasn't a Juventus fan who draped the scarf but rather an Internazionale fan and it wasn't on the nonexistent antlers of the boar but rather off one of his tusks.

Twenty-two maps of different cities—including Paris, Berlin, Rome, London, New York, Madrid, etc.—on which the same route is traced, longer or shorter depending on the map's scale. According to the author's note the original route was three kilometers long and these versions should strictly follow the author's indications, straying only when there is an obstacle and returning to the path as soon as possible. The route looks like a scar; though the author doesn't say it, this writer can confidently assert that the itinerary is the same as the one from Luca Borrello's house in Perugia to the house of a completely forgotten author named Romano Cataldi. Borrello was his friend and, circumstantially, his executor.

The manuscript of an essay or novel entitled "The Expunged Book," which, after a title page with Luca Borrello's name, includes only blank pages, followed by an index. The index, however, is crammed with completely unconnected names and subjects, and doesn't give an inkling of the content of the work, not even its genre.

A piece entitled "Maps of a Cemetery," which consists of a map of Italy left out in the sun, almost completely faded, making it impossible to discern borders or even major cities, which have been practically erased from this map and others.

Twenty-six copies of a poem entitled "The Sleepwalker," with the main text obliterated; numbered and signed by the author.

A box containing twelve photographs printed in a volume with die-cut pages that enable the photographs to be removed. The images turn out to be fragments of a larger image, which you realize only if you tear out the pages, which inevitably means destroying the book. Despite that, the box includes a metal wire and instructions stating that the photographs should be ripped out and exposed to the sun, which indicates that the author's original intention was exactly that, the destruction of the work—despite which, and as the note states, the destruction and transformation of the work into what seems to have been designed as a pendant doesn't detract from the work being considered, in spite of everything, a book. The text accompanying the images is a reflection on the immanent nature of the work despite its destruction, a recurring theme in Borrello's oeuvre.

Then, a folder containing eight images of buildings constructed during the fascist regime: the Casa del Fascio in Como; the Victory Monument in Bolzano (South Tyrol); and the Stadio dei Marmi, Palazzo dei Congressi, and Palazzo della Civiltà Italiana, all in Rome. The photographs seem to be part of a set of postcards commercially printed with the implicit objective of popularizing these buildings, and the explicit objective of serving as postcards. They have been scratched with some sharp object, possibly an awl or a pen nib without ink, making the buildings look as if they are in ruins: the statues surrounding the Stadio dei Marmi's track look mutilated; the columns of the Palazzo dei Congressi have fallen, as has part of the roof; the balconies of the Palazzo della Civiltà Italiana have also given way; the Victory who presides over the monument bearing her name in Bolzano has lost her wings and the inscription at her feet has been mutilated, leaving only the phrase "Hic patriae multas siste signa" with no reference to language, law, or culture any longer; the Casa del Fascio in Como has collapsed in the middle, splitting into unequal halves. He must have scratched the margins of some of the images in an attempt to make the buildings look overgrown with vegetation, though it's impossible to see what sort of vegetation, whether native to the Italian peninsula or some invasive foreign species. That depends in part on your interpretation of the images, which must have been created around 1944 at the earliest, as one of them—the photo of the Casa del Fascio—is decorated with swastikas, whose presence in Italy was relatively rare before that date. In most of the images the people who appear in front of or near those buildings—who seem unaware they are being photographed—have been left unscathed, but in a couple the people, not the buildings, have been scratched to the point of almost disappearing. One of those shows a mother and child; the arm that unites them has been erased.

(The ruins seem to be the result not of an unexpected event, but rather of years of neglect; if there's an accident here, in the piece, it is political: corruption, apathy, arrogance, etc.)

A series of *gialli* thrillers published by Arnoldo Mondadori, and amended by the Borrello. This "piece" seems to reveal a crisis of some sort in Borrello's political ideas. In the first, a translation of *Sad Cypress* by Agatha Christie, the lines have been hand numbered; the author's note, inserted on the book's final pages, consists of only a series of numbers—I quote the beginning: "74, 11, 67, 70, 12, 22, 40," etc.—which is disconcerting at first but later explained when you return to the book, because the numbers correspond to the lines in the text that reveal the crime. (The same procedure appears in a second copy of the Agatha Christie book, in which the selected lines do not reveal the crime plot but rather read as a completely different work, primarily focused on a romantic relationship between Elinor Carlisle and Peter Lord.) A third *giallo, Over My Dead Body* by Rex Stout, has some pages torn out; inserted in their place is a small typed booklet with a list of words taken from the original work that, hypothetically, allow you to determine—this writer didn't bother—who the murderer in Stout's book is: "women," "diamonds," "adoption," "British," "sword," "especially," "glove," "chocolate ice cream" (?), etc. In the next *giallo, Il mistero di cinecittà* by Augusto De Angelis, every word in the text has been crossed out, except for those that make up—spread out over the entire book but distributed into two grammatically correct independent clauses—the sentence "The monkey ate my hand; the monkey devoured my grief," which serves as the title for this series of amended books. Something similar happens in the fifth *giallo* in the series, *The First Time He*

Died by Ethel Lina White, where all the words have been crossed out except for "horror," which appears fourteen times throughout the text.

(These pieces all reveal the author's passage from the figure of "creator" to that of "modifier," or director, or however you want to put it. This doesn't point in a specific direction, and possibly Luca Borrello himself doubted his path, as seen in some relapses visible in works done after the modified *gialli*. It does seem that, for one reason or another, Borrello no longer thought of himself as a writer; or, more generally, he no longer believed in literature as a "creative" activity. Despite that, almost all his found work has to do with literature, in one way or another. It is also a deeply political body of work, not so much for its adherence to the guidelines of Futurism—the trend that did the most to turn aesthetics into politics, by the way—but rather because the *gialli* had been banned by the Italian Social Republic in 1943: B.'s use of them seems to point to, as much as or more than the images of fascist buildings in ruins, his discontent or disappointment with fascism. There is no need to mention that if that discontent or disappointment were absolute, then Borrello wouldn't have attended the Fascist Writers' Conference in Pinerolo, though there are those who claim he did so precisely in order to demonstrate his opposition and even convince others to join him in his stance. The key, in some sense, is that—as the *gialli* show—around 1941, the publication date of a good part of the original titles, Luca Borrello (as a fascist writer and, generally, as a writer) no longer seemed interested in holding any stance, because the author was disappearing, emptying himself out, ceasing to occupy the places he'd occupied, whatever they were.)

A cardboard box containing seven postcards, of the following cities: Rome, Florence, Perugia, Naples, Turin, Trieste, and Milan. The postcards were sent from, respectively, Milan, Trieste, Turin,

Perugia, Naples, Florence, and Rome—in other words, the one of Rome from Milan, the one of Florence from Trieste, etc.—all including the phrase "out of place," which probably lends its name to the "piece." (In many of them, actually, there is a third dissonance; the text written on the postcard doesn't correspond to the image or the place it was postmarked. So, for example, the postcard of Milan mailed in Rome talks about a visit to Florence.) This box is the first of Borrello's works concerned with the customary use of mailed correspondence. The other, entitled simply "> ≠," is Borrello's only known concession to the proposal made by Marinetti, in his May 11, 1912, "Technical Manifesto of Futurist Literature" (i.e., "abolishing" punctuation and replacing it with "mathematical signs"): it consists of the same images mechanically reproduced on large pieces of paper, along with envelopes and stamps to mail them, but the papers are too big to fit inside the envelopes even when carefully folded and, as such, are useless.

Another *giallo*, in this case *L'uomo dal laccio* by Mario Datri; the copy is carefully tied up, making it impossible to read without cutting the threads: if that is done, of course, the "piece" no longer exists as such. The same is true of other works in the series—titled "The Banned Books Segment"—in which the content of the pieces is inaccessible. One piece consists, for example, of what seems to be a book carefully wrapped in newspaper; determining if it really is a book—and which one—would mean destroying the piece, which perhaps constitutes some sort of reflection on what a book is exactly, though one can only speculate on the reasons why Luca Borrello would have believed that reading a work destroys it. In another piece a book's cover, which corresponds to a translation of *The Wall* by Mary Roberts Rinehart, seems to have been torn off and replaced by pages from a different work, but the problem is the copy has been sewn in such a way that it cannot be read without cutting the threads; in that sense—and perhaps that's the meaning of the piece—the book is only its outer walls, in keeping with the title that appears on the cover.

A series of poems that are made of appropriated and reordered poems by Cipriano Efisio Oppo, Ugo Ojetti, Luigi Spazzapan, Renato Guttuso, Quinto Martini, and Orfeo Tamburi; all the poems were published in Mino Maccari's magazine *Il Selvaggio* prior to 1939, as the author indicates. In the endnote, Borrello maintains that he considers the original texts "defective" drafts of his own work, in which the authors of the poems would merely be involuntary bit players.

A short story entitled "The Perfect Goodbye," whose lines are glued to an envelope in such a way that they make up a rectangle several millimeters thick, almost a sculpture made of paper.

A variant on the prior idea, with the title "A Landscape of Events," consisting of the typed transcription of the title poem onto a single line, the verses superimposed to the point of illegibility, a mere inkblot.

A piece entitled "Incomprehension of the Machine," consisting of six typed, numbered, and signed pages. According to the author's note, it is a short story written circa 1938: the author has no other copy of it and it's not a manuscript, it's finished. Despite that, the "piece" only takes on meaning when it is dispersed, for which each of the pages has to be sold independently: each buyer acquires something unique, but also something incomplete that forms part of a coherent whole he cannot access. The sale of more than one of the pages to a single buyer is ruled out: the buyer, states Borrello, must be satisfied with a fragment of text in exchange for participating in the production and enjoyment of a work of art, because the incomplete nature of the piece—what Borrello calls "its 'open' nature"—and the possibility of reuniting the fragments, which the author rejects but accepts as a logical possibility, is what makes it a work of art. The note goes on for several paragraphs; although sometimes confusing, what can be inferred from it is the distinctiveness of this "hidden" work by Luca Borrello (which postdates his abandoning the Perugian literary scene and, therefore, his "disappearance" as an author): pieces that are neither originals nor copies, neither truth nor lies, that exist as separate entities but depend closely on their environment, their context, and occupy a space outside of the usual categories.

A small untitled volume made up of rejection letters from the publications *L'Impero, La Città Nuova,* and *Stile Futurista.* The letters' lines have been die-cut in such a way that each of them makes a flap that can be lifted, revealing the corresponding line of text on the following page. The "piece"—it isn't easy to define any other way, a problem that affects many works produced by Borrello after, for lack of a better word, this "tipping point" in his literary production; "literary" is also a problematic term when characterizing his work—is made up of five pages made up in turn by five paragraphs of five lines each, which offer six hundred and twenty-five possible readings. (The idea may be to demonstrate the interchangeable nature of critical judgment, or simply to mock those who rejected his writing: perhaps the piece has some other meaning. The work referenced here, entitled "The Start of Spring," has been lost, by the way.)

(If this last "piece" sums up the—childish—drama of the writer whose work is rejected, it is a more than appropriate ending to the trajectory Luca Borrello seems to have taken in his "hidden" work, occupying and later abandoning the functions of writer, modifier, editor, and finally audience of the work of art. This trajectory could also be described as a voyage to the kingdom of the dead and the difficult task of returning from there, though in this case the kingdom of the dead would be literature, or art; or as a transformation from fascist writer to antifascist writer, as seen in the visual pieces where buildings of the regime appear in ruins and the use of the *gialli,* and the later adoption of an "antiantifascist" writer stance (if that stance is fascist or not is a matter of debate). Less controversial, however, is another type of journey, which to this writer seems very eloquent: the transformation of the author into artwork, into his own work. Perhaps the kingdom of the dead, in the end, was the condition of being an author, and Borrello only lived through his final years in order to escape it.)

Milan

DECEMBER 2014

〉〉

What does it matter that this pure fire merely consumed itself. It sincerely wanted to be pure.

ANTONIN ARTAUD, "Surrealism and Revolution"

At first he listens to A/Political and then to the Edgar Broughton Band, to Kronstadt Uprising and Flux of Pink Indians; later he discovers the Mob, KUKL, the Poison Girls and Zounds and Atari Teenage Riot. It all happens quickly, like the music he prefers, deliberately crude but also direct and often violent, and he only adds to the speed with alcohol and sometimes drugs. He lives in Quarto Oggiaro, a neighborhood in northwest Milan, with his maternal grandfather, who for much of his life worked with a team of housepainters. He hasn't seen his mother in some time; in fact, he doesn't even know where she is now. Sometimes his mother sends him postcards of lofty and not always beautiful temples in India, Pakistan, or Tibet. At one point she also sent him some postcards from Thailand, during a trip she took with someone named "Richard," whom she sometimes calls "Rich" or "R" and other times "he," and the trip must have been rushed because the content of the postcards and the images on them didn't match up: on the back of an image of the Wat Chaiwatthanaram temple she wrote about her stay in Bangkok, on the back of a photo of the mountains in the Luang Prabang Range, about her visit to the temple, etc. It all seemed very typical of his mother, of his mother's indifference to formalities and, in general, toward others, including her son: she wasn't actually interested in sharing her impressions of her trip with him, and she didn't have time for things like geographic precision; the whole point was to maintain contact with her son but, at the same time, avoid the inconveniences that contact entailed. More than his mother's lack of interest in him, he was surprised by her desire to keep up the illusion of contact. He hadn't been an accident exactly, but more of an anchor for his mother at a moment when she hadn't yet decided whether to give in to her nature and leave, or to teach a lesson to herself and others by staying. His mother was on what she dubbed "a voyage of self-discovery"; he thought it unnecessary to move geographically when what you really wanted—or said you wanted—was to reach a greater "knowledge" of yourself. Perhaps that knowledge would in fact be easier to find when your object of study wasn't so distracted by mountain landscapes, beaches, and ancient temples, though it's possible your discovery—if that discovery is possible— would be boring if it took place in, let's say, Milan's metropolitan area, where his mother had grown up and which, after meeting his father and conceiving him, she'd abandoned when he was eleven years old. He had only seen her once since then, on a brief visit she made to Milan for some dental treatment when he was fourteen; due to the hygienic conditions and diet in India, his mother had lost many teeth, and seeing her that way made him hate her, as if her neglect had been directed at him and not, as was the case, against herself. That was still during the "Richard"—or "Rich" or "R" or "he"—period, but the man hadn't come with her; reading between the lines, it seemed to him that Richard and his mother wanted to have a child and for a few days he thought that child would be him. At the time he felt euphoric despite having no interest in India and not liking the idea of living with a stranger; two strangers if you include his mother. They lived in an ashram in some place whose name he couldn't remember, surviving on what they managed to pull out of the ground or buy off the peasants. Their "guru" was a man who made watches "appear" on the wrists of his followers, his mother said, but he wasn't as impressed by that as by the other things his mother told him on that visit: practically no one slept in the ashram, as maintaining it took many hours and the rest of their time was devoted to prayer; his mother drank her own urine and ate balls of mud and ash, which she said had purifying effects; some peasants had violently burst into the ashram one night and stolen the two squalid cows that had been providing them with milk; several women who had wandered away from the grounds out of curiosity had been raped by the locals without the authorities doing anything to prevent it or to even pretend they were trying to capture and punish the guilty men. It seemed clear that the world his mother lived in offered no time for the introspection that had brought her there; perhaps the only function of the ashram was to dissuade people, through physical torment and intellectual exhaustion, from the possibility of thinking about themselves; if that wasn't the case, if the objective of the ashram was, indeed, for those who lived there to "find" themselves, it was even more ridiculous, since obviously that life transformed people in such a way that they were incapable of remembering what they'd once been like and what they'd wanted to understand in the first place. He however was already drawn to the idea of being "someone else," and for a few days fantasized about the life he would have in India with "Richard" and his mother; despite which his mother left alone after her dental treatment, dashing his hopes: the last thing he remembers seeing in the airport was her perfect and therefore completely fake set of teeth. Then his mother again cast out the line of postcards and brief letters that linked her more and more tenuously to him, and he hadn't thought of her much in three years. "Richard," "Rich," or simply "R" disappeared from the correspondence shortly after his mother returned to India, but the personal pronoun "he" continued to show up, first designating some "Markus" and then a "Tobi"—a nephew of Richard, who had left the ashram the year before—and a Spaniard named "José Antonio," like all Spaniards of a certain age. At some point he understood that there were going to be other men and that he would bear witness to their time as part of his mother's life, until his mother got old and men stopped being so interested in her, or until his mother stopped writing to him. Their correspondence was one-sided, of course, and was, as a result, all he needed to understand his mother, to achieve that knowledge of herself she'd gone off to India to find. She was the only one writing, with self-detachment but also with no interest in what her son might have had to tell her: none of the letters ever included an address where he could write her back, and it had been some time since he'd stopped wanting to anyway.

He ended up meeting Richard some years later. One afternoon a man knocked on the apartment door and, when it was opened, hastily introduced himself. Richard was tall and blond, and had washed-out blue eyes that he thought looked the color of laundry detergent. Richard explained that T.'s mother had given him this address and that he'd come because he'd always wanted to meet him—he said "Tomas" though his name wasn't "Tomas" but "Tommasso." Richard, who he'd thought was American, was actually Austrian and had decided to Germanize his name. He asked him to wait a moment and, after grabbing a jacket and writing a note, left the house. They went to Villa Scheibler, a nearby park, where Richard had parked his car, he said. As they walked over there, T. realized he had nothing to say to this man. Richard, on the other hand, didn't stop talking: he told him he was on his way to Tuscany, where he was going to spend some vacation time with his family, that he'd abandoned the ashram two years earlier but not the beliefs that'd led him there, which he then summed up briefly. He asked T. if he believed in them too, but T. didn't answer. "Your mother didn't tell me much about you, you were always like a mystery between us," Richard said when they sat down in the park. Finding out that he was a mystery to someone seemed strange to T. and he silently weighed what that meant. Sometimes he had the impression that he was empty, and that everything that happened to him came to fill him up somehow: he only had to contemplate how the experiences formed him and imagine how he would be in the future, when free of his grandparents' watchful eye. Richard told him that he and his mother had talked on several occasions about bringing him to live with them in the ashram but that his mother had opposed it every time: as T. studied this childish man who could've become his father, in a life he was no longer going to have, he felt relief and something akin to gratitude toward her. The Richard he'd imagined was, naturally, much better than the one there before him, among other reasons because he was made up of the characteristics of many people, including the aspects he liked about his biological father, though his father worked in Africa for a human rights organization and T. didn't see him very often. But the real Richard had never belonged to what—for the last few years, since two planes crashed in New York—was now called a "terrorist organization," he hadn't been in prison; he hadn't studied while locked up; he wasn't in some African country doing whatever T.'s father was doing, often something T. found unimpressive. Richard wanted to know why his last name was German, and T. explained what he knew about his great-grandfather, about his grandfather who'd been a carpenter, and about his father, who was in Africa and had been in prison. Richard didn't know what to do with that information; after a long silence he told him he'd started importing fabrics from India and selling them to his friends in Feldkirch, which was a city, he said, that T. should visit someday; he could put him up, he added; and then said that his plan in the midterm was to build a company that took people to the ashrams in southern India; he said he'd already spoken with the guru of the ashram where T.'s mother was living, and been given a parcel of land where he could build some guesthouses for visitors, but he needed to convince more gurus and have more ashrams available if the business was going to be financially viable. Richard could see it right before his eyes, he said; but T. didn't see anything before his eyes, except a man he didn't really know. Although he already knew more than enough about Richard—unlike in the past, which T. now sorely regretted—to completely disqualify him as a mirror of T's desire for a father. Absurd as it may seem, T. was going to continue to be a mystery to him, he could see that, and the man would speculate many times over the course of his life about what could have been, but T. would never think of him again in the same way. Perhaps Richard realized that, because he stood up, ending the conversation; a woman and a teenager T.'s age had approached them. "Is this him?" the woman asked in English. Richard nodded, and then he, the woman, and the teenager stood there, staring at T., who didn't know what to do, not then and not later, when the woman and the teenager headed to a car on the edge of the park and

Richard said he was going with them. So he too left a son behind to go to the ashram, thought T. for a moment; he wondered how many children were currently paying the price for their parents' desire to find themselves, and he felt sorry for them all. He also didn't know what to do when Richard slid a twenty-euro bill into his hand and smiled. Richard said he could spend it on whatever he wanted, although it's unlikely that he'd have approved of T.'s decision, had he known what it was. The next day T. used that money to purchase a cassette by a band called Capitalist Casualties. He listened to it so many times that the tape ended up breaking: every time he did, he thought for a fleeting second of Richard, a father—only hypothetically, briefly, and to T.'s regret—selling saris to women in some Austrian city, selling incense that smelled of some promising exotic destination, but also turning his back on him and walking to a car, with a woman and a teenager who weren't—but could have been—T. and his mother, on their way to a family vacation in Tuscany, perhaps with the intention of fixing something, but what, and how.

T. lives next to the train tracks—the line from Milano Cadorna to Saronna, and from there to Varese—and because he's never lived anywhere else, he feels uncomfortable in places where the earth doesn't move beneath his feet at regular intervals. He hears the trains before he sees them and, if he's in the mood, he leans out his bedroom window to look. From there he can observe the passengers, almost always absorbed in reading some free newspaper or on their cell phones. Sometimes someone reads a book too, but the train moves at a speed that makes it impossible for him to make out the title or the author on the cover. For years, the neighborhood kids have fought over the spoils found on the tracks—newspapers, wrappers, matchboxes, cans, a porno mag, pages torn from books, things tossed out by passengers—but recently, the train car windows changed to ones that you can't open, and the pillaging on the tracks ended. Since then, his friends organize fights, generally with the Egyptians who are numerous in Quarto Oggiaro; he's taken part in a few but really isn't interested. Sometimes he still walks down the tracks searching for abandoned objects, but there's hardly anything. Once he saw a dead dog that'd been hit by the train: its hindquarters were fifty meters from its front half, which had been dragged, and what impressed him most was that the corpse looked almost as if it had been cut with a knife—the animal's internal organs were whole and in place inside the casing of flesh and bones that had been the dog, like in an anatomical chart. The placid expression on the animal's face also made an impression, as if the dog—which he'd seen before wandering around the neighborhood, an enormous black dog who couldn't stand others anywhere near him—had died peacefully. He was intrigued by the matter for some time; at thirteen years old he'd come up with a hypothesis to explain the bliss on the animal's face at the moment of its death: according to him, the dog had died before being hit by the train, of cardiac arrest, poisoning, or some other way; coincidentally it had happened as the animal was crossing the train tracks. The hypothesis satisfied him for some time—until he told his grandfather, who responded that T. must be mistaken. While he could, he regularly visited the dog's corpse, which no one had picked up, to check on its beatific expression, which, of course, he couldn't describe in those words. When T. knelt beside the animal, its expression seemed beatific; but as soon as he turned away he doubted what he'd seen just a moment earlier. The problem shifted, in some sense, and ceased to be about how the dog had died, or the nature of the expression on its face—of its "smile" as he might have put it—to become a problem of the reliability of his impressions. For as long as the corpse's stench allowed, he visited regularly, trying to obtain information about it through the study and observation of the place where it was found. He acted like those characters so common on television in those days, who resorted to elaborate, often incomprehensible reasoning to solve crimes that always seemed obvious to him from the start, and that were always resolved, inevitably, near the end of the thirty-five or forty minutes the episode lasted. Although this wasn't the case with the dog, whose calmness in the face of death perplexed him, and T. never found a good explanation for it. He even drew several sketches of the scene in order to study them more closely. When his grandmother found them one day while tidying his room, she was horrified, and he had to promise her he would destroy them, but he kept them, hidden inside a large wooden box his father had given him on his first visit from Africa, when he'd made the decision to settle there for an unspecified length of time. The box held papers; his father had told him they were the books of a great writer, but to him none of the pages seemed to be any sort of book. His father had acquired them shortly before being imprisoned and hadn't been able to access them until he was released; in all that time, he'd been obsessed with the papers; according to what he told his son, he'd thought of them day after day, wondering what to do with them, what fate to give them. Perhaps, when he finally left prison and could read them, he'd been disappointed by those papers, because he hadn't done anything with them, as far as his son knew. His father's life had been difficult after his release, he'd worked sporadically in factories and workshops over half of Italy until his employers found out about his past, one way or another, and fired him or invited him to continue in his position with new, not always acceptable, conditions. There were varying versions of that past: his father's, his maternal grandfather's, and the one T. had been forced to listen to, and repeat, in school; it seemed obvious to him, from the very beginning, that none of the versions was completely reliable, and that the truth must fall somewhere in between. He didn't think his father or his mother's father was lying, nor did he think his teachers were, not deliberately, but they had all been tricked by their senses, as he was in the case of the dog's corpse and its blissful expression. When his father had handed T. the box, he'd showed him his paternal grandfather's signature, which had been chiseled into one corner, but he hadn't known his paternal grandfather and the fact that he'd made the box didn't seem particularly relevant. One day T. went back to inspect the dog's corpse and found it was no longer there: someone had taken it the night before, leaving only two stains of blood, grease, and hair where its hindquarters and front half were found. The stains would disappear shortly after, one more chapter in the story of the detritus the train left in its wake, which the adoption of new hermetic cars would put an end to, hindering children from the outskirts like him from accessing—even in that partial, parasitic way—knowledge of the lives of the inhabitants of the city's center, what they did and what they left behind. But the sketches he'd made remained in the box for some time. Whoever had taken away the corpse had kept it from decomposing and becoming part of the earth, which is what T. found, in some sense, to be the most natural and appropriate course. As that didn't happen, the dog's death had remained incomplete in his view. Then his grandmother got sick and died, and he destroyed the drawings, blaming himself, unfairly, for having been the one to bring death into the house where she, and they, lived.

T. envies his mother, among other things, for the fact that she believes things happen for a reason, which is the same as saying they exist in an orderly and therefore reasonable way. Her conviction that life is made up of cycles, that you can exert some sort of influence over them, in such a way that those cycles rise or descend, must interject some order into a life that would, otherwise, and as seems obvious to him, lack any. Just like most people who listen to the fast, anarchic music he likes, he yearns deeply for some order in his life, and for things to happen slowly enough for them to be comprehensible. Perhaps his father has a similar yearning, as the periods of his life seem to have unfolded in open opposition to each other; but it's also possible that in Africa—which strikes T. as a chaotic, violent place, based on the books his father has given him and the documentaries he's seen on television—he has found some type of order, or a less hazardous type of disorder than what appears to have ruled over his prior existence. His father has always seemed afflicted, and T. sometimes wonders if that affliction is a product of his time in prison and his conviction that he's guilty, though not of what he was accused of. Perhaps his father was different at some point, he thinks, but only because T. can't know that what he—if he could—would call affliction is a characteristic of every man in his family, all of whom have had to compare their convictions to the results of their actions. They have all, traveling along different paths, arrived at the certainty that you can only act blindly, equipped with a fistful of certainties that make it possible to believe in the legitimacy of your actions; when those certainties come crashing down, inaction results. The men in T.'s family have never been good at talking, paralyzed by their lack of certainty; however, he does sense something, because some years back, when he was seven years old, he was tricked, he fell into some sort of a trap. A schoolmate a few years older than T. convinced him to break into the school at night to wreck the geography classroom. It was revenge for them both: the teacher didn't like this boy, whom he considered dangerous; and T.'s grades in the subject were, as was to be expected of a child who had both parents snatched away by geography, very bad. His older schoolmate had already perpetrated a few minor actions, not very cleverly setting himself up: he'd destroyed a globe during recess; he'd lit a map on fire with a lighter shortly before class started; he'd stolen others, etc. Now he'd discovered that the school's night watchman abandoned his post around eleven, leaving only a few lights on to dissuade would-be intruders; if he and T. went in through the bathroom windows, they'd have the school to themselves to do whatever they wanted. If they wrecked the geography room, the teacher would quit, said the older boy. T. had never done anything remotely like this, and his interest in punishing the teacher was limited: his interest in his schoolmate wasn't, however, though it would take T. some years to understand it and a few more to accept it. What he'd felt for that schoolmate was sexual desire, a desire he would feel again for other men and some women throughout his life. In their nocturnal penetration of the school, in the execution of an illicit act with him, there was a sublimation of that desire, he would realize years later. And yet, as plausible as this theory seems, and as obvious, he would be wrong, at least partially, because the transgression was directed as much against the prohibition that men love men as against the paralysis and indecisiveness that was, without him having even an inkling, the only link between him and his father and his paternal grandfather. Despite knowing little or nothing about those two men, he wanted to distance himself as much as possible from them. T. and his schoolmate met up beside the train tracks, like two runaways, and went from there to the school, where the other boy leaned against the wall and interlaced his hands like a stirrup so T. could reach one of the windows and enter the building. When he had, they'd agreed, T. would extend his arms and pull the other boy up. The school was silent and only a few lights were on, just as the boy had said. When T. was pushed toward the window, he'd felt a pleasure unlike any he'd felt before, mixed with fear, the tension in his hands as he grasped the window frame, the scent of the other boy and of urine, which came up from the bathrooms. Once T. was through the window, he turned to settle with his legs hanging inside the building and his arms extending out, waiting for the other boy to grasp them. But when T. turned he discovered that the other boy had left. The lights came on behind him: the night watchman and the school principal were waiting for him in the bathroom. A few minutes later the older boy would join them, to reaffirm his version: T. was the one responsible for the prior acts of vandalism, as he had already told them when, in collusion with the principal, they'd decided to set a trap for T.

Some time later T. had run into that old schoolmate of his, who was still a student at the school he'd been expelled from, and also lived in Quarto Oggiaro. When he saw T., the other boy had tensed up, as if he feared that T.—shorter than him, a few years younger, as well as considerably weaker—wanted to punch him. But T. didn't punch him: he asked him, in a frail voice, why he'd done it, even though that seemed obvious. "It's a lesson; you won't forget it," the other boy had answered. Indeed, he had never forgotten it.

Before he stopped thinking about it, for years T. was convinced that death had entered his home through him and his drawings of the dog; perhaps, simply, that was the case. Some weeks after his grandmother found the drawings and demanded he destroy them, she got sick. She would cough, particularly at night: a cough that traveled violently up her throat, as if an animal had burrowed inside her and was just awakening from a long winter, making its way through her. The woman wheezed in a persistent panting that could be heard throughout the house. It was the flu, she said: she had grown up in the countryside, and would draw on the knowledge she'd accumulated there, about plants and infusions, as if returning to knowledge gained in her childhood and young adult years was an efficient way to return to the health she'd had then. T. had been cured by his grandmother on numerous occasions with plants she'd foraged and then taught him how to gather in the empty spaces between the buildings in Quarto Oggiaro and along the train tracks; however, it wasn't always possible to find the plants she needed, which only grew in the south or no longer existed. The woman went to the hospital twice; on both occasions, the doctors kept her at arm's length, the consultations were brief, the diagnosis was wrong. For a while it all seemed to T. a catastrophe, though a personal catastrophe, limited to him and his grandparents, the minimal unit the three of them had formed in the wake of his father's confusion and his mother's abandonment. She was in India, immersed in herself—a self the conditions of life in India were inevitably destined to change, or dissolve, until there was nothing left, no trace of her former self to search for and find, except the awareness of the search, completely befuddled by disease and hunger. T. finally understood, however, that the catastrophe didn't only affect the three of them, and that it wasn't a catastrophe: the family was poor; his grandmother hadn't been able to go to school; she'd been reduced by circumstances to being a housewife, which wasn't in and of itself a contemptible condition but did, inevitably, hold her back. T.'s grandfather had had to support the family with manual labor that left him exhausted: like most Italians, he had been fascist at some point or another and then gave it up, at least publicly. On one occasion, T.'s father told T. that he'd belonged to an organization that suggested putting an end to fascism, but T. knew, from his grandfather, that that wasn't exactly the case because, actually, ending fascism was impossible if there were still fascists, including people like his grandfather. The matter was more complex, naturally, and it doesn't now seem to T. that it could be simplified the way his father had simplified it, or how his friends saw it, as a confrontation between fascists and anti-fascists: the struggle was between the rich and the poor, between a system that served the former and exploited the latter, and the always delayed promise of a different system, which no one could imagine. Of course, his whole family belonged in the second group, and death had entered that family through his drawings of the dead dog but also through the doctors' mistaken diagnoses, dispensed with shocking indifference even in the face of their own fallibility. Recently, T. can't help but think: if his family weren't poor, if education and money hadn't eluded them over so many generations, his grandmother would still be alive, protected by the privileges they'd accumulated and by the general terror at the thought—the mere thought—of wealthy people dying. Because his grandmother wasn't wealthy—and neither was he nor his father, nor his grandfather— she had been treated with the indifference addressed to the poor, with a diagnosis that strove to prolong her life while it was useful, but which was shrouded behind certain facts—the difficult working conditions in hospitals, the cost of medications, the inability of less educated patients to adequately explain their symptoms, the excess of patients, etc. (all of which were true but didn't interest T., absorbed as he still was in the pain of his loss)—in order to justify the death of those less fortunate basically when their productive lives ended. Unnecessarily protracting life—which posed an interesting dilemma on the need for life, which T. didn't know how to get his brain around—was very costly. In Italy and everywhere, it was forcing the government to close schools, museums, and libraries; reduce hospital staff; raise taxes; and cooperate with corrupt and spurious governments in order to guarantee access to natural resources without which the entire system would fall apart. T. found the situation comparable to something his father once told him: that in "his" era young men had no possibilities, that everything was in the hands of old men and former fascists; in the end his generation had made off with those possibilities, though not in the way he'd thought, and everything was in their hands, he said, but now they were the old men. It had all been a terrifying joke, a slow, painful replacement ceremony in which they relinquished their bodies as vessels for the old ideas and precepts they'd fought so fiercely. When the ceremony ended, they were their own enemies, and the enemies of the young. "If the young were intelligent, they'd kill us old guys before we offered them our ideas in exchange for their bodies," he had said. It scared T. to hear it, knowing his father was right. This era's problems stem from the artificial prolongation of life, he thought; what was needed was a replacement that didn't become what it was replacing. Along a winding road he'd discovered the music that best embodied those ideas and he found the people who listened to that music, even though their ideas didn't always seem intelligent. His father didn't like those friends or that music, of course. T. had started listening to it shortly after his grandmother's death, following several weeks in the hospital, wasting away and walking blindly. She never had the flu, as they'd told her; a cancer had climbed from her pancreas to her lungs, slinking silently through her, taking advantage of the doctor's indifference, and her pancreas had been devoured by those things that devour the pancreas: overwork, poor diet, struggle, life on the margins of everything, including one's self. T. likes to believe and tell himself that he was able to "say goodbye" to her, but the truth is that their last conversation was trivial, like always: if there was some deep feeling inside her—the sense of an ending, for lack of better words—he wasn't able to perceive it and most likely she couldn't either.

Shortly after they confirmed the old woman's death, the doctors made T. and his grandfather leave the room; they needed the bed for someone else, they said. They carried his grandmother out under a blanket to someplace he and his grandfather weren't allowed to enter, and he had to cry in the hallway, in front of everyone, including a family entering what had been his grandmother's room behind a similar woman, intubated, convinced like them—like T. and his grandfather had been—that it was nothing serious. Then a nurse had come over and handed them a garbage bag: it contained his grandmother's medicines, some dried flowers, and a book T. had been reading. The book was about a family that had overcome all their difficulties. T. tossed everything into the trash when he left the hospital.

At first his grandfather refused to leave the house, just wandered around as if in each room he might, somehow, find his dead wife; later, however, and without any change in the situation, at least none T. could perceive, his grandfather began to spend more and more time out of the house: when he came back, he always brought something with him, which he would place in piles that soon reached T.'s height and then his grandfather's and finally were bigger than both of them. The old man would go out onto the street and come back with old magazines, newspapers abandoned at bus stops, shoes, screws, books, and bits of books, used clothing, bottles, signs, animal cages, a fish tank, useless broom handles and rags, pieces of rubber, boxes, a taxidermied shrew that had been partially eaten by insects, bags, chairs, broken toys, a supermarket cart that he'd bought from an Ethiopian family. He used the cart fairly regularly on his excursions; in his mind, he would say, he was setting up a business; sometimes he would talk about the fact that there were "better objects" in other places, in parts of the city that weren't as poor as Quarto Oggiaro: if he had a small van, he would say, he could extend his excursions to the city center, which he imagined as a place—thought T.—with more and better old magazines, newspapers, shoes, screws, bottles. Sometimes he returned battered and T. had to attend to his wounds; he had fought with a band of Romanian scavengers, he would say, who'd invaded his "territory." T. tried to dissuade him from continuing to go out on these excursions, but his grandfather insisted that it was a business with endless possibilities, though he never made any effort to sell what he'd gathered. He lost many of his teeth in those fights and on at least two occasions T. had to go through the neighborhood at night to pick him up and take him home to dress his wounds; on another occasion, two young men who were beating up his grandfather in a park, claiming he'd insulted them, laid into T. when he tried to defend him. Of all that, he only remembers sliding through the young men's arms, a completely painless slipping to the ground in which pain protected him from pain, and later the difficult return home carrying the old man. Around that same time, T. had started to listen to A/Political and Kronstadt Uprising: a dozen young squatters had been kicked out of a building in Cimitero Monumentale and had ended up in an abandoned factory between Quarto Oggiaro and Vialba. Naturally, T. had found out about that from his grandfather, who maintained that the squatters were trying to horn in on the objects he gathered in his territory, which he considered his property, even though it was clear, as was said around the neighborhood, that the squatters never left the house. One night T. dropped in and felt immediately attracted to the offhand chaos, which evoked his grandfather's apartment yet lacked its implications, where the loss of his grandmother was projected onto the accumulation and chaos. He was soon spending more time there than in his own home, where it didn't seem his grandfather was spending much time anymore either. T. was impressed by the speed with which he'd been accepted into the squat house and how quickly time passed there despite it being obvious that none of them did much; he was also impressed how quickly his grandmother's death and his grandfather's delusional accumulation took up less and less space in his life, as if they were missteps in a territory he was quickly moving away from. For the first time, he understood his mother, though their reasons for turning their backs on the past were diametrically opposed: for his mother, it was a voyage "in search of herself"; for him, on the other hand, it was a flight from himself, or from what he'd been up to that point. He took part in the repairs of the building, which were constant, as if the squat swallowed up each new repair; they let him sleep on the mattresses they'd laid out in the basement, next to the old boiler, which they fed with pieces of wood and cardboard they found on the street, in open competition with his grandfather. T. went to visit him sometimes, at night, and one day he discovered his electricity had been cut off. His grandfather gave him a flashlight, and he had to use it to light his path to his room through the piles of objects; when he lay down in bed he understood that his grandfather had created a labyrinth he would never find his way out of, no matter how hard he tried.

When T.'s father learned, on his next visit, of T.'s grandmother's death, he offered to go with him to the cemetery where they'd buried her, but it seemed unnecessary. His father wasn't aware of T.'s grandfather's situation and T. didn't want to alarm him. Nor did T. think it necessary to inform him that he no longer went to school. He had plans to go to university, at some point, but he still didn't know exactly what he would study. Admitting that he'd already read the book his father brought him as a gift also seemed unnecessary. T. had no desire to talk about himself, but he wanted to know everything about his father. Initially, his request was met with suspicion but then his father acquiesced and, finally and for the first time, spoke at length.

There were some versions of the story of T.'s father and what led him to prison that T. had put together as soon as he could, with his father already far away. His father had been part of an organization that had believed it necessary to respond violently to another type of violence that could be called, as he said, "structural." On March 16, 1978, that organization kidnapped a very important politician on Via Fani, in Rome, after killing his five bodyguards. His father had been told in Turin that something big was in the works and that, as a result, everyone not involved in the action should remain far from the scene, but no one had told him that the scene was Rome, though they'd suggested he not go to that city: nevertheless, his father was there. He was arrested that same day. Initially his father believed an old fascist writer (he said, with perhaps excessive emphasis on the word "old"), whom he'd been talking to and in whose doorway he was captured, had ratted him out. But it was, mainly, random chance, as his arrest had no relationship to the investigation going on and was just one of the many desperate acts carried out by the government that day in order to find the kidnapped politician. His father was interrogated for hours about "Maurizio," "Luigi," and "Monica," three names he was unfamiliar with, and they demanded he confess the whereabouts of Aldo Moro, which he didn't know. His father didn't say this, but years later T. will think they tortured him; if that was the case, the interrogation likely didn't aid the investigation in the slightest, because his father had truly not taken part in the kidnapping of Aldo Moro, whose lifeless body was found on May 9. In the months following, T.'s father was paraded through jails in Asinara, Sardinia, Turin, Voghera, and Bologna, almost always housed in the blocks for political prisoners, where the security measures were greater but, on the other hand, he was safe. On one occasion his father had recognized "Mauro," his superior in Turin, in a newspaper: his real name was Patrizio Peci, and soon after that he would give up his comrades, including T.'s father. By that time, however, his father had already been sentenced to eight years in prison: he did four before being released for good behavior. He didn't remember anything about them, he said, maybe because the adoption of an imposed routine was designed, successfully, to suspend individual life; if you didn't want to go crazy, said T.'s father, you had to mostly forget about yourself, cease to exist, so that your time locked up would be just a parenthesis. He had pulled that off, at least partially, though all those years he'd wondered who could've ratted him out, and how they'd found him. Despite that, the answer was obvious, so simple and easy to determine that he didn't understand how it hadn't occurred to him before: he had been betrayed by a man T. didn't know, he said, a different fascist writer he'd visited in Genoa a few days earlier, who'd given him the address of the fascist writer whose house he'd been arrested in front of shortly after. There wasn't a single day after that—not even when he was falling in love with T.'s mother and making his first efforts to keep her by his side and try to be a father for T.—when he hadn't thought about it: that his arrest had been simply a twist of fate, that he wasn't their target. Perhaps it all could have been different if he hadn't gotten caught up in a strange investigation—

incomprehensible even to him—into art and crime. Not even he could reliably express what it was he'd been searching for.

He listens to Blackbird Raum, the Hope Bombs, Culture Shock. Sometimes he gets the songs' lyrics and sometimes he doesn't, but he understands their underlying anguish; on occasions it seems that, despite their brevity, those songs make up a dark, violent tunnel at the end of which, however, he sees something like a light; in other words, a different sort of darkness. He doesn't know who to tell this to and he keeps it to himself. With the other squatters he talks only about music, and he pretends not to be interested in their political discussions: he doesn't have any expectations of those discussions and he doesn't like the invitation to violence they often conclude with. He doesn't think he knows more than the others, but he knows—from his father's experience, what he can understand of it—that if someone suffers, we all suffer; if someone kills, we are all murderers. He also knows, of course, that anything else they could do is worthless because freedom and justice are never given to the oppressed by an unjust government; he knows the oppressed have to fight for them, but even still he resists. Sometimes he looks at a poster for the Red Brigades that someone has put up on a wall, expressing a sympathy that everyone in the house shares. But he doesn't speak about his father's experience and he never listens. For a while he thinks he's in love with a young man from Viareggio who moves into the house for a while; they make love one night out on one of the factory's terraces, in the summertime; he goes with the flow and likes what he sees and does, but he decides that he isn't in love and isn't going to be. Later that young man, who is also named Pietro, like his father, leaves.

Now it is December 2014, the twelfth of the month, and the unions have called for a general strike: they are demanding the government not make firing people any cheaper. T. left the squat early that morning and headed to the city center to join the protesters. He only did so out of some vague sense of solidarity perhaps tied to the fact that his father and grandfather had been fired countless times throughout his life, under circumstances in which, unlike how he usually portrays it to the other squatters, their work was the only available way for them to be something or someone: when they couldn't continue doing it, their certainties about themselves, the identities they'd articulated around that work, vanished, leaving them empty. His father at least had his history, though it was incomplete because of his prison experience and perhaps other reasons, perhaps something analogous to regret. His grandfather had nothing except his confusion and the impossibility of conveying rationally, of verbalizing, what was happening to him; in the end, he'd only been able to express it through the accumulation of objects that, like he himself, had been cast off. T. had had to let him go, to distance himself, in order to not get dragged along. T. had also had to distance himself from his mother; he hadn't given her the address of the house, which, in any case, was temporary, and it was possible that, if his mother was still writing him, the letters were piling up in his grandparents' apartment or being returned by the postman. As the demonstration advanced through the streets of Milan, T. struggled to get caught up in the general enthusiasm, or even feel a part of the crowd: in some sense, the experiences of his father and his grandparents, to the extent he'd been able to know them, had taught him not to expect anything of others and to distrust ideas that enjoyed prominence; on the other hand, he believed he'd escaped from whatever bound him to a place and a time period. In some sense, he was clean, he thought, absorbed in the novelty of his individuality and only willing to lend it out—to drown his individuality in the river of people around him—briefly and conditionally. Around him swirled young people like him who carried flags he was unfamiliar with, and older people and senior citizens, men and women, who bore the insignias of their professions. Those were, of course, just symbolic, since most contemporary professions lack visibility and consist of the completion of procedures that are impossible to denote, actions done in front of a computer, in an aseptic, ahistorical space. T. could also see in that, if he so desired, a dissolution of the identity markers of the working class, if words like "working," "class," or "identity" meant anything to him: they would eventually mean something to him, including in a way that was hard to pinpoint, over the coming years, but T. doesn't yet know that. Nor does he know that his life will be more similar to his father's and his paternal grandfather's than he can imagine, as if the three were linked by something more than blood ties and family history, by an uncomfortable awareness of history and the place of individuals (even those who, like them, are completely irrelevant) within it. The marching stops, the people around him are no longer shouting slogans, and now, instead, the crowd issues a more frightening sound, loud and unclear, like some sort of roar that emerges from every throat and none, speaking in an incomprehensible language. T. hears shots and sees hundreds of pigeons take flight from the balconies and roofs of the buildings the crowd marches past, creating a dark cloud that looks alive and heads toward the Duomo, some hundred yards away. Then there is a moment of expectant silence and the crowd—which until now was some sort of living organism slithering through the streets—fractures: those in the front start backing up while those in the rear, who still don't understand what's going on, push them forward. The crowd, like a river when you try to contain it, overflows, and the currents that make it up, which up until now had converged, break into rows of people who, with more or less urgency, try to access the side streets, or search for refuge in the doorways of buildings lining the main street, or move along it toward the services and equipment. In the confusion, T. can't see beyond the relatively small circle he finds himself in: around him are the faces of older people, of women, people of various ages muttering and occasionally yelling that they have to go back. T., however, finds himself dragged forward by a row of young people who are making their way in a wedge through the protesters; their faces are covered with bandannas and their hair by black hoods and—T. sees it immediately—they're carrying sticks and shields and shouting "Come on, let's go" as if he were one of them. T. tries to get away, but the people fleeing the front of the demonstration keep pushing him back; in the air is something that T. recognizes immediately, and it's fear. Someone hands him a bandanna, and T. covers his face with it. Soon the river of people swimming upstream stops: he is in the front row, some ten or fifteen yards from a line of police shields; the policemen are also provoking them from behind. Someone drags a dumpster and sets it aflame with a bottle of gasoline and a lighter. The row of shields opens and from it emerges a man who throws a tear-gas bomb at them and one of the young men picks it up and tosses it back behind the line of shields: this seems to be a signal, because then the police charge. T. sees them coming closer and sees that, absurdly, the young men in hoods are running to meet them, and then he sees one of those young men on the ground, bleeding. A policeman is stomping his boot on the young man's head and it bounces against the ground again and again, leaving a bloodstain that grows and grows without anyone doing anything to stop the policeman. In that moment, T. feels responsible for what he's seeing and also for not preventing it; and he feels, for the first time, that he is the fallen young man and the policeman, both at the same time. T. thinks what he's going to do will come back to haunt him and that the damage he inflicts, if he manages to cause any, will be first of all against himself, and not exactly against his beliefs (which aren't much and never will be: just a handful of vague ideas about dignity and a nebulous notion of what, for lack of a better name, because the word often seems devoid of meaning, he will call "justice" always very regretfully, because of the echoes of his father he will recognize in it long after his father is dead), but against the very idea of believing in something, which is in opposition, he will always think, with the idea of doing. His father and his grandfather, he will think in the future, remain trapped by the contradictions inherent in doing and believing, in large part due to the fact that believing equals doing in every case, a very specific type of doing that also inhibits all possibility of doing anything. He will also think, throughout his life, that the lives of all these people—about which he knows everything and at the same time nothing—could be told as the story of how art always becomes politics and how politics, no matter what stripe, becomes crime. And he will think that there is a purpose for people like him: to inhibit the criminal elements in politics and turn politics into something like art, an activity that says something significant about being here, whatever "here" means: the world or society. He will learn all this over the course of a life that, like all lives lived with the desire to be politically and emotionally alive, is not very long or very easy. Of course, his life won't be short on situations that, for lack of a better term, people will call "art" or "artistic production," nor will it lack what those same people and others like them call "crime." T. finds both expressions superfluous, to the extent that he thinks of everything he does and has ever done as politics—even if unwittingly—because all that requires is the attempt to be coherent, and to leave a mark, no matter how small. Sometime in the future he'll think of that demonstration in Milan in December 2014 as the start of something, something vague he won't bother trying to put a name to. Right now it would be impossible and unnecessary for him to name it; even the mere fact of thinking about it seems absurd. T. doesn't think about it, just as he doesn't think about the asymmetries of violence, or its real or imagined legitimacy. In fact, he isn't thinking about anything: he picks up a cane he finds at his feet and rushes toward the policeman.

Already much more difference between death and death than between life and death. Already space measurable on the whole only in terms of death.

INGER CHRISTENSEN, *IT*
(Translated by Susanna Nied)

Azari, Fedele (Pallanza, February 8, 1895–Milan, January 25, 1930). In 1919 he wrote the manifesto "Futurist Aerial Theater," and presented it at the Great National Futurist Exhibition in Milan, showering down the pamphlets from his plane. In addition to his talents as a painter and writer, A. was gifted in advertising and business—starting in 1923 he exported Italian-made planes and Futurist works. F. T. Marinetti named him the first national secretary of the movement in 1924 and put him in charge of organizing the conference that year. He is also author of the manifestos "Simultaneous Futurist Life" and "Toward a Society for the Protection of Machines."

Bilenchi, Romano (Colle di Val d'Elsa, November 9, 1909–Florence, November 18, 1989). At a very young age he joined the left-wing sectors of fascism and was a regular contributor to its main publications in the Florence area between 1930 and 1934 as a writer and journalist; the Spanish Civil War distanced him from fascism, however, and by 1940 he was already a dissident. Years earlier he had published his novel *Pisto's Life* in the journal *Il Selvaggio* (1931), followed by *The Conservatory of Saint Teresa* (1940), *Anna and Bruno and Other Stories* (1938), *My Cousin Andrea* (1943), and the trilogy The Impossible Years, made up of *Drought* (1941), *Misery* (1941), and *Ice* (1983). B. took part in the Italian Resistance movement and its offshoots, including the creation of the newspapers *Nazione del Popolo* and *Nuovo Corriere,* organs of the Tuscan National Liberation Committee and the Communist Party respectively; in both cases, and as happened to him with fascism, his intellectual independence and rigor caused him difficulties, and it is no surprise that his subject, more than childhood—about which he wrote extensively—was actually disappointment. B. never stopped correcting his books, in a process of constant reduction. Among the most important are *Chronicle of Meager Italy or the History of the Socialists of Colle* (1933), *The Factory Owner* (1935), *The Stalingrad Button* (1972, winner of the Premio Viareggio), and *Friends* (1976); in that last one, B. writes about his friendship with Elio Vittorini, Ottone Rosai, Mino Maccari, Leone Traverso, Ezra Pound, Eugenio Montale, and others.

Blunck, Hans Friedrich (Hamburg, September 3, 1888–Hamburg, April 24, 1961). He studied law at the Universities of Kiel and Heidelberg, where he was part of the *Burschenschaften,* the student organizations that would form the basis of the National Socialist institutions. He was an officer during World War I and later settled in Belgium, before fleeing to Holland to escape the authorities, who pursued him for his pan-Germanic activities. In 1920 he began publishing novels and stories characterized by their rejection of modernity, which placed him in the orbit of Nazi cultural politics. His texts inspired by Nordic and Germanic mythologies, his fables and his sagas, as well as his texts on the history of the Hanseatic League and his poems in Plattdeutsch, seem to have been written specifically to justify the existence of what we call "National Social-ist literature," and he became one of its most important civil ser-vants, though he didn't join the National Socialist Party of German Workers (NSDAP) until 1937. B. was vice president of the poetry sec-tion of the Prussian Academy of Arts, while H. Johst was president, and, later, he became president of the Reich Literature Chamber and of the office responsible for promoting German cultural poli-cies abroad, the Stiftung Deutsches Auslandswerk. While holding such important posts, and fulfilling them with frenetic activity, B. published ninety-seven books and a hundred-odd articles between 1933 and 1945 (primarily for the *Völkischer Beobachter,* the Nazi regime's most important press organ). In 1944, Joseph Goebbels and Adolf Hitler included B. on a list of authors who should not be deployed because they, and their work, were part of Germany's cul-tural patrimony and, as such, essential. Despite that, the authori-ties of the Soviet occupation considered him simply a beneficiary of Nazism, which allowed him to continue writing. In 1952 he published his memoirs *Pathless Times,* followed the next year by another volume entitled *Light in Restraint*: in them he downplayed his role in the Nazi years, of course.

Borrello, Luca (Sansepolcro, December 9, 1905–Rorà, April 21 or 22, 1945). He did not finish medical school at the University of Peru-gia. He published his first texts in *L'Impero,* a magazine founded by Mario Carli and Emilio Settimelli that had a more openly fas-cist bent than the other Futurist magazines he wrote for, such as *La Città Nuova* and *Stile Futurista.* In mid-1936, B. left Perugia and, it seems, held numerous jobs, none of them literary, in the Umbria and Piedmont regions. After it seemed he'd abandoned literature, B. attended the 1945 Fascist Writers' Conference in Pinerolo, where he met his end. To this day no one has been able to determine whether his death was an accident, suicide, or murder. It seems that he continued writing between 1936 and 1945, but his literary production from that period, if it ever existed, has been lost.

Boulenger, Jacques (Paris, September 27, 1879–Paris, November 22, 1944). Philologist, poet, and novelist—as well as the author of numerous anti-Semitic pamphlets that were much more popular in France than any of his books—of whom Hellmuth Langenbucher said, "He allows his wit and imagination to drag him along in order to capture on paper an entire world of plots for the enjoyment of his readers"; this praise—while profoundly stupid—is not the worst manifestation of the pompous, meaningless literary criticism that would become, decades later, the rule more than the exception. B.'s body of work includes *Monsieur or the Professor of Snobbery* (1923), *The Literary Tourist* and *The Mirror with Two Faces* (both from 1928), *Crime in Charonne* (1937), *Anywhere, On the Front: Images of the Present War* (1940), and *French Blood* (1943).

Boyano, Espartaco (Ravenna, February 14, 1916–Ravenna, January 12, 1994). Despite being from Ravenna, he studied in Perugia, where he was a contributor to Abelardo Castellani's *Lo Scarabeo d'Oro* and came into contact with a local Futurist group in 1931. In 1938 he met Tommaso Marinetti and asked him to write a prologue for his first book; Marinetti agreed. An attempt to account for his work in an era concerned only with numbers would look like this: books, 6; publication dates, 1938, 1941, 1952, 1960, 1970, and 1971; genres, 1 (poetry); average copies sold of each, 60; reviews of said works, 8; positive ones, 3; negative ones, 4; those indifferent to value judgments or aware that value judgment is, in essence, the least important aspect of a critical text, 1; academic essays on B.'s work, 2; appearances in dictionaries and critical studies of twentieth-century Italian poetry, 0; number of unpublished works that B. left at the time of his death, 1 (unfinished); total weight of B.'s personal papers (which his widow got rid of, with the help of one of their sons, immediately following his death), 11 kilograms; total weight of his poetic work, 960 grams; number of poems written, 234; estimated average time dedicated to each poem, 271.41 hours; approximate reading time of B.'s entire poetic works, 7 hours; people who attended the poet's funeral, 8 (widow, three children and two of their spouses, as well as a granddaughter and a neighbor); average number of annual visits to his grave since his death, 0.80.

Bruning, Henri (Amsterdam, July 10, 1900–Nijmegen, December 17, 1983). Poet, essayist, polemicist, and Nazi censor. Some of his opinions diverged from those of the Nazi authorities he worked for—B. came from Dutch Catholic Nationalism and was conservative and elitist—but only some. In 1943 he published *Prelude* and *The Holy Union,* and in 1944 *Ezekiel and Other Criminals* and *New Horizons;* prior to that he had published an essay entitled *New Political Consciousness* (1942), which requires no explanation as to why it was new in 1942 and what it was conscious of. At the end of World War II he was sentenced to two years and three months imprisonment and banned from publishing for ten years, after which he tried to establish himself again as a poet, unsuccessfully, due to a boycott by editors, writers, and booksellers. Now he is celebrated, almost exclusively, in Catholic circles.

Burte, Hermann (pseudonym of H. Strübe; Maulburg, February 15, 1879–Lörrach, March 21, 1960). B. was a painter and poet in Alemannic dialect, two activities that could have easily allowed him to escape the scrutiny of his contemporaries without having to renounce an ideology close to the German popular and national essences that later made him a beneficiary of Nazism. But B. published the novel *Wiltfeber, the Eternal German* (1912) and the tragedy *Katte* (1914). Had he not written them, the river of history would have passed him by without dampening his shoes, but he did write them, and they were successful, earning him the Kleist Prize (1912), the Schiller Prize (1927), the Johann Peter Hebel Prize (1936), the Goethe Medal for Art and Sciences (1939), a personal gift of some fifteen thousand Marks from Adolf Hitler on his sixty-fifth birthday, inclusion on the list of writers "chosen" to escape forced conscription by dint of being considered German "national patrimony," nine months in jail starting in 1945, and censorship. In addition to the problems with his ideology, the book's reception, both before and after the Nazi regime, was marked by the fact that the swastika appeared for the first time in *Wiltfeber,* whose subtitle was "The Story of a Man in Search of a Fatherland," as a healing symbol and herald of a new era. Moreover, in 1924, B. announced the arrival of the Third Reich; another of his poems, published in 1931, foretold the arrival in Germany of a political leader who was later associated with Adolf Hitler, so his "Der Führer" was republished and widely anthologized. After his jail time, and after having lost his property as well as his right to perform political or literary activities, B. earned a living translating French poetry and was chosen as an honorary member of the far-right organization Deutschen Kulturwerk Europäischen Geistes (German Cultural Project of the European Spirit), which strove to reconstruct the ties between fascist writers who'd survived the war. The publication of his final poems with the title *The Face Beneath the Stars* (1957) generated some controversy due to their revisionist nature, which allowed one to think that B. did not have any regrets, was not offering any apologies, and had no bad conscience whatsoever.

Buzzi, Paolo (Milan, February 15, 1874–Milan, February 18, 1956). He worked his entire life in Milan's Provincial Administration, while writing comedies, opera librettos, poetry in dialect, imitations of Giacomo Leopardi, a prose poem, an essay on blank verse, a volume of Futurist poetry, a science fiction novel (entitled *The Ellipse and the Spiral: Film + Words in Freedom*) published in 1915 that was the first to use Marinetti's "words in freedom" technique), some works of "synthetic theater," various poetry books in a deliberately more conservative tone, translations (of *The Flowers of Evil* by Charles Baudelaire, for example), and another two volumes of poetry that can only be described as disconcerting: *Radio Wave Poems* (1940) and *Atomic* (1950). However, his most important work is *Conflagration (Epic "Parolibera", 1915–1918),* a World War I diary written entirely with "words in freedom," and many collages, published posthumously in 1963.

Calosso, Oreste (Rome, May 15, 1915–Rome, February 17, 2004). Despite his Roman origins, C. spent much of his life outside of Rome, in cities such as Milan, Florence, and Perugia; it was in that last city where he studied literature and became a Futurist and contributor to the primary Futurist publications. His texts appeared in *La Città Nuova* from Turin, *Artecrazia* (Rome, 1934–1939), and *Legiones y Falanges,* the magazine edited in Rome by Agustín de Foxá and Giuseppe Lombrosa, where C. was in charge of the film review section. His closeness to the cultural authorities of the Italian Social Republic and particularly to the minister of popular culture, Fernando Mezzasoma, led to his appointment to organize the Fascist Writers' Conference in Pinerolo in 1945; however, he cannot be held responsible for its abrupt ending. Although his production between 1931 and 1945 was vast, C. distanced himself from it after the war. Following a period of living discreetly in Florence, possibly waiting for his collaboration with the fascist government to be forgotten, he timidly returned to publishing literature in 1949 with a slim volume of poetry entitled *Prose,* whose title was as damning as the silence of the critics. It was followed by *The Unfinished* (1951), *Places, Moments, Journeys Through Time* (1953), and *The Foreigner Speaks* (1963), as well as a selection of short prose entitled *Sloth* (1973), which elicited that very mood in its potential readers and, like the rest of his works, went unnoticed. Among C.'s missing talents was the ability to come up with attractive titles for his books, but in his defense it must be said that he is one of the few twentieth-century Italian writers whose work isn't completely predictable, an honor he shares with Giorgio Manganelli, Carlo Emilio Gadda, and Maurizio Cucchi. Although he asked his family to destroy all his work, both published and manuscript, after his death, his papers are now held at the University of Padua, where his family members bequeathed them due to their library's interest in fascist literature and despite the fact that, apparently, C. swore off fascism and deliberately strove to write against it, which could have benefited him in aesthetic terms but damaged his image for posterity. On the other hand, he never seemed terribly interested in posterity.

Cangiullo, Francesco (Naples, January 27, 1884–Livorno, July 22, 1977). He met Marinetti and other Futurists when he was fifteen years old, at a "Futurist evening" in his hometown, and he immediately joined them and began to publish in their main magazines. In 1916 he published two small books of poems, *Piedigrotta* and *New Green,* and in 1919 *Café-Concert: Unexpected Alphabet,* one of the finest examples of the type of Futurist work in which typographical experimentation adds considerable visual importance. C. also became interested in theater, and contributed to creating "synthetic Futurist theater," for which he wrote, in 1916, the play *Detonation* and in 1918 *Radioscopy of a Duet* with Ettore Petrolini, and to the "Theater of Surprise," whose manifesto he wrote with Marinetti. Before distancing himself from Futurism he published *Pentagrammed Poetry* (1923) and, in 1930, a personal account of the "Futurist evenings" that, for some reason—as if C. couldn't resist their charm, which had drawn him to Futurism twenty years earlier—led him to return to their ranks at least temporarily: in 1930 he published the novel *Ninì Champagne* and, in 1937, the Futurist story "Marinetti on Mount Vesuvius."

Carduccio, Emilio (Palermo, October 12, 1904–Reggio Calabria, November 11, 1946). It is unclear whether he died in 1946—other sources mention 1947—or whether he belonged first to the Communist and then the Fascist Party, or if he was a fascist first and then later became a Communist to escape a formal accusation that finally did catch up with him and for which he died in prison. It's also unclear whether either shift between the two parties was out of conviction, or mere expedience. Nor do we know if he wrote the piece entitled "Farewell to the Wife Who Smiles in the Dunes" or the one called "Ways of Temporary Insanity" or simply "Temporary Insanity." Furthermore, it's unclear whether those works weren't just one single work, which could have been titled—there are accounts of this—"Farewell to Temporary Insanity" or "The Temporary Insanity of the Wife in the Dunes." As such, C.'s trajectory is one of the most emblematic of the Italian twentieth century.

Castellani, Abelardo (Castiglione del Lago, October 12, 1870–Perugia, March 8, 1942). He published, among others, the books *The Mirror of Ash* (1911), *The Thirsty Machines* (1926), *Night on the Acheron* (1929), *Cruel Gospel* (1931), and *Other Panthers* (1941), and for years ran the magazine *Lo Scarabeo d'Oro* (1921–1934). Some consider him one of the finest Italian short-story writers of the twentieth century, which may be less a compliment to C. than a statement on the calamitous, lamentable state of that literary genre in Italy over the course of said century. However, no one can deny that C.'s work has the merit of approximating literary quality while never actually brushing up against it, not even accidentally.

Castrofiori, Filippo (Florence, May 26, 1884–Florence, November 15, 1947). At fifty years old, in 1934, C. published his *Complete Works,* apparently inspired by Gustave Flaubert. Except for his correspondence, the *Complete Works* of C. are devoid of any interest despite having been very popular in their day; perhaps the diptych of novels composed of *Anxiety Visits the Via del Corso* and *The Way of the Flesh to Anxiety* is somewhat interesting as a document of a period drowning in boundless expressions of sentimentalism. His essay on the perpetual motion machine he invented is disappointing due to the fact that, after listing his numerous failed attempts, and without any explanation, C. states that he's finally found the solution to the problem, although he refuses to reveal it for fear that it will fall into the hands of the enemies of what he calls "Italian civilization," which may or may not have been a joke. An opera about the "anthropogeography" of Friedrich Ratzel for which he wrote the libretto and the music has never premiered because, among other reasons, it requires twenty-six mezzo-sopranos and it's rare to find more than a pair. He never published again after his *Complete Works,* in what may be the strangest literary career of the Italian twentieth century.

Cataldi, Romano (Cantiano, March 14, 1893–Ethiopia, possibly Aksum, October or December 1935). Several arrests and some jail time for minor offenses during his youth; during which, he claimed, he learned to read and write, creating a series of somewhat autobiographical stories that the prison authorities destroyed for immorality. One of them, reconstructed by its author, was published in the Turinese magazine *Stile Futurista* with the title "A Long Shadow Dog" in August 1934. The following year, C. enlisted along with other young fascists from Perugia in what would be known as the Second Italo-Ethiopian War and disappeared for some months after his regiment helped take the important city of Aksum, on October 15 of that same year. (Other sources state that C. died a few weeks later, during the mustard gas bombings on December 22, 1935, when a gust of wind dragged the gas clouds over to the Italian lines, but that was never proved.) Despite his own statements, and the testimony of his friends, who insisted on the quality and quantity of his poetry, C. left no known posthumous work.

Cavacchioli, Enrico (Pozzallo, March 15, 1885–Milan, January 4, 1954). F. T. Marinetti referred to him in 1909 as one of the "incendiary poets" of Futurism, but—despite belonging to that group, and being particularly valued for his role in the confrontations with the public that took place at each "Futurist evening"—he only superficially adhered to the Futurist aesthetic, which was too heterodox for his poetic tastes. C. was best known as a playwright, and there is a fair amount of consensus around the idea that his finest piece is *The Bird of Paradise* (1920), despite majority opinion also agreeing that its grotesque elements do not conceal its bourgeois comedic nature.

Corra, Bruno (pseudonym of Bruno Ginanni Corradini; Ravenna, June 9, 1892–Varese, November 20, 1976). Although he distanced himself from Futurism in the 1920s, publishing some rather unsophisticated novels and, particularly, earning renown as a dramatist, there were very few writers as important to the history of Marinetti's movement. In 1912, C. (whose name, just like that of his brother, Arnaldo Ginna, was given to him by the important Futurist painter Giacomo Balla, who saw in them the embodiment of running and gymnastics) founded the magazine *Il Centauro* along with Mario Carli and Emilio Settimelli, signed the main Futurist manifestos, enthusiastically supported fascism from 1915 on, and created and codirected with Settimelli *L'Italia Futurista* in 1916. That same year, he collaborated with Balla and Marinetti on *Vida futurista,* the film produced and directed by Ginna of which all that remains are a few stills and a broad-strokes idea of the plot. *Sam Dunn Is Dead,* his "synthetic" Futurist novel, was published in 1915; it was followed by *The Enamored Family* (1919), *Blonde Woman* (1921), *Yellow Marriages* (1928), *International Loves* (1933), *The Dazed House* (1942), *X-ray Eve* (1944), *Midnight Rose* (1945), *Full of Surprises* (1949), and *The Mystery Lover* (1953), among others.

Cuadra, Pablo Antonio (Managua, November 4, 1912–Managua, January 2, 2002). "He began with the avant-garde *Songs of Birds and Women* (1929–1931), followed by, in 1935, *Nicaraguan Poems,* in which he achieves a remarkable poetic version of popular life. Following that, his poetry took on more religious tones, losing some of its freshness but none of its quality, in the volumes *Temporal Song* (1943), *The Book of Hours* (1946–1954), the lovely *Poems with Dusk on My Back* (1949–1956), *Garland of the Year* (1957–1960), *The Jaguar and the Moon* (1960), where he recovers his country's indigenous mythology, a subject he returns to in the masterpiece of his later years, *Songs of Cifar* (1971). In 1976 he published *Those Faces in the Crowd,* containing both short stories and poetry, and, in 1980, *Seven Trees Against the Dusk.* His *Complete Poetic Works* (1983–1991) fills nine volumes. Cuadra also wrote good prose. [. . .] For the stage he created a little avant-garde piece, *The Dance of the Bourgeois Bear* (1942), and a Brechtian social drama, *Down the Paths Go the Peasants* (1937), considered the culmination of Central American rural theater. His work as an essayist was abundant" (César Aira, *Diccionario de autores latinoamericanos* [Buenos Aires: Emecé, 2001], pp. 159–160).

Fleuron, Svend (Keldby på Møn, January 4, 1874–Humlebæk, April 5, 1966). Athough he spent his youth following a military career and in 1941 stated he was "thrilled with war," F. was, primarily, a lover of nature and animals, to whom he dedicated much of his work. A residential street in Søborg named after him in 1925 was renamed immediately after the war and the Danish Writers' Association expelled him from their ranks: in both cases, due to his participation in the National Socialist Weimar Poets' Gathering of 1941, from which his reputation never recovered.

Folgore, Luciano (pseudonym of Omero Vecchi; Rome, June 18, 1888–Rome, May 24, 1966). *Early Hour,* his first book of poems (1908), adheres to the conventional poetic forms of the era; a year later, F. meets Filippo Tommaso Marinetti and becomes a Futurist: rarely has a book been repudiated by its author in a shorter amount of time, but its author, or at least his name, was also soon repudiated; his next book of poems, *The Dawn Aflame* (1910), was still signed by Omero Vecchi: two years later, in 1912, *The Song of Motors* and the poems included in the important *Anthology of Futurist Poets* were signed by "Luciano Folgore." He also signed the manifesto "Synthetic Lyricism and Physical Sensation," where he develops his poetics, with that name. He publishes in *Lacerba, La Voce, La Diana, L'Italia Futurista, Avanscoperta,* and *Sic* [sic], meets Pablo Picasso and Jean Cocteau, moves to Florence. In 1930 he compiles his poems in *Poetries,* and after World War II he opts for other literary forms, such as prose, and occasionally humor, drama, and parodic children's poetry. Between 1930 and 1945 or 1946 is the most important period in F.'s life, though the author himself later tried to minimize its relevance: it was in those years that his publications included *The Book of Epigrams* (1932), *The Colorful Trap* (1934), *Little Fables and Stray Lines* (1934), *Novellas in the Mirror: Parodies of D'Annunzio and Others* (1935). He was a civil servant in the Ministry of Justice, and he was an accountant.

Folicaldi, Alceo (Lugo, February 7, 1900–Lugo, January 4, 1952). At seventeen years of age, he met Marinetti and joined the Futurists. In 1919, he published *Folders* and, in 1926, *Rainbow over the World,* his most important book. Marinetti included it in his anthology *The New Futurist Poets* (1925) and always seems to have considered him one of his best students, but F. stopped publishing shortly after that date, as is known.

Garassino, Michele (Arezzo, September 27, 1902–Rome, April 29, 2002). He was born into a prosperous Arezzo importing family; it may have been his mother who encouraged his literary vocation, which seems to have been precocious. In 1933, while studying literature at the University of Perugia, G. earned considerable prestige within the young local scene thanks to some poems of African inspiration published in various places and then in book form in 1934; in 1936 this was followed by another volume of poems published previously in the magazine *Artecrazia*. Throughout the following years, G. held minor posts in the Perugian fascist cultural institutions, but in 1939 he moved to Rome. That same year he published the book of poems *Helpless Childhood* and, two years later, in 1941, an essay entitled *The Song of the Whip: Literature and Its Critics*. After the July 19, 1943, bombing of Rome, G. returned to Perugia, where he was working on the launch of a new newspaper commissioned by the authorities of Salò when he was invited to the Fascist Writers' Conference held in Pinerolo between April 20 and 23, 1945. He left the Social Republic shortly afterward, and, following a period of relative obscurity, already back in Rome, he became one of the most highly respected Italian literary critics of the 1950s and 1960s. G. liked pseudonyms, and, according to O. Zuliani's memoirs, he used them profusely to review his own books in the press and to stoke controversies with himself in confrontations he didn't always win; according to R. Rosà's autobiography, G. could have (using another of his pseudonyms) made public the discovery that much of his work is inspired by the work of an obscure American writer named A. Maddow, although it's hard to imagine that he wanted to unmask himself in that way. In the 1970s, G.'s luck took a sharp dive, and in the 1980s he was already basically forgotten. He spent his final years in a senior home in the Monte Sacro neighborhood in Rome. His papers remained in his apartment downtown until his death, shortly after his hundredth birthday; no one knows what happened to them after that.

Gentilli, Filippo (Colle di Roio, December 24, 1894–L'Aquila, January 17, 1951). A true scourge of those aspiring to prosper at the expense of literature and of its readers, G. didn't hesitate to criticize the bad practices of his contemporaries in the Italian press; his confrontations with Gabriele D'Annunzio and F. T. Marinetti are well known, as is his denunciation of G. Rossi for plagiarizing D'Annunzio. Among his many works—mostly historical dramas and essays—are *Colloquy Among the Illustrious* (1932) and *The Spanish Fortress* (1939), a book of poems that celebrates both the imposing building constructed in L'Aquila between 1534 and 1567 by order of Charles I of Spain, King of Naples, and the victory of Francisco Franco in the Spanish Civil War. G. was a firm defender of the abolition of private property, from the safety offered him by the private property of several hectares and considerable rent profits; his death—which occurred, according to witnesses, during a fit of laughter over dinner in his home—thwarted his first trip to the Soviet Union, planned for that year: at the end of his life, G. was a profound admirer of Josef Stalin.

Ginna, Arnaldo (pseudonym of Arnaldo Ginanni Corradini; Ravenna, May 7, 1890–Rome, September 26, 1982). The experimental short films that G. made between 1910 and 1912 in collaboration with his brother, B. Corra, were lost in a bombing of Milan during World War II; it is known that in them G. experimented with what he termed "cinepittura": the application of colors onto untreated film celluloid, in a succession of images accompanied by abstract music G. himself composed; also lost is the film *Vita futurista* (1916), in which G. collaborated with Marinetti, Giacomo Balla, and, once again, with his brother. He wrote pieces of "synthetic theater," manifestos, prose, political texts; he published in magazines such as *Roma Futurista, L'Impero,* and *Futurismo;* in that final one he published his work *The Future Man:* prior to that he published *The Locomotive with Trousers,* which included a prologue by B. Corra and illustrations by R. Rosà. In 1938 he signed, with Marinetti, the manifesto "Cinematography," after which he focused less on his artistic production and more on occultism, a subject that had always interested him, highlighting it in the context of Futurism, usually concentrating on the most material aspect of the art. In addition to his esoteric works, which by their nature were not widely popular, G. was a painter and film critic.

Govoni, Corrado (Tàmara, October 29, 1884–Lido dei Pini, October 20, 1965). He joined the Futurists in 1905, though he began publishing in 1903. *Electric Poetry* (1911) and *Rarefications and Words in Freedom* (1915) are the clearest examples of his adherence to Futurism, which was nonetheless superficial. In 1922 he took a job at the Ministry of Popular Culture and later held significant posts in professional institutions such as the National Union of Writers and Authors, always with the support of Benito Mussolini, to whom he dedicated a laudatory poem. However, the execution of his son Aladino in the Ardeatine Massacre on March 24, 1944, caused him to break with fascism. G. continued to develop his solid, prolific body of poetic, dramatic, and prose work until his death but, by its very nature, the standout book in his oeuvre is the one dedicated to his son and to his former convictions, *Aladino: A Lament for My Dead Son* (1946).

Herescu, Niculae I. (Turnu Severin, December 6, 1903 [1906, according to other sources]–Zurich, August 19 [16, according to other sources], 1961). In 1944, after the coup d'etat against Ion

Antonescu that shifted Romania to the Allied side, H. went into exile in Portugal and then France, where he worked as a Latinist and bolstered the expatriate Romanian literary scene. Among his books are *Latin Poetry* (1960) and a posthumous novel, *Agony Without Death* (1998).

Hollenbach, Hans Jürgen (Untermünstertal, May 28, 1911–?). Author of the books *Notes on a Philosophy of History* (1941), *The Theory of Discontinuity* (1943, revised editions in 1976, 1979, 1988, and 2000), *On Dissatisfaction* (1954), and *Some Observations on Uncertainty* (1974), among others, H. was a student and later collaborator of Martin Heidegger, as well as a professor at the universities of Freiburg, Augsburg, Alexander von Humboldt of Berlin, and Heidelberg between 1935 and 2008, approximately. H. wrote: "What we call history is the effort assumed as a supraindividual task by those who came before us, to impose order on seeming chaos, on a series of discontinuous events that cannot be explained. It is also the task of elucidating what remains hidden, eclipsed by horrible acts that are omitted (when at all possible) and the suppression of the visible and obvious. History is what justifies us, what legitimizes our institutions and our practices, thus only a positive vision of it can offer us the salve of knowing that our atrocities are not gratuitous, but instead necessary links in a chain that illuminates a path. This invention of a fictitious time line of a horrific map of atrocities is a paradoxical task, because it means inventing something already surpassed in order to pave the way for the inevitable atrocities in the future." For more information on H., see Martin Lachkeller's book *History of the Philosophy and Philosophers of National Socialism (1927–1945): An Approximation,* published in 2011.

Johst, Hanns (Seerhausen, July 8, 1890–Ruhpolding, November 23, 1978). Primarily a playwright, J. was president of the Reichsschrifttumskammer (Reich Literature Chamber) and, as such, the most powerful man in German literature during the Nazi period. When it ended, he faced detention centers and denazification, but by 1955 J. was considered rehabilitated, despite which he was unable to resume his literary career. He ended his days writing poems for the magazine *The Intelligent Housewife* under the pseudonym "Odemar Oderich." His moment of glory took place on April 20, 1933, with the premiere of his play *Schlageter,* dedicated to Adolf Hitler "with devoted veneration and unwavering loyalty."

Junco, Alfonso (Monterrey, February 26, 1896–Mexico City, October 13, 1974). Member of the Mexican Academy of Language and an extraordinarily prolific writer, J. was one of the most eminent defenders of Francoism outside of Spain, as well as a detractor of ideologies such as liberalism, communism, and fascism, which found no place in his deeply Catholic view of existence. Among his works are *Señora Belén de Zárraga Defanatizing* (1923), *Eucharistic Anthology* (1926), *A Radical Problem of Guadalupe* (1932), *Cassocks of Mexico* (1955), and *Gongoristic Questiunculi* [*sic*] (1955), all books that deserve to be back in print, if not for their quality, at least for their extraordinary titles.

Kolbenheyer, Erwin (Budapest, December 30, 1878–Munich, April 12, 1962). He is mainly remembered for his trilogy of novels Paracelsus; or, better put, would be mainly remembered for his trilogy Paracelsus if anyone remembered it, which doesn't seem to be the case. Although he joined the National Socialist Party of German Workers (NSDAP) in 1940, he had been a sympathizer since 1928 and a very active writer in that decade and the following one, even though his efforts to prove the biological origin of the supposed superiority of German literature over the literature of other countries were discredited, and with them his work. In 1945, the occupation authorities banned him from publishing for five years; except for that, one could say that K. emerged from National Socialism and the war relatively unscathed.

Maddow, Arthur (Philadelphia, September 27, 1903–Casablanca, December 24, 1947). Born into a wealthy family who turned their backs on him when he came of age, M. lived in Sicily and Tunisia. He published his only book of poetry in Algiers in 1938. The scant testimony from his contemporaries describes him as sickly and with few friends.

Marinetti, Filippo Tommaso (Alexandria, December 22, 1876–Bellagio, December 2, 1944). He elevated hysteria to the category of aesthetics, he invented Futurism, he was one of the first writers who thought of himself as a businessman, he fought in two world wars and in other lesser conflicts, he was a magnificent publicist. Once an orange was thrown at him, and, after catching it in midair, he peeled it calmly and ate it to the exasperation and admiration of his audience. "We destroy, but only to later rebuild," he wrote.

Masoliver, Juan Ramón (Zaragoza, March 13, 1910–Montcada i Reixac, April 7, 1997). Essayist, journalist, literary and art critic, and translator. As happens with certain celestial bodies, his light was not his own but rather came from those around him: James Joyce, Ezra Pound (whose secretary he was for a while), Luis Buñuel, Salvador Dalí, etc. Among his publications are *Guide to Rome and Italian Itineraries* (1950), *Presenting James Joyce* (1981), *Anthology of the Poetry of Ausiàs March* (1981), and *Profile in Shadow* (1994).

Massis, Henri (Paris, March 21, 1886–Paris, April 17, 1970). The magazines *Roseau d'Or* and *Revue Universelle* are among his lesser contributions to French literature and culture in the first half of the twentieth century; more important is his "Manifesto of French Intellectuals in Defense of the West and Peace in Europe" (1935), in which he proposed an alliance of all the right-wing European powers, particularly the French and Italian, and a suspicious attitude toward Germany. During the war he formed part of the Vichy elite, and, as a result, his name appeared on the list of "undesirables" drawn up by the National Writers' Committee in 1944, despite which M. was never subject to any purge and in 1960 became a member of the French Academy. M. was a Catholic writer, right-wing and perhaps somewhat sentimental, but, primarily, an enemy of all literary modernization. Among his works are *How Émile Zola Wrote His Novels* (1905), *Romain Rolland Against France* (1915), *Judgments I: Renan, France, Barrès* (1923), *Judgments II: André Gide, Romain Rolland, Georges Duhamel, Julien Benda, the Literary Cliques* (1924), *The Cadets of the Alcázar* (1936), *From André Gide to Marcel Proust* (1948), *Maurras and Our Time* (1951), and *Over the Course of a Life* (1967).

Mencaroni, Diego (Perugia, February 14, 1906–Milan, April 23, 1945). Respiratory problems forced his family to move to Rome from Perugia when M. was four years old, in search of less polluted air. The decision turned out to both terrible and excellent at the same time: terrible because M.'s respiratory problems multiplied in Rome and excellent because the Italian capital was the perfect place for him to make an early impression with his many talents, which included writing film and theater scripts, and composing the sound tracks and creating many of the sets for his films. At fifteen, after having made a name for himself as a set designer and pianist in the Roman theater scene, M. directed his first film, a silent sword-and-sandal movie about the life of Messalina entitled *Thirty Thousand Men* (1921); it was followed by another eighteen films, many of which were lost during the bombing of Milan and Rome during World War II. Of his film *The Start of Spring* (1938), for example, only two scenes remain: in the first, two characters talk about a third, someone named Hans Jürgen Hollenbach, about whom the audience knows nothing and, seemingly, will never know anything; in the second, some Aryan-looking young women dance partially naked in a forest. Not even reviews of the film could illuminate the relationship between the two scenes, and it's possibly there never was any. M. was a pioneer of films whose scenes aren't as important as their sequencing, in an early acknowledgment of the fact that meaning in cinematographic narration, as well as other types of narration, comes through only in montage. This characteristic, which links his film work to avant-garde proposals that would take place decades later, during what some critics named "postmodernism" and others "the late avant-garde," didn't impede the relative popularity of his work in its day. Despite his early adherence to anarchism and some aesthetic ideas whose proliferation and lack of any system were diametrically opposed to conservativism—or precisely because of it, considering the fact that most vanguards are produced on the left of the political spectrum while adhering, to greater or lesser extents, to political positions on the right—M. was celebrated by the fascist regime as one of its most kindred artists. However, this was not an obstacle to their stripping him of all support as, at the start of the war when their need for propaganda films increased exponentially, M. proved himself incapable of producing a film for those ends. It seems his only incursion into the genre was a film entitled *A Crow in the Snow* (1941). In it, a soldier—played by M. himself—whose legs are cut off by a grenade at the start of the film, lies dying for an hour and a half; during that entire time, the camera remains on the ground on its side so that all the viewer sees is a part of a snowy trench on which a crow finally lands: except for some explosions and howls of pain from M., which fade into a murmur and finally disappear with the arrival of the crow, nothing happens in the film. It was destroyed by order of the Italian High Command after a private viewing attended by B. Mussolini, F. Mezzasoma, A. Cucco, and G. Almirante, among others. He took part in the Fascist Writers' Conference held in Pinerolo in 1945, but shortly after was executed by the fascists. M. had confided to a couple of the attendees that he was working as a double agent for the Americans; he seemed to have counted on being imprisoned by the fascists and then freed soon after by the Americans, but the American advance was halted for some hours on April 21; meanwhile, M. was accused of high treason when he reached Milan and immediately executed by firing squad. There is no evidence that M. was in contact with the Americans, though there is evidence that those who ordered his execution were: perhaps M. knew of that link and invented his story in order to be protected by the fascists who had already surrendered to the imminent victors of the war—but they decided his execution would keep up appearances until the Americans guaranteed their safety. His plan was a good one; it merely failed due to being carried out at the wrong place and time and due to the actions of others.

México, Pobre (?–?). It is not known whether he lived between 1899 and 1956 or between 1889 and 1946, nor whether his was a pseudonym or a real name. None of his works have survived.

Möller, Eberhard Wolfgang (Berlin, January 6, 1906–Bietigheim, January 1, 1972). Although he was one of the most important playwrights of the National Socialist period, and the Nazi authorities, particularly Joseph Goebbels, named him to the Theater Division of the Reich's Ministry for Public Enlightenment and Propaganda, M. is remembered only for his participation in the film *Jew Süss* (directed by Veit Harlan, 1940), the finest example of German anti-Semitic cinematography. Apart from that, M.'s dramatic works (for example, *Douaumont or The Return of the Soldier Odysseus: Seven Scenes,* of 1929, *Rothschild Prevails at Waterloo,* of 1934, and *The Fall of Carthage* of 1938) are of some interest due to his use of techniques from the avant-garde and the theater of Bertolt Brecht to write plays characterized by anti-Semitism, misogyny, and enthusiasm for war; in other words, for values generally opposed to avant-garde ideas. For these works, M. received the 1938 National Prize and other honors, though his star faded somewhat when, in his book for teens *The Führer,* he compared Adolf Hitler to Martin Luther and attributed characteristics of a pagan god to him: despite selling half a million copies, the work was taken off the market for being too "kitsch." Between 1940 and 1943 he formed part of a tank division, and, later, when already an SS officer, he continued his literary work, though without his earlier success. M. was in prison between 1945 and 1948, after which he tried to resume his literary activity: because his plays were no longer staged, he began to write historical novels; their content wasn't very different from his previous texts; in fact, they contained such marked anti-Semitism and antidemocratic tendencies that it becomes impossible to believe in the efficacy of the purification procedures that took place in German cultural life after 1945, and of which German society is so proud. M. is a perfect example of the type of fascist writer who continued his literary activity after the fall of the regime that had sheltered him, without having to repent or show any doubt as to the correctness of his activities prior to 1945. In 1963, for example, he attributed the lack of success of his anti-Semitic novel *Chicago* to a conspiracy rather than blame its content. The news of his death was reported only in the neo-Nazi press of the period.

Montes, Eugenio (Vigo, November 24, 1900 [Bande, 1897, according to other sources]–Madrid, October 27, 1982). He was an author in Galician and in Spanish, as well as a journalist and civil servant. His works include *The Old Fisherman Suns Himself, and Other Stories* (1922), *The Traveler and His Shadow* (1940), *Italian Melody* (1943), and *European Elegies* (1949).

Morlacchi, Flavia (Piove di Sacco, February 27, 1905–Padua, February 26, 2005). Pseudonym of the Italian poet and playwright Gaetana Morlacchi. Her works include the books of poetry *The Chinese Nightingale* (1927), *The Partridge of Isfahan* (1930), and *An Approach to the Parrot of Cordoba* (1931), which make up the ornithological trilogy whose verses Pier Paolo Pasolini quoted—possibly mockingly—in speeches delivered by the actresses Rossana Di Rocco and Rosina Moroni in his film *The Hawks and the Sparrows* (1966). Her *Scorpion Tail Poems* (1935), *Spiderweb* (1938), and *The Monkey Ate My Hand* (1949), attempts at incursions into the realms of entomology and the study of animal behavior respectively, were coolly received and M. soon returned to the birds she'd based her poetic reputation on: she wrote about them in the books *Pigeons of the Piazza San Marco* (1967), *The Swedish Blackbird and Other Poems* (1971), and *The Cuban Trojon* (1974). Very few people remember her now, but her poem about the Palatine, comparing its ruins to "blind eyes / shaded eyes / of the fierce and glorious Roman specter," etc., is still recited from memory by all Italian elementary school students.

Munari, Bruno (Milan, October 24, 1907–Milan, September 30, 1998). Author of the first "mobile" in the history of art, his *Aerial Machine* of 1930; creator starting in 1933 of Useless Machines and, from 1951, of the hilarious Arrhythmic Machines; maker of "projected" and "polarized" paintings, and ones resulting from the decomposition of light; writer of children's books and responsible for the first laboratory for children in a museum; pioneer of kinetic art with his work *Hour X* (1945); inventor in 1958 of a sign language using what he called "talking forks"; creator of a series of found objects including *The Sea as Artisan,* from 1953, and the *Fossils of 2000,* from 1959; author of abstract series such as Illegible Books, the Imaginary Museum of the Aeolian Islands, the Theoretical Reconstructions of Imaginary Objects, the Travel Sculptures, the Illegible Writings of Unknown Peoples, etc. M. is one of the most important Italian artists of the twentieth century.

Nazariantz, Hrand (Istanbul, January 8, 1886–Bari, January 25, 1962). Studied in Paris and London, was an important journalist in Istanbul, moved to Bari (1913) and became an Italian citizen; but he never stopped writing in Armenian and was possibly the only Futurist writer employing that language.

Olgiati, Carlo (Novara, November 15, 1908–Novara, July 2, 1945). Despite the author's precociousness (publishing at twenty-three), and his lack of a formal education, the three volumes of his *His-*

toric Metabolism (1931) are surprisingly mature and ambitious, but the work does have some ambiguities and contradictions. We can no longer question the author about them, as he took his own life after the destruction of his family business, which he had planned to have support his essay writing.

Ors, Eugenio d' (Barcelona, September 28, 1882 [1881, according to other sources]–Villanueva y Geltrú, September 25, 1954). "The carnivalesque aspects, of both the man and his philosophy, are defect and virtue at the same time, and the collection of his glosses in *Glossaries*—new, highly original, and definitive—is a monumental and invaluable legacy, even above his other masterpiece, which sinks into the angelic stratosphere with the heaviness of a weighted diver" (Andrés Trapiello, *Las armas y las letras: Literatura y Guerra Civil (1936–1939)*, corrected and expanded third edition [Barcelona: Destino, 2010], p. 574).

Palazzeschi, Aldo (pseudonym of Aldo Giurlani; Florence, February 2, 1885–Rome, August 17, 1974). Despite fanatically (in other words, with fanaticism) joining the Futurist movement after meeting Filippo Tommaso Marinetti (in other words, engaging with him), P. never approved of the group's militarism (in other words, its enthusiasm for soldiers and war) and he broke with it (in other words, with Futurism) at the start of World War I; by that point (in other words, up until that moment) he had already published the book of poems *The Incendiary* (1910), the novel *Man of Smoke* (1911), and the manifesto *Controdolore* [*sic*] (1914). That break led to a particularly prolific period (twelve works in almost forty years) followed, beginning in 1956, by a decade without publishing anything of importance (in other words, anything of relevance), which ended in 1966 with *The Integral Comedian;* which gave rise to the publication of five other works until 1972, two years before his death (in other words, his demise). He died as the result of a poorly treated dental abscess: in other words, of an inflammation produced by the accumulation of pus in his gums stemming from an infection; in other words, from the penetration and development of pathogens within his organism.

Popowa-Mutafowa, Fani (Sewliewo, October 16, 1902–Sofia, July 9, 1977). Author primarily of historical novels that aspire to psychological profundity, P.-M., who was the most popular woman writer in her country before and after writing panegyrics to Adolf Hitler and Benito Mussolini, was condemned to seven years in a detention center for her participation in the Weimar meetings. She was exempted after eleven months due to a lung disease. She didn't publish anything between 1939 and 1972, the date of her final novel, *Dr. Petar Beron,* about the well-known Bulgarian educator.

Pound, Ezra (Hailey, Idaho, October 30, 1885–Venice, November 1, 1972). "I hadn't seen Ezra since 1938. Thirteen years had not aged him particularly. He still looked leonine, big-chested and swarthy. Wearing a yellow sweater that gave him the appearance of a tennis coach. [. . .] 'You see why I like deck-chairs,' he said, packing them flat against the wall and indicating the dimensions of his cell. The room contained an iron bed, chaos of clothes and a muddle of magazines and paper. We had to shout at each other even in his cell because a large television set outside in the corridor blared away. 'They try to reduce us idiots to the level of insanity outside,' Ezra confessed. 'Have you written any poems in here?' I asked. 'Birds don't sing in cages.' We didn't mention poetry again" (Ronald Duncan about his visit to see P. at St. Elizabeth's psychiatric hospital in November 1948).

Rebatet, Lucien (Moras-en-Valloire, November 15, 1903–Moras-en-Valloire, August 24, 1972). The most important works by R., author of *A Contribution to the History of Russian Ballets* (1930), bear titles that leave little room for debate about his political ideas:

Bolshevism Against Civilization (1940), "Jews in France" (1941), "Foreigners in France," "The Invasion," "Loyalty to National Socialism" (1944), etc. In 1942 he published *The Rubble,* an anti-Semitic pamphlet in favor of collaboration with Nazi Germany, of which they printed sixty thousand copies during the occupation and which led Charles Maurras to call him a "maniacal coprophagist and an impulsive, sick dwarf." Some time later he sought refuge in Sigmaringen Castle with the main figures of French collaborationism, including Louis-Ferdinand Céline, whose *Bagatelles for a Massacre* he'd openly celebrated in 1938. He was arrested in Feldkirch (Austria) in May 1945 and condemned to death in November 1946; some months later, in April 1947, the sentence was reduced to forced labor in perpetuity and one hundred and forty-one days in chains, despite which he was freed in July 1952. A year earlier he had published one of his most important works, the novel *The Two Banners,* followed by *Ripe Ears* (1954) and the essays *For Jean Paulhan* (1968) and *A History of Music* (1969). His most important works, and the ones that best reveal the scant or nonexistent evolution of his political ideas following the debacle of fascism, are the ones published after his death, however: his *Memoirs of a Fascist* (1976), *Letters from Prison to Roland Cailleux (1945–1952)* (1993), and *Dialogue of the Defeated, Clairvaux Prison, January–December 1950* with Pierre-Antoine Cousteau (1999).

Rosà, Rosa (pseudonym of Edith von Haynau; Vienna, November 18, 1884–Rome, 1978). In 1908 this aristocratic Austrian woman married the Italian writer Urlico Arnaldi; seven years later, when her husband was at the front, she came into contact with Futurism and joined the movement. She wrote *A Woman with Three Souls* (1918), a strange and early example of surrealist science fiction with a feminist theme, and *There's No One but You!* (1919), another Futurist novel. In 1917 she illustrated B. Corra's book *Sam Dunn Is Dead,* and in 1922 she illustrated A. Ginna's *The Locomotive with Trousers,* as well as other literary works; her graphic work, which is more extensive and integrates elements of expressionism, Futurism, and art nouveau, and is powerfully reminiscent of the work of Gustav Klimt and Aubrey Beardsley, still awaits rediscovery by critics. She also, late in life, published two essays, *Eternal Mediterranean* (1964) and *The Byzantium Phenomenon* (1970), and left two unfinished novels, *The House of Happiness* and *Flight from the Labyrinth,* which were considerable departures from her earlier Futurist style, as well as an autobiography entitled *The Danube Is Gray.*

Rossi, Giovanni (L'Aquila, February 12, 1920–Rome, April 14, 1994). In 1942 the publication of some poems plagiarized from Gabriele D'Annunzio led to his denunciation by F. Gentilli and the ensuing scandal; he didn't publish again until 1972, that time a very commendable book of poems, encumbered only by the somewhat excessive influence of F. Gentilli.

Sân-Giorgiu, Ion (Botoșani, 1893–Udem, 1950). Writer, expressionist, professor, art and literary critic, playwright, and journalist, S.-G. is not remembered for any of those things, but rather for his anti-Semitism, his sympathies for the extreme right, and for having held the position of minister of education in the Romanian government in exile when it was expelled from power by the Allied advance during World War II. He was condemned to death in absentia by a Romanian court after the war and died in exile in Germany.

Sánchez Mazas, Rafael (Madrid, February 18, 1894–Madrid, October 18, 1966). Journalist, novelist, essayist, poet, founding member of the Spanish Falange party, and minister under Franco, S. M. came up with the not very imaginative slogan "¡Arriba España!"— basically "Long live Spain!"—and wrote the poem "Prayer for the Fallen Members of the Falange" as well as taking part in the composition of "Cara al Sol," the Falangist anthem. His body of work is one of the few among Falangists that leaves a positive impression on readers, as long as they never read it and avoid ever laying eyes on a portrait of the author.

Santa Marina, Luys (Colindres, January 5, 1898–Barcelona, September 14/15, 1980). Pseudonym of Luis Narciso Gregorio Gutiérrez Santa Marina. Writer. Journalist. Falangist. Representative in the Francoist courts. Author of works on Queen Isabella I of Castile, Joan of Arc, Francisco de Zurbarán, and José Antonio Primo de Rivera. A Spaniard, with all that sadly entails.

Settimelli, Emilio (Florence, August 2, 1891–Lipari, February 12, 1954). He founded the magazines *Il Centauro* (1913) and *L'Italia Futurista* (1916), the first official organ of the group, where he published texts he'd written about "Futurist science" and the "synthetic Futurist theater"—the latter in collaboration with T. Marinetti and B. Corra—*Futurist Rome* (1918), and *Dynàmo* (1919). S. is also author (again in collaboration with B. Corra) of a revolutionary theory on the objective evaluation of artistic objects that was published as a manifesto entitled "The Weights, Measures, and Prices of Artistic Genius" (1914). After *Spiritual Adventures* (1916), *Futurist Masquerades* (1917), and *Survey of Italian Life* (1919), S. published texts that clearly state—from their very titles—his adherence to fascism, which happened in 1921: *Benito Mussolini* and *The Fascist Coup d'Etat* (both 1922) and *The Souls—B. Mussolini* (1925). Marinetti expelled him from the Futurist ranks at the Bologna Conference of 1933 and Mussolini had him jailed for his criticisms of some fascist leaders and his anticlericalism; he spent five years in prison: his bad luck with those whom he admired and supported is typical of the Italian twentieth century, one could say.

Somenzi, Mino (Marcaria, January 19, 1899–Rome, November 19, 1948). Pseudonym of Stanislao Somenzi. He took part in the occupation of Fiume and became a Futurist, then headed up the movement's principal magazines: *Futurismo* (1932–1933), *Sant'Elia* (1933–1934), and *Artecrazia* (1934–1939). His was a left-wing Futurism, as seen in his text *I Defend Futurism* (1937); naturally, his stance was shared by very few.

Sybesma, Rintsje Piter (Tjerkgaast, January 22, 1894–Heerenveen, February 5, 1975). Dutch veterinarian and author, a volunteer in the SS of that country, and an employee of the Reich's Ministry for Public Enlightenment and Propaganda. He lived until 1975 without ever having to answer for his past.

Tessore, Atilio (Florence, November 15, 1910–Bottai, on the outskirts of Florence, September 22, 1978). Pseudonym of the Italian writer Atilio Castrofiore. He published his first book of poems at seventeen years of age thanks to the intervention of his father, the writer F. Castrofiore. The performance of his erotic play in Rome's Monumentale theater in April 1937 is remembered as one of the biggest scandals of the twentieth-century Italian theatrical scene: the drama, whose subject was the rape of a young Italian woman by Austrian soldiers, in what constituted some sort of allegory about the eastern Italian territories, was considered in poor taste by the audience due to the nudity of the main character, played by the actress Luce Caponegro, and some of the Austrian soldiers; the play was not performed again. T. published two more books, with prologues by his father, *We Honorable Barbarians* (1939) and *Many Targets on Every Map* (1940), which the Italian critics rejected because of his abuse of hypotaxis. In April 1945 he was captured by partisans near the Milan train station, where it seems he was trying to get to Florence; his father's payment of an unspecified sum saved him from being shot by firing squad, but not from his trial for collaborationism: despite that, and a sentence against him, in March 1947 he was free; his attempts to reestablish himself as a writer failed because of his shyness. Those attempts included the publication of the memoir *White Flag* (1949) and the historical novel *Evil as an Effect of Ill Will* (1961).

Troubetzkoy, Amélie Rives (Richmond, Virginia, 1863–Charlottesville, Virginia, 1945). Beginning in 1888 with the short-story collection *A Brother to Dragons and Other Old-Time Tales,* and until 1898, T. was an extraordinarily prolific writer who published four books in 1888 and three in 1893, including *The Quick or the Dead?* (1888), her most popular novel and a true best seller of the period, and her drama in verse *Herod and Mariamne* (1888). She published a total of twenty-four books, plays, novels, stories, and poems, with titles like *Virginia of Virginia* [*sic*] (1888) and *The Queerness of Celia* (1926); they all put forth a mix of religious piety and sexual desire, passion and remorse, which must have been exceptionally attractive in that period, given her success as a playwright on Broadway. Her undeniable physical beauty as a young woman, her first husband's insanity, her divorce, her friendship with Oscar Wilde, and her addiction to morphine only added to that attractiveness. She lived much of her life in Europe, primarily in Italy; her literary friendships included Henry James, Louis Auchincloss, and Ezra Pound.

Zago, Cosimo (Venice, October 11, 1860–Venice, May 4, 1945). Despite starting to write at a young age, Z. didn't make a name for himself until he arrived in Rome, where he was on May 23, 1915, when Italy declared war on the Austro-Hungarian Empire and Z. enlisted with the Italian volunteers. According to his own declarations, he lost his right leg in Valsugana or Val d'Adige, he couldn't recall exactly, during the Austrian punitive incursion of May 15, 1916, when he stepped on a mine. He said that in his boot he was carrying the manuscript of an almost completed novel whose subject was said to be, on some occasions, the experiences of a young Italian man on the Tyrolean front, on others, those of a young Italian woman on that same front. Z., whose memory seemed fragile at best, did however remember that his novel was absolutely extraordinary, despite which his attempts to reconstruct it after the war bore no fruit. He was one of the first writers to publicly support fascism, and he was repaid with cultural and diplomatic missions to South America and the United States that seemed designed to relocate his troublemaking over there as opposed to in Italy and, more specifically, so he would feel no need to write, and, moreover, have no possibility of doing so. This is why his whole body of work barely fills one modest volume and is almost entirely composed of circumstantial poems, which he repeated in his diplomatic destinations with slight variances that reflected the local traits, about which, actually, he seemed to know very little. As Z. was naturally extremely slender, the rationing and scarcity of the war years took an undue toll on his health, and he died shortly after the conflict ended.

Zillich, Heinrich (Brenndorf bei Kronstadt, May 23, 1898–Starnberg, May 22, 1988). His entrance onto the literary scene came in 1936 with the novel *Between Borders and Eras;* his entrance into the history books took place three years later, when he called Adolf Hitler the "savior of the Reich and the people" in a poem written in his honor. Beginning in 1945 he denied any links to National Socialism, however: incredibly, he was believed. A fervent anti-Semite, he maintained to his last breath that the number of Jews killed by the Nazis was not as high as is typically believed and he continued to consider Germany the "protector of the West."

Zuliani, Ottavio (Venice, December 2, 1913–Turin, December 9, 1977). Author of a memoir on his literary activity during the fascist period that is essential to understanding the era despite its exculpatory nature and strange title, *Let the Chickens Graze* (1977). Giulio Ferroni states, in his *History of Italian Literature, the 20th Century* (1991), that Z. published a single book of poems, entitled

Pentagrammed Poetry, in the January 1923 issue of the magazine *Nuovo Futurismo.* That's true, except it wasn't in *Nuovo Futurismo* but in *La Testa di Ferro* and it wasn't published in January 1923 but in August 1921, the title wasn't *Pentagrammed Poetry* but *The Bird of Paradise,* it wasn't a book of poems but a play, and Z. didn't publish it but rather reviewed it: the piece was actually written by Enrico Cavacchioli, the incendiary poet.

AUTHOR'S NOTE

The struggle was, and still might be, to preserve some
of the values to make life worth living.
And they are still mousing around for a significance
in the chaos.

EZRA POUND, *GUIDE TO KULCHUR*

Some of the quotes and several passages in these books require
some explanation. The statements about the "absurd, unfortunate recipe for a self-centered, mercenary, cautious peace and
avaricious mercantilism" and others that follow it are taken from
texts by Filippo Tommaso Marinetti, including the "First Futurist
Manifesto" and "The Necessity and Beauty of Violence." The story
of Carlo Olgiati is based on the story of the same name by Juan
Rodolfo Wilcock, in the book *The Temple of Iconoclasts* (1972). The
bit about Mussolini and his particular relationship to the sky over
Salò comes from Justo Navarro's book *El espía* (2011). The idea that
dehumanizing and totalitarian art is accompanied by an opposing
current that shifts the destruction onto the artist himself comes
from Al Álvarez's book *The Savage God: A Study of Suicide* (1972).
The poem by Flavia Morlacchi is found in Luigi Pirandello's book
Her Husband (1911). The story of Justo Jiménez Martínez de Ostos
is superficially based on the book by Max Aub *Antología traducida*

(1972), as are the stories of Arthur Maddow and Juan Antonio Tiben. The speech by Hanns Johst is made up of passages from texts by Juan Ramón Masoliver, Ezra Pound, Octavio Paz, and Arturo Serrano Plaja. The phrase about war as a cleanser comes from "The Founding and Manifesto of Futurism," by Marinetti, published in *Le Figaro* on February 20, 1909. The address by Eugenio d'Ors is taken from passages of José-Carlos Mainer's study in the anthology *Falange y literatura* (expanded edition, 2013) and from "Pedagogía de la pistola" by Rafael García Serrano. The words spoken by Fani Popowa-Mutafowa come from a speech Miguel de Unamuno gave in 1934. Bruno Corra's text belongs to "Hermes en la vía pública" by Antonio de Obregón; D'Ors's reply, to "La fiel infantería" by Rafael García Serrano. The title of Romano Cataldi's story "Un lungo cane d'ombra" is taken from Luciano Folgore's poem "Fiamma a gas." The story of the astrakhan is from Sigizmund Krzhizhanovsky, *The Letter Killers Club* (2012), although it departs considerably from the original; the bit about the pack is from Chekhov and appears in his *Notebook* (2008). Michele Garassino's defense against accusations of plagiarizing Romano Cataldi's work is plagiarized from the defense Laurence Sterne made for his appropriations, which, in turn, is plagiarized from a similar defense in *The Anatomy of Melancholy* by Robert Burton (1621). The dream Espartaco Boyano describes comes from Joseph Brodsky's book on Joseph Roth (2011). A substantial part of the questions about "monsters" are taken from Fernando Montes Vera's article "Penny Dreadful," published in *Otra Parte Semanal* in September 2014, and some ideas that appear in David J. Skal's book *The Monster Show: A Cultural History of Horror* (1993). The idea that Futurism was too revolutionary and anarchic to be the art that represented the fascism in power was formulated by Giuseppe Prezzolini in 1923, in "Fascism and Futurism." The idea of the "self-portraits" by Luca Borrello comes from the work of Jaume Plensa. Some of the ideas about political violence and individual responsibility are taken from the conversation between Margaret Mead and James Baldwin published as *A Rap on Race* (1971). All the titles by Atilio Tessore are taken from the names of songs by the Spanish band Triángulo de Amor Bizarro.

Some titles from the bibliography deserve special mention. For a panoramic vision of the Italian Social Republic, see *La repubblica di Salò* by Diego Meldi (2008); for a discussion of its internal security forces, *I Servizi Segreti nella Repubblica Sociale Italiana* by Daniele Lembo (2009); for a—very partial—analysis of Ezra Pound's relationship to what was also called the "Republic of Salò," Antonio Pantano's *Ezra Pound e la Repubblica Sociale Italiana* (2009). Although *The Cantos* do not seem to be the most organized way to approach Ezra Pound's ideas—if those ideas ever had an organization to them—they are essential, as are his Radio Rome broadcasts, *ABC of Reading* (1934) and *Guide to Kulchur [sic]* (1938), and the following books: *The Pound Era* by Hugh Kenner (1973) and *A Serious Character: The Life of Ezra Pound* by Humphrey Carpenter (1990). For more on Futurism, consult the books *Dizionario del futurismo: Idee, provocazioni e paroli d'ordine di una grande avanguardia* (1996) and *Artecrazia: L' avanguardia futurista negli anni del fascismo* (1992), both by Claudia Salaris; *Futurism and Politics: Between Anarchist Rebellion and Fascist Reaction, 1909–1944* by Günter Berghaus (1996); *Futurismo: La explosión de la vanguardia,* edited by Alessandro Ghignoli and Llanos Gómez (2011); and *Estética y arte futuristas* by Umberto Boccioni (2004). About and by the movement's founder, *Marinetti: Arte e vita futurista* by Claudia Salaris (1997), *Synthetic Forms of Futurist Expression,* and *The Necessity and Beauty of Violence.* For a discussion of the state of literature during the Nazi period, see *Literatur im Dritten Reich: Dokumente und Texte,* Sebastian Graeb-Könneker, editor (2001); for a discussion of Spanish literature during early Francoism, the aforementioned anthology by José-Carlos Mainer and the fascinating *Las armas y las letras: Literatura y Guerra Civil (1936–1939)* by Andrés Trapiello (2010, third edition); for a history of French collaborationism in literature, *Die französische Literatur im Zeichen von Kollabora-*

tion und Faschismus by Barbara Berzel (2012). There are dozens of books about the experience of the partisans in Italy; I recommend one of the most recent, by Sergio Luzzatto, *Primo Levi's Resistance: Rebels and Collaborators in Occupied Italy* (2015). For those who want to dig deeper into the events of 1945 in Europe and the immediate postwar period, I recommend the hair-raising *Savage Continent: Europe in the Aftermath of World War II* by Keith Lowe and *Year Zero: A History of 1945* by Ian Buruma (both 2013). On the Red Brigades, *Europe's Red Terrorists: The Fighting Communist Organizations* by Yonah Alexander and Dennis A. Pluchinsky (1992) and *Strike One to Educate One Hundred* by Chris Aronson Beck, Reggie Emiliana, Lee Morris, and Ollie Patterson (1986); for the history of the Milanese Red Brigades, *Le Brigate Rosse a Milano: Dalle origini della lotta armata alla fine della colonna "Walter Alasia"* by Andrea Saccoman (2013). More about the anarchist scene in Milan can be found at https://federazione-anarchica-milanese-fai.noblogs.org/ and https://torchiera.noblogs.org/, for example.

Much of this book was written at the Civitella Ranieri artists' residency near Umbertide, Perugia. I want to thank my hosts, Dana Prescott and Diego Mencaroni, as well as those there with whom I shared conversations and experiences that are reflected in this book's more positive aspects—if it has any—to some degree: Ed Bennett, Estrella Burgos, Mary Caponegro, James Casebere, Helene Dorion, Lise Funderburg, Dan and Becky Okrent, Russell Platt, Tonis Saadoja, and Gayle Young. I am also grateful to my editors, especially Diana Miller and Claudio López de Lamadrid (in memoriam); to my agents at William Morris Endeavor, Claudia Ballard and Laura Bonner; and to the translators of my books. Thank you to Mónica Carmona, one of the earliest and most talented readers of this book, and to Raffaella de Angelis and Graciela Montaldo, who let me attend a private viewing of the exhibition *Italian Futurism: 1909–1944: Reconstructing the Universe* at the Guggenheim in New York in exchange for pretending I was Sergio Chejfec: surprisingly, the ruse worked. Thanks also to everyone in the offices of Penguin

Random House in Madrid and Barcelona, and to Rodrigo Fresán, José Hamad, Pablo Raphael, Anna Maria Rodríguez, Juan Cruz Ruiz, Iker Seisdedos, Javier Rodríguez Marcos, Andrea Aguilar, Daniel Gascón, Matías Rivas, and Eduardo De Grazia. This book, along with everything else, is for Giselle Etcheverry Walker: "All my powers of expression and thoughts so sublime / Could never do you justice in reason or rhyme."

A NOTE ON THE TYPE

This book was set in Chronicle Text, a typeface designed by Hoefler & Frere-Jones in 2002. It is a Scotch face, created to withstand the effects of newspaper printing, in which low-quality paper and rapid printing speeds often caused delicate hairlines and serifs to disappear and enclosed spaces to become ink traps. Chronicle Text is offered in four press-sensitive "grades" to cope with these various printing challenges, and works well in different kinds of media.

Typeset by Scribe
Philadelphia, Pennsylvania

Printed and bound by Berryvile Graphics
Berryville, Virginia

Designed by Pei Loi Koay